2Q AND
SIN BYRON'S
BROKEN CRYSTAL
MIRROR PIECES

JOSHUA RA DUNDAS

 ARCHWAY
PUBLISHING

Archway Publishing books may be ordered through booksellers or by contacting:

Archway Publishing
1663 Liberty Drive
Bloomington, IN 47403
www.archwaypublishing.com
1 (888) 242-5904

Because of the dynamic nature of the Internet, any web addresses or links contained in this book may have changed since publication and may no longer be valid. The views expressed in this work are solely those of the author and do not necessarily reflect the views of the publisher, and the publisher hereby disclaims any responsibility for them.

Any people depicted in stock imagery provided by Thinkstock are models, and such images are being used for illustrative purposes only.
Certain stock imagery © Thinkstock.

ISBN: 978-1-4808-5695-0 (sc)
ISBN: 978-1-4808-5696-7 (e)

Library of Congress Control Number: 2018900331

Print information available on the last page.

Archway Publishing rev. date: 01/25/2018

DEDICATION

First I would like to thank the lord of heaven who intervened in my life on many occasions, sending his angels to watch over me during my tribulations and battles with demons for my very soul. Second I would like to thank my family who stuck by me and listened even when at times my mission didn't make any sense, their words of wisdom and advice were invaluable in my internal battle against myself. Third I would like to thank the people who left me for dead, the ones who hurt and betrayed me, the ones who plotted and conspired to destroy me, the ones who hate me and will always say ugly things about me now and forever. Without you I would not know the power of the crystal mirror inside of me, because of your hate I have been to the depths of my very soul and have learned and seen things you can never imagine. Because of you I am 2Q and Sin Byron, the light and the dark, I am no longer the same, I have been reborn.

WHAT BOOK IS ABOUT

I am 2Q, I live in your world but I have a dark secret. Deep inside I have a dark side named Sin Byron who lives in my soul, every night he talks to me through a mysterious and powerful crystal mirror. While I am cool and confident my dark half is hot and arrogant, our push and pull upsets the balance and shatters the mirror to pieces, now our world and different dimensions within have crossed. With the protective veil destroyed demons have taken over wanting the crystal pieces for themselves, if they succeed the dark will wipe out the light for eternity. Follow me as I travel through the multi dimensions of my very own mind and soul, meeting love and other emotions that are being targeted and killed. Can I bring love back to the desolate heart, stop the demons insidious plot and help save myself, or will I be consumed by the demonic influence that may have corrupted my other half the infamous Sin Byron?

I am Sin Byron; I live in the eternal dimension inside the limitless soul. While sitting on my diamond throne I can see what 2Q doesn't, through our heated and aggravating conversations, through all the times I have forced my way on my to forgiving and to soft other half, I did not realize the mirror was cracking until it was to late. Now with the mirror shattered I must find a way to restore the balance, missing crystal pieces have disappeared into the outer dimensions of shadowing darkness. Follow me as I travel the dimensions of my broken world on a mission to collect them, meeting demons like anger, revenge and arrogance, were being a emotion means certain death. Will I stick to the mission or become corrupted by the promise of power and my insatiable weakness for women, giving in to lust, desire and temptation?

PREFACE

There are things in this world that cannot be seen, for if it were life's perfect illusion of perceived reality would change, as we know it. Never before has any book taken you into the depths of the eternal soul. What will you see in the reflection of my crystal mirror, now that it is broken into crystal pieces what will you decipher about 2Q and Sin Byron, both sides of my light and darkness, for I am the author.

Through the portal of this book view the secret places of my soul, travel through it and the ever-mysterious dimensions that form its essence, an existence that has become intertwined due to a spiritual unbalance. Know that the deeper you go there can be no turning back, the war against myself and the demons have begun, the perils of the darkness within threaten my souls inhabitants. Which side will win? Will 2Q and Sin Byron become one again?

Through this unforgettable journey meet 2Qs love, light and passion, and his dark half Sin Byron's lust, desire and temptation. Amongst my souls beautiful riches lay a personalized and coveted gift for all women. My loves under the sun will you be made spell bound by the red rose of 2Q, or eagerly drawn by the black rose of Sin Byron, and what of the living white rose that searches the heart of all those who vide for it, Giving itself only to the one who is worthy of its purity, symbolizing the union of the two who have become one, the infused harmony and marriage of romance and seduction.

(CRYSTAL MIRROR)

Everything I am, everything I perceive, illuminates with bright intensity, in my wondrous soul surrounded by eternal treasures, the powerful crystal mirror looms in its center, I am bewitched by its spectral elegance, its crystal luminescence transparent in solace, oh how I marvel at this heavenly miracle, its dream like presence, stunning in its magnificence and mysterious appearance, through its reflection view the spiritual things unseen, both conflicting forces of the light and darkness, at war for supremacy

(ALIEN)

Sometimes I feel I am not from here, a sphere with a different atmosphere, no gravity, no core, no sun to rise or fall, so you see this planet revolves around me, what keeps it centered cannot be seen, but if you could you would come to me, the light is a friend of mine, it came to me when I died, showed me things I couldn't see, evidence of the inner me, so it helped me build a wall, from a world that cast me off, possessed me now I am reborn, an alien to its form

(BOOKS)

When you open up a book you are transported to a world that saturates your mind, the story's, knowledge, and information inside the words confined, each sentence paragraph and line burst forth coming to life, leaving everything behind you learn as you go, looking forwards to what's next to unfold, an adventure, a struggle, a poem, a mystery unknown, action, suspense, a plot, a twist, fiction or non fiction, something will grab your attention, something will stir your interest,

anything you can dream if you take a look, opening a portal
Inside this book

(THE WAR)

Wake up friends, family, people near, far or around, there is a
war that's been going on before time, before you were born and
cradled in your mothers arms, the battle of good versus evil,
that comes from the spiritual world that cannot be seen, that
ultimately effect you and me, the things people do, whether it
be kind or cruel, simple tests of cause and effect, for the body
without the spirit is dead, so who is it we place blame on when
things go terribly wrong, how quick it is to say someone is sick,
mentally insufficient, not fit for what we deem appropriate, I
urge you to look deeper, to guard yourself with the knowledge of
the cunning weapons of the every day demons who destroy us
from within, giving us a false pretense that it is us in full control,
when in fact it is them that play a role in our self destruction,
playing the ultimate trick, convincing man kind they do not
exist

(INTERNAL ENEMY)

My worst enemy is inside of me, he comes in my name, he
may look like me, his job is to lead fluctuating thoughts, lost
to pitfalls and traps that cannot be seen, to do what I feel and
not what I need, to lose my way in whatever he deems, a sense
of right, my twisted left, taught blindly to believe if it comes
from me trust nothing less, my ideas come from what source
I ask, will the answer be absolute or half the truth, or far in
between a mortals means, how alluring is a choice made as
sure as me, yet the outcome received is not what's foreseen, to

take it back is far out of your reach, was the decision yours or truly your internal enemy

(WISH)

I wish a piece of me would latch on to you, so you could see inside of me and know my point of views, to empathize my love and hate observe my darker half, an advisor to disordered thoughts structured to a path, to visit levels in this vessel and encounter no resistance, communicate directly linked to the man with my description, look ahead and don't dread this exalted cryptic vision, for in this wish is a gift, my elusive intuition

(THE SOUL)

Under the veil of the metaphysical travel deep into my soul, however you perceive it, is how you will see it, here boundless energy flows freely, a gift from the divine is all inside but distractions lead our daily lives, stealing essential focus away vital to tapping into your limitless energy, an endless well of riches beyond the comprehension of your wildest dreams, the exterior on the outside may seem imperfect or even feeble, but you are abundant on the inside with wealth unimaginable, with every valuable thing comes someone who wants to posses it, the physical realm effects your spiritual connection, the further you are away, the more oblivious you are to the damaging hole you are opening, inviting malignant influences that will latch on to you and drain, taking your life, then eventually taking your soul away

(HELL)

Because you do not see it, does not mean it does not exist, hell is full of the damned, it is not silent, how can it be when its chilling lament echoes throughout the spirit world constantly, haunting the physical plane in certain ways, hell is under our feet, hell is in the very air we breathe, hell is in the things we see, hell knows its own, all those that are connected to its aura vibrates with its energy, those brief moments of seemingly knowing something or someone is not right, the goose bumps or cold chill running down your spine, may just be your internal self discerning what it knows to be the truth, that hell in fact exist and it's calling out to you

(DEMONS)

From hell they rise to blot out the eyes, materializing at the door of your open mind, lurking in the corridors of the heart, seeking secrets to the portal of the soul, the whole of your being they wish to control, with a sinister hunger for destruction and a fiendish need to taste the sweet nectar of life, they can assume any shape and take any form, wearing down the will to resist them, subtly seeping poison to the sub conscious, hidden underneath the layers of insecurities and troubles, building a wall made of a intricate façade, gradually drawing you away from the light, taking possession, then leading you into the darkness where they are

(PERIL)

Walk with me through the valley of the shadow of death, were all that we have become will be tested, were all that we are can be altered, were reality and dreams flow into one stream, the peril of evil materializing from the unseen, nightmarish demons in high places resurrecting death, conjuring the gateways to secret places, take my hand on this adventure of truth. Hope that our feet are swift and the light guides us on the pathway to life, all the way through to the hidden world beyond our naked eyes

(HIGH PLACES)

Malevolent evil in the heavens above, as numerous as the stars in the life that you love, in safety and peace, their evils unleashed, to wander the world as demons and beasts, your body, your heart, your soul and mind, the targets of rulers with blood thirst devised, to separate you as far from the truth, through temptations and lies, to conquer and divide

(INVITE)

The portal lens has been opened, inviting you to see the world differently, inviting you to dream, looking through the eyes of a hybrid, viewing beauty and mystery, hidden secrets of hidden depths where no one has been, visions of the things no one has seen, I invite you to believe, to unlock the many doors of your mind and receive, opening the greatest gift that one can be given, letting go of fear, doubt and inhibition, embracing the unknown harnessing the power within, I invite you to 2Q and his dark half Sin Byron

(WELCOME)

I welcome you to my pain, love and darkness, to the corners of my soul that are haunted, to that vast riches that lie in abundance, to my desire, lust and temptation, to the two sides that make up who I am, to the three roses of symbolism, to the mystery, danger and secrets, to the monsters, nightmares and demons, to the threshold of my heaven and hell, I welcome you to the power struggle inside of myself

(THE SOUL MANUAL)

Everything in me, within everything you read, becomes every crystal piece, the past, present and future, lying at your feet, knocking at the door, no one could for-see, so take another look, take it personally, because everything you take, may one day come to be, especially on this path, where nothings as it seems, my every tool will build, the souls manual

(ARMOR)

For love I am, to love I commit, the wholeness of self, the armor within, so arm yourself with the mystery inside, to travel the depths through the darkness and light, right here now, yet also in time, every level throughout the heavenly sky, take up your weapon, piece by piece, the kingdom is nigh, the armor of life

(ESSENCE CONTINUUM)

What lives in essence eternal, an everlasting loop, what's me and you, multi dimensional, never ending, a prism of affinity dimensions, the infinite applications of a mind with no limits, the beautiful soul of all things connected, the transcendence of many forms in an continuum warp, the mortal body nothing but a paradox of what really lies beyond, what essence, a divine piece of intricate complexity, the universe within, yet all wonders hidden, under the veil of our reality's perception

(THE SPIRIT WORLD)

When you close your eyes in the physical, you open your eyes to the spiritual, death is only a means to a beginning, shedding off the flesh releasing the inner being, crossing the void in between two points, a world next to ours parallel and conjoined, a world of metaphysical energy, its connection a frequency, a channel that our naked eyes cannot see, yet there are some that are gifted with the super-natural abilities to see, hear and talk to the mystery's that be, influences aware of you and me, entity's and spirits, the light and dark, there are those that would argue that this is false, that once you die it is over and done, that life ends here and doesn't go on, everyone has there time and all will see, that despite there views, in the end you will know the truth

CHAPTER 1

2Q

Every night I close my eyes and fall into a star-lit sky. Weight-less I land in front of a ruby door, I have done this many times before.

This door leads to a candle lit room full with precious stone and jewels, but this is not what I am drawn to. A stirring mirror stands in its midst, its crystal brilliant in its luminescence.

Looking into its crystal clear reflection I can see someone who looks like me, with the exception of his strikingly red eyes and fanged teeth there is no mistaken our mysterious relation, his deep and melodic voice I hear constantly.

Though our conversations are brief, I get the feeling he wishes to control me. He shows me things, he tells me how I should be, when I reject his views he grows angry, his tone harsh and sharp, his features flaring in a burning red countenance.

Falling to my knees faint and weak, I open my eyes only to realize I have been sleep.

I am relieved to be back to reality, though I can never shake this eerie feeling, that I am being haunted by my other half who calls him-self Sin Byron.

(ME)

My other half is cold, his core detached, its made of narcissism and wears a mask, a tint of black its shaded past, its smooth demeanor cuts a path, through everyone its eyes can see, it is its own entity, it moves self sufficiently, two half's of a whole symphony, a twin brothers chemistry, identical my other half and me

(BEHIND THE RUBY DOOR)

Behind the ruby door lies a world unlike which the eyes of humanity have never seen before, a parallel dimension, a cross between two flows of existence, where reality is in the distance, where something more exalted is in your midst, it cannot be fathomed, it just is, as if it has always been, the heights of the un-attainable some-how in your grip, this feeling, yet you don't know what it is, as if reaching into the endless sky at night pulling the very stars from there place, in awe as its luminous glow lights up your face, seen in the pupils of your wide eyes, secrets through-out and abroad, there is more behind the ruby door

(THE BEHOLDER)

In my eyes, I can see more then you can imagine, more then what's paraded out on the surface, I can see magic, your essence, a world without blemish, endless treasure alive, secrets so intimate, your souls hidden desire, her loves rose blooming, both its rise and sunset, its spilling over passion, nothing can contain it, the golden staircase to the stars, the living mystery afar, the morning will dawn, but the night is coming, yet there's beauty twice over, in the illuminating eyes of the beholder

(MY DARK CRYSTAL REFLECTION)

In my crystal reflection I see this dark side of me, he speaks a caliber of levels beyond physical reach, beyond the mere façade of poised reality, yes I am more then carnal intention, more then emotions governed by human impulses, no my world is motivated by mysterious forces, in the core of my being, the depths of my spirit, my wondrous soul is alive and infinite, something my complacent mind would not fathom, could not imagine, and so I try to forget, to try and deny my very face in this flawed reflection, but every night I am brought back to this startling presence, reminded that no matter how I perceive this, what stares back at me is apart of a chosen fate, my unique existence

(LOVES DESIGHN)

The architectural source of all things spiritual, the auras unique signature of the essence within you, every single breath, every waking moment, what feelings and sensations *in the world you inhabit, the mysterious soul of the divine equation, a universal paradigm, apart of loves grand design*

(SHADOW LIASON)

What relation does light have with darkness? With both sides different what could possibly bond them? How could this have happened? This mystery perplexes my understanding, a paradox of a shadow liaison, a split within a oneness of spirit, yet the same in its twist of an intertwined essence, a beautiful soul of endless treasure, yet a change of reflection in the core of its center, though it is me in which I speak, in which way would I begin to contradict this reality, balanced, yet shifting, existing here, yet also in an alternate dimension, a universe infinitely connected, but also diverse in various perception

SIN BYRON

The soul is my home, a beautiful place where I live alone. Its eternal structure uniquely carved by precious stones, the view of your world sits before my diamond throne.

Here I could see the enemy lurk and study there cunning ways, the unawares of spiritual warfare secretly invading hidden havens of worth, a curse, an abomination of true evil that will do anything and assume any shape, scheming its way into your sacred place for control to posses your very soul.

Here battle plans must be drawn to protect self from certain harm, here I guard my territory jealously, here I will kill if deemed necessary, here I will do whatever it takes to preserve the soul and keep it safe.

Yet my other half refuses to see things my way.

How I abhor his misguided kindness, this light that exploited his blatant blindness.

A fact debated when his day turned to night, my tangible world taken view in his subconscious mind.

Through the crystal mirror we communicate face to face, his ignorance of the world around him would boil my brewing rage.

Oh how I wanted to taint his peaceful ways, my heat to infuse threw his coursing veins.

I mysteriously came to being when his anger arose; such a fury of fire beckoned me close, awakening with a vengeance, stirring the soul.

I manifested when he needed me most, yet he pushes me away when it is I that could see the insidious things that could use his naiveté as a way to desecrate what I hold dear and safe.

He does not listen, nor does he understand the true nature of his existence. The human world made those living in it vulnerable, casting a veil of the illusion of time and reality.

I have watched people become possessed, not even knowing there souls have been ransacked by demonic monsters, countless victims life's decaying by a slow death, I would not let that happen.

First I would force myself to protect him from his own idiocy. Eventually I grew tired of his liable weakness, savoring the satisfying sensation of consuming him, loving the feeling of control, growing a particular hatred for the human side I felt made him weak.

Part of me wanted to rid myself of the attachment, becoming the soul proprietor of the physical vessel.

So I pushed harder, using every situation as an excuse to alter his mood, likened unto a ghost haunting his every move.

With no thought of the heavy pressure applied, I became negligent to the damage being done to the crystal mirror inside.

Now that I am aware it is to late, the mirror has broken into pieces.

(REIGN)

On my diamond throne I Sin Byron reign supreme, in the
midst of riches of a glorious vision, lies a boundless power
that flows endless, a gift from the darkness that does not give,
inherited for I was born in it, but he who was granted the
gift of life was also given the gift of light, together a world
of no limits of sight, the freedom to cross the forbidden line,
to co-exist is to defy the boundaries of time, an unwanted
alliance between different sides, a hybrid of earth that upset
what lurked, the high place of an insidious evil disturbed, yet
a purpose I am and a purpose is he, for I Sin Byron reign
supreme

(MYSTERY)

What will you find in the deep crevices and secret passages
of these interchanging words? For the things that seem easily
interpreted may be easily missed, going over the head of the

adventurer who searches, yet the treasure lies right before your eyes and is for all to grasp, for the power was and has always been yours to command, but there are those who would stop at nothing to see its potential lost, which in turn loses your identity of who you truly are, the mystery dates all the way back since the beginning of time, but its up to each and everyone to discover where that lies

(ASTRO TRAVELERS)

To all travelers I warn you to travel with assurance, to scrutinize your surroundings and watch your every step, for you have entered another world where nothing is as it seems, where the metaphysical and the spiritual are within reach, for because the internal crystal mirrors broken the fabric of mere reality has been shifted, there are no boundaries, therefor different interpretations to what may be, for there are two things that are sure, 2Q and Sin Byron, the light and the dark

(ILLUSIONS)

Time moves ever closer to the threshold of eternity, for what is time but an illusion of a human analogy, when time has run out what will be left? if we label things and say that it is, then who is to argue its logic, a thought that says it is real, must be, for thoughts become things and things the perception of the beholder, so what is a dream if it is vividly seen, does it not mean that it existed in that present reality, does not the stars intrigue you, or the intricacy of the brain, what about the mysteries that cannot be explained, who are you really, what have you been told to believe, if all were revealed to you now, would you accept it, or deny its existence, if you knew the truth, what would you do, if that meant the dramatic change of what everyone thought or knew, would the knowledge be hidden and kept away in secret, or treated as a guise, under the illusion of the individualized mind

(CHOSEN)

Why was I chosen to receive this luminescent gift? Given the sight to see the millions who have been made to be blinded, the cunning of the wolf, the relevance of the sheep, the burden of the few outweighed by the many, for who am I to judge when I was just the same, searching everything else, but myself, who was the one to blame, but everything that happened could not have happened any other way, I accept all that I am, for I have come to understand, the beauty of my purpose, the pure light beneath the surface

(CRYSTAL BALANCE)

Meshed, delicate, precious, symbolic, elevated, concentrated, balanced, sacred, harmonious, focus, pure, universal, heavenly, spiritual, a paragon, a miracle, the sky, the stars, what's light, what's dark

(MY UNIVERSE BEYOND AFFINITY)

My soul, my universe, what wonders in the form of a crystal mirror, a multi dimensional element, an affinity of the infinite, Through my eyes a window to the realm of the spiritual, my treasures, my gifts, my will, my ability to transmit whom or what I wish, to bend reality in the continuum of my perception, to show you pieces of passages before or after the source transcended, awakened to what it has always been, a bright star formed in the celestial heavens

(SCRAMBLED PASSAGES THE MULTI DIMENSIONS)

Past, present and future, ever-changing, multi dimensions, seemingly separated pieces of my universe within, yet one souls essence in the bond of a crystal element, where will you land once entering my portals infinite, for what I am is limit less, an illuminating spectrum of precious focus, under control by my will, directed wherever I wish, in light you transcend to heavens beyond comprehension, my soul has been written, yet in essence ambiguous, given flesh within you, but in truth, what has always been, underlies the veil of reality's perfect illusion

(MOTHER NATURE/HUMAN NATURE)

Mother nature how beautifully inconsistent and unpredictable you are, summer, winter, spring, fall, four seasons in all, each with a different job, a cycle that goes on and will never stop, cold then hot, mother nature can become unstable, with massive earthquakes and erupting volcanoes, dangerous hail, sweeping tornadoes, devastating hurricanes, cold fronts, heat waves, frost bitten blizzards, heavy down pours of flooding rains, paying the price for natures active ways, yet this is not always that way, it is human nature to appreciate warmth from her sun rays, to enjoy cloudy days, to take refuge under her shady trees, to view as a whole natures astounding beauty, yet it is also human nature to be ungrateful for these things, to destroy land, abusing natural resources, polluting the air ways, seas, rivers and oceans, wanton dilution of waste and toxins, yet human nature and mother nature must co-exist, both unpredictable, both beautifully inconsistent

(THE UNIVERSE)

This blue orb in which we live there is a vast universe surrounding it, how little our existence seems compared to the billions of stars in the galaxy, the question if we are alone, so far unknown, we cannot fathom or comprehend the deeper space so infinite, the many moons, the different planets, we send machine to answer questions, hoping for a better understanding, collecting data, computers testing, scientist analyzing, giving birth to what others believe, theories and conspiracy's, yet we have barely scratched the surface, a tenacity that keeps us searching, a mystery, an unanswered question, the universe that keeps us guessing

(THE WORLD)

The world connected by land, divided by sea, so much diversity in the beauty I see, through different races, distinct faces, special people with unique languages, vast cultures with various traditions, their way of life in sacred religions, rich history's of civilizations, crafted art from inspiration, different regions in exotic locations, yet with every difference comes a switch, for the good you see to the bad that exist, for it cannot be exempt, for it hides just beneath the worlds surface, tainting the good when it surfaces, the wars for resources and land, corrupted blood money exchanged from hand to hand, the hate, people racist ways, discrimination for the color of your face, different beliefs with different views, if its not their way they turn their back on you, the famine, the sickness and plagues, with nothing equal this is seen more in a poorer place, the insistently selfish rich, hording their wealth instead of giving to the poor or helping the sick, loathing those who are beneath them, the governments who find a way to oppress the people with the laws they make, making the rich richer and the poor poorer, spawning legal horror on there secret path to control, yet among these are those who are good people, who feed the poor and help the sick, finding vaccines to cure plagues running rampant, fighting for equal rights, opposing all of the bad, they are the balance, in this beautiful world of madness

(OPINIONS/ARGUMENTS)

How can you win a argument based on opinions, it will only lead to your frustration, back and forth with what you believe is a fact, that the other doesn't see it as, based on what you heard or observed put into your own words, will only be viewed as coming from you, there will always be the opposite of what you perceive, to the other end there knowledge supersedes, yet in between there is something missing, you cant win a argument based on opinions

(MOURN)

I mourn for my old self, it died broken and weak, alone in the dark with tears of blood staining his cheek, shivering from a broken heart cold and empty, no love would comfort him in his time of need, no one cared for they shunned his face, they turned their back on his cries of pain, only death could have relieved this deep sadness, and now I mourn for him over an internal casket

(NUMB)

Away from you I sit alone, my secret pains my broken soul, I am nothing of what you think I am, your fickle ways I cannot stand, I do not fit in your kind of crowd, I can see through your friendly smiles, I do not wish to have you near, I have come to love this isolation, its coldness adopted me in my anguish, the light became my souls salvation, but you did not care, because you were not there, my naked dignity exploited and ridiculed, my vulnerability and innocence bullied and abused, my weakness used against me to further condemn me, its despicable taste spewing the vomit of regret and disdain, I have loathed myself for opening doors of acceptance, in the end to be spit upon and rejected, a ghost in the eyes of false illusions, dead to the ones I thought would understand, all this has opened the gates to what I now see, I have become numb, I have become Sin Byron

(MY WORLD)

My worlds foundation was built on the brink of a dream, yet it exist tangible where as only I could reach, anything is possible, wish and it shall be, a never ending magic, a well of energy, everything is one, its essence origin, bears a branded mark of the light and the dark, since the beginning of time both sides have been at odds, for the very riches that make you who you are, in the temporary world nothing there will last, but the universe is forever, past, present and future

(COVER)

I see darkness in the light, they use it to cover and hide, to gain access to the deepest layers of the heart and mind, appearing as a lamb when they are the wolf, they have come to terrorize the innocence of your intentions, taking advantage of your ignorance, you so trustingly accept them amongst you, your insecurities are a wide tunnel to walk through, not knowing they have chosen you to posses, the internal effects abuse and wastes you, your portal to your soul becomes easily accessible, in this socially vain world you worry about what others think or how they view you, you are easily corruptible, not worrying about yourself, cast a cover of an illusion of the shadow of acceptance, I fare thee well, when you are the unsuspecting target of a malicious hell

(SUPREMACY)

Tortured on the inside I seek relief from the hell I created, I am shunned from rationalization, to show you me is to show you pieces of the light and dark that battles for supremacy, my soul is a warzone, my mind and heart the casualties, what you see on the exterior cannot define me, you would be foolish to try and save me, when you cannot save yourself, because u cannot see what hides in secret, you cannot see the demons who have willingly made your body a base of operations, so to me, you are a enemy sent to destroy me, because it is I who sees clearly, it is I who threaten their seat of power, will the war be won I do not know, till all is calm and no longer I seethe, on the frontline I fight against the demons in me

(TINTED SHADE)

I view the world in a tinted shade, what you see and I see are two different things, your up is my down, a world upside down, parallel dimensions exchanged, my eyes view stars in a dark distance, this is how far I am from you, to become this way you must live in dark days, when everything becomes different and new

(SIGHNS/MESSAGES)

You must read in between the lines, to decipher the coded messages inside the signs, for signs can be warning that some thing is not right, that something needs a watchful eye, you can better prepare for what's ahead if messages are earlier read, caught before the signs manifest, you can prevent something from going to far, or you getting involved, you must read in between the lines, to decipher the coded messages inside the signs

2Q

In my daily dealings I am ambitious with a drive of tenacity, this is what keeps me ahead of the rest, where others would fail, I would win.

I am humble, yet determined with no time for non-sense; there will be no deterrent in my surroundings, No one to stop me from achieving nothing but the best.

I have a secret; deep inside there is this living darkness.

Whenever I found myself growing angry or upset I would feel like I was burning alive on the inside. Some caged beast clawing its way outside trying to control my mind.

The object of my anger could not possibly know what I would do to them if I let myself go.

Something about today felt especially strange, I felt detached from myself like something was missing.

Could it be because of the series of unusual visions that have suddenly began to plague my reality? Since these visions started my usual dreams of the mirror and my dark half have ceased.

Could that be the issue? Was my being aware of this part of me causing me to doubt my own sanity?

With no clear answer to the question I disregarded it, pushing it to the back of my mind. It probably was nothing, no point wasting my time thinking about something that was irrelevant. There was only enough time to focus on me, and how I wanted my life to be.

(MY WAY)

My way is the only way I know, your way is no way I want to go, an internal compass on an invisible road, the things I know cannot be shown, it can only be followed, it cannot be sold, it is what is a skill to be honed, a gift of precision to navigate with ease, a blessing of the spiritual eyes in me, a way to be made out of none, my way and your way can never be one

(CONSUME)

I pray demons don't take the part of me that's alive today, to consume the piece that managed to survive those dreadful days, to provoke my inner darkness I struggle to suppress, coercing this latent part of me that wants to snatch your breath, to stop a run away train derailed from its tracks, trampling and destroying everything that's in its path, there are things in my world caged that cannot be loose, for if it was so help me god everything will be consumed

(MORE THEN)

I am more then you know, I am more then you can handle, less cannot appease my destiny, you will be overwhelmed by my tenacity, I loathe your acceptance of nothing, it is a powerful magnet that attracts what-ever just like it, becoming a stain that cannot be cleaned, a putrid odor, a pheromone for failure, I am more then average, my mind levels an elevated

status, there are unlimited destinations to a masters atlas, my
potential lies at the cornerstone of the universe, perseverance
and ambition are the leader while inhibition and subjection
are the follower, I am original in all that I do, I am the canvas
of the successful, I am relentless, I am the few, I am the way
out of none, I am 2Q

(NARCISSUS)

Narcissus I channeled you, in turn you have given me a
better view, to see that the wealth in myself is unimaginable, a
value that cannot be priced, a wealth that is greedy to my eyes,
a treasure that is undoubtedly mine, it is a voice that causes
you to stir, it is unique, so therefor it is not for everybody,
my attention is not to be taken lightly, for most of my time
is used only for me, the world is cast out into the cold until I
feel such time to open back my door, anything I feel like will
be dispensable, I will loose no sleep when I get rid of you, for
I focus on what is best for me, tell me what do I merit from
dealing with the likes of you, there is nothing that I don't
already have, there is nothing I cannot do, I can see more then
meets the eye, when narcissus channels through

(WHAT YOU THINK)

Whatever it is you think about me, I am in hysterics at what
this gets you, absolutely nothing, sometimes it is better to say
nothing, at least that would conceal your true value, sadly
I can see right through you, the negative you feel about me
deep down inside only afflicts you, so let it all out and see
where that gets you, what you think about me makes me
truly happy, for it shows the effect I am having, needless to

say I'm only thinking of me, so it is impossible for me to care what you think

(DARK SECRETS)

My secret of spite a venomous bite, metamorphous of nightmares conjuring fright, I know not why it haunts me at night, the echo alone a soulless demise, wherever I run it always finds me, evanescent its touch insidious and grimy, idly it waits to claim its prize, with an obsession to take what's rightfully mine, the blood thirsty hunger of a savage beast, at night it takes root in the subconscious mind, infused contorted dark secrets of mine

(HELD BACK)

Evaluate those around you, will you find them doing the same thing? Now switch the focus and ask yourself what have you gained? How much time did you waste? Did you accomplish anything? What steps have you taken to reach your goals? If your answer is nothing, or no, something has to go, things have to change, you are being held back, perpetually stuck where your at, making no progress, likened unto the dead, the only way to thrive is to cut all ties, severing the link to your old life, this cancer that's held you back this whole time, must die, friends, etcetera pushed to the side, its time to think of yourself taking control of your life, when at long last you open your eyes wondering after all this time where it is you have been, like a projectile the answer will hit you hard and fast, a revelation will be revealed, you have been held back

(HARDWORK AND DEDICATION)

There are no shortcuts, to get what you want takes hard work and dedication, passion, work ethic, steady motivation, with a set goal in mind, understand that nothing just happens over night, to reach success takes time, energy and focus, nothing is just given, you have to work for it, distraction can come at a heavy cost destroying everything you worked hard for, with dedication, there is not time to waste with meaningless things that will only get in your way, because in the end you lose and is the one to pay, you must put work before play, if you mean what you say, you will find a way to prioritize everything, the path to success is full of sacrifices, but if you are to win, it will take hard work and dedication

(STUDY/CHEAT)

Study and prove yourself, what you have learned will come handy in your future, why cheat yourself? Because in the end only you will fail, this hurts no one else but you, never knowing when what you said will be of use, the end results for cheating is to truly lose, using a temporary fix Is the way of fools, just getting by the tools that should be utilized steals substance for your mind, if cheating has gotten you further then where you were at, instead of steps forward, you have taken steps back, you have neither gained nor retained the very least, you benefit the most if you study and don't cheat

(AMBITION AND SUCCESS)

Be ambitious, go for yours, do not stop until you reach the open doors, walking through the gates of success, eager to be the best, watch for the unknown toes, they will feel stepped on, *for who-so-ever they belong will prey for your downfall, seeing your rise as a threat to their position, feeling that the throne they sit in is being challenged, climbing through the ranks of life triggers hate, potential possibilities creates enemy's, do not let this daunt or hold you back, continue on the same path to the end, passing the test, reaching the finish line, from ambition to success*

(SET DEFINITIONS)

To view the world in a set definition, only builds up the barriers that create your limits, the authority of your mind is the ruling perception, your will the force that pushes your direction, what you say is, is because you said it, what you say cant, cant because you allowed it, what did not take root, never existed because it wasn't planted, you stop your own progress, you stunt your own growth, but if you change your perception, the span of possibilities are infinitely endless

SIN BYRON

Sensing a shift, a searing pain detonates inside of my jumbled head giving me the feeling that I have also been broken into pieces.

The crystal mirrors shattering has caused an unbalance giving vulnerable access to the secret places within, creating the very situation I tried so hard to prevent.

My worst fear has become a living nightmare. Demons are at the portal of my soul, I can feel their cold presence drawing near.

I knew what they wanted, their whispers amongst each other spoke of the crystal pieces and their need to acquire them, how at long last their day had come and their master would be pleased.

These malevolent entities' referred to me as a sub-conscious hybrid that had to be seized.

Something else was different, I could feel there was something missing, this inner void calling out to me growing more intense, urging me to follow it into the unknown.

I had no choice but to leave the soul, the only home I had ever known.

But I would need to do something vital before leaving. What I had to do needed to be done quickly.

Even if it killed me I had to right this wrong, or everything I had known would forever be gone.

(TRUTH AND LIE)

Truth and lie are feuding brothers, that cannot exist with one another, for truth will always expose a lie, in the cover of darkness lie secrets hide, despising the light of truth, for all it has built could become undone, revealing its under-handed moves, lies plot to do away with the truth, burying it forever then burning its roots, whoever is connected to truth are subjected, to being erased for secrets protected, the truth is hard to handle, far reaching and powerful, some would prefer lies because they are more desirable, others spend there whole life searching for truth, finding nothing at all, or pieces of proof, for once something is done its hard to undo, truth and lie a family feud

(PAIN)

The pain it eats away and leaves a hollow feeling everyday, if everything is left unchecked, the pain slowly spreads, its moves follow three steps, invade, takeover, progress, until nothing is left but a bottomless hole in the hearts home, the clouds of pain, turn acid rain, that cuts through to the bone, escalating boiling heat, to frost bitten bitter cold, the pain it knows no peace, a wanderer it roams alone a haunted soul

(THE LIGHT)

In the light where all could be seen, where nothing could hide from its revealing beams, a place you would hope to be, because then you could see the enemy's trickery, all the snares and pitfalls set, to deceive then destroy till nothings left, in the light, open doors you can clearly see, to walk through the gates of prosperity, for the light dwells In those who receive it, an open mind and a heart to believe it, through everything faith is the key, to awaken the light inside you and me

(THE DARK)

In the dark monsters lurk knowing they cannot be seen, weary of the light that exposes their dirty deeds, here in the dark they can be free to release the evil they hide so carefully, to move anyway they choose, to kill, steal and destroy, victimizing peace, bending rules to insidious use, here in the dark there are no boundaries, with roles reversed, right becomes wrong and wrong becomes right, for a moment this shift has its time, for even darkness must rest, but know this my friend, darkness will come again

(EVIL)

Evil does not sleep or rest, lock all of your doors because evil will come in, invited or not it will find its way, to destroy the things held dear and safe, to darken the light, to dispel the truth, to saturate the mind until its consumed, to dismantle, oppress, defiling goodness, to take all it can to the abyss, to *disturb serenity and love, conjuring hell where it is from, its followers blindly follow its cult, to lay waste to the world and those not their own, to drain the blood from lifeless body's and devour the meat from their bones, never satisfied evil roams, like a cancer it finds a way to spread, for evil does not sleep or rest*

2Q

My eyes betray reality as I see a silhouette of astounding beauty.

A portrait painted, as if God himself commanded the sun so radiant to anoint his creation with tender strokes of patience.

A gift made for amazement with true dedication; there could be no waiting.

This urge to covet her love as my own, this desire to possess and control the whole of her glow, this untamed soul, this angel heaven let go, for it could not contain her pureness so true.

This want in me screamed in pursuit, this voice a whisper invading my mind, awakening dormant senses hidden inside.

The heat of my want coming to life creeping up my spine, dancing images emulating titillating sensations of a fantasy come to life.

Walking hypnotized in desires grasp, the image of my affection suddenly disappeared with a flash. Gone from my vision, a spell that seemed to be broken, casting my false dreams in a frigid ocean of despair.

This cruel fate leading me to believe that things are never quite what they seem, yet I cannot forget the seductive image of the mysterious silhouette that set my heart aflame, leaving me flustered and breathless.

My instinct told me something was wrong, and that these series of dream like visions were the quiet before a raging storm.

Yet again I threw my troubled thoughts aside, I would not let these irrelevant occurrences take away my focus on a promising life.

(ELUSIVE DREAMS)

In my dreams I chase a love that always runs, at the earths edge I pull back before I jump, looking over I can see a heart I will never reach, why does this elusive ghost have this powerful hold over me, who is she to command my full attention, so beautiful the sight, stuck in mid suspension, frozen In place, thinking of another way to capture her infectious love before she runs away

(SIREN DREAMS)

I can hear her calling, saying my name, come closer my love on a spiritual plan, finding myself in an ocean of waves, in the middle of no where lost in a haze, hypnotized I move to follow her sound, drawn to the music that comes from the clouds, I see a bright light it pierces the dark, the key to an endless chorus of hearts, what is this melody that enchants my soul? who is this angel of diamond and gold? Could she be whom I have always known, a goddess of beauty, a symbolic rose, before I reach she's out of my reach, who is this siren that haunts my dreams?

(TUNNEL VISIT)

In my dreams this tunnel I see surrounds her silhouette, it's hard to see in front of me but these things I cant forget, the feeling of knowing who you are with no evidence you exist, you must be this apart of me, this enigma I cant resist, a picture poorly taken hard to make a description, I reach for her in desperate need, in turn she slowly mimics, as my view fades from sight I grow more frantic, the more I chase it slips away, my tunnel visit vanished

(GIFT/CURSE)

I am endowed with the gift of a multi changing love, it is sweet and attentive, yet feral and addictive, I am the chemistry of every emotion that causes burning passion, yet I am the contradiction that locks your attention, it is wild and dangerous, seductively contagious and insatiably restless, I am cursed with a need to search the depths of the heart, yet blessed with a soul to navigate its ever changing corridors, I search tirelessly for the beauty who conjures inside of my dreams, until she is mine, in the grip of her spell I am bind

(YOU)

You are all I need, my elusive love that haunts my dreams, do you know what you do to me, my lonely heart cut in two, for you watch how It bleeds, in the depths of hell I will make my bed, if you were there to give me rest, for your kiss I would slit both wrist, to die in your eternal bliss, my angel will you give me peace or watch me broken into pieces, search me my love and condemn my demons, for there is no room for nothing else but you

(STORM)

Be the more vigilant in peaceful times, do not become slumber, lax in your ways, for a storm can come, unexpectedly sweeping the shores of your ignorance, uprooting the seeds that have not been properly harvested in procrastination, what will you do when you are unprepared for the silent storm? The waves of mayhem over-taking the house built on un-even ground, will you call upon those who have always known? Thus fortifying their foundation with brick and stone, or will you drown in

your complacent grave? Being swept along with the others who
did not prepare for the trying days

(DANGEROUS DENIAL)

What I know I should do, I do not, in the way of acceptance
I foolishly put off, overlooking the evident problem, turning
my back on my liable ignorance, anything to hide the fact
that I am vulnerable and open, naïve to a world driven by
madness, innocent in ways that are tragic, what is wrong
with me? I hear a underlying voice of reason, yet I purposely
reject its meaning, all to come up with my own complacent
interpretations, my own way of dealing with my shadows
reflection, forgetting the future, only thinking of now,
disregarding the perils of dangerous denial

(SOLACE BEAUTY)

As I look up I see my love, her immortal beauty illuminating
the eternal heavens above, painting her joy in solace
contentment, radiating through the soul of a crystal element,
I watch in adoration at her carefree freedom, delighted to
know more will soon transcend in spectrums of happiness, I
see a crystal sea in an aurora of faces, all hearts unique, all
sparkling spirits like diamonds celebrating in jubilant melody,
my scattered loves, if you can imagine, then you can see, that
you to can shine, if you only believe

(LOVES PREMONITION)

I see them, to many to number, the stars of transcended spirits
in the universal palace of loves immortal splendor, a crystal
sea of hearts a-flame, blazing in the dimensions of essence

continuum, creating a streaming aurora of bewitching beauty,
painting breathtaking horizons on the ether of new heavens,
I can feel her fluttering excitement, the utter euphoria of
limitless freedom, a supernova birthing passion fire in the
heights of special alignment, I see endless treasure sparkling in
spectrums of a crystal element, illuminating the reflection of
my souls wondrous depths, unveiling loves world in a startling
premonition

SIN BYRON

I have become a fugitive and a vagabond from my home. No longer can I stay, for demons have found their way inside searching for the broken crystal mirror pieces.

Taking special precautions that the wealth of my soul would remain safe I have hid them away.

They will search high and low finding nothing, of this conclusion I was confident. They would need me to unlock its secrets, but even then they would be sorely disappointed.

There are crystal pieces that are missing, the feeling is too hard to ignore. Its cry leads me further into the shadows away from my soul.

This pains me deeply, I feel alone and empty, as if I have been abandoned and left to die.

It was imperative I find the missing pieces, reconstruct the crystal mirror and become one with my other half again. Till then we were both susceptible to outside influence.

Reaching a mysterious gate I stared into its dark abyss looking into a bleak hollow tunnel that seemed unending, a light would be needed to travel through it.

In my hand I held a blue flame, its burning light illuminating brightly in a clear cylinder case.

What I held was the flame of hope, a power source derived from the boundless energy inside of the soul.

Despite the possibility of my demise I had to press forward, once inside I could not look back, to the end I must endure this trail that inevitably lead to a certain hell.

To recover my missing pieces I would have to face demons. Who is to say I make it out safe or even return the same. I guess that would be my fate, to be consumed by this mysterious dark place.

(HAUNTING GHOSTS)

When haunting ghosts arrive, I hide, I have hidden before, lost, alone, scared of my own shadow, evil ghosts, insidious souls, agonizing recitations, endless insinuation, constant provocation, leaving me with scrapped knees and bloodied hands, wishing my vulnerable life would come to an end, the haunting ghosts eventually leave me alone, but with their every visit, I become more cold

(COLD HEART)

My heart cold as ice, wonders through the blackest nights, I can blame no one but myself, an empty vessel void and pale, like a thief who came in and stole all I had, then burnt my fortress down to ash, now a beggar internally stained, a heartache, a restless need, you only appreciate once you truly lost, a glacier forms when warmth is gone, temperature reads zero degrees, my heart is cold as winters breeze

(LONELY HEART)

My heart is a loner traveling far and wide, searching for a love that left it far behind, exiled to a place searching for a sign, in the night crying looking at the sky, how could it endure so much pain, scorned by the light, oppressed by the rain, tears dried up the pain is underneath it, the streaks are overwhelming, he hides so no one sees it, what he would give to leave and just vanish, disappearing from those who wouldn't understand it, yet the heart remains and somehow manage, the lonely heart distant and stranded

(DEEP INSIDE)

Deep inside I am empty longing for something to fulfill me, my search tires my eternal soul, perpetuating my never-ending question, has destiny chosen me to never be whole? To wander with half a heart, half its home encased in stone, who can reach me when I am so far away? When what I do and what I say is two different things, when what's real and what's fake cannot be deciphered, for my own sake I push you away, mentally at a distance I can feel no pain, immune to the hell that's tormented me for so long, deep inside I retreat from the outsides raging storm

(DARK PATH)

The path I chose is dark and cold I would not recommend it, insidious it draws one and all, its humor is demented, it will infect the deepest parts of the human psyche, don't get lost, you will lose it all, coming back is unlikely, dejavu through and through, twilight in a matrix, patience calls, decipher all if you want to make it, no map, no help, look in yourself, watch every step you make, cause on this path is full of traps, fall and that's your fate

(HOPE)

Hope is to trust your desires to come through, to rely on expectations in and outside of you, for there is no control over said situations, hold steadfast, unyielding in patience, tenacious, persistent, firm in your belief, that what you wish will soon come to be, do not change, waver or falter, to have hope, your will must be as a stone in rushing water, no matter what may come do not budge, for hope is a foundation you must stand upon

(MISSING CRYSTAL PIECES)

From the darkness, each missing crystal piece cries out to me, what have I done, abandoned in the land of the dead each and everyone, my head reels, fast heartbeats, cold tears fall, I am empty, the insides of my ears bleed from the sound of their tormenting, I have been likened unto the vulnerability of a child, distracting myself from the inevitable truth, but I cannot hide, demons have broken through the barrier of my mind, whispering there insidious intent to take my life, the walls of my sanity are closing on reality's perfect illusion, how long will it be before the riches of my eternal soul are pillaged and my heart drowned in hells poison? Will I be torn asunder and fed to the mindless beast? Or by some miracle of heaven may there be some hope for me

(IN THE MIDST)

In the dark my tears fall alone in a isolated place, far away from your ever judging face, I cannot take back what I have done, the hurt I caused came back around and has made my life a living hell, now in these perilous times I wish I could end the pain, nothing will ever be the same, in the midst of death I cried aloud and was answered by two different sides, a blazing fire inside of me coming to life, the crystal mirrors luminescent light, everything I now see in clarity, a hidden world now open to me, my soul a glorious palace full of the riches of eternity, glimpses of my haunted dreams, a dark path, a aura, a diamond seat, a beautiful silhouette, an addictive need, a never ending well of energy, in the midst of this transformation I am truly awake, I have been reborn and given a new name

(BEFORE ME)

Before me there was nothing but emptiness, before me there was no love, just pain and sadness, before me I cried in the darkness hoping no one would see, before me the hell of my past tormented me, before me I was all alone, before me there was no one to depend on, before me I hid from my evident weakness, before me I was haunted by demons, before me I

closed my eyes, before me life passed me by, before me I awoke
adorned in the light, before me another was born in the night

2Q

Muddled thoughts weighed heavily on my mind. What was once disregarded and deemed irrelevant seemed to be resurfacing. I now wondered if something could actually be wrong with me.

The feeling of displaced detachment grew stronger as days passed, so instead of going about my normal routine I decided that taking at least one day off to clear my head would do some good, maybe this is what I needed to get back on track.

What a beautiful day, the birds were singing there songs of contentment and harmony, people going about their way seemingly without a care or worry, the radiant sun shining her rays of warmth on to my skin. Yet still doing nothing for this deeper coldness.

This empty feeling of hopelessness and despair causing me to dread my very own breath, my demeanor likened unto a living dead void of the substance of life, what is wrong with me? Why couldn't I focus on more important things concerning reality?

Analyzing the rationality of my troubled thoughts, I was oblivious to my surroundings and a second to late to get out of the way.

In a blink of an eye came a speeding car swerving recklessly, its impact knocking me off my feet and into the air.

In an instant my eyes opened in disbelief, did that really happen or was I dreaming again?

Finding myself lying on the ground I got up quickly, moving my legs, arms and hands, with no scratches, bruises, injuries or pain I brushed it off counting my lapse of reality as another daydream. Maybe today I would go see a shrink to see if in fact my sanity was to blame, I thought to myself continuing on my way.

Stopping my stride, I was unexpectedly startled by a crowd of screaming people, pointing and running in my direction.

Wondering what the problem was I remained still, confused at their eccentric behavior?

Within seconds a crowd gathered around with shocked and forlorn expressions, maybe I was day dreaming after all and had actually been hit by a car, but I was ok, wasn't I? Maybe it was the driver who got hurt?

Upon my observation I could see no car in sight. If I did get hit the car must have took off, it had to be me that was the reason for this commotion.

"I'm ok there is no need to worry," I said putting both thumbs up indicating I was fine.

But the crowding people just looked past me ignoring my existence completely.

Even more confused by their lack of acknowledgement I followed the direction of their attentive eyes. Turning around I looked down, surprisingly my lifeless body laid sprawl on the ground.

(UNSURE)

I am unsure of me sometimes, what side of me will show in time, my humble good or dangerous bad? What situation will bring about that thin line that easily snaps? The mirror of broken crystal pieces, a collage I fear will never resolve, but instead dissolve self control, causing me to hastily let go, oh the damage that would be done to my eternal soul, the likes of which I have never known, to avoid the colossal catastrophe to come, together myself and I must be one, to establish a balance this strain demands, everyday control is steady slipping from my hands

(DEATH THE UNEXPECTED)

Live everyday as best you can, because the unexpected can suddenly happen, when its time to go you never know, at any given moment death can come for you, for there is a time and a place for every living thing to return to its essence, from where it began, it so shall end, what state will death find you in? For all must return to the creator from whom he breathed the breath of life in, so who is to say that something belongs to them, when life can be so easily taken, what is it do you take when you go? What is it you say you have under control? When no one knows when it is their time to face the grave, ready or not it still will come, to return you to what you were made from

(CLEAR DETACHMENT)

You must look outside yourself to form a clear detachment, to see the things you cannot, letting go of all the attached burdens you must neutralize all emotion, for this is the weight that will lose your focus, seeing things for what they are, evaluating your flaws, you will attain the ability to see things for what they appear, no longer distorted, your vision will become clear, you will become aware of actions and patterns never perceived there, an internal presence, a metaphysical mirror, an infinite mind reaching an elevated status, looking outside of yourself to form a clear detachment

CHAPTER 2

SIN BYRON

Taking the first steps into the mysterious dark dimension outside of the soul, a loud echo bounced from wall to wall, a disruptive sound traveling further along into its endless darkness.

Startled I stopped and listened, alert for anything that could potentially be in the shadows lurking. Realizing my footsteps were the cause for the disturbance I continued on, stepping ever so lightly, even the smallest sound seemed to amplify in this dark world.

As if reacting to my unwanted presence the ground began to shake wildly, with an earsplitting bang the entrance to the dark gate closed behind me cutting off my only way back to the soul, there truly was no going back, I had to move forward.

Deeper and deeper I traveled into the unknown abyss determined to find the missing pieces I would need to make me whole again.

Hearing the sound of rushing water ahead, the luminous light of hope fell on a curved wooden bridge going over a vile river.

Moving slow and steady I walked over the bridges creaking wooden boards, my eyes going ahead of me looking for signs of a potential weak point.

But before I could get across, a black cloud of fogging smoke materialized before my anxious eyes.

Startled by its sudden appearance I prepared myself to face a monstrous demon, but what came out of the dissipating cloud was not what I expected to see, instead my eyes went wide, my legs felt weak, my heart skipped a beat at the sight of the two seductive beauty's.

Their name is their power, lust and desire diverted my focus away from the mission.

Spell bound by these beautiful women I followed them blindly; the first encounter is where it all begins.

(OBLIVIOUS FOG)

Diverted by the fog of desire you perilously stray from the right path, losing your will to get back on track, possibly reverting the long way you've come, whatever progress made dwindling to none, whatever focused plan cast by the wicked wayside sinking in stagnant sand, the further you wander in purposeless tread, the more oblivious you are the soulless demons of death

(WICKED WAYSIDE)

Many have fallen by the wicked wayside, all in eager pursuit of empty desire, unknowingly seduced into the fanning flames of a deathly fire, blinded at first, the spoils of pleasure enjoyed in contagious laughter, debauched without a single thought, disregarding that underlying sense, warning they have gone to far, but still you continue to follow the path of the demented others, who care not if your soul has wandered, the damned are consumed by the wayside of doom, trapped in the bottomless pit of shadowing death, lost in the outer regions of wicked darkness

(CLOUDS)

Stagnant energy, blocking the shine of your radiant positivity, drifting into your existence unexpected, coming together shrouding your focus, these are nothing but whimsical hindrances, never knowing in what direction they are floating, easily blown off course by the gusty winds of circumstance, the stormy atmosphere dragging you into a loop of turbulent nonsense, obscuring the clarity of your goals and vision, to rid yourself of an unwanted burden, the hazy clouds of distraction have to be parted

(PROVOKE)

You provoke me to chase you, to lose all thought thinking only of you, lured into your web by your siren call, how clever and calculating a seductress you are, when I am with you nothing seems to matter, overwhelmed by your smile distracted by your laughter, spellbound by your touch, enslaved by your sex, your beguiling eyes leave me with no defense, what are you after? Is it my addictive love, do you selfishly want it for yourself? To bring me the pleasure of your highest high, yet coming to know your lowest low, are these your motives? The way you lick those kissable lips charming my desire by your sexual whims, taking control losing my will to resist, provokes my urge to taste your skin

(CAUSE AND EFFECT)

One circumstance leading to the next, every action a reaction, every cause and effect, everything you do, every place you move, has an influence on your choices, pursuits to be pursued, introduced to countless options with many doors behind, once you have walk through one, others open wide, every step echo's your foot prints in the future, be careful were you tread, for every cause has an effect

(DISTRACTION)

Come to me my love, let me distract you from your worries, let me lead your heart, don't stray away from me, look into my eyes and see a radiant sunrise, through a crystal veil as beautiful as the sky, focus so serene, a sparkling sea of glass, where all comes together, present, future, past, every captured moment, more special then the last, come to me my love and never look back

2Q

In shock I panicked, my life nothing but a vapor in the midst vanished. To the world dead, yet here I am an eternal ghost with no end. Who could hear me scream? Who would answer my pleas? What of my family?

I will not accept, nor will I believe that me with so much potential could easily disappear into the wind.

Where is this God? Has he forgotten me? Am I cursed to roam the world captive in my emptiness, an apparition of a former self stuck in between heaven and hell, life and death, how I wish I wasn't born or given life's breath, if only my beloved mother spewed me out a bloody mess, a worthless waste to be discarded, disregarded, then forgotten as quickly as I was conceived, this alone would comfort my soul trapped in this empty dream.

As I continued venting in bitter despair and discontent, to my alarming disbelief a casually dressed man walked over pleasantly, his big bright eyes that seemed to be judging, calculating, and yet assuming nothing.

He was tall and intimidating with skin that illuminated a bright fixation. Panicking, my first thought was to run, but I couldn't move.

Awe struck and utterly clueless I tried to speak, but my tongue was as glue.

"I'm sorry my friend but if you promise not to run, I will remove the hold from your limbs and tongue," said the easygoing man.

Coming to grips with this unbelievable situation I incoherently mumbled to tell the man yes. Snapping his fingers, my breath was instantly released simultaneously freeing the hold on my limbs.

With a heaving chest I dropped to my knees breathing heavily.

"Who...are you," I managed to say.

He then responded,

"I am the reaper of souls here to take you away."

(BLESSINGS/COMPLAIN)

Why do you complain when you receive so many blessings? When there are those who have less, those who would die to be in the position your in, those who would receive and be content with just a small portion off of the bountiful table of your blessings, yet you complain of the littlest things, not giving thanks, consistently searching for flaws and weak links, ungrateful for the things given and what those things could mean for someone else, your blessings are far in between your complaints and pitiful views, selfishly ignoring what has always been right in front of you

(FAMILY)

My family, dear family, I owe a debt that cannot be paid, for you gave me joy that I replaced with so much pain, a life built solely on my faults, now the hell brought on myself is my just reward, selfish I have been for everything you give, now the underworld of death is where I made my bed, a tombstone pressed in weeds is where I lay my head, to the ends of hell over its edge I fell, all the blessings from the heavens are the things I took for granted, unfair to the care I always knew was there, now I could only blame myself if it was to disappear

(WHERE WERE YOU)

Where were you when I needed you most? When I was down, you let me crawl, when I stood up, you let me fall, when I cried out, you ignored my existence, my weighted pain a heavy burden to lift, every hellish day took a piece away, every single minute took my heart with it, no longer the same washed away by the rain, all that was me died in a wave, it drowned a boat I thought couldn't sink, a ripple effect on an empty shore, lost at sea a part of me gone, where are you now I can see you no more

(KARMA)

What karma loaned me I am still in debt, to pay for sins I cannot forget, a law, a scale, a balance and check, a constant reminder when it comes to collect, its equation of life is always correct, it measures each moment and weighs each step, a tally is took when a baby's conceived, the sins of the parents, the life that it will lead, all that is owed can stick to the breed, what's done unto others can come unto me, for who are we to blame, it's the universes way, its cosmic action and reaction, its yin and its yang

(SORRY)

Your sorry you let me go, you let me down, all because I was not around, out of sight, out of mind, no thought of what you left behind, you thought me lost not to be found, so you switch sides and turned around, now your hearts left in the cold, when I'm the one you needed most, your words are empty, to late for your pleas, your shallow tears have no substance to me, I'm sorry

SIN BYRON

As the ever-burning flame of hope lit the way through the darkness I followed the sirens aimlessly, hopelessly ensnared like an infatuated child by the persuasive beauty of a naked lust and desire.

Stopping at a massive stone, its solid structure materialized into a door made of tanzanite.

In awe I entered into their boudoir, my eager eyes following the burning torches aligning a glowing path towards their tantalizing bed, excited by the irresistible sight of its ambivalence my baited heartbeat sped.

Sashaying in front of me lust and desire began fondling each other slowly, their smoky eyes boring seductively into mine, their throaty voices moaning as their wet fingers stimulated the others sex.

With wide eyes I stood captive by my desire, immobilized by the pure feeling of lust, the pent up pressure of my aching libido dying to be released by these erotic beauties.

"Come here Sin Byron, come play with us" they both said in unison walking backwards like a floating specter towards the inviting bed.

With no thought of the mission or the possible consequences I pursued them mindlessly, mesmerized by there beckoning, likened unto an easily molded piece of putty constructed in there manipulating hands.

Reaching the foot of the opulent bed they began to undress me strewing my clothes all around the room, taking turns whispering into my ear and caressing my fully erect cock.

Now naked and to the point of no return I gave into my animal like urges, grabbing then roughly penetrating lust who simultaneously pleasured desire with her tongue.

My entire body felt on fire as I rigorously pumped in and out of her dripping sex, her screaming orgasms drenching me in succulent juices.

Once finishing with lust I entered desire next, the room seemingly spinning as the sound of our grinding bodies clapped, her sharp nails digging into my back as we collided together with reckless abandon.

Seized by the euphoric distraction of pleasures intoxicating high, my breathing became heavy, my legs began to weaken and shake, desires clenching sex seemed to tighten even more around my stiff cock, any second my spurting seed would explode inside the demon of body shuddering ecstasy.

Hearing a scuttle, I impulsively turned my head in time to catch a little green demon sneaking away with the flame of hope.

Not giving the thieving creature a chance to escape I swiftly got off the bed chasing after the pilfering demon; startled by my suddenness it dropped the flame of hope disappearing in a smoky haze.

Disenchanted by this unforeseen interruption lust and desires spell over me was broken. Without saying a word I grabbed my belongings, feeling foolish for falling for their trick, this little slip could have been the end of the mission I thought to myself, angry at my vulnerable mistake.

"Come back to bed we are not finished" said a brazen desire sulking.

"Never again you filthy demon bitches! I must admit that was a nice attempt, I applaud you for trying, but it will take more then that to stop Sin Byron!" I stated proudly.

"Oh how foolish, the demon deceit should be the least of your concern, for every demon you accept, in turn makes you just like them," said lust snickering.

"So Sin Byron will you come taste this again" said desire spreading her legs with a devious smile, her moist fingers moving feverishly in and out of her velvety sex.

"Never in your miserable eternity you filthy demon whores!" I snapped angrily before turning my back on them walking out of the tanzanite door.

(LOSE YOURSELF)

Come with me my love and lose yourself in the dark, be with me forever, lost in a lovers daze, into another world spread your wings and defy restraint, here you can let loose your repression without fear of judgment, here the pure defile themselves in lustful need, a willing slave of insatiable exile reveling in the craving I ransom, a sexual eternity, a timeless poetry immortalizing the essence of my love perfectly, reaching beyond the fabric of mere reality to rapture her radiant energy, take my hand and let us be free, come lose yourself in the deep well that is me

(LUST)

I want you here, I want you now, your clothes ripped off and strewn around, who cares who hears, who cares who sees, on your back or on your knees, screaming loud or tender pleas, to the point of your release, I want it in the worse way, drown me in pleasures deep, tasting your sweet fruit, pouring all over me, I pull on your hair, you mark up my back, lost in our lust, no escaping how we act, something nasty the way Sin Byron likes it, our aphrodisiac lust, there is no way to fight it

(DESIRE WANTS)

Desire grasp is a potent narcotic, it finds me in want as I undress you with my eyes, my provoked mind painting images of hot sex under foreign skies, my disguise elegant and smooth yet underneath brash and loose, never apologize for brazen behavior my love, we are what he made us, so drown out the haters and give into want, take your clothes off and do what you want, my body is your playground for as long as you want, in desires grasp desire will want

(ONE TOUCH)

One touch and your mine, one touch will send shivers down your spine, one touch will open up the flood gates to your pleasurable release, one touch will bind you to me, one touch will free the love from your beating heart, one touch will release the dark, one touch will make you obsessed, one touch will make you give in, one touch will make you moan, one touch will make you sin, one touch will be your days, one touch will be your nights, one touch will possess you for the rest of your life

(BOUDOIR)

In your boudoir I bring my sex, the taste of my lips, my enticing scent, an addictive love, secret wants, trapped inside your hungry lust, dreams of me inside your legs, my voice dominating your submissiveness, I am your weakness making you wet, my touch turns on your body's faucet, opening my mouth to take a drink your juices spill all over me, here your free to do as you please, to do whatever you want to me, to tear apart the open seems, filling it once more with shuddering ecstasy

(PLEASURE)

I live for your pleasure, no strings attached, sensuous sensations, pure extract, capture your essence to entice you slow, to bring you through the highs and lows, let go of control give it to me, lets leave reality and float away, into a dream, a fetish place, relax my love and revitalize your parched flesh, give in to pleasure a realm of sex

2Q

Many questions I wanted to ask this spiritual being, but my mind was overwhelmed.

If what he said was true, and he was in fact the reaper of the dead, that meant he was there for me and there was nothing I could do.

I didn't want to leave the world so soon there was so much in life I wanted to do, so many things I never experienced and wanted to accomplish. If I could only start over a brand new me, I would appreciate life more doing things differently.

"I can read your mind, your words are sincere but your soul is in distress," said the reaper in a grimly manner, his unassuming eyes beaming intensely into mine as if he could see right through them.

Not knowing what he meant I summoned the strength to say some words in my defense.

"I know I wasn't the most caring person, and to be totally honest I may have been a bit of a narcissus in my endeavors, but I never was a hateful person and I have always remained fair to people even when they did not deserve it. Sure I may have gotten upset losing my cool a few times, but who hasn't, that's part of being human. I guess what I'm trying to say is that I'm not ready to move on yet, please give me another chance at life again, if you do I promise you-"

Interrupted without a chance to finish my plea, the loud sound of thunder drowned out my speech.

Suddenly a cracking lighting bolt flashed across the darkened sky violently striking the reaper where he stood.

Staggering back, my popping ears belted a deafening ringing sound leaving me stunned and barely able to stand on my quivering legs.

Through spotted vision I could see the reaper standing in the same place calm and unharmed, in his hands he held a large black book.

Opening the book its animated pages flipped rapidly, stopping abruptly.

"Now let us see if your good out weighs your bad, but pray as you might have a hope to fulfill yourself again… now that's interesting," said the reaper with his eyebrows raised.

Bracing myself for the revelation of what would be my fate, there was no doubt in my mind that this was judgment day.

SIN BYRON

Even with the flame of hope lighting the way through the dark path like a lantern I still couldn't pinpoint where I was or how long I had been away. All I knew was the longer I traveled down this road the light of burning hope was slowly fading, without it I would be lost in the dark. I needed to find the missing crystal pieces, but where to look or start?

In this dark world were many paths, ridges and even pitfalls with who knew what at the bottom. So to give me a sense of direction I stayed on the original path not veering from it since my first run in with the siren demons lust and desire, their last words to me replaying over In my head.

I would never be like them! The only them that would transpire from my actions would be to kill anything like them.

Right now I could only contemplate what was going on with my other half 2Q? I could no longer feel his life force, was it somehow being engulfed by this dark place?

The absence of this vital feeling caused me to wonder if something could of happened to him in the physical world due my spiritual absence. I was his eyes and ears for the supernatural, without me 2Q was internally blind and empty, his soul uninhabited and vulnerable, without the crystal mirror he was defenseless.

With the welfare of my other half on my mind I neared the end of the path, reaching a battered sign at the beginning of a fork in between two new roads, the right arrow read to prosperity, the left read to demise.

Was this some kind of joke? Why would an entity need a sign? Was this some imaginary fixture made up by this strange place?

Trying to rationalize this would force me to rationalize everything else that didn't make any sense in this place, so I would go with the obvious choice.

Taking the right road, a good feeling warmed me; I was finally making progress I thought to myself. But little did I know a little green demon had changed the signs direction, leading me down a gloomy path towards my demise.

(CHOICES)

Everyone has a choice, everyone is given free will, what is chosen leads to paths bearing fruit, or being stripped ruined and desolate, for a choice could be your last or the beginning of something excellent, looking beyond what is, to what could be, opens up options beyond limited comprehension, why give something a set definition, when the possibilities are infinitely endless

(THE DEMON DECEIT)

The demon deceit causes countless souls to lose their way, it leads many to their deaths not caring who it leads astray, all for self satisfaction and personal gain, the grave is full of its victims, the road paved with good intentions, misguided direction that can avoid detection, everything that glittered seemed gold, until it robbed and desecrated the remains of the soul, the truth, the demon deceit truly hates, so it will do everything in its power to have you lose your way

2Q

"It seems the lord of heaven has a plan for you yet, but I fear your mission is one you will fret," said the reaper closing the book causing it to vanish.

"Plan...mission, I don't understand, does this mean I will not pass on instead?" I inquired hopefully.

"If you so wish, I will spare you from what you must do, but the decision will be up to you, know that if you choose to accept, you will have to enter the depths of darkness to save yourself, but know this well, if you are to fail, your soul will be forever trapped in a perpetual hell."

Thinking about the raw words of the reaper, my thoughts went back to the start of the trance like visions.

Since then I had lost contact with my other half, could all of this be happening because of this damaged connection? Was the coldness I felt inside myself actually Sin Byron lost?

I had to make an important decision. Despite all that Sin Byron had put me through how could I leave the other half of myself in distress, if I was to leave with the reaper of souls I would never be whole, so how could I rest.

The spirit of this alternate consciousness called Sin Byron derived from my conscious objection on moving to a new place.

I remembered begging my mom and dad not to leave the only home I had ever known.

Though we were moving to a better location, I would be leaving my childhood friends and familiar settings of comfort-ability and attachment. But I was a teenager and therefore to young to make any big decisions, besides we were finally getting what we always wanted and prayed for, a house in a better neighborhood.

A gift from God my mom called it, but to me it was nothing but a mistaken inconvenience.

Trying to get a feel for my new surroundings I ventured out on my brand new bike embarking on a mission to make new friends.

Eventually finding someone named Johnny, a boy around my age I thought was cool.

Within seconds of meeting him I was asked permission to ride my bike, being that Johnny was fascinated with it and he kindly asked me I quickly agreed with this person I just met, making it out in my mind that this small gesture of trust was a token of our budding friendship.

But that trust was readily broken when Jonny rode away never coming back in the "few minutes" he said he would, so I went searching, finding him thirty minutes later laughing and joking with three other boys.

Approaching with a good attitude and a smile I politely asked for my bike back, but instead of good cheer and gratitude I was met with hostility, shoved to the ground, punched and kicked, beaten down by all four of them.

All I could think about was how I begged my family not to leave and how nobody wanted to listen to me, because of that, this was happening.

I felt my presence didn't matter to anyone, burdened by insignificance, enslaved by my vulnerable tolerance, I became filled with rage, so sweet the payback I regret to this day.

I remember the feeling, a euphoric release to let loose with a vengeance.

Blacking out, not able to remember what happened next, I awoke to all four of my attackers unconscious, their dripping blood cascading droplets from my shaking hands.

Every night since then whenever I slept my dreams would take me to where this crystal mirror stood.

At first I just saw it as a dream thinking nothing of it, until it became consistent and more real then the world I was living in. So I kept this dark secret to myself, Sin Byron was my first friend in a foreign place, though we were different, we were also the same, he was apart of me, I had to help myself.

(BULLYS)

I can see through them for they are shallow inside, what is it bully's hide there exterior defines, for you see the outside is a desperate cry from the burden inside, making things worse becomes there curse, ultimately sabotaging themselves in the end demeaning there worth, lashing out from the internal help denied, the vessel of the bully Erodes, a gradual decline, detesting themselves they do what they can so you can feel what they feel, a twisted version of empathy hiding the bitter bully destitute and empty, one who will soon self destruct ceasing to be

(BUILT UP)

Emotions built up on the inside beg to be released, eating away mercilessly causing you to seethe, this wont go away, it will chip at the wall of your resistance till its structure breaks, flooding through the dam you tried desperately to restrain, breaching the outer exterior that can no longer be contained, it is only a matter of time before the built up emotions you harbor can no longer be caged, building one on top of the other collapsing from its weight

(BE YOURSELF)

Be yourself, change for no one, who is it you are trying to be? When how you act doesn't fit who you are personally, becoming something your not, portraying a fraud, not being true to your heart, is it acceptance your after playing the role of someone else? at the end of the day your still yourself, is it when you look in the mirror you hate what you see? Why, when inside of you is full of beauty, you are special and unique, there will never be someone like you, stay true to yourself, not changing who you are to appease someone else

(EXPRESS/SHY)

Let it be bright, express your light, let it pierce through the darkest nights, transform yourself, be full of life, you cover brilliance by being shy, let it go, let it show, how intriguing your colors glow, you are so much more then what you know, in you there is promise and potential

(KIDS)

Kids are a special gift from heaven, you must pay extra attention, for they can become the greater good or bloom into the greatest evil, for they learn from watching you, imitating the impressionable, not necessarily the best of you, because the things that slip, what's not noticed, is in their sight in full focus, their premature minds soaking in this volatile solution pollutes them, be vigilant and good, so the things that rub off stick, becoming the best in them, how they act becoming a testament to the proud parent whose time was invested in, what we do in the present lives, shaping the future of our kids

(PARENTS)

Parents so much rest on your shoulders, what you do effects your child as they get older, you may not see it, you may not recognize your actions as being a reason, but inside your child is changing, feeling different emotions, they are being molded, they will either learn to hate or love you, they will learn through the things they go through and reflect it on other people, there can be no one else to blame but the parents whose job is to raise and properly train, the child who goes the wrong way didn't start off that way, their minds are impressionable at a young age, absorbing what they see and feel, helping shape them in what they will be, a burden or an upstanding citizen in society, parents open your eyes and see. That what you do affects your child deeply

(HAPPY BIRTHDAY)

On this special day you were born free from your umbilical cord, sweet kisses showered your little face, with love you were given a name, with a soothing coo and a lullaby to sing, you rocked back and forth cradled in your mothers protective arms, your pretty eyes like marbles twinkling like a star, with wonder what you will be and will you be happy, promises were made to keep you safe, to give their life in your place, to give you everything you will ever need, to shelter, clothe and feed, with love you were conceived, so celebrate today, when you took your very first breath on your happy birthday

(PEER PRESSURE AND MANIPULATION)

Who are you? Can you tell me? Why let someone else decide, have you no dignity or pride to take control of your own life? Can you not see you are being used for all the wrong reasons? A puppet by a string being manipulated for hidden agendas disguised as peer relations, tricking your mind to think that you will be accepted, but the truth is you are being pressured to do something they will never do themselves, a scapegoat if everything was to fail, as disposable as trash to be thrown away, turning a back to you just as easily, it is nothing to them because it is you being manipulated and used, knowing who and who not to do it to, they pick and choose, preferably a gullible fool, so they choose you, only you know you, so the question is, who are you?

(DIGNITY/INTEGRITY/MORALS)

Do you know your worth? How do you view yourself? Because how you view yourself becomes how you treat yourself, your appearance, your actions, your health, all reflecting your morals and integrity held, with no dignity it becomes as if you sold your soul, falling for anything and standing for nothing, your morals and integrity cast to the side, with no standard of pride it is like you are not human, likened unto an animal with no direction, void with no self judgment, free yourself from this indecency, awaken from this stupor and have some dignity, embrace morals and become open with integrity, looking at yourself with total honesty you will awaken urgently, holding yourself accountable through self expectancy you will start to see yourself succeed, a change from negative to positive energy, your presence expressing growth and development, knowing your worth the better you will be, with dignity, morals and integrity

(THE TURNING POINT, THE BIG BANG)

Nearing the brooding edge of the deepest depths, I hang my dispirited head, my cry, my tears, and my darkest fears, echoing off the solemn walls of despair, wallowing in my exposed filth, the more I am shunned by all the meaningless feelings I had ever felt, pushing me closer towards the deadly fall of my looming hell, why resist, who would care if I die or lived, I'm hallow, damaged, muddled, emotionally distant, but something strange seems to be happening, I am slowly becoming numb to the madness, excepting my inadequate and shameful position in this hopeless situation, I am wavering in anticipation, utterly euphoric, for soon pain will dissipate along with the release of my ever burdened weakness, what comforting emptiness would bring solace at the conclusion of my grave torment, as I now drop tumbling towards my fate, a bright light exploded into being, the turning point, the big bang

CHAPTER 3

SIN BYRON

The first thing I noticed was the flame of hope fading fast. Next my strength leaving, my every step like draining a life sustaining battery, my eyelids heavy, my head starting to spin, my weary legs reluctantly moving though wanting to shutdown and rest.

Blinking my weary eyes, a set of red eyes blinked back; red as the blood I could now see covering this path, could I be seeing things? Was this an illusion?

Looking down, I was surprised to see that my legs were covered with blood streaming like a river, yet grungy and dense like mud.

Slithering by silently catching my unawares, something unexpectedly snatched the flame of hope from my grasp.

Before I could react darkness surrounded me while the flames illuminating light quickly moved away.

I hated to be slighted; this thief would feel my rage.

Running in the endless dark I could see nothing around me just the light up ahead, my hurried movement echoing the sound of my feet splashing in the bloody river.

With every step my mind painted retribution in a vivid picture, oh what I would do to this filthy creature when I caught it, how dare it steal from me, did these creeps think I was weak, that I Sin Byron would allow this thing to do whatever it pleased.

For this blatant disrespect I would sever its head from its neck watching on in glee as whatever it was squirmed in its own piss and shit, then every demon, monster or otherwise would know to stay the fuck out of my way or they to would suffer the same fate.

Nothing mattered to me, just getting even and taking back what was mine.

Up ahead the light stopped in place as if challenging me, taunting to come and get it if I dared.

Not thinking clearly, I should have been aware of the insidious trick being played, from the very beginning my decisions being swayed, a game of chess, a loose pawn trapped in a maze, this was their world and I was their pray.

(SNAKE)

Beware of the snake, but also respect the snake that's stays true to its name, what is it to sneak around in secret, with the potential to bite the hand that feeds it, it can camouflage appearing normal, inconspicuously cordial, then changing in an instant to betray or harm you, know the snake for what it is capable of, through the way they move, you will know what to do when confronted with this type of animal

(DARKNESS FALLS)

Once you are open and all hope is lost, evil darkness rampantly falls, whatever resisting faith or love is dashed, blackening your precious soul with the burning portals ash, the consuming contagion spreading restless anguish, its fiendish grasp violently seizing your helpless being, the hungry shadows rampaging in a malicious frenzy, defiling and usurping your feeble energy, once the stage has been properly set, next the spiritual invasion the demonic duress

(ANIMAL)

Trapped in this hell where I cannot escape, where every corner is treacherous and no place is safe, where there is no difference between an animal with two legs our four, here they are governed by no laws, naturally driven off of impulse, what is it that makes me distinct is the very thing that draws them in, my uniqueness locks them on to my scent, I have become the hunted, but to run is to only spur them on, to become them is to lose who you are, the only option is to understand where it is they stand, to always think ahead, out maneuver and follow threw with your plans

(THE DEMON ANGER)

The anger comes from deep within, caused by legions of multiple sins, a malicious cancer seeping strength, it does not care who it offends, family, friends, authority figures, the more it grows, the more its bitter, be cautious and leery of its sensitive trigger, for it does not think it lashes out on instinct, on the brink of rage leaving ruble in its place, the anger destroys what it cannot relate, its fickle demeanor eccentric its ways, the demon anger comes then goes away

(THINK/ACT)

Think before you act, or you will find yourself mixed up in something bad, stuck in a place you never thought you would be at, stuck in a situation you never thought you would be in, the keyword is thought, something that should have been clearly formed before pursuing whatever your actions brought forth, the outcome you would have been prepared for, but instead off balance you go with the first thought, your actions *afterwards become forced, now chances are the decision made was wrong, making a hard bed only you will have to lay on, to stay on the right track think before you act, or become apart of the very problem you can never take back*

(CHESS)

Life is a game of chess, you are the king protecting your interest, finding the best alternating positions through offense and defense, the opposition will try to knock you off of your square, through devious tactics used in modern warfare, all in a twisted plot to make what's your there's, sacrificing resources no matter how scarce, through manipulation lies infiltration, preparing their forces for an invasion, doing whatever it takes to strategically move closer to your kingdom, using traps intentionally set for you to stumble, nefarious plans to breach your walls, to triumphantly burn it down, securing the victory when it falls, prepare what's yours, for this is war, strengthen your castle, barricade the doors, see to its armor it must be strong, go over every nook and cranny until you are sure, defensive and offensive specifications are up to par, prepared and ready to perform at its best, you are the king, life is a game of chess

2Q

"Yes I will accept the mission and brace the darkness to save myself, but there are questions I need answered, if I am to be truly prepared I need to know what dangers I'm facing and what enemy's I'm up against," I said facing the reaper.

"As you wish," said the reaper holding out his right hand, "take my hand and open your eyes to the unseen things on the other side."

Was I ready for this? What if something went wrong? I thought to myself hesitantly reaching for the reapers hand.

Immediately after contact the sky turned black, the earth shook angrily, the ground started to crack, the combination of shock and panic gripped my heart in fear.

With wide eyes I looked at the reaper for answers, but his face remained passive lacking emotion.

Suddenly the ground split open, out coming a dark smoke with an unbearable heat plaguing the air with the stench of death and burning flesh.

In disbelief, my bulging eyes took it all in as I stood suspended over a scorching pit.

"This is what happens when souls become trapped in a perpetual hell, there are seven levels of torment, here what you see is the first where it all begins."

Agonizing cries could be heard below.

In horror I watched one mans head smashed open over and over again with a large stone, then caused to regrow, beside him a women's face viciously cut open with a jagged knife, and as it healed ripped back open again as it closed. Countless others being tortured in the same heinous fashion with no rest, just endless torment.

Closing my eyes, I turned my head from their cruel fate.

"Please lets move on from this," I asked feeling nauseous.

Nodding his head, the reaper of souls replied

"As you wish."

(SPIRIT GUIDE)

Under the veil of the spirit we carefully move through the chilling darkness, our souls a brilliant lamp illuminating our every step, enveloping our hearts in the pure light of the heavens, at the front lines of loves battle I blaze a path through barriers of inhibition, making way in a royal chorus of dwelling transcendence, lashing out in a out-cry of deep passion, to draw all loves through the portal to the stars, to find her intimate treasure, alive in the celestial paradise of immortalized splendor

(THE OTHER SIDE)

Light why do you elude me, I search but cannot find what makes me whole, the shadow of pain envelops my soul, my physical being, my mental well being, all that I am is constantly fleeing, trapped in a dark room where no one can hear me, the demons of death fight to be near me, a secret pain, a secret past, a hellish department first and the last, empty smiles, void emotions, vast seas, raging oceans, on the rivers of hades I have my token, but what is my life if my fate has chosen the other side

(SIN)

Sin what is said we fight against, how difficult this is, for towers and mountains of various pleasures, to valleys and corruptions of vast measures, the things we allow to consume our lives, the battle of what's wrong and what's considered right, morality disregarded, temptations of immorality's flaunted, priorities banished for feelings of reckless abandon, sin a river that runs through us all, a raging waterfall that pours abroad

(QUESTIONS AND ANSWERS)

An answer starts with a question, how would you know were to go if you don't ask directions? Answers in the dark will elude your grasp, questions are a compass, answers are the needle pointing towards the path, how could you get lost when *there are multiple arrows directing your knowledge to what it wants, endless sources in rows of information, waiting to be freed from proper investigation, there is nothing off limits and nothing out of bounds, to find something out, ask questions and answers will be found*

SIN BYRON

Throwing all would be caution to the wind I rushed ahead.

Reaching the floating cylinder I was alarmed to see it left alone, what sense would it make to just abandon my only source of light when it had me right where it wanted me? Was it baiting me waiting for the opportune moment to strike? One thing for sure, something wasn't right with this picture.

I got the feeling of an eerie expectancy in the dead silence, as if it to was also waiting for something.

Squinting my eyes through the flames fading light I found my suspicions were sorely right.

A grayish smoke contaminated the air.

Despite my instinctive movement to cover my nose from the poisonous cloud, my bodily functions started to gradually shut down.

Fading in and out of consciousness I kept moving forward fighting to resist, questioning myself with my every step weather I would die or live.

Suddenly the sound of a malevolent hiss echoed threw-out the perilous abyss.

The creature must have returned to finish off what it started, I was being ambushed, and this was a trap!

What was worse I didn't have the strength to fight back.

Materializing, Anger and arrogance stood side by side in the form of snakes equipped with human limbs and lethally curved teeth, an excited swarm of frenzied flies flying around them as if attached to there foul smell of decaying flesh, causing my eyes to water and my head to turn away in disgust.

"My friend you look like you had better days, if I didn't know any better I believe in your eyes I see some hate," anger was the first to say, his repulsive face contorting in a grimace.

"I think your right anger he's upset because he cannot have his way, I do recall reading his mind he wants to make us pay," said arrogance with a hiss.

"What the fuck do you want with me?" I asked almost retching on my own spit in revulsion at the forms of their disgusting manifestations.

My head was reeling and my wobbling legs threatening to collapse, but I would rather soon die then give these creeps the satisfaction.

"You must not know where you are my feeble friend, you better get with the program if you want to live that is," said arrogance with a snicker.

"No continue to get mad, id rather him like that, it shows he has a will to strike back," said anger rubbing his disfigured hands together.

"Go fuck yourselves!" I retorted sharply, weakly dropping to my knees spitting up a black colored blood.

I was held captive by my vulnerability, and soon the inevitability of death would come to claim me.

(NEVER HOLD BACK)

What must be done I never hold back, underestimate my intentions and suffer my wrath, if you play with fire you will get burned, anger to cremate ashes to urns, no barrier can withstand my relentless consistence, my push will pull any resistance, for nothing in heaven or anything living, can stop the sentence to carry out my mission, I will not heed until I succeed, till my life force is gone and no longer I breathe, I will never hold back this fire in me

(GIVING UP)

Once you give up you sign your will to surrender, automatically losing the fight, your actions have become a sanctioned suicide, laying down willingly, voluntarily suffocating waiting to die, not only just you, but everyone who has ever supported you in your entire life are also buried with you inside, the question now becomes why? Do you think you are alone and that you carry yourself? How foolish and selfish you are to think you are the only one who has it hard, somewhere someone's life is far worse and death would relieve their hell on this earth, how little do we count the blessings in turn even when some blessings not even deserved, think of this when your feeling stuck, think once for yourself, think twice for those you love, think before giving up

(THE DEMON ARROGANCE)

The demon arrogance could care less, don't even waste your breath, words would only fall on deaf ears, their is only itself no one else is there, always coming first you are beneath it, the demon arrogance could careless if you die or live, its only concern and focus rest on self, you could say it is unfeeling and empty inside, if arrogance could reply it wouldn't, why would it when your opinion is worthless as dirt and your existence lowly as a worm, the way it sees it you do not deserve anything, for everything that is worth acquiring should only be for it, and all for its uncaring arrogance

(SILENT NIGHT)

They watch from the shadows plotting your grave demise, they are insidiously evil, wanting to possess the portal to your soul so they can abuse and waste you, once in there clutches your inhabitants will die, your vibrant world will become empty and silent inside, a shell you will be, perpetually swallowed up in consuming misery, if you only knew what nightmares lie in wait, you would laugh less and think more of your inevitable fate

2Q

Opening my eyes, I was relieved to see everything as it should be, regular people headed to their destinations crowded together on city streets.

For a moment I felt like I could walk away with them and put everything behind me, but I couldn't because I was in the spirit, dead to the world, reminded by the ever haunting presence of the reaper standing next to me that I was nothing but a ghost.

"Behold I will show you the living curse that is and the effect they have on the living, the first demons you will see go by the names murder and hate," said the reaper pointing to a short man dressed in worn out clothes, shoes and a baseball cap.

In an instant my vision became as a magnifying glass causing me to see two unsightly demons whispering horrible atrocities to the distraught man.

As far away as I was there should have been no way to hear them, but I did.

"Look at these stupid people rushing off to their cozy homes and lucrative jobs while you so worthless have been crawling and begging your whole life, they never will know what its like to struggle for scraps while they sit back and get fat," stirred hate.

"Yeah you don't got nothing to live for anyway, its not fair how life's treated you, you would think one of them would stop to help a poor man, but no! They are to busy to notice your sad existence, what's so different from you and them, oh I forgot, your garbage in the eyes of society, these arrogant selfish privileged scumbags need to pay for there sins," pressured murder.

The influential pressure of the evil demons caused the distraught man to snap becoming enraged.

Clenching his teeth with a wild look in his eyes the man pulled from his waste a semi-automatic pistol.

To the delight of the demons and my horror the demented man started shooting blindly into the crowd slaughtering men, women and children in cold blood, a tragedy of epic proportion, pandemonium and confusion.

Frantic people took to the streets causing a reckless stampede, the unlucky caught in the commotion, trampled to death underfoot.

Looking on in horror and frustration, I could see the two demons celebrating in mock of the foolish man who fell for their evil plan.

"One soul for the master and one less for him!" they cheered and chanted over and over again.

Ejecting an empty clip from the smoking guns chamber the shooter loaded more rounds in, just as he did three police cruisers came screeching to a halt boxing him in, other emergency sirens could be heard in the far distance.

"Who cares if you die, kill all of them! What's the point in living," incited murder.

Taking cover behind there police cruisers with their guns drawn law enforcement ordered the crazed man to drop his weapon.

"You have been spit at, abused and stepped on, you will never be, or have anything, fuck this petty life of misery, take as many as you can with you, do it now you worthless fleabag of a human," provoked hate.

Ready to die, the demented man raised his gun squeezing the trigger three times before going down in a ballistic hail of booming gun fire, not before one of his bullets hit its mark, striking a rooky officer in the head, both closing their eyes to welcome death.

(LIFE/CHALLENGES)

In life there will be challenges to face, everyone worried about themselves going there separate ways, in life there is no easy way, you have to stare challenges down face to face, going through the fire to find your place will either make or break, bringing about an iron will, or a tombstone with your name, life is what you perceive, what you do inevitably is what you will receive, a cause and effect of eminent responses, advantages and disadvantages, life and challenges

(MONEY)

Money is the root of need, an advocate for evil deeds; the cause of countless wants yet seemingly not enough, the drive behind many forces, the reason for many losses, the battery for motivation, blue prints for kingdoms of administration, why wars will always be fought, money we are dying for, for loyalty to switch and change, banished morals for capital gain

(THE DEMON HATE)

Hate does not discriminate, it never gives it loves to take, good qualities you have, prosperity that shines, it lives to bring about your demise, to suck the bright light dry from your eyes, it would love to see the life drained from your body, your demeanor cold and bitter as it is, it could hide in the heart like a cancerous grime, coming alive in the most opportune times, hate destroys things made of substance, the demon hate disintegrates anything that can potentially accumulate, corrupts what can possibly rejuvenate, taking space in the mind, growing more tumorous

(SABOTAGE)

Why sabotage yourself, purposely destroying the good done, anything given to you unraveled coming undone, what is it you have done? Why can't you see you deserve good things to happen? No one is perfect, why single yourself out like your not worth it and worthless? Everyone in this life has a purpose, some spend their whole life searching, hard on themselves when they come up short, when the truth is life is not easy and its not their fault, all you can do is play with the cards you have been dealt, count your blessings, don't sabotage yourself

(THE DEMON MURDER)

Murder so mindless and senseless has no conscious; its motives have many reasons though it does not need them, weather you are awake or sleeping, no matter what day or season, this fiendish demon anytime can be creeping, scheming with no respect for life, it laughs in delight when what you love dies, it loves to relish in the tears of grief falling from your eyes, it squeals in joy of the walking dead whose insides are as hollow as death, it will never be satisfied until you are no longer alive, when it snatches your last breath and your heartbeat flat lines

(PANIC)

Overpowering panic suddenly strikes, thoughts of your well being swirling storms through your mind, chances are you miss something vital to help keep you alive, everything combined rushing in at once, given limited time to process information, will you think about others or self preservation, panic, how unthought-of a situation, anxious, no rationality, pushy, impatient, unpredictable, dangerous, capable of widespread mayhem, contagious and very easy to catch, without a focused driver to drive, the navigator will swerve and crash

(RULES AND ORDER)

Without rules things would run out of order, chaos would spread running rampant, blood would paint the streets red, evil darkness would openly lurk, death would be eminent for the weak, who would protect your family? Will you be enough to shield them from the inevitable atrocities? Rules keeps things in check, order things in its place, a balance to keep what matters safe, looking at things in honest perspective, rules and order have to be implemented

(MORTALITY)

For what is a man but a spec of dust easily blown away, or a vapor that easily dissipates, when it is hot we burn, when it is cold we freeze, the sun rise and the sunset is the nature of our mortality, a brittle breath whisked away by the slightest breeze, for we navigate a chaotic world of uncertainty, piloting vessels made vulnerable by life's unexpected twists and turns, for each day the hour glass depletes, and humanity reminded of its mortality

(GUNS)

So much controversy surrounding guns, do we need them? Should we band them? So much killing, so much damage, a good percent mostly violent and random, yet we have to use guns to solve the problem, used for protection, creating laws that govern the use of a weapon, at a safe distance, unloaded, concealing possession, different avenues, but they still are used to commit crimes in neighborhoods, burglary, armed robbery, manslaughter, or murder numbered in different order, its all the same cup of water, but a hard pill to swallow, that guns will be needed to protect our tomorrow, but at the same time without guns less people will die, I guess the choice is up to the view of each and everyone, when it comes to both sides, when it comes to guns

(WHY GOD)

Upset I am at you sometimes, though it is clear that your ways are not mine, I wish I could see what it is you see, so I could understand why these things happen to me, sometimes I wonder if what I go through is a test because of some higher plan, something that your creations not meant to understand, why my god is there so much death? Why do you allow evil to exist? Babies to die, mothers to cry, the innocent to suffer, the corrupt to thrive, the poor to go hungry, kingdoms to be built on mountains of lies, the blood sweat and tears to fall from our eyes, when these things happen I look up to the sky, the worlds looking for answers, why God why?

(DARK SHADOW DIMMENSIONS)

Among the stars of the heavenly sky's, in between the spectrums of celestial light, in the corners of the barely perceivable eye, exist the planes of endless night, its darkest depths eternal, its conscious inhabitants alive, its atmosphere oppressive, its reach transgresses beyond the veil of what seems evanescent, lying invisible worlds of shadow dimensions

(HELLS CLUTCHES)

Once it has you, it will fight before letting you go, latching on to your mind then fortifying its stronghold, its effect leaves your spirit shivering and cold, at first it may seem that it is nothing at all, just a regular occurrence of a bodily function, until striking problems rise to reality's surface, what was disregarded now painfully evident, that your once vibrant heart feels empty and afflicted, your attitude then shifts to one of indifference, unbeknownst that on the other side of the veil your soul is a target, pushing you further into an isolated depression, a gradual suffering of perpetual madness

SIN BYRON

"We are the only chance you have left, welcome Sin Byron to the valley of the shadow of death," bantered arrogance.

"Hmm I thought you was stronger then this, guess you're the one who's going to be rutting in their own piss and shit, ill show you what rage really is!" cried anger kicking me hard in the stomach.

Falling over, my body submerged beneath the waves of the bloody muck.

Pushing with all my failing strength I struggled to get back on my feet.

Suddenly elongated and disembodied arms rose from the blood, its razor sharp claws digging deeply into my back like malevolent clamps dragging me back down in its hellish clutches. Crying out in excruciating agony my limbs went slack, my face and chest hit the bloody water with a smack.

Inhaling off of reflex my nose and lungs opened to a burning sensation, the aching pain rendering my body useless.

With no control of my limbs I had to keep my head above surface, or drown in the valley of the shadow of death.

(SUFFER)

Here in this place to suffer has become normal, the normal is my pain, I have forgotten how it felt to be without it, traveling with me like a faithful companion, my thoughts drift continuously on the edge of destruction, the fire is close, I can feel it, almost touch it, breathing in its suffocating air of toxins, but instead I find myself running away from it, holding on to the pain, the only evidence that blood runs through my veins, evidence I am indeed alive, though at times I wish for my own demise, not caring if I was to die a lie, not caring what you perceive is wrong or right, not caring if the casket was closed and still I breathe, suffering covered by darkness surrounding me

(TIRED)

I'm tired of living in a superficial ignorance, they say ignorance is bliss, yet if you cant see in front of it you will fall into a ditch, the blind leading the blind, a captain without a ship, operators thrown overboard drowning in their sins, crabs in a barrel pulling each other back, no progression but acceptance of their limits and there lacks, excuses piled high, affirmation till they believe it, a never ending cycle, foolish to rival reason

2Q

When the aftermath of the bloodshed was finished the survivors lay hurt and writhing while the dead littered the street.

My heart burned in my chest as I watched the family members of the dead loved ones crying in grief, the traumatized and confused expressions of innocent victims trying to piece together the last few minutes of this life altering experience.

Even after all the pain and loss beyond measure the two demons rejoiced, looking at their handiwork in pleasure.

"Why is it that these foul monsters can get away with this?" I asked clenching my fist, ready to vent the pent up emotions I could no longer hold in. "Where is God in all this? How could he allow this to happen? How is that fair when we as humans don't even know these heartless animals are there!" I shouted bitterly.

"Look," said the reaper pointing, turning towards me with an emotionless face.

In wonder my eyes widened at the sight of the massive beings clothed in white descending from the sky, each one of them different in shape and size, some with two wings, others with four, some with six, ten or more, some where beautiful, others ugly and menacing, all of them massive spirits meaning business.

"The lord of the heavens commands all that you see, now witness the spirits awaken from sleep. How un-aware humans are for they do not know and are blind to see, the angels of the order do not tire or sleep, the laws of life commanded they keep because this is how it must be," said the reaper.

Invisible to the naked eye, the mighty beings of light landed instantly raising the spirits of the dead, comforting and taking them in peace to their eternal resting place.

But as for the shooter, his spirit was snatched out of his body screaming and kicking, dangling between a muscular angels massive hand, the squeamish spirit cringed in fear at the sight of the mighty angels menacing glare.

"Please don't kill me I want to live!" pleaded the shooter.

"Vile spirit you have violated the law of life and therefor the lord of heaven who sees and knows all, you smell like the blood of his creation, now you will reap what you have forbiddingly sown, no mercy will you will receive, your cries of torment will fall on deafened ears until the final verdict on where you will be for all eternity," commanded the angel.

Enclosing its massive hand over the spirits head its screams of terror was muffled in the palm of the vengeful angel, who then disappeared into the ground at lightning speed.

(LOVES ARHITECT)

It is my core belief that the lord of the kingdom made love to balance all sustaining life that you see, for he knew what an opposing force darkness could be, so in turn love was born to bring universal harmony, the greatest power in creation freely given in its perfect purity, the essence of the eternal soul centering all created beings, within each a piece of a underlying divinity, the energy connected to the ultimate source, in whom all things in existence were formed

(LORD OF THE KINGDOM)

The lord of the kingdom of light, the creator of the cycle of life, the mysterious architect of the heavens, the sustaining source of the eternal essence, the perfect being of love and blessings, the everlasting father of all universal spirits, the ultimate authority of all in existence, the almighty sovereign king of the highest, the sheltering refuge in the holy temple of the sacred, the reigning peace that surpasses understanding, the alpha and omega, the beginning and ending

(CHERISH LIFE)

Love, cherish life, for you have only one vessel on the veil of this side, why regret, why be stagnant with troubles and burdens, forgive others, do unto others how you would want them to do to you, adore the enigmas of what's beautiful, shine your starlight in the presence of shadows, believe in your heart all the good things to come, be of high spirits in harmony as one

(HAND IN HAND)

Love and you will be loved, give and you will be given, what goes around will come again, what energy expended rebounds with spinning momentum, the universal force of attraction, what signal put out received in just acceptance, hand in hand all beings are connected, through every dimension of the intimate spirit

(ANGELS)

Heavenly hosts, angels of the order, winged guardians of the sky, to many to number, herald the kingdom of light, orders given to each from the creator of all, the sovereign lord, *different sizes and shapes, different number of wings, different ranking positions, all fall into place, some bring life, others death, but like other beings they still have their own free will*

(TEARS)

As your tears fall like drops of rain you remember all the pain, what it is your going through like waves crashing inside of you, on the shores of a heavy heart, the flooding tide begins to start, a tempest raging back and forth, your tears releasing a waterfall, out of your eyes the water drains, crying until its dry again

SIN BYRON

Struggling to keep my head above the bloody waters gunky surface, my skin started pulling and ripping from the grasping clamps digging deeper into my pierced back.

Opening my mouth to gasp I gagged as the bloody water went into my mouth, the holding strain on my neck threatening to give out.

"We will give you one more chance to give in, submit now or you will die here in this darkness!" shouted anger.

"With no hope to find what you so desperately need, but if you let us in you will find what you seek," encouraged arrogance.

Spitting the vile sludge out of my mouth I spoke back defiantly.

"Fuck you! Do what you have to do you disease ridden flukes, if it wasn't for your cursed tricks I would kill both of you filthy snakes."

"Now that's what I call arrogance all the way to the end," said arrogance grinning with satisfaction.

"You will pay for your foolish insolence, good riddance, we will join you in hell when this is finished" said anger stomping on the back of my neck burying my head beneath the bloody surface. I was being drowned in gross glop and there was no way out, I had to give them what they wanted, there was no other option.

The last second before running out of breath, in my mind I cried out "I surrender you win!"

Then consuming darkness over took my consciousness.

(NO AIR)

I suffer in this tiny space, the walls mock my solemn face, with no escape it's closing in, cutting off my oxygen, how am I supposed to breathe when you took the better part of me? Naked exposed for all to see, a numb effect in my Iv, a masquerade, a change of face, puts everything in its place, I show you what I want you to see, because in this tiny space, there is no air to breathe

(CROSSING OVER DARKSIDE)

On this dark-side no light shines, no love, only despair, plaguing nightmares, wrenching fear, to resist only brings worse demons, the doubting thought that gives up and relents, crosses the power of your will over to them, accepting your beings frailty, submitting on your knees, slavishly embracing conformity draws you to the edge of the precipice, what pain numbs brings a sense of ecstasy, strangely enough, but then your shadowing hell has only begun

(SPIRIT INVASION)

Desolate, cold, a draining dark hole in the now vulnerable portal, strife within self, horrifying enmity, meshing hell, deeply rooted affliction in wicked darkness, savage disposal of saving goodness, dead-en empathy of core feeling, internal loathing in eternal emptiness

(SHADOWING ATTACHMENT)

Be careful who you allow into your home, for evil knows no closed door, in ill will it attaches to others, its ulterior motives spawning nightmares monsters, deriving manifestations of self hatred, reflecting to those who know not your anguish, slowly destroying the light in your world, to one of change from a shadowing curse

(CONSUMING DARKNESS)

What has taken advantage of my ignorance, brought about a defiled innocence, insidiously lured me into the dimensions of darkness, drowning me in the temptations of evil corruption, using me as an object of carnage and destruction, implanting consuming poison of emotional mutilation, plotting the self demise of my souls invasion, blinding my eager eyes in a promising illusion, then seizing my ravished mind in a hellish revolution

(STAGES OF SLEEP)

Like the many pieces of my crystal mirror, you to must find the balance in the heart of your center; your conscious in stages of sleep burdens you dearly, the covering blanket of an illusion settles over your life in complacency, seeing what you want to see, believing blindly in the surface of your reality, all the little things taken for granted, all the insecurities and burdens baggage, all the prideful delusions of a delirious *existence, the un-aware mind creating negative energy that later attaches, for your eternal soul is a universal magnet, the spiritual essence of your own perception*

(SURVIVE)

You only have two options when faced with a grave situation, either die or survive, to survive you must do what you normally wouldn't, putting aside all pride, to die comes easy, what is it you leave behind is what's hard to decide, you will be tested on your mental capacity, what it is you can withstand without breaking, the pain can be breath-taking, panic and frustration will only worsen the situation, what also will be tested is strength, your body forced into different positions through certain conditions, the pressure can break you down despite resistance, only through perseverance and persistence can you make it through this, what you need is lying deep inside, this is the only way to survive

2Q

Appearing in a serene neighborhood, with beautiful homes, cut lawns and a gentle breeze wafting through the trees.

I scrutinized everything around me trying to find something off, some kind of disturbance in this calm and peaceful suburb.

"Just wait and witness how beautiful evil can be, how it can subtly lurk in the face of the friendly, how something as virtuous as trust can be used by the enemy," said the reaper pointing.

Coming out of a colonial style home onto the porch was a stunning woman with long black hair, smooth brown skin and dark brown eyes. Immediately I could see something was wrong with her, a shadow hung over her head like dark clouds in a coming storm.

With the revving roar of an engine a sleek new model sports car sped around the corner stopping abruptly in front of the colonial style home.

Stepping out of the drivers seat a handsome man dressed in dapper attire, his passenger a woman of obvious beauty.

Taking her lips into his, the passenger giggled in suspended bliss locking themselves in a brief and intimate embrace, their open display of affection causing the black cloud hanging over the girls head to take its true form, materializing grotesque demons from every direction.

Envy, hate, desire and deceit appeared, whispering with ill intent into the troubled women's ears.

After a brief stay, the trim man waved to the lady on the porch then got back into his sports car and sped off, leaving my focus on the extent of the passengers breathtaking beauty.

With auburn colored hair, hazel eyes, long sensual legs and flawless skin the color of porcelain, it was obvious that her beauty was far more prominent then that of her friends.

Little did she know her friend on the porch was surrounded by malevolent demons, and her unjust dues were a nightmare soon to begin.

Fusing together, desire and deceit formed a slimy two-headed beast, its drooling puss covered body and festering flesh a bubbling sight for sore eyes. Agitated it ate ravenously out of the outstretched palm of envy; in it were four black seeds that caused the excited beast to grow restless, yet envy had full control of this seemingly senseless fiend. The beast then regurgitated one black seed that doubled in size into the hand of hate, who then placed the infused seed into the troubled women's head.

Disappearing inside, the seed sprouted roots penetrating deep into the troubled women's mind.

"Now grow and feed off of the bitterness in her soul, dig deep, inside is what you will need to thrive," hexed hate.

Those cursed words vanishing with the demons, while the seeds roots like a leech grew, feeding off of her innermost insecurities, bringing to the surface all the unstable feelings buried deep, leading false words in spite of her best friend, who noticing nothing different trusted blindly in them.

After catching up on current events the giddy girls made plans to meet up at night where they would have fun by partying at different clubs, but fun was the farthest thing from her friend's tainted mind.

The demon envy would see to it that what she wanted most would soon come to be, in her twisted view this was a dirty game, nothing was given, you had to take it.

Who was she to have something over her, flaunting her shapely body and premadona like beauty, walking about as if she had it all, as if being in her presence was a blessing, no not this time, now she would be the one losing.

With an ulterior motive, the demon desire would steal her man with the lustful intent of having her way with him in bed, all while the terrible demon hate carried out her evil plan.

(VANITY)

Empty vanity some see and nothing else, convinced in fullness of self seeing more then what is, looking deeply into a shallow pit of nothingness, all that would be if you could only see past vanity, a useless quality of futile pride, convincing blinded eyes that it sees riches inside, when in fact it is as brittle as glass, if it were to break it would as easily disappear, pouring its false wealth into a pool of fear and insanity, seeing that it is nothing more that it could be, dying for its vanity

(LOVE YOURSELF)

Love yourself, if not who else will? For who could love you like you? Who else knows yourself like you do? For people are inherently vain only worrying about what's going on with them, not caring what happens to you, in the long run all you have is you, so take care of yourself, be good to yourself, think of longevity, think of your health, healthy relationships, healthy well being, inside there is wealth, love yourself

(THE DEMON ENVY)

The demon envy wants what you have, it harbors ill will wishing all things bad, it resents you for what it wishes to covet, your life it sees as a precious object, conniving and evil this silent enemy, for its subtle warfare on the face of the friendly, its diabolical scheme to sit and wait, blindsiding unexpectedly when resistance has waned, when the back has turned its attacks are more severe, when you least expect that envy is there

(FRIENDS)

The definition of a true friend is one who will lead you in the right direction, one who will sincerely help instead of leaving you to fend for yourself, yet though this may be, friends can easily become enemy's, take heed to my words, both eyes must observe, learn to never close them, for the closer they are leaves your defenses open, for who will know you better then them, valuable pieces of personal information, your goings and comings, strengths and weaknesses, being blind to this fact, you become your own liability susceptible to attack, while you watch your front, a true friend will watch your back, if nothing else remember this, anyone can wear a mask

(PARASITES)

Watch for those who would only drain you, who only come around when they see something attainable, once you are no longer useful you become disposable, you are only as good as the last thing you did for them, no matter what's done in kind, parasites live in grime, ungrateful by nature, finding victims to take from, a parasite almost invisible can be undetectable, using friendship as a way to get close to you, easing through suspicion you lose your will to resist them, finding it hard to say no, as time goes on your awareness will grow, but by the time you are able to see the parasites trickery, from you it would have acquired the sustenance it needs, to move on to the next, repeating its process over again

(SOMETIMES TRUST)

Sometimes trust is a two edged sword, your damned if you do, your damned if you don't, the truth is you never know an ulterior motive behind closed doors, until it is revealed, your decisions there-after pulled by another's will, sometimes trust can help, to go further, to succeed beyond yourself, with sincere trust, not secretly out for want, in general beware of trust in its entirety, for it can lead to your ruin, a treasure map, or a stabbed back, there is no easy way, the choice is yours, sometimes trust is a two edged sword

(MISPLACED LOYALTY)

To find true loyalty is a rare jewel, a high commodity, its aspect in a cause evens the odds immensely, but beware of misplaced loyalty this can cost you greatly, to who you pledge your allegiance can jeopardize your safety, the company you keep will tell who you are, drawing a line where you stand can place you in a circumstance, to find true loyalty the rewards are great, but on the other side of this find can lead to your grave

(MOTIVE/INTENTIONS)

In this pay attention, for motives and intentions on the outer exterior can be unseen, moving in mysterious ways, the motives reasons can be far away, unclear for the stranger looking in, there is confusion in intentions which can be interpreted in different ways, yet not to the person whose motives had intentions, a goal set in methods not meant for you to have laid out direction, for it was concocted and conceived in the mind, causing the objective to become unclear, when viewed from the outside

(GOSSIP)

Gossip is like quick sand, it pulls you in causing you to want more information, you become addicted to the constant fixation, with no filter or investigation, you find yourself listening to rumors heard from others, yet the whole truth could not be further, a lie sounds better and holds more attention, stuck in suspension you wait for the next addition, eventually believing what it is you are hearing, the news becomes close to you almost endearing, like poison it spreads from the mouth to the host, a parasitic leech, gossip takes hold then grows

(IDLE TALK)

Foolish conversations with nothing to learn, idle talk, wasted words, to whom these things do concern, with no foundation, nothing firm, entertaining to say the least, you can gain nothing from these, time consuming and nothing more, no flame could spark with idle talk

(HYPOCRITES)

You say the way things should be, showing conviction the way you teach, it all would seem so convincing if you only lived it, you are a sore sight for weary eyes you habitual hypocrite, how to move you swear you do, following some guiding rule, something you don't follow threw, yet you expect me to listen, to implement this falseness how I live, be gone from my presence, your feigned life makes me sick, oh how I despise hypocrites who contradict

(DEMENTED OTHERS)

Hidden in the shadows the evil darkness awaits, to find a vessel to consume and deprave, once a victim is found the eerie haunting begins, to weaken the portal giving access to them, deeply chilling and unnerving to know, that the others they consume is open to control, through perceived delusions thought as there own, demented all the while gradually losing there soul, so carefully watch whoever deemed close, the unknowingly possessed who will threaten your own, weather family, friend, neighbor or stranger, anyone can potentially be in spiritual danger

(DEEP INSECURITIES)

On the outside a beautiful home seems pleasant and content, but underlying this elaborate façade is something unseen, a burrowed tunnel of deep insecurity, its hollow substance of hazardous walls are highly unstable with deadly potential, under any circumstance the foundation of this sensitive structure can cave in and collapse, trapping the unbalanced occupant underneath layers of ruin, in an instant, whatever

crushing burden there undeniably feeling are buried with
them, solidifying mounds of pent up frustration, suffocating
growth in an unstable location

(NATURAL BEAUTY)

My love your uniqueness comes in many shades, why change?
Why wish to cover your heavenly blessing? to distort the sheen
of your natural beauty, you are perfect the way you are,
learn to accept your flaws, see them as the difference that
distinguishes your existence, apart from the others who have
become spiritually imprisoned, whose empty vanity traps them
in the unstable depths of insecurity, reveal the prominent side
of your personality, the special side that causes your radiant
light to shine outwardly, what you think about yourself is
important, because in this perception you can miraculously
transcend, entering the portal of a crystal element, emerging
in a vibrant spectrum, taking your rightful place amongst
the starry inheritance, the internal treasure in the universe
of loves palace

(BACK BITING)

No matter what you do, there is always someone who will
have something to say about you, behind your back when it is
turned, to your face they dare not say a word, when you are
gone there is no pressure, freeing there tongue to say whatever,
what they always felt, but did not say, will come out of hiding
when you walk away, if you could hear, you would not believe,
the intrusive things discussed spitefully, but do not take it
personally, it's the light of your special individuality, brightly
shining on their insecurities, exposing all of its ugly qualities

(LIES)

Your eyes full of lies draw me near, you planed to pillage and burn my castle bare, to ravish my home a love lived there, to plunder a poor beggar stripped expressionless, a pain that rapes false promises, reeled in then killed for substance, your soul a cold decrepit dungeon, your lips pose in seduction, to betray the heart in brutal destruction, to drain each drop in eager consumption, to keep in the dark suspicious assumption, to isolate, disturb, usurp and lurk, to bury a body then cover with dirt

CHAPTER 4

SIN BYRON

Opening my eyes slowly, it took a few seconds to adjust to the light.

Finding myself in a luxurious room laying on a deluxe bed dressed in a robe of fine silk, what I saw next had my head reeling.

On the bed sleeping beside me was a naked woman I had never seen before.

With a battering heartbeat my eager eyes traced the curves of her naked beauty, from the tip of her small and pretty feet to the contour of her hips, tracing the line of her jaw stopping at her succulent lips.

In awe I could not stop starring, my mind was fuzzy and my thoughts somewhere lost and scrambled, how had I gotten here? Where was I? Taking my eyes off of the sleeping beauty I looked around further inspecting my surroundings, my eyes widened in astonishment at the different pictures of erotic art framing the wall, pictures of gorgeous women flaunting there desirable bodies shamelessly and exploiting their sexuality provocatively.

Suddenly the events of what previously took place came bombarding my mind at once, this tormenting anguish invading my memory in flashes, it was all coming back to me now, how could this be I should have been dead!

Hoping off the bed I rushed over to the adjoined door handsomely crafted out of an amber red chalcedony gem, opening it I stood still in wonderment.

Suspended about twenty feet above me sat a miraculous spiraling gold staircase that elevated to heights unknown, extending an impressive reach impossible to climb.

I stood on the ground floor of an expansive hall full of exquisite furnishing, massive paintings of peculiar art and exotic objects of splendor. Everywhere before me walked exotic women, all naked and distinguished in their prominent beauty, all going about their duties, until one noticed my attention.

In an instant they all stopped what they were doing and lined up in front of me from smallest to biggest.

"What shall you have us do Master!" they all said at once in a synchronized chorus.

Flushed and at a loss for words I remained speechless, all I could do was stare dumfounded until my daze like focus was broken by a startling embrace from behind, it was the mysterious beauty awoken from her sleep.

"The Master will call you when he is ready, go back to what you are doing," commanded the beauty with authority.

Without missing a beat the excited women went back to their duties.

"You probably have many questions," said the women looking into my eyes reading my shocked expression, "Allow me to introduce myself, my name is Temptation."

(WOMEN)

A women is one who understands her place, who handles herself in such a way, one who works, supports and nurtures, one with potential who pushes further, one who is caring and a guiding light in her children's lives, one who surrenders her unconditional love, one who you never take advantage of, one who stands by her man as best as she can, one who never lets her emotion supersede her intelligence, one who's reflection is seen in his, one who handles her business, one who's beauty is not only physical but mental and spiritual, one who knows what they want and is not afraid to go after it, one who at

times can be tough, but warmth and affection runs in their
blood, one who despite the road is tough, one who does things
out of love

(THINGS)

The finer things, that you cannot see, intrigues me
The desirable things, that you have, are beneath me
The wondrous things, of the spirit, are true riches
The selective things, opens up, to her senses
The secret things, a mystery, not yet told
The eternal things, timeless, within my soul

(BIGGER PICTURE)

What was once a portrait became a bigger picture, the
surrounding scene becoming clearer, the overall space only
fit for the mind, no where else could capture the meaning
inside, the thought a paintbrush on the canvas of life, the art
a collage, because the art is alive, the moment is frozen to the
eye of the beholder, time and eternity, a harmonic mixture,
once I had formed the bigger picture

(THE DEMON TEMPTATION)

Oh temptation, how enticing and inviting you are on the
outside, beguiling ones appetite for the sublime, drawing us in
uttering sweet words of poison to the senses, lowering defenses,
leaving us defenseless, how pleasant it is until reality sets in,
that we have been betrayed to destruction, given away to the
enemy, to know the weaknesses in the walls we build around
the treasures of our own free will, by the time you become
aware of temptations plans to Infiltrate, by then it is to late,

in the armor of your exterior there is a kink in its place, to fall apart in ruin, when temptation shows its face

(TASTE)

As I stare at your breathtaking beauty, I can't help but think how your love tastes, is it bitter as the aftertaste of whine, or sweet as a pomegranates inside, will it entice me with a magnetic lure, will I find myself in denial, telling myself I will have just one more, or will it completely turn me off at the very taste, turning my stomach outside, fatally curious I wonder close, but is it you I see, or a mirage artificially, for my eyes also taste, then decides just the same

(PICTURE PERFECT)

My love you are picture perfect, but even this does your beauty no justice, for no picture could capture your intoxicating essence, let alone the glow of your aura in an intimate reflection, one can only imagine the taste of your kissable lips, or the way you shake and moan from a satisfying orgasm, one can only dream of how it feels to enter your warm sex, or to be mesmerized by the winding of your hips, one can only wish to caress your soft skin, or there tongue to roam your special places, one can only fantasize of your melodic voice, your seductive eyes drawing them close, one can only hope for the pleasures you give, my only definition for reality's slip, is to tell you my love, you are picture perfect

(GOLD STAIRS)

The gold stairs composed of seven, every level, every heaven, every existence, all in one unison, all one universe, always moving, a different dimension in separate sections, but all one energy shared between them, to reveal the mystery when the time is near, to climb every level of the golden stairs

(DECLARATION)

To all my women is a declaration of love, for you a doors open to the riches of my soul, your hearts are welcome to the crystal well that never runs dry, drink in merriment and be full of life, if you are lost, or cannot find your way, follow the torch that burns wildly, through the unknown path of life, through the wrongs and rights, through the days and the nights, what you will find cannot be denied, its call conforms to one and all, loudly proclaiming loves declaration

(GIFT)

My gift to the world is exclusive for her to rekindle a profound desire, a masterpiece, masterfully crafted In her honor, to adore her image, painting a picture in ways to the heart, a shrine, an idol, radiant rays piercing through the dark, a glow, a torch, a fire burning wildly with my love, the heat and passion sending toxic lust through her blood, euphoric, contagious, seductively tailored, designed for her attention, this gift is yours to covet in your arms, to conceal its true intention

(COVET)

My unique love, this spiritual world is a wondrous haven made for you, this is more then a book, its your emerald portal, weather pedestal, treasures, levels to visit, you are all special, endangered, precious, this place of beauty has

been prepared without prejudice, without judgment, without
baseless assumption, it is yours to covet, yours to imagine,
yours to seize, alive for your heart to feel, for now that you are
apart of me, the beholder, you know loves world is real

2Q

Kissing him goodbye, the girl with the porcelain colored skin got out of her boyfriends sports car. Purposely-changing direction she walked down a series of blocks cutting down a dimly lit street towards an alternate rendezvous point, a secret place she and her friend agreed they would meet. Excited she skipped along lured by the thoughts of the adventure and possibly forbidden fun they would have.

Being the first to see a loathsome shadow following her lead, I wanted to scream out warning her to run, but I knew that was impossible, I would just be uttering wasted words that could not be heard.

Spotting someone out of the corner of her eye standing still under a blinking street light, was a tall man with a sunken in face and a nervous twitch he couldn't restrain, his right hand holding a bat making kissing noises with a chilling laugh.

Frightened she walked away as quick as she could, only to find her path blocked by another man wearing a hood.

Panic-stricken she turned to run in a different direction and was suddenly hit with a forceful blow; toppling over unconscious her face hit the cold pavement with a thwack! Orchestrated by a third man hidden in the shadows waiting.

Then I saw them; six ugly demons congregated greedily anticipating in a thirsty expectation.

"We have to do something, we can't allow this to happen!" I vocalized to the reaper excitingly, ready to spring into action.

Fuming at how the evil men harassed her, dragging her unconscious body were anyone passing by couldn't see, quietly groping and forcefully molesting her delicate body,

While the demons hate, pain, panic, reckless, rape and fear whispered into the ears of the heartless men giving them more incentive for evil ideas.

My biggest fear was that if no one came to save her in time, they would not only sexually abuse her, but after they had their way kill her and get away with it, I would not let that happen.

"You are right there is no other way, here you must face demonic entity's of pure evil, for true evil originates in the spiritual, once you cross over the veil of protection I can no longer help you, do not let them consume you, for the darkness will drain away your light until nothing is left, then you will die a true death, do you understand?" asked the reaper sternly.

"Yes," I acknowledged, taking his warning into account, but more eager to rush towards the innocent girls aid and end her suffering.

"Give me your right hand, and remember, if ever you lose your way, lose yourself and pray," said the reaper.

Not knowing what he meant I took his hand firmly, instantaneously my body went numb, an electrically motivated current shooting through my rippling body jumping out of my charged pores like a bolt, I had become the magnetic rod rerouting its currents live wire. I had become its source.

In the blink of an eye I transformed into a soldier of the light clothed in righteous garments of white, on the right side of my sash sat a white sheath with the symbol of an engraved Celtic cross, the gold hilt of the enclosed sword was fashioned as a lion and in between its voracious jaws an illumined red stone. Inscribed down its side were words I could not read, its language like nothing I had ever seen.

Tucked inside the left of my sash was a burning flame flickering brightly in a clear cylinder shaped case, but with no idea what it was and no experience on how to use a sword properly, for lack of knowledge I could easily be over-run by the enemy, I clearly didn't think this through.

With so many questions on my mind I turned to ask the reaper, but he was gone, and what surprisingly stood before me was the women in harm, the evil men and the demonic entity's who were now fully aware of my presence and undoubted interference.

(THE DEMON RECKLESS)

With no warning the demon reckless loses control, why have something less when it can have it all, destruction, corruption and devastation left ruins in its wake, beware the more you give, the more greedily it will take, if given an inch, it is sure to run a mile, be cautious it does not think, it is tireless, destructive and wild, ever gravitating towards the unstable mind, impulsive and explosive, reckless by design

(THE DEMON FEAR)

Everywhere this demon lives, it grows stronger by stoking its fire underneath your skin, known to cause certain paralysis, uncertainty creeps and begins to lead, a voiceless voice, a restriction of choice, abandoning self to random circumstance, your foundation has no place to stand, so it must fall, by design human nature is riddled with flaws, the demon fear exploits those flaws and draws out your weakness, your insecurities opening a wide door, welcoming more demons

(THE DEMON RAPE)

The demon rape stalks its prey, what it wants it takes away, not caring who it hurts, whose insides rot in decay, who's every waking moment is a nightmare relived each day, it defiles innocence and pillages villages, it causes the light to be darkened, hope to be forfeited, by use of force for loathsome gain, the demon rape is a monster, a blot, a stain of disdain

(PRAY)

You cannot repent unless you sinned to know temptations face,
to curse the one that did you wrong and give them hell to pay,
the demons feed off energy to carry out your plan, deceit and
lies cover your eyes truth is you work for them, a subconscious
contract based on a need to know, what you don't know they
hide so you can dig your hole, the hate you send comes back
again on you it grows two fold, prayer expose those wicked loop
holes, void it from your soul, pray

(SHOW ME)

My love words are only as good as the action they carry,
in the end what will you show me? Was it real, or what was
said to get what you wanted at the moment? My love you
need someone who is mature in all of there ways, not childish
and indecisive with no sense of responsibility, in the matters
of your heart are you to do the work alone? To carry the
burden of loving someone who is supposed to be grown, why
subject yourself to an inevitable hurt? When it is obvious your
love they do not deserve, nor is your love a main priority in
their childish outburst, will you idly sit back while your deep
emotion is played in jest and your efforts of affection mocked
by there being inattentive? Will you just accept anything? Is
your love worth nothing? Show me now and do not wait, or
my attention will settle on another's face

(MISTREATED)

My love why are you mistreated, beaten, cheated, not seen as
even? Why do you allow this to happen when you deserve so
much more? I can see you love hard, but is that worth the pain

and scars, you second guess yourself, questioning should you let go, my love you are so special, a treasure to be treasured, but you need to be the one to sever the ties, to what should have been done from the very beginning, starting over is never easy, but for something that is what worth is it having, it is better to gain something hard to get, you will appreciate more cherishing it, reluctant to let it go, open your eyes my love and see this, that you should never be taken for granted or mistreated

(EXPERIENCE)

Experience is the best teacher, for some despite words must learn, some must touch the fire to know that it burns, to think first before a decision, experience is knowledge implemented, through trial and error of past endeavors, even though this is known the novice craves to be initiated, whatever it takes, wherever the pendulum swings, there is one thing that remains the same, regardless of the conclusion, experience is knowledge proven

(TRY AND FAIL/CANT)

How do you know you cannot do something if you don't try, you must give your best and nothing less, if you fail try again, there is no such thing as cant, cant is an excuse from trying, for it is better to fail in an attempt, then to not attempt and fail because of it, you will never accomplish anything, your potential will never be realized, disappointment and what if will shadow your life if you do not try, cant is a cloak that covers and hides, your willingness to accept failure and be satisfied, the road to success had many fail, but by pushing none the less, the one out of the millions who cant achieved what they so diligently pursued, remaining persistent, not accepting failure, driven to improve, driven not to lose

(TRANSFORM)

With the power inside I transform, three roses in all, each essence come forth, the red and the black, the light and the dark, 2Q and Sin Byron, a white rose between, as bright as a star, a love when released, the crystal mirror, a glorified mystery, scattered abroad with beautiful stars, adorned in the sky, that light in my eyes, the child of heavens, a special connection

(GRAVE PRICE)

Pick a side, for the price can be grave, to put someone before yourself can complicate everything, in your sole perception what choice chosen becomes the most important, even if elsewhere your presence is needed, right now in the present the situation at hand demands your undivided attention, either you are all in ready to pay the asking price of personal admission, or do not bother with the commitment, because straggling both sides of this volatile decision, may in the end charge all recipients

(CRYSTAL VEIL)

The spirit realm lies before your eyes, its ether illuminates with heavenly spectrums of light, a change of perception opens the connection, but can also attract evil entity's of shadowing darkness, for some it is better to exist oblivious, blind and comfortable under the illusion of the reality there living in, for once the veil over there eyes has been lifted, the portal to *there soul is open to control by possessing influences, ravenous demons wrecking the secret places within, the mind left desolate, its substance violated in ruin, evil monsters ravaging the vulnerable body, consuming its blood like malevolent leeches, draining the source of your vibrant essence, the crystal veil protects you from these, because the lord of the kingdom commanded it be*

SIN BYRON

Speechless I stared into the most beautiful eyes I had ever seen, both lavender and scarlet with a hint of green, if this was a trick, it was an elaborate hoax meant to distract me further, I had to show these demons I wasn't soft and damn sure nobody's fool.

I fell for pretty faces before, these demons were the cunning masters of disguise, but I would strike first, this time I would have the upper hand.

"Do you think I am a joke?" I snapped, grabbing temptation by the throat pushing her back into the room slamming roughly against a wall.

"Tell me what the hell is going on!" I demanded.

"Yes I like it rough, show me what you're made of!" cried temptation provocatively; her light fingers swiftly loosening my sash exposing my nakedness underneath.

"Ether you give me the information I need or you going to find it hard to breathe," I threatened.

"I will tell you everything you need to know if you fuck me the way I like it, you know you want me don't try and fight it," whispered temptation.

Like a sauna the boiling heat of her poisonous words began to seep into my mind, shaking my head to clear my lustful thoughts I strangled temptation as hard as I could,

"Stop playing with me bitch who do you think your messing with!" I barked, feeling strange and off balance, slowly losing myself to these conflicting feelings.

My snapping anger sent her over the edge, in a heated frenzy temptation locked her legs around my waist moaning loudly, gyrating and grinding her pressed hips into me insinuating the intensity of sex.

"Fuck me hard the way I need it, the way I crave it, take your frustrations out on me, choke me, beat me, make it nasty!" temptation pleaded with an unhinged look of madness.

Losing control of myself, a ravishing beast was released; with both of my hands wrapped around her tiny neck I forcefully penetrated her sex, trapped in the thrall of brazen passion.

In sync with my every thrust temptation cried out in pleasure trembling in frantic ecstasy, her whining voice of submissiveness further provoking this lust crazed beast inside of me, hooked I could not stop I had fallen for her trick, something deep down I knew I would regret.

(DARE)

I dare you to open up your heart unto me, to blind fold your eyes and give me the reins, I dare you to relinquish control letting me in, influenced by my power on a spontaneous whim, I dare you to jump and don't look down, in hopes I will catch you before you hit the ground, I dare you to block out the world and everything else, to follow the voice of a seductive spell, I dare you to walk into the fire in search of 2Q, to see how it feels for his love to consume, I dare you to seek Sin Byron at the heights of your pleasure, screaming his name for him to come enter, I dare you to be mine for all of time, and cross over with love to the other side

(DIRTY THOUGHTS)

I can see your dirty thoughts, because these thoughts are mine, we lust, we fuck, we make love in our mind, a window to your desire I can see through your eyes, submissive to my will yet your pleasure is my high, aggressive tables curve now's the time its your turn, to cover dirty maybes between the lines of your words, when we are away I think about it all day, our lustful dirty thoughts never go away

(EYE CANDY)

I am your eye candy, gaze upon my sweet beauty, hungrily your eyes roam my chiseled body's muscle tone, a subtle and succulent thirst to take me and do your worst, to lick, suck and taste the object you crave, to savor every drop of me, your appetite anxious to devour all of me, devising to posses me jealously, selfishly not wanting to share an inch of me, because I am your eye candy

(TEASE)

Oh what a tease I can be, oh the power of my seductive possibilities, drawing you close then pushing you away, oh how infuriating and exciting my little games, finding yourself hopeful, yet discouraged at my meaning, I become your addictive craving without you knowing the reason, becoming a mystery to yourself and what you thought you knew so well, what has come over you, have I poisoned your needs, have they enslaved your wants, are you lost in the entanglement of emotion, an obscure temptation so potent, I am the very obsession that will lead to your madness, oh how I love the way you squirm in my presence, my power will make you crawl to me on your knees, but that is only if I Sin Byron choose to tease

(BRAZEN PASSION)

Come to me, rid yourself of all burden, soon we will enter the moment, becoming lost in the wilds of brazen passion, give me your sex, give your pleasure to Sin Byron, learn the highs and lows of blissful suspense, succumbing to submissive or aggressive whims, you will be mine, enraptured in the forbidden fruit thy hearts desire, the danger that excites your heightened delight, give in to the heat of the blazing fire

(WILD ECSTASY)

Trapped in the in the throws of wild ecstasy, unable to focus, your jittery eyes glaze, sizzling in frictions pressing heat, ravishing agitation crashing against your frenzied heartbeat, shaking the core stability of your fluttering body, blending deep into the euphoric depths of pleasures thrashing waves, recklessly penetrating the base of your sensitive place, possessing the dangerous intimacy of your eager sex, raptured, enslaved by your careless actions, hopelessly manic, sensual madness, brazen passion, open to thrilling highs, yet craving to taste the dirty lows, Sin Bryon's addictive desire, pulling you in, never letting you go

(TRANSGRESSIVE EXCITEMENT)

Forbidden, tempting, an animalistic call of transgressed excitement, a wild rebellion against dutiful slavishness, a change of the predictable repetition of burdening boredom, a turn from the polite acceptance of the obvious direction, a guilty pleasure that engages the senses, a limitless high of thoughtless drifting, a secret of an abandoned conscious, a satisfying affair under the cover of darkness

(TEMPTATIONS LUST CRAZED BEAST)

What have you done to me? What is this intense hunger that ravages my being with greedy
Expectancy? This insatiable demon fighting for bodily control, with the scent of her sex I turn into a lust crazed animal, anxiously rattling its primal cage, uninhibited, an unrestrained beast rampaging unhinged, barreling through barriers with reckless abandon, drawn by her siren like beckoning, slavishly aimed to please, endowed with unlimited stamina and energy, enthralled by the desire of her mesmerizing femininity, yet turned out by the pleasure of her sick cruelty

(RESIST)

Resisting me will only become the spur to a deeper desire, the mystery that is 2Q and his passion fire will cause a subconscious spell to be cast on your love, while his dark half Sin Byron will see to it that he awakens the cravings of pure lust, creating an urge that cannot be controlled will draw you to me in ways you never thought possible, you will no longer be apart of your limited reality, but spirited to were everything will seem like a dream, where your eager wants and repressed needs all come to life when your heart is free, for in my world there will be no one to judge and fresh air to breath, no matter if you choose to resist this atmospheric gravity

(POISON)

Your poison in my blood washes over me like a flood, it commands my full attention, a purely concentrated lust, an oasis to my vision, your sex enthralls me to a higher elevation, my mind saturated in your naked persuasion, conjures insatiable beasts in my lustful imagination, to materialize reality subject so dangerous, that it threatens to constrict my veins and nerves, your poison coerces my tongue possessing my words

(RAW)

Come out from under the cover of a safe love, become raptured in the essence of raw lust, give in to the feelings with-held, let go of the control limiting yourself, release your wants, open up, unwind and become one as you come undone, don't think and let what is begin, a new life with the black rose of Sin Byron

CHAPTER 5

2Q

Going into the thick of the situation the demons eyes and mine locked in an unflinching stare.

The abducting men unaware of our presence continued in their savage obsession.

Now conscious, the distressed women screams of horror were being muffled as her attackers continued to beat and force there way onto her, this injustice and sickening display of malice motivated me to action.

Unsheathing my sword, my eyes grew wide in disbelief at the realization that there was no blade, in desperation and confusion I blinked my eyes turning the gold hilt over and over again hoping this was some kind of mistake, that somehow this was an invisible blade that could scare the monsters away.

But the odds of that were becoming less likely. When the demons started to laugh a feeling of dread washed over me, no this couldn't be, why would the reaper send me into battle with no weapon to protect myself?

While the demons cackled in hysterics the sexual abuse got worse, the evil men were getting tired of their conquest, more rough and less concerned with their inaudible secrecy, the badly beaten women was holding on by shallow breathing, there wasn't much time left I had to do something bold despite the cost.

"Hey you filthy bottom feeders leave her alone!" I snapped with authority in my tone.

This just made them laugh more blatantly brushing me off; to them I was nothing but a joke not a threat to be taken seriously.

I had to say something to draw them away; maybe then I could buy her some time by stealing the focus away from the thought provoking demons.

"Hey I'm talking you shit heads! I know why your laughing, it just dawned on me that you bastards are scared, you cowards are softer then a stool on laxative, the light gives me power over you, and when I'm done whipping your filth of garbage off this planet I'm coming for your grime ball master to."

No longer laughing the demons bared their razor sharp teeth glaring at me menacingly; seeing I had their attention I continued my verbal assault.

"Your master isn't worth squat, even the dirt on earth is more rich then him, what a loser he is by sending you clowns its obvious he was to scared to face me himself, are you mad…well to bad, matter-of-fact all six of you get on your knees because I am your new master now, your old master just phoned in and told me he was to busy giving blow jobs, now do as I say you servant bitches!"

My verbal assault did the trick but gave birth to something more insidious. In a series of disturbing snaps their bodies contorted, their grotesque limbs dislocating themselves bubbling in a steaming black liquid fusing into each other growing gigantic in height, my eyes bulged as I shrunk from this frightening sight.

With an earsplitting roar a six-headed dragon was formed.

Fear gripped my heart as I stared into the multiple eyes of nightmarish monsters, saliva drooled profusely from their razor sharp teeth, they all shared two massive arms and feet equipped with razor sharp claws that with the slightest swipe could easily sever a body apart.

When the dragon spoke its infused voice left a lingering echo.

"You little dog I will rip out your beating heart and feast on your disemboweled insides, you have come to your demise, I can smell your ripe fear, denounce your inferior light, bow down now, swear your undying loyalty and allegiance to the darkness and I may let you live," snarled the dragon.

With no weapon and no help I felt paralyzed in my fear, how could I stop this monster? What made me think I 2Q a mortal from earth could make a difference in the spirit world?

Looking towards the women in distress I could see the evil men talking amongst themselves leaving their victim alone at least for a moment, my plan was working, without the demons giving life to their ideas they were wondering what to do next, this temporary victory gave me the courage to push harder further upsetting the beast on purpose.

"I would never join you losers, id rather die then be considered an associate of your tired ass master and you inbred demons, my place is in the light, how about this, I will let you live if you bow down now kissing my feet admitting I'm better then you, then just maybe I might consider giving you a more pertinent job like scraping the shit from a dog."

Snarling the dragon advanced, all six of its heads bearing its razor sharp teeth, its giant steps causing the ground to tremor, the chances of me surviving weren't looking good.

(APPEARANCE AND IMAGE)

To judge based on appearance is common, making a conclusion about something or someone and thus responding, image becomes standard in society's book, you will be treated based on how you look, treated with respect, or eyes cast down in reject, the image you project sends a message of who you are, or where you from, not necessarily correct, but none the less looked at by a bias aspect, a stereotypical view that places you in a category of the image assumed, telling a story without words being used, your appearance is an impression that speaks before you do

(FACE VALUE)

Never take anything for face value, for a unstable face can change, representing something entirely different, yet its expression remaining the same, never judge a cover without being sure of its content, know before you commit getting yourself involved in something, you might find yourself swallowing a hard pill, signing a contract for shoes that cannot be filled, for the devil is in the details, once the fine prints revealed its true intent will become evident, every mistake has a consequence with the potential to ruin or kill you, never take anything for face value

(CATEGORY)

With the tendency to look from the outside you categorize, yet you know not the person place or thing inside, basing things on what you see is partial and inaccurate, the slander done to the character is damaging, not opening a door because of what you think might be behind it is ignorance in its purest form, only when you are sure do you realize things are not what they appear to be, but actually a switch in perception leading to better judgment, looking beyond a mirror of a reflection, going beyond the shadow of a doubt, in depth knowing the book instead of settling for half the story and its blank pages of a made up category

(WIN OR LOSE)

While you must fight to win, you must not be afraid to lose, it is all about perception, the way that you view, for a loss could make way for a win, opening doors for progressive options, with your mind changing the dynamic no longer will you see losing as a disadvantage, but an opportunity to learn from defeat, by seeing your mistakes made previously, for a win is a win, but it is the knowledge gained that creates an unstoppable momentum

(NEGATIVE WORDS)

Negative words have the power to destroy, to tear down walls, to cause straight paths to be crossed, to divide multitudes, to damn the lost, to kill the weak and rob the poor, to bring doubt to clarity, sane to insanity, thoughts into turbulence, corruption from innocence, respect to insolence, for a love to turn into hate, negative words breed negative ways

(POSITIVE WORDS)

Positive words have the potential to build, to structure a stronger will, to bring life to death, what's wrong to right, thoughts to the thoughtless, Heart to the heartless, anger to happiness, joy to sadness, poor to riches, the off balance to better positions, light to the dark, a map for the lost, ignorance to awareness, positive words have a positive influence

(WORDS/ACTIONS)

Words can speak what they don't mean, but actions speak loudly and are more clearly pronounced, exposing what a word is truly about, for words are untrustworthy, anyone could use them by dressing them up falsely, its garments flowing beautifully like poetry, yet venom filled and spiked with bad intentions, it is actions that give words its definition and undeniable position, without action words are easily disregarded as another contradiction, with actions backing

them words have weight and substance, taken more seriously,
no longer empty and redundant

SIN BYRON

Awakening from a deep sleep, the sweet smell of a cinnamon smelling incense wafting in the air greeted me pleasantly.

Satisfied and rested I felt comfortable on the plush bed covered in sheets of satin, though a part of me felt dirty and used for enjoying such luxurious perks during these perilous times. I had to admit I could get used to this kind of treatment.

"I will have one of the servants draw a bath and clean you," said temptation appearing abruptly as if from the very drifting smoke of the incense. "Anything you desire can be yours" she cooed lifting her hand caressing the side of my face.

Springing up unexpectedly I grabbed her hand bending back her wrist with a wrenching twist,

"Fuck that! Its time you answer my questions, who are you? What are you? What is all this? Is this some kind of trick? Who brought me here and where can I find them? I'm searching for something special, something that has disappeared into the darkness leading me here. I want it back! I know you have information on where I can find it, are they here? So help me if you lie because this time I will see that you die," I threatened sincerely.

"Don't threaten me with a good time" said temptation casually flashing me a sly grin.

Not in the mood for her bullshit I applied more pressure on her wrist,

"Answer my questions damn it!"

"And if I were to refuse you and your ridiculous demands" quipped temptation unconcerned. Bending back her wrist as far as I could I glowered into her scheming eyes loathing her non-caring face of audacity, simmering with anger at my failing attempts to coerce the information I wanted but couldn't acquire.

The only way to get what I wanted was to take it by force; I would enjoy putting this crafty temptress to a well-deserved death.

"Then you would suffer death at my ugh-"

In a reverse grip motion it was my wrist being twisted then bent, the pain was excruciating.

"Haven't you learned by now you cant hurt me, all your succeeding in doing is pissing me off, so yes, to answer your first question what I am is a demon, and if you expect to get any answers from me I suggest you be more nice or it is I that will end you misinformed life, do you understand?"

Through clenched teeth I forced a "yes" out of my mouth, though my raging thoughts were saying the first chance I got I would take her life.

"Oh I don't think you do," stated temptation bending my wrist back to its max. "Do you understand now? Huh do you!"

"Yes let go of my hand!" I cried out bitterly.

"Now lets try this again, and this time we do things my way," said temptation releasing her hold, "Just so you know I can read your mind, so if you think you can get away by tricking me you wont make it out alive, and judging by your condition your running out of time.

(RESPECT AND DIRESPECT)

Respect goes a long way, taking you to high places, getting you were you need to be, things are made obsolete with the taint of disrespect, things can be made in abundance with the seeds of acknowledgement, giving regard will take you far, but disrespect will cause rejection, resulting in grudges and resentment, nothing good can come from this, but respect is rich in contentment, rising in the highest heights of acceptance, its applications are infinitely endless

(FACIAL EXPRESSIONS/BODY LANGUAGE)

What your thinking I can read through your facial expressions and body language, your looks betray your heart and the feelings involved, the way your body moves I can see through you, knowing what it is you are fixing to do, talking to me in its own special way, your expressions have an intimate place, it can hide and it can fake, but eventually the façade recedes showing exactly what it means, interpretation in its exposure through looks and composure, looking at me is like looking through a mirror and receiving an instant message, through your body language and facial expression

2Q

Striking me with a jarring blow I landed disoriented on my back yards away.

Taking a second to register threw my blurred vision that the red substance streaming down my face now smeared on my fingers was my own blood, for there to be blood I had to be alive, but how when I was dead? None of this was making any sense.

But I had no time to hunker down on the seizing pain or ponder this new revelation because the multiple scowling heads of the angry dragon was now staring down at me waiting.

Reaching down, the dragons massive arm disappeared inside of my abdomen, the searing pain growing scorching hot as the effects of its consuming poison spread.

Not able to cry out from the unbearable heat I watched on in a trance like horror as a shadow formed at the soles of my feet, slowly creeping upward ingesting the whole my body.

For a fleeting moment I could see my other half trapped in darkness, I could feel his pain as if I was there. Growing faint, I shook my head trying to clear the repetitive images of evil demons and hideous monsters racing threw my mind.

If I could focus on one thing maybe I could get a grip on my sanity I thought to myself.

In desperation to block out the pestering madness I looked for something to focus on, my split focus falling on the gold hilt of the bladeless sword I noticed lying free next to me.

The images of the demonic monsters sped faster and faster, groaning voices of the damned invading the sanctity of my mind repeating my name over and over again, I was trapped in a hellish nightmare, being swallowed up by the soul shredding grip of a perpetual hell.

"Higher power if you are with me please save me from this nightmare!" I cried out,

As if in reaction to my pleading words the red stone between the lion's powerful jaws on the golden hilt began to glow, lighting up the words down its side that I could previously not understand.

As its letters began to animatedly change itself, I could suddenly make out what it said.

(FORGET)

My eyes open to the pain, I wish to close and never open again, reminded of things I have done, the people I have hurt, each and everyone that did not deserve, I want to forget and leave the past where it is, dead no longer haunting my every breath, my dreams have become repetitious playing my conscious of messed up decisions, agonizing visions I can now see for what it is, I am to be punished for my sins, cursed to role over and over again in the same grave, all the wrong I did I pray to forget

(DARK GLIMPSES)

What is this I see as the creeping darkness consumes me, bloodthirsty demons lying in wait to taste the flesh of the simmering fate, evil monsters lurking in the shadows of hate, plotting to invade the portal to the souls secret place, haunting the aura of an eternal existence, this and far worse I see in dark glimpses,

(MOVING SHADOWS)

Creeping shadows, materializing, moving uncertain, its existence hidden to a world unknowing, it seems that these are malevolent entity's, or maybe the driving force behind a demonic source, but even I only see what the shadows will, knowing very well at any time or place, these eerie things can suddenly manifest themselves

(PERPETUAL MADNESS)

Haunting nightmares, storming, flaring, swirling in a twister of perpetual madness, clawing, uprooting, flinging the horrid past into the beat up face of misery, no comfort, no escape, no outlet for the numbing pain, what has been buried deep dug up callously, desecrated savagely, what decomposed remains jolted and animated, what unwanted beasts of burden brought back to reality's surface, what has hurt and daunted you creating an insane cycle of an never ending loop, a stirring tomb, the undead carcass of an agonizing truth

SIN BYRON

Fizzing in my bubbling irritation I took deep breaths bringing my rapidly hammering heartbeat to a calm and steady rhythm.

"What condition?" I reluctantly asked through clenched teeth.

"That feeling of our demon blood curdling, can't you feel it slowly consuming you and its poison coursing threw your veins? Can you not feel what you are becoming? Is it not refreshing to let loose, the way you ravished me I could tell lust and desire has touched you, mmm and the way you choked me thinking of no one else but yourself I could tell you had anger and arrogance to help you, and now I have contributed, thanks to me you will not have this one-sided view of burdensome obligations, you will be free to give in to your repressed temptations, I can be everything you need and more," said temptation caressing me.

Smacking her hand away, it took another series of deep breaths to calm my sizzling anger.

"What else do you have to tell me?" I questioned sternly.

"You are in a place where anything you can imagine can happen, here you are the ruler and all that you see subjects its-self to your will, here whatever it is you seek you can find, welcome Sin Byron to the mind, were there are seven levels and different ways to reach them. On the seventh level you will find what you want, but if you are to change you will no longer be the same, your perception as of now will mean nothing, you will not care who or where it is you come, you will become one of us, you will become a demon."

"I've heard enough! You or anything like you I will never become, so enough talk, save it for a fool who would be dumb enough to believe you, you demons are known for your foul tricks and filthy lies."

"What is it do I have to hide!" replied temptation sharply, getting close to my face staring into my eyes challengingly, "Tell me what do I benefit if you are dead or alive, to me your just a good fuck, easily acquired and easily disposed of, deep down you know what I'm saying is the truth, so if you wish to waste your time I will be happy to welcome you amongst my kind, or you can come with me and I will show you how to achieve your levels peek, for right now we are late for your welcome feast.

(THE MIND)

In the mind there are many doors, different levels of different floors, the ever-changing thought running in and out its core, here things manifest from processing ideas which then passes on, linked through the channels of an intricate system, amped by feelings from different locations, interchanging by design, it adapts to the signal its receiving, assessing its many connections then re-routing its actions, its reaction carry's out orders the body forwards, in obedience and absolute compliance, all falling in line, in alliance with the mind

(IMAGINATION)

Imagination is your minds limitless freedom and infinite possibilities, there are no boundaries, there are no hindrances to what can be made, you control the world you create, bending it to whatever form or shape, you are the author, the narrator, the king of your domain, there is no higher authority, all are subjected to what you think, here magic exist, whatever character lives, here you are more then just human, you are any and everything you choose, in your kingdom, your castle, your imagination rules

(INSPIRATION)

Inspiration can come from anything or anyone, its potential is highly influential, varying in differences, its work is evident, for it is all around us, even laying dormant inside of us, coming awake when there is a need to express individuality, inspiration becomes a clock tinkering on the brink of mastery, an engine pushing us with such an invisible force we rush to answer its call, inspiration for one, inspiration for all

(STRANGERS)

Take caution when encountering someone new for they are strangers to you, their ways and intentions are unknown, their actions have not yet been shown, analyze and watch how they move, don't be to quick to allow them close to you, take the time to find out who you are talking to before opening up, because once you do, your personal life becomes easily accessible, knowing things about you makes you familiar and easily approachable, you must learn to see things from a skeptics point of view, don't be so readily trusting when encountering someone new

(PRIORITYS)

Putting things to the back that should be brought to the front, for importance to be shunned, is stupidity and nonsense, an ignorant complex, handle your priorities first, learn how to make things work, there is a time and a place for everything, know when to expend your energy, utilizing its use wisely so its seeds can bare the proper fruit, becoming more to you then what it is, will cause you to take more pride in it, seeing that the acquired specifications are met, handling your priority's with more respect

(RE-IMAGINE)

What if you were to re-imagine, all in a reverse of things, where it may seem that love saved me, rescued from the darkness of nothing, the bitter confines of deeper coldness, solely created to live only for loves purpose, a Romeo pining for his Juliet, can you re-imagine how it would be to live in a home that's barren and broken, but this home is your heart beneath the physical surface, beyond society's since of rationality, beyond what you see, now dare I, dare you, to re-imagine me

(WELCOME FEAST)

Come and dine with me my beautiful love, for this feast is in honor of your souls transcendence, eagerly made for your thirst to be quenched, your hunger to be satisfied by the treasure of your palace, given whatever thy heart wishes, a plentiful harvest for the roses of the harem, what your famished spirit needed, what your vibrant body wanted, is yours for the taking, if you really want it, a brand new perception, faith and belief, the essence of your passion, at your welcome feast

(MIND FRAME)

The core structure of the active mind, the genetic make up of the mental design, the constructional working of the outcome on the inside, projecting the screening signals of the attitude on the outside, the multi shifting framework subjected to perception, the overall outlook of the subject in question

(RESPONSIBILITY/NEGLECT)

Handle your responsibilities, it is your obligation to see that what needs to be done is taken care of, not left to its own devices in neglect, for anything can happen to it, under your watchful eye and guidance minimizes the chances of *something going wrong, irreparable damage being done, it is your decisions that will show if you are trustworthy to hold important positions, or tasks given showing competence and consistence, levels will never be reached if your character shows irresponsibility, in life, to get where you want to be, you must handle your responsibility's*

2Q

Blinking my eyes hoping what I was seeing wasn't an illusion, the words read (Believe to receive what faith can increase an everlasting fountain with power moving mountains)

As the shadow continued consuming me I began to feel weak, my strength leaving me slowly, my lungs starting to constrict, my vision becoming distorted and spotted, the cold feeling of deaths icy grip slowly creeping up my hip and climbing, I had to figure out what these words meant or death was eminent.

"What will you do when the sun doesn't shine and all that you love has withered and died? When you have become one of us craving evil the light will leave you, the darkness inside will let loose, your heart blackened and consumed will drive you to oblivion, seeking ruin you will desecrate all that's pure and good rejoicing in the destruction of what's right, celebrating the embers of a burning fire in the darkness of night, when you have ended your rampaging carnage and all has met there doom by your bloody hands, only then will you be satisfied, until your blood thirsty hunger comes again!" snarled the malevolent six headed dragon.

On the verge of death all feeling of my lower body went numb, with my quivering right hand I grabbed the bladeless gold hilt beside me swinging it with all my might, it was all or nothing, if I lost now the girl would die, and all hope would be lost for me and my other half lost on the other side.

(FAITH)

Something that can be seen yet believed, the air felt its caressing breeze, I know your there my beating heart, the heavens amongst the twinkling stars, for millions to bow there head in submission, to a loving god they know is listening, for love to be a powerful feeling, just knowing you fell deeply in it, jumping not knowing if you will land, going to sleep not knowing if you will wake, leaving your home not knowing if you will return safe, in everything you must have faith

(BELIEVE)

Believe in yourself, believe in love, believe in all pure things that come from above, believe in your heart, believe in your soul, believe that anything you dream is possible, believe in hope, believe in faith, believe in the light that shines through the hate, believe unwavering, believe in your strength, believe in your will, the way out of no way

CHAPTER 6

SIN BYRON

Alert to my active presence, the host of eager women stopped what they were doing, following along giddily, caressing me provocatively, pleading and whining suggestively, aggressively beckoning, one after the next fighting so I could notice them, fighting to have me, the whole of these tempting sirens beautiful and submissive mixed with an innocent naughtiness, a sensual corruption, persistent and needy until temptation shooed them off.

All along something inside of me was stirring, an insatiable appetite forming, I had tasted the forbidden allures of temptation, exposed to the highs and lows of blissful suspense, I wanted them all in my bed crying out in passion, captivated by lust, shaking uncontrollably, exploding in ear splitting orgasms…

Shaking my head I tried thinking of something else, but my debauch thoughts came more and more each time, I would have broken and given into my lustful cravings had we not reach our destination.

Walking through two magnificent pearl doors I could not believe the amount of food prepared for me, a sumptuous feast, table upon table of mouth watering delicacies, and all around for dessert naked beauty's with soft subtle bodies varying in variety.

"You can have anyone of them, they will be more then willing to do your bidding, but none of them will give you the feeling like I did, anytime you want this you can have it, now sit and be fed by your eager servants," said temptation leading me to a gold throne that sat exalted at the head of the banquet.

Immediately after sitting down she clapped her hands together, thereafter I was fed and pampered by women of every kind, all vying for my attention, waiting on me hand and foot, caressing me, offering pleasure, the feeling was intoxicating, I was there ruler and there was nothing they wouldn't do for me.

As the spell bound women celebrated and danced to harmonious songs being sung in honor of my name, there suddenly came a distraction, the deafening sound of something screeching and scratching.

(MY LOVES)

My women so special how could I choose amongst you all, I would sooner be consumed and my heart torn apart, as far as the east is to the west, north to south, the pieces of me are spread abroad and threw-out, hidden treasures of different measures, sections of selective messages, from deep wells to abandoned desserts, my loves a weakness surrounded my keenness, because I know your silent power that causes empires to fall, the mighty to crawl and great walls to be destroyed, how can I hide this burning passion that speaks through my eyes and spills out my actions, warned of your seductive distractions, dangerous how a heart could cool and bring about doom, but I am to be shared, until such time I am aware, of the one to whom my heart compares, my women, my loves, find me near

(TROPHY)

I am a trophy to be won, all will gaze upon what the other wants with a desire to be the chosen one, at the alter they will congregate in fascination at its pedestal and breathe in its seductive fumes, could what they have dreamt of there whole life possibly be close enough to touch, yet far from there grasp? With a strong urge and an even stronger curiosity they ponder the sweet thoughts of victory, some will leave going there own way but turn back because there heart Is yearning, a magnetic need drawing them back to the elevated trophy, why is this trophy so alluring when there seems to be others just like it? A multitude of why fills the air, then suddenly the trophy speaks bringing silence and expectancy, "I embody all that is your desire, there is nothing above, below, before or after the power of this prized possession, I am to be coveted above all else, I will never die, I am your love, I am a trophy to be won"

(SEX SYMBOL)

The enthralling temptation, the elusive rapture of sensual elevation, an aching need to possess the whole of this symbol, a covetous desire shaped in forms of the spiritual, a pedestal, a rose, an elemental crystal, in essence the yearning soul burning within you, a lit torch in your world blazing dimensions away, what gives life to this flame, is forever alive in me

(HAUNTING DESIRE)

Everywhere I turn, everywhere I go, the thirst in me arises, to revel in my want, to lay drunken and corrupt, debauch by her sex, with no thought of a conscious, or a care for my actions, oh the things I would refrain in my hopes to fight it, but the feeling is addictive, the craving so obsessive, it makes my being cringe with an urge to sin, this taunting temptation haunting by desire, spewing an inferno of lust, from which I cannot run

(CONCENTRATE)

I am your love in a concentrated form, your volatile lust coursing through your blood, like a tidal wave its purity submerges your heart in a devastating flood, as you awaken from a concentrated stasis your head may waver, your body quiver, your speech incoherent, in a state of euphoria you spasm and flutter, you seem possessed, no longer do you worry about the things you cannot control, or how you used to see things before, you concentrate on me and the pleasure you wish to receive, you wish the feeling to ravish you completely, overtaking your reality, you begin to slip on the slope of a concentrated obsession, haunted and hypnotized by the visions of desire and temptation chased aggressively, but what will you do when one piece of my attention does not satisfy the craving of your first taste of Sin Byron, or 2Q and his burning love of reflection and devotion? Will you self-destruct or remain patient? When I have become concentrated

(ADDICTED)

I am addicted to the sensuous sensations of love, it makes me crave desires touch, the heat of want courses threw my blood, it makes me weak to her drug, susceptible to pleasure and pain, both to me one in the same, I love it so I cant get enough, there is no help from what I'm on

(PASSION FIRE)

The fire of passion burns wildly in me, dangerous it spreads, uncontrollably threatening to consume all of you, all my women, cant you see, the reason things have to be, the burden of every piece, distributed evenly, for I know you want all of me,

I can see you are emotionally greedy, this I can understand, but my loves my mirrors broken, therefor unpredictable, if I were to give it all to you, you would burst into flames, instantly combustible, fire would devour you hungrily, I am unaware of who you will be? If you will change, remain the same, or curse my very name, unstable blazing with desire, you will be consumed by passion fire

(INEVITABLE)

It is inevitable you come to me, and someday soon you all will belong to me, enslaving your sweet love swept in my dark breeze, a depth intoxicating the very air you breathe, in a trance trapped in a deep seductive hypnosis, nothing can be closed, your door will forever be open, my audacity venomously infusing passion, my love entices your slavish reaction, so don't fight it, delight in my everlasting likeness, a serene madness, inevitably I am consumed by your essence, our souls intertwined, an intimate connection

2Q

In a brilliant flash my swinging sword of light severed the deathly appendage, putting an end to the demented effects of the consuming burden on my strained body.

Shouting profanities, the dragon cried out as its severed arm saturated into the hungry ground, degenerating into a steaming pile of oozing black goop.

Everything was starting to make sense now; in my hand I held a blade that was, yet was not, only if I believed it, having the unwavering faith to accept that what I needed was right there, then its blade of light would appear.

"How did that feel," I quipped with a smirk, "now its my turn, I will give you one chance to leave, go back to hell now or die!" I snapped with an ultimatum and no fear resonating in my eyes.

With a rumbling roar a suffocating cloud of black smoke steamed from the dragon's nostrils. With a chilling snarl it Blew a sultry inferno out of the mouths of each of its six heads, whipping flames engulfing me in its searing hurricane of death, its eye a blazing tornado with me in its center.

Assured of its victory the dragon laughed diabolically, but stopped abruptly when the smoke cleared revealing I was still standing with not a singe on one hair.

"Is this the big bad dragon, your pathetic," I said spurring the dragon on, planning to bait it by using its own anger against it.

"Oh the big mean dragons a bust, I knew you were worthless, run back to your master with your tails tucked in you clowns."

With a guttural cry the maddened dragon lunged at me presenting just the opportunity I needed. Once the dragon came within range of my blade, I cut off each of their scowling heads with a single swing.

(MASTERY)

True Mastery lies within yourself, to control your compulsive desires felt, to have subjected your body in utter obedience, monitoring it, knowing what it is receiving, keeping focused on a straight path, not veering off the side track, ending up in the back where you started at, but to push ahead of the pack, becoming one of a kind, your body in line, in tuned synchronizing of the mind, inhibited thoughts slowed, its inhabitants controlled, now you can clearly see, that what lives within is true mastery

(CONFIDENCE AND INSECURITY)

Hold your head up and walk tall with confidence, believing in yourself that you can do whatever it is you put your mind to, insecurity will daunt you, having you doubt your potential, at times even overwhelming your mental, but you must not let that stop you, use it as a tool to motivate, know how to differentiate, keeping things positive, for insecurity will try to infiltrate, turning your mind to the negative, leading you astray, stress and frustration making it hard for you to think, take a step back, a deep breath then breathe, believe you can do all things, then you will find the strength that confidence brings

(PATIENCE)

Have patience and ripe fruit will soon fall at your feet, with patience pain soon will cease, difficulties and hardships will come to an ease, ways around obstacles will be revealed, hone your patience for such is a skill, to see ways made out of none, to analyze situations finding ways around them, to piece together the impossible puzzle you must learn self control, for patience is a treasure map to an endless supply of gold

(OPPORTUNITY)

Pay attention and you will not miss opportunity when it comes by, for it may come many times, or once in your lifetime, it is up to you to catch it, revealing itself through peculiar circumstances, opportunity could disappear in an instant, coming subtle and inconspicuous, or loud and boisterous, opportunity must be seized by any means, taken advantage of immediately, if it is to come your way there must be no delay, you must move with haste, or find yourself left behind with no way to make up for lost time, no longer placed within your reach, there is no guarantee when it comes to opportunity

(LIGHT BLADE)

Symbolically forged from the illuminating ascension of 2Qs higher purpose, its blade radiates in its pureness, a revealing harvest of internal enlightenment, its culminating form shaping from faith and believing, its origin derived from the lord of heaven, no evil can stand in relation to its presence, if spiritually unbalanced it can erase your existence, its unrelenting truth cuts threw the darkness, wielding this light blade the power within awakes, giving energy to the inner being from an elevated place

(PURE LIGHT)

In supernova radiance, pure light suddenly exploded into my existence, enveloping my being by its shocking immediacy, this phantasmal radiation overwhelming intrusively, where was the source of this energy coming from, this dazzling phenomenon creating a miraculous rainbow of brilliant spectrum, I am blinded to my every turning direction, likened unto a bumbling mad men, stuttering repetitiously, frantically uttering why me, but then this spontaneous anomaly generously resides, leaving behind an illuminating glow, more whys escape my quivering lips, frightfully wondering what this could mean, but I have instantly come to snap realization, though at one point I could not see, I 2Q am beauty's beholder, this pure lights source comes from me

(OVERCOME)

Do not be consumed by evil, possessed by the insecure whims of fickle circumstance, but counterbalance the adversary's dilemmas with good, viewing vicious attacks and jolting setbacks as a way to always learn and advance, do not sway hopelessly in any torrents direction, easily tossed about by troubled winds, but in patience and perseverance will you build up an arsenal of faith and courage, during trying times do not become wear-fully stagnant, toppled by the weight of worrisome burden, but believe in yourself that you can do all things, and the pestering problems of the enemy will have no choice but to flee in retreat

(UNLIMITIED POTENTIAL)

Greater the spirit in you, then anything insidious or evil, we are the stars unlimited, our potential beyond normal comparison, for it far surpasses simple understanding, it is superior, deeper then the reflection seen in the mirror, but it must be realized by the individual beholder, believed in the innermost core of your center, the faith to walk into the danger of a blazing fire, an iron will, a soul of crystal

SIN BYRON

Brought dragging through the dinning hall held by each arm were two frail old men bound in chains. Held captive by four muscle bound beasts, mutant dogs bearing wide jaws, razor sharp teeth and sickle like claws that retracted and shape shifted.

"These Demon dog soldiers serve as your security, and there are many like them to do your will," said temptation.

"What would I need with security, this is my mind," I retorted arrogantly.

"How right it would it be if your will went unchallenged, and the decrees uttered from your revered lips worshipped, held sacred above all others. But to utter such lofty lies now would only deceive you, these fickle emotions oppose your rule and stand in the way of your growth, they are the clotting weeds on the fertile ground of your glory and need to be exterminated," said temptation handing me a black sword that materialized into her hands, the hilt fashioned as a dragon with smooth gripping scales. "This dark sword has been made to channel your growing power, you were made to be a king, made to rule, show these two fools and all those who would dare to oppose your way that death will be there only fate."

"What could these two possibly do to me?" I asked, looking over the sad appearance of the two sickly looking men.

"They plot to take what is yours, it is these burdens called emotions that stand in the way of your destiny!" snapped temptation, her raw hatred emerging, shooting from her condemning lips like a boiling pot of spewing spittle.

Looking at the two old geezers I still couldn't see how they could pose a threat, though I knew from experience that looks could be deceiving, to me there was nothing that indicated that these old guys weren't capable of anything physical.

"Let go your restraint, I see no threat here," I ordered the demon dog soldiers.

Upon my command both men fell to the floor with labored breathing. Their mangy hair follicles stuck to their worn faces by perspiration and their malnourished bodies weakened to a slow moving grind.

A pitiful display watching a defeated man spared right before the grave, pulled back, beaten, starved, held prisoner, subjected to the torment of a prolonged life wasting away.

"Help them stand now!" I demanded.

On their feet the old men staggered in a daze wavering clumsily, their brittle legs wobbling shakily but eventually finding steady balance.

"Who are you two? Because apart of me refuses to believe that you could possibly stand in my way let alone harm me."

"Don't talk to them, you don't know what there capable of, kill them now before they trick you!" shouted a devilish temptation.

"Enough! Everyone will have a chance to speak, you are free to speak" I said to the men, growing irate with the unappealing issue.

"My name is kindness, you say we are rebels, yet you have forced us from our homes, we will not rest until we reclaim what was ours to begin with, we will not bend nor see things your way, we will fight against you accursed demons night and day until there are no longer any of us left standing."

I don't know if it was the tone of his rising voice or the bold audacity of its delivery but I felt disrespected, this disembodied voice slowly creeping inside of my head screaming to behead these heretics before another slanderous word came out their false lips.

Moving suddenly a snarling demon dog struck kindness in the gut dropping him to his knees; the dispensed pain on behalf of my dislike for the disruptive emotion stroked my sense of satisfaction, euphoria and power.

"I am happiness, we refuse to give in to your devious tactics of intimidation, we refuse to live under a tyrant like you, I remember this place how it used to be before you came and ransacked its beauty, pillaging its treasures, killing off emotions, preying on the weak, you monsters are abominations, incarnations of blood sucking parasites, we emotions will restore this cesspool to its former glory!" shouted happiness with defiance.

Now I was outraged, whom did these two think they were accusing me of something when before this and even now I had my own situation to sort out.

In response to my vexation a demon dog struck happiness in the face knocking him to the ground.

"You have defiled the sanctity of the mind with whores and demonic mongrels, you all will pay!" shouted kindness back on his feet, struggling with surprising strength against the demon dogs fighting to restrain.

"Are you a ruler who would allow two insignificant emotions to speak to him in such a way, disrespecting his house and his property!" stated temptation loudly proclaiming for all to hear.

Flying into a fit of rage, with one easy swipe of my dark blade kindnesses head rolled away, turning on happiness next, my swinging blade left his head partially decapitated, his severed neck dangling freely from the skin stuck in a permanent expression.

All around there was nothing to be heard but silence.

(DARK BLADE)

Symbolically forged from the provoking fire of darkness, supernaturally crafted at the source of its sole origin, a pure harvest of all the secrets of the shadows within, linked to the culmination of the hidden mysteries and depths of the forbidden, wielding this dark blade steadily engulfs the eternal soul, in the grip of its possessive hold one can become spiritual desolate, damned to the lost, for there must be an existing balance to stabilize its core, or be consumed and forever no more

(KINDNESS FOR WEAKNESS)

I praise the kind and their loving ways, they would give there last from there heart and not think twice of withholding anything, but there is a downside to being kind, for there are those who would wish to take advantage of this, seeing their kindness as weakness to oppress and mistreat them, for a number of reasons, finding an opening to exploit, they can come quietly or with great noise, in some cases kindness was misinterpreted, the picture not fully painted, one side kind the other underestimated, both leading to the oppressor's devastation for missed information, though this may sometimes be, there will always be those who see kindness as a chance to prey on the weak

(TITLES)

So easily are titles given to those who do not deserve it, for a leader, a friend, a brother, to this end titles should be proven, not so easily abused, only given to those who earned its use, for a title carries meaning, it is so because actions speak it, if nothing was done to attain the name, it is in vain, taken away the right of those who have paved the way, don't claim something you have no right to, don't take on false titles

(ADVICE)

Be careful of the advice you give, for the receiving end could give life to it, acting on false guidance, be careful of the advice you receive, for it can leave you sinking from no foundation, marooned on a raging sea, from the words you trusted in, from the words you believed, if there is something you don't know, find out or leave it alone, or potentially risk becoming a catapult, leading someone on, taking advice you don't know is right, can create a situation that cant be made right, if asked how you would handle something on your side, be sure to make sure its good advice

(MAN)

A man is one who stands on his own two feet handling his responsibilities, one who understands the importance of priorities, one who takes care of family raising his kids as an extension of him, one who know how to put things in proper perspective, one who knows how to accept and give direction, one who knows how to provide and if need be improvise, one who wants the best out of life, one who is willing to work achieving set goals, one who never says cant whatever the task demands, one who despite the obstacles formulates a plan, even if the plan fails and things get tough, a man pushes forward and never gives up

(VALIDATION)

Why is it you seek validation, caring what other people think when inside of you is something great? When all you need is yourself to believe and validate, your heart is where things should be based, your will is where things should be built, instead of trying to find quality in someone else start by looking deep inside yourself, only then you will find what it is you seek, putting off the old you that searched frivolously, looking for acceptance, going in the wrong direction, your life is what you make it, there is no need for validation

(JUDGE)

Oh the audacity of those who judge, forgetting where it is they came from, all the things they have done in private away from prying eyes, inside hiding facts covered by lies, not looking at there faults and all its wrongs, ignorantly claiming false dominion over all, looking down as if endowed with insight to see what cant be seen by the naked eye, how far from the truth, you are blindly smug, oh the audacity of those who judge

2Q

Falling, the dragon's dead weight instantly degenerated into gunk, it's grossly malformed heads and conjoined body sizzling in a tar black substance before dissolving into the famished ground.

Without warning, the blade of light willed from my faith emitted a ray of energy, though the no good men could not see me physically, they witnessed the blinding glint of lustrous light shining from the unseen, reaching through the thin crisp night air physically manifesting from the veil of the unknown.

Fleeing in fright they left their victim unconscious and badly beaten but thankfully still breathing.

Suddenly a flurry of gusts whipped and whirled from a gathering band of stormy dark clouds, at the cue of rolling thunder a lone bolt of lightning fell striking the ground with a deafening crack; there a beautiful six-winged angel stood, its countenance glistening in stunning brilliance.

"My name is Gabriel, the lord of heaven has commanded me to bring you to what's next, the time has come for you to move on from here.

"Wait I have questions, what will happen to her? Where are you taking me? And I figured out how to use the blade of light but what is this burning flame?" I said excitedly pulling the fascinating object from my waist.

"The women will heal, she will be shielded from what she had to undergo, not remembering anything of her trying ordeal her life will go on as normal, as for you, I will cause to fall into a deep sleep, then I will spirit you all the way through the veil to the crossroads where you will then be on your own, what you carry is the flame of hope, you must protect it and bring it to the right place," responded the angel Gabriel.

"Where can I find this place?" I asked looking at the undying flame of hope in amazement.

"I am permitted not to say, but have faith and you will find your way," said Gabriel avoiding my question.

"What will become of the women's friend who set her up and those vile men who attacked her?" I asked, still angry with the foul people who played a hand in the vicious plot then got away.

"I cannot say for I am merely a messenger, there is only one who can judge, for it is the lord of the kingdom who has the ultimate authority in these spiritual matters, but there will come a day when all evil doer's will answer for there evil ways," replied the angel Gabriel vaguely.

With only a bare minimum of my questions answered I didn't feel anymore prepared then I did from the beginning, but who to complain to? Who else could help me? I was a soldier in a war older then time, I just had to play with the hand I was dealt, bite down and bear with my afforded resources until things started to make more since. The worst-case scenario was that I die with no solution to restore things.

On the Brightside, at least I was starting to get used to the divines aggravating and unclear way of answering things.

"One more thing, if I am to find my other half and he is consumed what to do? How do I get through to him if he is already consumed by demons?"

"This answer you must find on your own, but when the time comes you will know, now come take my hand," said Gabriel holding out his right hand.

"You are going to be ok" I said to myself, briefly looking back at the abused women with concern. With my attention back on the angel Gabriel I took his hand, in an instant my conscious vision was covered by darkness.

(THE LORD ANSWERS)

The lord works in mysterious ways, he answered me in the subtlest of ways, and he told me he sees all the hurt and pain, yet also his favor bestowed each day, but his creation rebelliously disobeys, ungrateful for all the things he gave, destroying or altering the things he made, so he lets them go their own way, for everyone he grants free will, yet they choose to stray, then places the blame on his bountiful grace, when death and evil show its face, yet goodness and mercy prevail triumphantly, they fail to know or appreciate, the author and finisher of our fate, the king above all kings, who is it among you that say they are great? What in this world did you create? All the beauty within the earth he has created, yet his creation worships it instead of him, a wrathful God could wipe us out yet still he sends his blessings down, the world is a test, sometimes the worst must happen to bring out the best, he wouldn't give us a task that we could not handle, but as quick as something is built, the lord of heaven can dismantle

(PURPOSE)

Move with a purpose, you must be determined, to master whatever it is set out to do, with a focused effort you can conquer any endeavor, doing anything you put your mind to, whatever's pursued put your heart into, and you will find barriers easier to move, remain focused and doors will open, to win you must earn it, move with a purpose

(CARE/WORRY)

To worry about someone shows that you care about their well being and how they fare, what happens when they are out of your sight, worrying that something's not right, no longer can you keep them safe, to protect them from different things, that could hurt them and make them feel the pain you desperately tried to shield from them, for your experience has taught you many things, the bumps and bruises this world can bring, but in the end you know you have to let them go, oh how you care and worry so

SIN BYRON

Retiring to my chamber, I told my multitude of servants I didn't want to be disturbed. The twisted feelings inside of me seemed to grow worse, I felt as if I was coming undone.

This was a different feeling then my already shattered psyche from the broken crystal pieces, no this was something far more malevolent, and what scared me most was the fact that I was starting to like it.

Every since I became aware of the unbalance between me and my other half 2Q I tried focusing on the task at hand, putting how I used to be behind me for both our sake, but I was starting not to care, slowly reverting back to my old ways, as my thoughts grew more turbulent in walked temptation.

"Congratulations you have completed your first task as well as your demonstration of power," she said clapping her hands sitting next to me on the bed ruining my self-meditation "Now you can advance and are one step closer to reaching your unlimited potential."

"I want to be left alone!" I snapped.

Turning up her nose with an attitude temptation dismissed my displeasure.

"Don't be so snippy this is our last time together before you go advancing to the next level, for the next time you wake you will be in another place, so I have come with a special parting gift."

At the snap of her fingers in walked two beautiful women, both identical twins with a honey brown complexion, both eager to please.

Immediately after my anxieties left me and my lustful thoughts focused on one thing, bringing these exotic beauty's pleasure and release.

"And me makes three" said temptation rubbing my arm softly whispering into my ear.

Our time together was full of passion and sex, I enjoyed penetrating temptation and each twin one after the next, our pungent musk feeling the air as we gave into debauch desires, the taste of each others sex on our tongues, the smell of our scents on each others breath.

When we were finished I closed my eyes in a fitful rest, the sensation still lingering after they departed.

(ALONE/RELAX)

Sometimes its better to be alone, to sit back colleting your thoughts, analyzing your mind, re- evaluating yourself from time to time, for distractions are constant, its repetitious patterns of life's problems and responsibilities taxes your mind and your body, to fall back and relax revitalizes your position of who you are, where your at, what you have to do when you get back, it all will seem easier to cope with when you are alone, you will acquire that rare feeling of being neutral, as you relax tension and pressure dissipates, pushing its cloying reminders to the back, to become a better you, sometimes its better to be alone and relaxed

(CAN'T LEAVE YOU ALONE)

I am incapable of leaving you alone, I tried but cannot crack your code, your deep effect has cast an incantation on my will, and I try to fight, try as I might to struggle against your steel, it wont bend, it wont break, a hopeless inhibition, to turn away only frustrates, my reserve is further tempted, so then I hide deeper inside my multi dimensional soul, to my surprise defensive lines were cast to rubble stone, my aggravating revelation, I cant leave you alone

(SCENT)

Like an animal I'm attracted by your scent, its odor like attraction draws my passion, the scent of enticing flesh, its vapor rises filled with sex, a calling from deep inside, Sin Byron willingly answers, the primal instinct within becomes alive, with no control or thought I am lured becoming yours, your smell carried by the breeze possesses me, turning me into a insatiable slave aimed to please, with my appetite increased, you use me selfishly pursuing your release, the scent awakens animals in heat

(DRUG)

You have become a dangerous drug from which there is no rehabilitation from, my body strung out from the sensations,

I must have you now there can be no waiting, the aftereffects are not on my mind, with your drug I feel alive, without it, its as if I might die, going threw the withdrawals of an obsession, the more deeper I go the more sense of lost time and direction, creating a void I'm hopelessly left in, held captive by my insatiable habits, only time will tell how much caused damage, if even at all, your sex is a powerful drug that runs threw my blood

(STRAWBERRY CREAM)

Your sweet taste of strawberry cream, my tongue so excited, kissing those succulent lips to your thighs and hips, trailing circles of wet lines around your creamy center before I dip in the middle, until your eyes roll in the back of your head, shaken and tremble, your relief is my satisfaction, kiss my lips and taste your sex, your sweet strawberry cream dripping down your legs

(FORBIDDEN PLEASURE)

For whom do you care? Do you really? Is not your obligations stressful daily, let us disappear into deep passion, hot sex with no strings attached, your monotonous life has become a weighted burden attached to disappointment and frustration, boredom and predictability has dulled your passion dying to re-awaken, you are in need of my sweet distraction, your heart aching for pure lust found in heightened sensation, focused devotion your pleasures waiting, wet from excitement and anticipation, knowing you are in the dark doing things you shouldn't, yet open, lost in the waves of pleasures ocean, if your conscious is dented let me renew it with vengeance, for you deserve better, come taste a forbidden pleasure

(UNDONE)

What has become of me? Why do I wish to make you bleed, to spill your blood like the control leaving me? I am coming undone, what comfort can calm this beating drum, what rest will I find in this pestering distress? This curdling cry invading the peace I wish swiftly unraveling in my contempt, creating the burning seed my shattered reserve has planted, why do I curse my existence, yet at the same-time wishing yours to be silenced? Why can I not run? From the disturbing madness causing me to come undone

(NO ATTENTION)

It would be devastating for me not to look at you, it would be better to be abandoned and left to die then for you to be a ghost to 2Q, it would be better for your casket to be closed then Sin Byron not give you his black rose, it would be better that you not exist then for me to turn my back and give you no attention, it would be better you remain mute then for my words to have nothing to say to you, it would be better you stay in the physical realm of your expectance then to come to me and be rejected, it would be better you sink and do not swim then for my undeniable love to give you no attention

(FORBIDDEN FRUIT)

To acquire the euphoria of the forbidden fruit you must first sever your attachments walking the dark path of no regret, taking the hidden fruit into your love and engulfing it in your sex, by tasting its sweet rebellion in secret and savoring its intoxicating satisfaction in selfishness, for it is all about you nothing else matters, its scintillating excitement gives life to all of your repressed desires, its texture a gratifying conclusion, for you may leave and return to its fresh abundance as you wish, but the appeal of the taboo must be locked in the whisper of your lips

(TIME/CHANGE)

Change is inevitable for nothing remains the same, everything has its time, every time has its place, the way things are meant to be, to grow and then cease, everything in harmony, in sync naturally, why fear change when it will happen regardless? Despite disagreement, denial or argument, comfort-ability has its time, but to disregard change is blind, there is no way around this, you can try to cover it, to act as if it does not exist, but the fact remains, time will change

CHAPTER 7

2Q

I am detached and still; yet floating through the current of a perceived dream.

Passing through a warped passageway I feel a strange feeling of there being no sense of time, the darkness revealed a full moon in a bloody sky, my heartbeat merged with the silence of night, my naked thoughts were exposed to a spritzing mist, the images I saw were contorted and mixed, seemingly trapped in an endless world-wind, round and round everything spinning.

Slowing, I could feel the warmth of the sun; its rays like shining gold arrows piercing threw the heavy cloak of darkness.

Opening my eyes I found myself alone on a dirt road.

Looking around I could see no difference from the material world, instead of living in a suburb or city this would be the rural country in the middle of nowhere.

Seeing something barely visible far out in the distance I started towards it, I didn't know what it was or what I was looking for but hopefully this wasn't anything evil and a start to help fixing whatever went wrong.

On the way there my surroundings changed dramatically, the time of day, weather, even the terrain instantly changed in a split second.

In confusion and astonishment I probed my bizarre surroundings, was I hallucinating? Somehow I had materialized without my knowing it into a super sized forest.

I was the smallest thing compared to the abnormally tall trees the intimidating height of massive skyscrapers and its enlarged shifting and unnatural environment.

There was no telling what kind of dangers lay in wait behind the scenes of such a perplexing and unstable location.

Jolted by a high pitch shriek, I moved through the forest towards the source of the distressing sound, the further I went the thicker the smoke reaching out into the forest.

Hiding behind a brush near a clearing, to my horror I saw a home engulfed in flames, frantic people being slaughtered, heads decapitated, arms ripped apart, demented dog like creatures in a frenzy feasting on mutilated corpses, there smeared instruments of death covered with the blood of a fresh kill. It was clear to see these carnivorous predators would spare no survivors.

Not to far away from the massacre and conveniently closer to me were three dog like beasts surrounding the most beautiful women I had ever laid eyes on, going wide with disbelief when I saw she was stark naked and the source of the startling shriek.

This time instead of jumping into unknown waters and giving away my position, I would wait for the perfect opportunity.

From what I gathered there would be no way to save her now without drawing an unwanted crowd from the enemy. Judging by the severity of the situation I made up my mind that I would launch a sneak attack when the time was right, with the element of surprise on my side I would have the upper hand.

Counting all opposition in the surrounding area I summed up ten, if I could manage to take out the three closest to me quietly, there was a chance of slipping away unnoticed by the others.

But if I miscalculated my approach by the slightest things could get bad.

Despite what could possibly happen I was ready to accept the consequences.

Slowly inching forward I strategically placed myself close enough to eaves drop on their conversation.

"After all this time tracking you down we finally got you now, we have been waiting for this day did you think you could get away," said dog number one haughtily with a look of triumph.

"Maybe we should bite off her pretty little face," snarled dog number two salivating profusely.

"I wonder if she tastes as good as she looks," replied dog number three shoving the helpless women to the ground.

Shape shifting its retractable appendage into a veiny disfigured hand, dog number two swiped at her bare legs locking on to one of the ankles of her feet.

Fighting to resist, the beauty in distress flailed her legs frantically putting up a struggle, cocking her free leg back it met her aggressor with a colliding impact mashing dog number two directly in the nose, yelping in pain it let her go rubbing its sore snout tenderly.

When the other two dogs saw its wimpy reaction they started to wisecrack and howl in hysterics at the others expense.

With a crushed ego dog number two grew hostile and mad.

"You stinking emotion I'm going to pull you apart then rip out your bloody heart!" snapped the enraged dog.

From that uncontrolled outburst I knew I would have to react and risk the timing being bad.

Bearing razor sharp teeth it snarled menacingly, lunging madly at the frightened women.

Coming out of hiding prepared to intercede my blade of light cut down the rabid beast easily. Startled, both demon dogs one and three stood momentarily stunned by my sudden entry, but once over their initial surprise, they both came after me at the same time.

(ADAPT)

You must be able to adapt becoming flexible in any situation, forming a tough skin that can't be penetrated, a layer able to last the duration, capable and reliable through any terrain your placed in, weather complicated or basic you must be well rounded, properly trained, adapting to inevitable stress and strain, the trials and tribulations sure to live up to its name, the pain, heartbreak and all the games, these and far worse will come to attack, in this must be ready, able to adapt

(SOMEONE NEW)

Discovering someone new sparks this flame inside of you, a journey threw uncharted territory, an exciting adventure, a new story, all the potential possibilities, all the new insecurities, all the secrets to be revealed, all the new feelings to feel, all the pain and heartache to come, all the people comparing from, all of the ups, all of the downs, when someone new comes around

(UNAPPRECIATED)

My love, I know you are unappreciated, you do so much yet receive so little, living in this special world were peoples motives are questioned, not knowing what's next and from what direction, not knowing if they are for or against you, to sincerely want to help, or just out to use you, I can see you my love through a different lens, I can see how hard you work, the pressure your in, how things can seem one sided, what's fair blatantly distorted and divided, none the less stay the course and finish strong, there is a light up ahead, and an award waiting for the unappreciated

(FIGHT/WALK AWAY)

A fight takes places on many levels, physical, spiritual, each in itself a battle, a war raging on, what are your odds, what is it you gain from walking away, is it your life, your piece of mind, your morals of what's wrong and right, these things need to cross your mind, why do you fight? What are you fighting for? Is this even your war? Would you give your life for this cause? Are you prepared to lose it all? What the outcome could be, is there a chance for peace, at the end of the day two choices remain, you could fight or walk away

(STRATEGIZE AND PLAN)

It would be wise to strategize and plan so you wont become a victim of circumstance, prepare yourself even when the situation has not yet been, this will prevent sudden events from taking you by surprise, losing your footing and stride, because now you will know how to handle what comes along with everything that needs to be done, to keep moving forward you need a clear path to advance, not knowing the unknown strategize and plan

(EPIC LOVE)

Epic, elevated, witnessed on the horizon of an aurora lit sky, its vibrant passion ever ascending the starry heights of the celestial heavens, descending into the lowest depths of the covering veil of reality's darkest illusion, loves legendary presence has existed before life's budding essence, becoming apart of our souls divine genetics, what heroes of old, what stories told of chivalrous deeds, a selfless influence that blended into the universal waters of the worlds conscious, subtly seeping into languages fluent as flowing streams, collecting in the hearts of races vast as oceans and seas, out pouring in a waterfall of loves fascinating legacy

2Q

Stepping to the side I deflected a swinging blow from dog number three, coming at me dog number one swiped its lethal claw at my throat, stepping back to dodge it I noticed the women still on the ground, her mouth agape staring wide eyed and still, was she to frightened to run? To stunned at the sudden turn of events to move?

Taking my mind off the mystery women I watched both of my adversary's sickle like claws elongate, its curved tips growing sharper, thicker and more pointed.

Thankfully still occupied in a bloodthirsty state of ravenous slaughter, killing, feasting and chasing there prey were the other seven demon dogs who had yet to take notice of me or the moderate noise being made by there counterparts.

This confrontation was turning out way longer then I expected, these savage demons were muscle bound, unnaturally strong, brutal and versed in the art of combat, whereas me with no combat skills at all fought with a lone belief that I could do anything, the faith in my will fluently becoming one with my movements, freeing me from the doubt and fear I realized could only hold me back from achieving my potential, I would not be held down again.

Deflecting a heavy blow from dog number one, I shifted simultaneously catching dog number three in mid swing, my first blow terminating its right arm, my second and third mercilessly splitting then severing its head, now I was down to dog one, both of us circling each other in a defensive position.

"Who are you?" asked the demon dog curiously.

"I am 2Q, and I have come to rid this place of monsters like you!" I replied boldly.

"Is that so, well I regret to inform you that you will have a lot of ridding to do, I am the general cruelty, these are my soldiers! Lay down your weapon now and I will pardon your transgression allowing you to leave in peace."

"The only way I leave is if she comes with me," I said pointing towards the stunning women who did not move since the beginning of the battle.

"I'm sorry that I cannot do, for you see this emotion is wanted and therefor must be punished according to the ruler."

"Who is she to you? And who is your ruler?" I asked fully aware of the dwindling time I was playing with, at any given moment one of his soldiers could come across us or notice there general and fellow comrades were gone and come searching, but despite the danger I needed answers.

"To show you that I am a good sport, I will answer your questions if you triumph in a battle against me, but if you lose, you will wish that you have taken my generous offer to leave in peace, you will know anguish until you are consumed and your beating heart ripped out of your hollow chest, you will change into a heartless demon and I will happily watch you tear her apart, devouring her delicious flesh mercilessly bathing in the warmth of her spilling blood, then you will fall in line assuming the role of my bitch underling!" shouted cruelty attacking spontaneously.

Off guard, the point of its claw came inches from my face. Taking advantage of my being off balance cruelty went on the attack, but luckily I saw this coming.

Pivoting, my blade met its claws, clashing, clanging, maneuver for maneuver, swing for swing, block for block, locked in a battle to the death.

Pulling back he went for my abdomen, dodging, its claw caught hold of the left side of my sash tearing it, freeing were I concealed the flame of hope, tumbling from my waist its clear cylinder case clinking as it hit the ground, bouncing, spinning then coming to a stop.

In that brief moment my opponent put his guard down I struck.

Taking advantage of this vital mistake I sent my sword plunging through its left shoulder, the skin sizzling as the blade of light exited the wound smoothly.

With a loud yelp cruelty hit the ground crying out in high-pitched agony, the roaring sound alerting the rest of the blood-lusting devils to our whereabouts.

In a rush I looked around for the flame of hope quickly realizing it was gone and so was the women I fought to save.

Further ahead in the opposite direction I could see her fleeing.

Not only that, howling and coming at me full speed from another direction was the rest of cruelty's soldiers who had spotted me.

With no answers to my questions and the flame of hope taken from me, I had no choice but to chase after the women.

For a moment I could see her not to far ahead and calculated it wouldn't take me long to catch her, then she astonishingly disappeared.

Paces further I found out why when suddenly the surroundings, environment and time of day instantly changed into a mountainous terrain in the pitch-black darkness of night.

Pausing in fascination, my eyes scaled the foot of a massive mountain; further up, the cloudy fog shrouded its invisible peak.

Willing my swords light I moved forward, the pyramiding path elevating the face of the mountain, my every step giving me the strange light headed feeling of walking into the sky. With my climbing height the ridge became dangerously steep, a sure death if you fell over its edge.

Hearing the demon dog's sinister howls I knew they were near, it was only a matter of time before they tracked me here, I had to find this mystery girl before they did.

Walking the path in search of her I heard something, so I stopped and listened.

Hearing a barely audible sound I instinctively knew it was her panting breath, she was hiding somewhere, but where could you hide anything in an open place like this? I thought to myself.

"Come out I wont hurt you!" I pleaded but got no response, "listen I know you don't know or trust me, but there is no time I was followed, the rest of those demon beasts are close behind."

"Where did you get this ever burning flame?" she asked, her voice barely audible above the tone of a whisper, still not giving up her location.

"Listen I swear to tell you everything you want to know, but right now I could use your help and I'm sure you can use mine, I can help you, but I can guarantee if we stay stagnant any longer chances are we are both going to die."

Surfacing, the remarkable women miraculously materialized out of the mountains wall; to the untrained eye she could have remained unseen, what seemed apart of the mountains structure was really a hidden passage, a barely noticeable gateway to a connection of places.

"How do I know that your telling the truth," she asked still hesitant and unsure of my motives.

"Because if I was lying to you, why would I go through these great length's just to rescue you, I do not wish to harm you, but please we must go now," I urgently implored.

But before having the chance to leave, a bloodthirsty snarl traveling with the nights gusty winds reached me chillingly.

In alarm I could see beady red eyes just a few feet below the elevating path, the good news, the advantage of higher ground, the bad news, its dangerous conditions.

"How do we get out?" I asked, focused on the approaching threat.

"On this mountain are special passageways to different places, going threw this one will bring you to a valley," responded the women.

"Go now and take the flame with you, I will meet you there when this is over," I said preferring it in her hands then anyone else's.

"No I will not leave you all alone, this is all my fault!" She argued.

Advancing, the beady red eyes grew closer by the second.

"I don't think this is the time to object, now go before they get here, I don't want to have to worry about you to in the process."

Walking up to me she kissed me on the cheek,

"Be safe," she said sweetly then swiftly retreated.

Hidden under the cover of darkness I quickly formulated a plan of action.

Once the beady red eyes of the demon dogs were close enough, I revealed the swords blinding light causing the first startled dog to cover its eyes, giving me enough time to plunge my blade deep into its heart then kick its body back into the dog behind it.

Throwing that one off balance I immediately rushed forward plunging my blade into its neck, as it fell backwards the second dog knocked the third over the mountains edge, its howling an echo as it plummeted to its death.

With no more enemy combatants to engage, I looked down the mountains face to the winding path below.

Seeing the faint glow of torches I concluded that the remaining demon dog soldiers were still further behind, they must of sent three up ahead hoping they would be enough to take me.

Turning back around, I was confident by the time there back up arrived I would not be followed.

(THE DEMON CRUELTY)

Ready and willing to disregard all feelings, with no mercy, with no recognition, eager to deliver its worse punishment, eager to make you suffer, your fate is in the hands of a monster, it does not care, it lives for oppression, reveling in your fear and desperation, feeding off of your emotional distress, the demon cruelty wants you to cry and beg

(SKILLS)

Important to know in a variety of use, a learned skill is helpful to you, when faced with a problem to know what to do, will show that skills are valuable, to not need help able to do it yourself, will set you above everyone else, with knowledge of skill, to fix or to build, a job opening will always be filled, its future value holds a multitude of purpose, with worth in yourself as well as your service

(CHASE LOVE)

Chase me my love I wont make it easy, for what's worth in something easily acquired, chase me till your heart is tired, then

I will see if you are for me, you pursue harder when something you really want is out of your reach, tell me my love what will you do for me? Games are not to be played for I am not to be swayed, your intentions will be brought to the forefront, one way or another, my observant eyes will see what it is you do, when my precious time is given to you, in these trying days, I will know if your worth my time or to go another way

(LET ME)

I know you are hurt my love, not quick to open up to someone, afraid to give your all, not knowing if your all will lead to a broken heart, let me in, don't close yourself off to my presence, let me show you the beauty of your reflection, showing you a women of confidence instead of inhibition and subjection, let me free you from insecurity, to tell you what it is I see when you look at me, to answer in truth and sincerity, bringing you peace and clarity, that no matter what shape or size, how tall or short you are, the real substance lies in your heart, its steady beat reminding that you are still alive despite the odds, if you cant be seen for who you are, its there loss, let me right the wrong, let me be your all

(HIDE AWAY)

Come hide away with me in the dark where no one can see, let us create a lasting beauty in an everlasting dream, may we never wake forever this undying flame, that cast a lovers spell binding me to your gaze, here in the flesh, but our spirits far away, in romantic abandon we lock ourselves together, the world is left behind, all connection to us severed, lingering in a breeze, my fresh air you breathe, my love lets hide away, then come back as we please

(LEAN ON/TALK TO)

When things get tough becoming hard to handle, I encourage you to find someone to talk to, this I know, no one can do it alone, there is someone out there who cares willing to lend a helping hand, lean on them for support, don't be afraid of falling short, because you can always get back up, its not weakness to lean on someone, a lot of things could be prevented when problems are small and not as serious, but you have to seek someone, to talk to and lean on

(DANGEROUS)

Dangerous to know yet she wants me alone, how could you love what your unsure of, addicted to my type it feels so right, her body blocking rational thoughts of the mind, you should of known what you were getting yourself into, I tried to warn you before you fell into my issues, the man inside is split in two, the good and the bad, the kind and the cruel, your emotions weighed you down so you couldn't see, that you were tied up with a train coming full speed, kicking and screaming looking at me for help, my dangerous love, my dangerous self

(I UNDERSTAND)

I understand you my love, even when you feel like no one else does, from me you can hide nothing, for every emotion has come in contact with me in its pureness, and you my love are made of them, they shape the whole of your being, they are the gateway to your heart, mind and soul, you are beautiful and unique, a precious jewel, every man may not see your value, everyone may not be the one for you, but hold your esteem on a pedestal, be patient, and in time the sun will shine revealing your materialized desire unto you, if you only believe, what you wish will come true, but do not rush your special love risking the fragile strings of a broken heart, for the rain will bring scornful clouds that will block your discerning eyes, closing your heart from a true love that's destined to arrive, why give yourself away if it is not to your soul mate? The one whom your heart will love for all eternity, a connection that will follow and comfort you in this life and the next, until you meet again, for I truly understand

(BASED ON)

What have you based your love on, is it looks, money, empty promises, sweet words of nothing, what you base your attention on will lead you to a flourishing heart, or a temporary foundation that will crumble from the start, all your hopeful dreams of the possibilities that have yet been, disappearing into the wind, all your invested emotions carelessly cast to the wayside, my love how many tears must you cry, how many times must you reassure yourself of your beauty or your personality, that it is not your fault that these things are happening, you are setting yourself up for disappointment and a broken heart if you do not know what it is based on, for a precious jewel like you deserves the world, relationships cannot stand solely based on, the weight of your supporting love being the only one

(IDENTIFY LOVE)

Love lies deep within, intertwined into the essence of your beautiful spirit, you must find it, chase it, capture it, but over all identify what makes it authentic, is it indeed what you have been searching, the other half to a soul of fulfillment, you must first be specific, for what may seem real may just be imitation, for love is intimate, intricate and infinite, a bonding energy in wavering feeling

(ENVELOPE LOVE)

Intimate love, never let it go, for now that you have found it, identified it, chased and captured it, you envelop it in whole, becoming the diamond, the crystal, the gold, an immortalized treasure in the center of your soul, a sparkling star adorned in the heights of spirit, one in special alignment with an eternal element

(SWEET KISSES)

My every devotion, my every wish, my every desire, her sweetest kiss, every crystal piece, for loves melody, drawing her ever, closer to me, a marriage, a union, a spiritual movement, a touch of affection, a caress of the senses, the contact of pure souls, leaving a reverberating echo, on worlds of hearts, the palace of stars

(CAPTURE LOVE)

Once love has been found, capture it, remember the feeling, savor its emotion, lose yourself in the moment, you are alive and vibrant, a brilliant star in the universes celestial palace, a rising sun on the horizon of heavens, the soul that matches your own is priceless, a prized possession, a rare treasure to covet, make sure no one can take it, protect it, for nothing can replace it, this intimate connection is born of your essence, the completing wholeness of spirit, the other half of your union

(LOVES PYRAMID PLATEAU)

To reach the celestial plateau within loves pyramid takes time, its many levels illuminating in special alignment, materializing the heavens within the dimensions of a crystal element, the soul seeking maximum attainment must first build its base foundation, elevating piece by piece, striving towards the realizable goal of your dreams, only by knowing yourself, stabilizing a core will of faith, belief and acceptance, can you shape the important things that are missing, bringing immortal beauty in harmony and solace, the new birth of a light spirit, traversing the starry heights with the freedom of no limits

(EDGE)

Knowing where you want to be, you look how far you have to go, such a long way down, hesitant, the stagnant fright from the depths defensive edge, a fall, a slip, a slight shift in position leaves things unbearably tense, instead of wasting focused energy on inhibiting dread, take a good look at where you been, with ignorant fear in proper perspective you can boldly face your sought out objective, coming to terms with what has to be done, you can now look back, truly appreciating how far you have come

(FIND LOVE)

To find love it all starts within, to accept yourself and give up burden, to free your heart of barrier limits, uncovering the portal to loves quantum dimension, a celestial realm, the universes soul center, painting brilliant spectrums of beautiful auroras, illuminating crystal in stars of the ever eternal, bringing life to light, shining on the love I find

(LOVES FORMES)

Your love will be seen as uniquely as perceived, how deep, what forms will the needs of your passion breathe, everything will come to life, the light spirit illuminating heavens of your desire, but you must believe, undoubted, wholeheartedly embracing self acceptance, channeling this pure feeling in precious focus, your secret dreams will miraculously come true, because you formed it inside of you

(ALONE)

You are not alone, as I sit here you are all with me, your hearts I will gladly carry, for it is in you I find relief, one love is all, and all is one love, for when time has ended this is what will live on, what has been built will preserve and hold, my love together we are not alone

(LOVES ESCAPE)

This world I create is for loves escape, to release all inhibition past beauty's gate, its depths and its planes, its secrets attained, a vastness unending, her desires aflame, what's more is forbidden, deeply attracting her gaze, the more she is free to revel in her ways, weather danger, taboo, or desires destiny, it is hers to decide in her brand new life

(TIME TRAVEL)

All inside the time is bright, to travel wherever thy hearts desire, highly complex, for there is so many pieces, a mirror of

*power, a crystal light luminous, different levels to go, but one
vital connection, different portals and doors, to your beautiful
essence, to hidden places of secrets, into depths unknown, to
unattainable heights, threw passages in time*

SIN BYRON

Awaking, I found myself lying on a bigger and cozier bed in an even more extravagant chamber. No longer wearing a robe of fine silk, what surprisingly adorned me was black armor made of a light material that contorted to the flexible movement of my body. On my waist sat a dragon fashioned hilt made of black scales, drawing it, I was reminded by its girth and death dealing blade that I had just mercilessly killed the emotions happiness and kindness with it.

Bursting into the room interrupting my thoughts unexpectedly were two demon dogs.

"Master come quick! They both shouted in unison before bowing then turning to leave in a hurried haste.

Walking out the adjoined door to the room, I had to cover my eyes from the beaming sunlight, where was I? Covering to adjust my vision I squinted my bothered eyes as radiance gleamed through the branches of massive trees, how did I get in a forest? This was impossible I seemed to be outside, then temptations last words came to me, this had to be the next level she spoke of.

Wondering what the problem could be I walked out into a clearing.

The demon dog soldiers had set up camp next to a burnt down house and the commotion was coming from under a canopy.

Spotting me, the crowding dogs scrambled lining up in there ranking order.

In the middle of the parted crowd lay five dead bodies, among the five, two were mutilated and one beyond recognition.

"How did this happen?" I asked out of sheer curiosity.

Falling before me in response was a demon dog clenching his wounded shoulder.

"My great ruler I am the general cruelty, upon finding where the fugitive emotions were hiding we were blindsided by the one who call himself 2Q, one who bares a uncanny resemblance to you."

Caught off guard by this revelation I was shocked. As the general kept on speaking I could hear nothing but my own thoughts.

My other half was here in this world but how could that be? Did I have something to do with it? What was his purpose? Could he be searching for me? Did he know about the crystal pieces? Had he found them? I had to find him and stop him.

I no longer had regrets, I was free to let loose how I wanted to, I enjoyed no burden of another side who cared about frivolous things I despised, I am the one everyone followed now, I would never go back to the way things were, I never felt more alive, 2Q must die.

"Where did they go?" I questioned the general eagerly.

"After we were attacked 2Q and the emotion fled into the mountains, we gave chase but it was to late, they both had escaped."

"Where are they headed?" I asked keenly.

"My lord more emotions have been captured," interrupted a demon dog soldier running to the front of the line bowing.

To figure out where 2Q was headed I needed answers to my questions, so I decided to interrogate these incessant emotions.

Drawing my dark sword I followed the demon dog soldier leading the way.

On the ground were three men and one woman on their knees.

"You petty emotions are really becoming a problem for me, but I have great news for you, if you answer my simple questions I promise you can leave, now stand!" I demanded.

Once they did I asked my first question,

"What are your names"?

Getting no answers I grew impatient standing in front of a tough looking young man to start with him.

Instead of complying with me he just stared back defiantly as if challenging my authority. In a burst of anger I cocked my fist back slamming hard knuckles into his stuck-up face, blood pouring from his nose as he landed on his back roughly.

"Now I am going to ask again and this time I wont be so nice about it!" I stated in agitation.

In startling fright the rattled older looking woman was the first to answer me.

"Please don't hurt him he is just a boy, his name is loyalty, my name is care, and these two are humbleness and forgiveness," said care stammering with trembling anxiety.

"Hmm how interesting, now care, instead of asking the rest of them I am going to leave the questioning and there lives in your capable hands, For every answer that is credible you save one of there lives, but if you know and do not say, or so much as lie to me each one will die, there blood will be on your hands do you understand?

Shivering, care nodded in frightened acceptance.

"Well let us begin."

(DON'T CARE)

Ask me why I don't care, and I will tell you simply you were not there, you don't exist to me, I'm surrounded by my enemies, I caused people to suffer, thought only of myself and no one other, ran to sleep only to find, the demons were close behind, nightmarish prison, my sanity is but a weed in desolate ground, how long must you test my patience you repetitious thorn in my side, you nor your patronizing sympathy is warranted here, because the truth of the matter is, for my sake, it is best that I don't care

(UNPREDICTABLE)

Why would I be anything else but unpredictable? I would rather you assume then know my moves, for what's done in the dark cant hurt you, this is where I have to stay, worlds away, to myself eternal night is your everyday, looks can be the most deceiving thing, it gives false impressions, leading you away to your infinitely open mind, yet sadly closed, predictably bias, because you judge what you see first without understanding the essentials, so I must be a mystery, I will not challenge your conclusion, but allow whatever it is you conclude, why would I change your mind? I prefer you mislead yourself, these are the way things must be, why would I be anything else to you, but unpredictable?

(BELIEVE/WISH FOR)

Be careful what you wish for in the dark, for it may come true, becoming more then you can handle, the saying is true, you can do anything you put your mind to, directing your energies to what you wish, your actions will start to work towards it, what can be achieved, must be believed, what words you speak, can manifest just as easily, like a seed, what you believe will grow, but be careful what you wish for

(HUMBLENESS)

I have seen the fruits of the humble and their shining lights of humility, their hearts assuming a formless identity, appearing insignificant yet strong in its differences, not holding on to meaningless instances, free of malicious intent or other disruptive emotions, their uncanny ability to read people are keen because they are not burdened by common things, the humble spirit is light and free, and as smooth as a summers breeze

(ENVIRONMENTS)

You must not allow the environment to dictate who you are, becoming the misplaced product of a system flawed, the innocent die from the influences abroad, whatever dreams and hopes crushed and lost, the innocence and goodwill snatched and gone, seeing the world as you know it, cold and frozen, resorting to what you see, influenced by what others believe, slowly becoming a product of the environment, the only way to beat this negative conformity is to separate yourself completely, becoming the odds, to a percentage based on a belief that people from certain environments wont last long, you must be strong, you must know who you are, change wont happen overnight, change can only happen one perception at a time

CHAPTER 8

2Q

Emerging from the other side of the passage, my surroundings changed into a vibrant valley full with the lush abundance of life; the suns brilliant rays piercing threw the cloudy sky drifting aloof in a gentle breeze.

Waiting for me patiently was the women with the biggest smile I had ever seen.

Running she jumped into my arms embracing me intimately, I could feel myself getting hot and the rising thump of my beating pulse flustering in fervent yearning.

Now that I could focus and see all of her pronounced beauty I fell in love instantly.

"Your wounded," she said with concern.

Not noticing it before there was a deep cut on my waist where my sash was torn.

"Let me," she said covering my wound.

In brilliant inspiring beauty both of her nurturing hands started glowing a bright blue hue,

At first it stung, then it cooled and soothed,

When she removed her hands I was healed.

Shocked at her special gift I stared at her dumfounded,

"Who are you," I asked in awe and admiration.

"My name is love and I am a emotion, seeking refuge I hid amongst others like me, but my whereabouts were discovered, I would be dead now if it wasn't for you, my hero," praised love embracing me with affection.

Facing each other, I stared into her beautiful and unique pink eyes, there was something about her that seemed familiar, something that awakened this need to be her protector, her friend, her everything. I needed answers, but I couldn't ask the questions if I kept staring at her nakedness. Looking down to steady my rapidly beating heart, I began my questions from where I wanted to start.

"When I was fighting that monster cruelty why didn't you run? And when you did taking the flame of hope with you, what purpose did you need of it? Do you know of its significance?"

"I did not run because you bear the face of the ruler who would wish to cover the sun with darkness, yet in you I saw the light, now I know who you are, we must travel to the center of the heart with hope to restore its vitality and revive the emotions."

"Who am I to you? Where are you from? This ruler you speak of is his name Sin Byron," I asked enlivened, wanting to bombard her with more questions.

"You are the balance to the equation no one could solve, these emotions are yours, I belong to your heart, you are the source of these multi dimensions, its creator, in another existence we have been with you from the beginning, but your dark half has an alliance with demons and would have us killed to further instill more evil, until nothing is left in either dimension but a cold desolate wasteland."

"I still don't understand, how is it you belong to me yet you are here? What caused this unbalance? What world are we in?" I asked, unable to fathom her perplexing words.

"There have been stories told of a crystal mirror that lived in the soul, its power keeping everything in harmony and peace, until one day its power shifted shattering the crystal mirror into many pieces, causing the unbalance, aligning different dimensions, it is said that if the mirror were ever put together again everything would be restored as it once was, bringing solace between the balance. But the story of the mirror is just a myth; no one truly knows what happened. Ever since I could remember this is how its been, other emotions guarding me always keeping me hidden, the elder emotions said I had a gift and one day it would be needed, they always spoke of the healing powers off hope and how it could reverse the damage done to our home, but as far as anyone knew that to was a myth, but I believed, so wanting to save it I left despite the warnings of emotional danger, later on realizing my home had been overrun by demons, all the emotions inside either slaughtered or being hunted down. I am there queen, it is me these monsters truly want, but now that we have hope I can save my home."

My head was spinning trying to process all of the information, not only was I in a different dimension, but this beautifully stunning and stark naked women was my love and a queen of emotions that supposedly belonged to me, in a world I supposedly created, or came from, or whatever, how could any of this make sense? I pondered.

Everything began happening once the connection between me and Sin Byron was broken…with a jolt I stood up excitedly,

"Of course! We have to go where everything started, to get the answers we need we have to go to the soul."

(UNIQUE)

Your style, your grace, your kiss, your taste, there is no one that can take your place, you are phenomenal, special, unique, beautiful, a breathtaking sight no one could compare to, you are perfect, worth it, desirable, deserving, all the traces of your hearts beneath the surface, the bonds of your love that can never be broken, your pedestal illuminates with my three roses

(DESTINY)

Has destiny brought us together? I wonder if it was your souls yearning desire bringing us closer, perhaps coincidence, no I am convinced, the past of a long lost connection, the

universal law of attraction, when I first admired your breath taking beauty I instantly knew I was made for you, magnetic, magical, yes destiny it is, that spiritual insigne, claiming your love from stars yet born, the celestial appointment of a glorified dawn

(LOVES MAGIC)

Spellbound, enamored, I am rendered speechless by loves bewitching presence, her healing properties treat blemishes, changes doleful moods and soothes insecure wounds, I am astounded by what love can do, the internal feeling she invokes, the focused attention despite faults, with loves magic, past, present and future loose meaning, the deliriously delightful effects inflaming the very lease bit of resistance, charming the one of hardness to a state of emotional innocence, following loves lead seems as if you are being carried, distracted, changing by loves seductive means, but not truly knowing where that leads

(LOVES HORIZON)

I can see you all, each of your yearning hearts on the horizon of a new dawn, with wide eyes I shudder at this awesome sight, its beauty bleeds passion fire into the sky, the color blended, a mixture of living consciousness, multitudes speaking of the wonders of my soul, the awe of its treasures echoing praises threw-out the gusty wind, natures elements greeting me warmly with well wishes, yet I am in awe at the sight of this, overwhelmed by this indescribable feeling of bliss, no matter how many heavens I have climbed I am still amazed by this gift, that has been made eternal in the starry sky, forever immortalized, forever glorified

(MY LOVE)

My beautiful love I have finally found you, bringing to life the burning desire of my frustrating dreams, the innermost depths of my deprived needs have become incarnate in my unbelievable reality, are you a figment of my wanton imagination? An illusion of my peculiar vulnerability, all doubts allay just by the way you look at me, the way you touch me, I am comforted by my loves assurance, yet unsettled by this world of mystery, but with you I have found its elusive meaning, the portal and the key, to the haunting connection of each crystal piece

(SUN RAYS)

My love is the sun, my soul the rays that envelope her beautiful countenance, shining together adorned in our eternal union, dancing above in a dreamlike world of starry heavens, what we share is intimate, timeless, poetic, symbolic, romantic, when love rises all beating hearts draw towards the radiant warmth of her presence, and there she happily sets to forever center my universe, in the pure light of her celestial palace

(MIRACLE LOVE)

When I needed you most you quickly came, when I stumbled near the edge of hell, you pulled me away from the consuming flames, when evil darkness sought my soul, you sheltered me in the light of your celestial home, when I cried in the dark broken and left for dead, you heard my lament, bringing me comforting gifts of the spirit, when fear and inhibition brought doubt and weakness, you freed my heart of barrier limits, when my whole world was cold and torn, you dawned the healing sun of your radiant warmth

(LOVES ATMOSPHERE)

Transcending in a brilliant spectrum, your hearts awaken in the atmosphere of loves everlasting moment, weightless, suspended, free of burdens limits, with no judgment you play in un-inhibited abandon, reveling in the pleasures of your passion, your dreams painting the reality of your choosing, you are the center of a marvelous universe, the inheritor of sparkling treasures in a palace of wonders, all within, made to adorn your essence in a diamond tiara of happiness, a long overdue gift for your vibrant spirit, set on the celestial pedestal of a crystal element

(MODEL LOVE)

I am loves model, her living image, the painter, the portrait, the canvas, the crystal structure of her universal influence, the yearning hearts volatile example, the inherently enticing carnal pedestal, the symbolic portal to a dimension of dreams, the brilliant runway to a design of beauty

(THIN GRAY LINE)

Since the first time I laid eyes on you my heart skipped a beat, I wanted your love I kept it discreet, my secret desire making me weak, a dangerous fire this gray line between, I think of things I dare not repeat, forbidden pleasures you wouldn't believe, romantic escapes, sweet kisses in dreams, holding you close fulfilling your needs, the sweetest bliss my star in the sky, a euphoric love that mirrors my mind, if you dig deep then you will find, there is no such thing as a thin gray line

(ACID)

My heart burns like acid in the presence of your beauty, not knowing why this feeling takes over me, I try to be subtle as smooth as can be, there is something about you that causes unease, I can feel my skin burning when your staring at me, I turn away wondering if your looking threw me seeing my heart rapidly beat, my reserve slowly melting from the furnace like heat, telling myself I should get up and leave, far away from this strange effect your having on me, in my mind I can see me walking away, but I never do, I'm stuck in place, the acid burning my resistance away

(TELL ME)

Tell me my love your hopes and dreams, what it is you see when you look at me, tell me your lustful fantasies, together you and me can reach them, tell me all your secrets, I promise to keep them, tell me you want me and cant live without me, and I will forever be apart of your life, tell me what demons haunt you at night, and I will shine a light releasing there stressful hold on your mind, tell me what makes you smile and laugh, so I can make you happy when your angry or sad, tell me what you love and hate, so I can be what you love and appreciate all the things that make you this way, tell me the truth, no matter how ugly we will make it through, tell me what I have to do, to hold on to your love, to hold on to you

(YOU DESERVE)

My love you deserve better, you deserve not to be cheated on, you deserve a man who is strong, you deserve someone to lean on, you deserve appreciation, you deserve affection, you deserve attention, you deserve compliments, you deserve acknowledgement, you deserve gifts, you deserve a tender kiss, you deserve adventure, you deserve romance, you deserve your heart to be open, you deserve sex, you deserve love, you deserve to feel like the only women, you deserve the land, you deserve the sea, cant you see, that you deserve me

(BREATHE)

Its hard to breathe when you are around me, my chest tightens, my head spins, it feels like I'm drowning, when you smile, when you laugh, I could hardly think, spellbound, my heart melts, the way your voice sings, hypnotized, paralyzed, when you walk my way, caught in the moment cant find the words to say, I love and hate this toxic effect you have on me, because every time you come around, you make it hard to breathe

(STABILITY)

My love you need stability, someone who could give you love constantly, someone who knows how to treat you, treating you as a treat to, licking and touching you like supposed to, someone who knows how to hold you making you comfortable, every night coming home to you, someone who gives you attention, communicates and listens, someone you could spend your life with, someone who never stops surprising, someone who would love you no matter what, someone who would rather die without your love

(STORY'S)

Beware of story's told for the source is unknown, the question then becomes, is this all, some, or none of the facts in which the

tale was spun? Who did you hear this from? What credibility
supports this conclusion? For story's can be exaggerated, far from
the real situation that brought about its reiteration, stretched for
effect, diluting the truth, for idle talks expense, story's are used

SIN BYRON

"Now pay close attention because I will not repeat my words again, where is love going?"

"I…I don't"

"Before you say you don't know think hard," I said grilling care with a threatening glance.

"She…she maybe going back to the heart" said care compelled to speak under menacing duress.

"Care what are you doing don't tell him anything!" shouted a defiant loyalty back on his feet.

With a bloodthirsty snarl a swarm of demon dog soldiers moved to put him in his place, but I raised my hand stopping anything from happening to the disruptive youth.

Ignoring his disrespect I continued.

"Why would she go there?" I asked so far pleased with the information I was prying.

"Just know that I am doing this out of care," said care looking at loyalty with tears in her eyes, in response an angry loyalty gnashing his teeth in glaring disapproval.

"She wants to restore the hearts vitality bringing back its restoration, she wishes to revive all the emotions that were slaughtered by demons," said care with a weary and defeated look.

"Good care now we are getting somewhere." I said with a grin, my caressing fingers sliding down the side of her shivering neck.

"No don't give him any more information you can't trust him!" interjected the rebellious emotion loyalty.

Once again the snarling pack of demon dogs moved to silence his disruptive disrespect and yet again I held up my hand stopping punishment for his boisterous insolence.

"Rest assured you worthless twerp next time there is another outburst you will learn to speak when it's your turn," I said with waning patience and a murderous glare.

Turning my attention back on care I continued my interrogation.

"How would she accomplish this?"

"The only way to revive the heart is to bring hope to its center, but there is no way of telling if hope actually exist, this is just a legend an unproven myth," stated a nervous care.

"Thank you for your cooperation," I said satisfied.

Hearing everything I needed to hear I now had a feeling were they were going, I still needed to do one other thing before going on a campaign, before that it was time to take out the trash.

"Execute all of them," I said coldly turning my back walking away.

"You liar!" loyalty shouted lunging at me angrily, instantly a blood raving dog snatched loyalty by the throat, sinking, twisting and wrenching its razor sharp teeth into his soft fragile neck, blood spraying the air as loyalty was wrung and torn apart savagely.

By the time I had moved on to the next phase of my forming plan, all four dead emotions beaten and gnarled bodies were hanging from a tree.

2Q

"Then this is where we will go," said love determined to heal her home.

"If you don't mind me asking, how long has it been since you heard this myth about the crystal mirror?" I inquired curiously.

"About a thousand years give or take a century," answered love plainly.

Taken back by her answer, confusion and anxiety battered my struggling comprehension with a slight queasy feeling of nausea.

"I can see you're bothered," said love studying my stunned expression.

"Is it that obvious," I said in awe and disbelief.

"Time is not apparent here, one of your years is multiple in this dimensions omnipresent atmosphere," said love matter-of-factly.

"Then how could it possibly be that my other half is the cause for all of this damage? Could one dimension affect another? Could we unknowingly have started a ripple effect from our world to this one? Did we cause this?

"I know its a lot, but I believe everything will be restored as it once was, we have the flame of hope and you its source, that means the legend is true, and the balance can be stabilized closing out the demons forever," said love excitedly.

"Well there is only one way to find out, we must use your knowledgeable expertise of this dimension to navigate through this unpredictable world of uncertainty," I stated feeling optimistic.

"I know how to get to where we must go, but we have to be careful, moving cautiously, for there are powerful entity's in high places who would stop at nothing until they capture me," Stated love grimly.

"Do not worry, if we watch each others back we will make it, I will never let anything happen to you, after all you are my love and that makes you special," I said gazing into her pink eyes.

Drawing closer, together me and love became lost in the moment, kissing with burning passion, spellbound from this magnetic connection, held captive by my affection. The feeling of having no need to search anymore, of finally arriving after have waited for so long, as if opening my eyes for the first time realizing how I could have been so blind.

Love was the mysterious silhouette that haunted my dreams I was sure of it, I needed her, I needed love, if only my other half could see the relevance of this miraculous beauty then maybe we could co-exist in harmony. But as for right now he was the enemy, and if he tried to harm my love I would rain death upon him and every last demon he supported.

While my thoughts raced, loves kiss put them at ease. Locked in each others embrace we fell onto the soft grass, our hands exploring wildly while our tongues magically danced, ending up on top, I looked down on loves innocent face having second thoughts, not wanting to take advantage of her vulnerability.

"Don't leave make love to me," said love sensing my hesitance holding on to me tighter.

"Are you sure?" I asked looking into her pleading eyes.

"I never wanted something more, I want to feel you inside of me, together we are one heartbeat," said an eager love.

Freeing my fully erect manhood I entered her sex gently, slowly easing my way in until love got used to its feeling. Releasing a satisfying sigh love wiggled beneath me taking my fullness in, moaning in ecstasy, moving her hips in sync with my slow thrusts until we both let go in a shuddering release, laying cuddled in each other arms happily.

(YOUR EYES)

Your eyes speak volumes a language of its own, a heavenly melody that captures your soul, an enchanting hypnotic musical spell, its beauty is silent, its heartbeat is still, there is no star brighter in the heavens above, full with such passion, its depths full of love, it sees through me so I cannot hide, this attractive adoration you see in my eyes, my heartbeat pounding, my pulse amplified, your hidden desires I see come to life, a lunar eclipse, a morning sunrise, a beauty worth a thousand words all in your eyes

(MY HEART)

Take my heart as it is with all its cuts and bruises, in your
loving embrace it becomes perfect again, in your eyes it comes
to life beating with purpose, its coldness thaws leaving its cage
where it was imprisoned for so long, it flourishes when you kiss
my lips, healing the pain that took advantage and burned it,
my heart opens in acceptance when its only known rejection,
in your presence it is free, to love you endlessly

(LITTLE THINGS)

My love it is the little things that make you shine, it is what's
on the inside that brings being to life, like the stars in the
heaven that give humanity her light, I am blessed a thousand
times to be in your life, your presence brings great happiness
that cannot be measured, your smile a gift that cannot be
priced, your touch a warmth in the coldness of night, your
kiss leaves an imprint on the corridors of my dreams, my love
you are beautiful because of the little things

(CRYSTAL REFLECTION)

Through my reflection see your beauty, look close my love
and know that truly, you are a goddess Devine in nature,
a special creature, a special creation, unique, significant,
Aphrodite descendants, bearers of life, fluorescent independent,
sexy, audacious, emotional beings, strong lovers I wonder
through change of seasons, creative feats amongst the elite, my
reflection is yours, so what do you see

(IN THE HEAT OF LOVE)

In your sensuous embrace we lose ourselves in the heat of love, we careen madly into each others hypnotic touch, enthralled as if by magic's magnetic pull, drawn into a whirlpool of longing lust, hungrily snatched kisses, my whole being racked with ravenous physical need brings erratic thoughts, my body mindless in nature and in its pursuit of pleasure gives into the erotic and provocative tastes, the intimate haunting connection which renders my heart aflame, in the heat of love

(DANCE)

Tangled in each other arms we dance to a sound only we can hear, all we see is our love nothing else is there, in a trance our body's rhythmically dance, twirling then falling into intertwined hands, like tonight could be our very last dance, as if any minute the world could end, holding together tight like where never going to feel each others warmth again, our pining eyes we look deeply in, looking for the love that keeps our hearts beating, we urgently kiss the faster we spin, in our own world were dancing in

(ADONIS)

I am Adonis and you are my Aphrodite, I demand you to hold back nothing, spill your repressed desires all over me, under the waterfall of a potent love persuade me by your seductive magic, lead me to rest on your heavenly bed, what will you do with me my Aphrodite? How will you make me touch your body? Alas, I admit my guilt of being naïve, my heart may be open for you to control me, what is it do you have in mind? Is it dirty or clean? How will you use me? When you look into my eyes will you defile that hint of youthful innocence, or will you bathe me in your tender kisses? How will you show the appreciation for the object of your affection? Will you build a shrine with your intoxicating scent and feminine wilds of sex? Or will you chant dark spells of binding love, calling upon lust and desire with the heat of my boiling blood? At once I demand you hold back nothing, for you are my divine goddess, and I your Adonis

(DON JUAN/CASSANOVA)

I am the reincarnation of Casanovas love infused with Don Juan's seductive tongue, in union these two have become one, they have recognized the strengths in there differences and use me to channel them, all women must be receptive for it is your beautiful love and burning passion in which they were born, so will you not let them in your inviting home, will you not willingly become a slave to what you dream and you crave, my love what beautiful image shall I paint? Where shall we make lust? Where shall we kiss and touch? I can take you anywhere, I can be what you want, I can live in your mind and rest in your heart, if this is not obvious it soon shall be, that you will be mine, that you will be free

(USE ME)

Use me intimately, use me as a need, use me for an outlet for what is hidden deep, use me for your pleasure, use me as the key, use me as the mirror for the reflection of your beauty, use me as your love, use me as a sign, use me as the constellations that shine through the night, use me for your heart, use me for your soul, use me for eternity, use me how you want

(OUT THERE)

On this plane of time are souls whose hearts are bound to their one true love, once together traveling the celestial ether their energy would flow as a peaceful river, fate would have it to separate their serenity in an ocean of madness, what was once simple and beautiful became complicated by a world of distractions, troubles and burdens pushing them further apart causing them to forget who they are, creating a wedge between the illusion of reality and their true essence, but the one thing that will forever remain is their intimate connection, your true love is out there, no matter who you are there is someone connected to your traveling soul mate from the stars, you may get lost along the way, but if you search without ceasing, you will find that piece of your eternity that went missing

(INTENSE LOVE)

Touch me, feel me, take me, become raptured in loves intensity, the thunderous drum of my rapid heartbeat playing in sync to loves melody, the pain and pleasure of embracing bodies, rendered innocent, lost in feeling, giving in to natural impulses, spiritually connected, naked and intimate, the deepened breath, the sensitive sex, the focused attention, the release of tension, giving what's special, to the one worth giving, your love soaked in each others spilling essence, a raw passion, burning and intense

(ENTER THE MOMENT)

Once our eyes lock it has begun, the ever present moment knocking the door of anticipation, hanging over our heads loosely, expectantly looming, in essence a guns cock and loaded chambers ready bullet, next the carnal abandonment, the sensuous touch turning the wheels of passion, the scintillating key to an imploding emotion, now nothing in a world of distraction has any meaning, isolated, distant, disengaged time has obediently frozen, our combined energy igniting, convulsing in eager suspension, the shroud of sweet tension begging to be vented, leading up to an inevitable climax, yet still building in frantic momentum, in a frenzy of pure pleasure our magnetic lips crash together, finally succumbing to rabid release, the trembling sex exploding dangerously

(INTIMATE JOURNEY)

Intertwined, connected, me and my incarnate love together on the crossroads of multi dimensions, she is the bewitching silhouette of my frustrating dreams, the burning passion of my hearts desolate need, all that I am and ever will be, born in the heart of light and starry beauty, further within to mysteries unknown, levels through out the mind and the soul

(HEAVEN ON EARTH)

Our heaven on earth is now, let us ascend majestically drawn to the clouds, let our bright light invade the thickest of shrouds, may we toast from the highest mountain then bathe in a crystal fountain, may all your dreams come to life dancing before our eyes under the cosmic starlight, to live in a pleasures paradise with no more pain or troubles of life, angels will ease your mind to rest, my eternal love is what you deserve, everything is yours in this heaven on earth

(ROMANCE)

Take my hand let me lead you away, to a secret place between
time and space, a timeless world our hearts in seclusion, all
I see is you nothing else is moving, a passionate kiss brings
me to nirvana, our heavens on earth there is no tomorrow,
your touch opens doors, exclusive allures, romantic connection
bring me to your shores, we escape from those intrusive hellos,
to isolate our love, to render it slow, so take my hand let me
lead you away, hand in hand to a secret place

(FANTASY IN THE FLESH)

He is the man in your dreams whispering words of love till
you succumb, you have read about him in books since you were
young, sweep you off of your feet in the dark of the night,
whispering secret and loves hypnotic delight, dancing under
the stars, kissing in the moonlight, the passion of fire your
radiant eyes, he could read your mind and know your heart,
to live only for you and worship every part of your body, the
sex is patient, fantasy, fantasize well to your cravings, and
desires deep dark aching's, he serenades your provocative lust
with Don Juan and Casanova language, he is the man of
your dreams, fantasy in the flesh

(NO ONE)

No ones got to know what we do, lets keep it a secret just me
and you, secret locations, rendezvous, unlock hidden depths
in a world we choose, an adventure our own lets run away, to
rule the night and seize the day, our love is worth the price
we pay, lets spread our wings and fly away, never listen to

the hurtful things they say, you only live once lets live today, with no destination we choose our fate, they don't know us they cant relate

(ANNIVERSARY)

On this anniversary, our special anniversary, the day we first met, the very first time you let me in, when I looked into your eyes I knew right then, that we would share this very moment, do you remember how it all started? Your first kiss, the way your heart pounded, can you remember the feeling? How it was in the beginning, when hugs felt like you were melting in them, when the first time you made love your orgasm shook your body senseless, the very feeling your addicted to, so on the anniversary, our special anniversary, I dedicate it to pleasing you

(CUDDLE)

There are times I see you need to be held, when life has you down I will pick your head up and hold you, my love we are in this together no matter what stormy weather, here as we cuddle I assure things will get better, kissing you softly I lean over and whisper words of affection that cause you to shiver, holding you close I can feel your heart beat, this feeling of love washing over me, this feeling to protect you from whatever might hurt you, here I discovered something special, experiencing this different part of you I never knew, holding on to you as we cuddle

(BEAUTY)

I admire your mind, body and soul, possess me oh beauty temptation so bold, to the ends of the earth wherever I go, destiny aligns a timeless abode, forever be mine an intimate loop, magnetic attraction pulls me to you, eternally bound the chains of the truth, the stars of heaven tied in a noose, the essence of love how could you see, all the things that's dear to me, take my heart do as you please, beauty oh beauty come to me

(BITTER SWEET)

My love everything about me is bitter sweet, I would tell you to leave, to run far away from me, yet you are drawn to me, there is no escape from this fate, our destiny's have crossed tangling in its place, the beginning is here, but the end is lost, you prepare to give your all hoping to receive the same equally, yet you only have one piece of me, a devastating reality, one which the ending cannot be foreseen, the games, the heartache, the disbelief, I wish this weren't so, I wish this wouldn't be, your emotion for me is bitter sweet

CHAPTER 9

SIN BYRON

"You miss me already" stated temptation with a smirk.

"Don't flatter yourself I only summoned you for answers" I said in annoyance.

"Yes, but once I answer you must give me something," said temptation eagerly.

"Whatever, anything you wish if you give me the right information," I replied, though not meaning a bit of it.

"What is your question?" said temptation licking her lips with a sultry gaze.

"Before I got to the mind I had in my possession a burning light called the flame of hope, where is it?"

"I'm sorry to inform you that this flame was destroyed before you were brought in from the shadow dimension," said temptation shrugging her shoulders laxly.

Growing angry at her indifference I seethed in contempt as I asked my next question.

"When I first came threw the shadows gate it closed locking me out from the soul, is there another way to get there?"

"In this realm there is a way anywhere, do you wish to go back home and here I thought we were having fun," said temptation with a jeering sarcasm.

"Bitch! Do you think this is a wayward game, my lively hood is at stake, so help me if I am to lose it then you will be truly sorry," I retorted angrily.

"Temper, temper Sin Byron anything can be arranged threw the proper channeling, we demons are linked threw a network, there is nothing we cant do and no place we cant be, there is just a way to go about things."

"Is that right, well then I demand you demons to bring me what I have been searching for."

Not answering me she stood bewildered my statement, her feigned expression of ignorance making me want to snap her slender neck in half.

"Don't play coy with me, your coquettish games wont work you know exactly what I speak of, where are my missing crystal pieces!" I shouted

"Oh why didn't you say so, they are speculated to be in different locations, but we ourselves could not find them so-"

"So you want to use me as a puppet on a dangling string, is that it!" I snapped.

"Don't look at it that way, I know you would be more then willing to help for a fair exchange," Replied temptation.

"Oh yea like what, what could you demons possibly have to offer besides what has been taken from me already."

"More then you can imagine, anything you wish can be yours, but those crystal pieces wont reveal itself to anyone but you and your other half 2Q, one I know to be on this side of the veil as we speak."

"So what you been spying on me," I said unimpressed.

"I have been watching, I know of your troubles, your desire to be free of his burdensome existence, there are those in high places who have the power to assist you in getting rid of your problem," said temptation.

"So what, you want me to find the crystal pieces and bring them to you, is that it."

"Precisely,"

"Why should I do that I could get rid of 2Q myself, were exactly in this so called exchange is it beneficial for me because so far all I hear is a vague promise of whatever I wish, what does that entail and for whom?" I inquired, ready to get down to the real reason behind this pop up proposal.

"If you retrieve all of the crystal pieces and capture the emotion love you will rise to meet the demon king, it is well within his power to give you whatever thy hearts desire, do this and he will."

Liking what I was hearing I silently brooded upon the unlimited possibilities.

Not only would that weakling 2Q be eradicated, but also I would be king of my own domain, the only authority I would have to answer to would be me, I thought to myself.

"Why is this emotion so sought after? I inquired wanting to know every little detail as much as possible.

"This emotion holds the power that keeps the other emotions defiant in there rebellion. The emotion love is their queen and the ultimate threat to your rule, if she is captured the emotions have no more will to oppose us, of course you must bring her to my king alive, anymore questions."

"Not at this moment, but there is a little problem, besides the missing crystal pieces I'm sure to find, the remaining pieces are another thing, I know they are in my soul, but where inside I don't know."

"How is that possible?" asked temptation with a puzzled expression.

"I am not sure, strange as this may sound my recollection does not recall, could be because of those foul creatures who destroyed my flame of hope and tried to kill me. Speaking of which, if you ever come across those disgusting maggots anger and arrogance again tell them I will find them and render there mashed heads unrecognizable by my dark blade, and this time I would be sure to display there putrid bodies on my mantle. Anyway knowing my tenacious other half he will also search until he finds the crystal pieces, this is the only reason I could gather that he would be on this side of his physical reality, once he does, I will be there to take them and end his life. I accept, now if you will kindly tell me the information I need I will happily be on my way," I concluded.

"Not so fast Sin Byron, part of me answering your questions involved you giving me something."

"You got to be kidding me, I already accepted the proposal for the exchange of services, what more could you possibly want?" I asked incredulously.

"I told you what the king wanted, not what I wanted, you will ravish me Sin Byron, you will fuck me with no mercy, this is what you will give me," said temptation snapping her fingers causing the room to change in an instant, with dim lighting, lit candles and light smoke filling the air from sweet smelling incense.

Along the walls were chains and whips; I was now standing in some sort of sex dungeon, a place for transgressed pleasures.

"I will be your submissive harlot and you Sin Byron will dominate me, but first I must give you the incentive," said temptation getting on her knees in front of me.

I could not believe her audacity, the way she forced herself onto me made my heart beat uncontrollably, she knew how to entice, to get under the deepest layer of my skin filling my thoughts with nothing but sin.

Suddenly a black cloud materialized engulfing the air, when it dissipated my eyes bulged in surprise as I recognized a naked lust and desire.

"You will not touch them, they will only touch you," said temptation loosening my sash freeing my cock.

"We knew you had potential," said lust.

"Since the first time we touched you," said desire simultaneously.

Both of there leering eyes hungrily roaming every part of me, before sashaying over joining temptation on their knees.

At a loss for words chills shot through my body as all three began to fondle, suck and lick me mindlessly.

Gasping and shaking wanting to cry out from there unforgiving pleasure I tried to move, but quickly found out I was unable to, something invisible was holding me in place, I was there toy, the slavish object of there whims.

The sensation like a wave crashing continuously, my toes curling, my legs buckling and weak, my eyes rolling back tearful and glossy, I was being turned out by the insatiable demons of corruption.

The hold on me let go when I climaxed, their open mouths trying eagerly to catch my every squirting drop coating all three with my seed. Falling to the floor flushed, my body spas-med from the shock of the lingering sensation.

"Get up you are not done, how can you rule anything if you cannot handle me" said temptation mockingly.

"Just like men with no stamina or energy" said lust.

"Maybe we are to much for his virility," said desire.

Bursting with anger I lunged at the tormenting instigator of my expense.

Grabbing temptation by her throat I squeezed with all the energy I could muster, who the fuck did she think I was some pansy punk she could easily make a fool of? No not this time, this time she would die for playing games with me.

"Die you no good whoring filth, die!" I shouted with boiling wrath.

But despite my efforts she once again started to moan in pleasure, enjoying my attempt to cause her pain.

"Yes…yes, squeeze me harder, lust, desire, do with him what we discussed!" shouted the insatiable sadist temptation in ecstasy.

Walking over to me at the same time lust and desire whispered into my ears, at once I lowered my hands standing entranced.

In a dream like blur I could see temptations arms get tied to a bed post, the bed must of materialized out of thin air because I could not remember it being there before, but I could not think, nor would I have cared to.

With a devilish grin temptation invitingly spread her legs, with an animal like urgency I eagerly mounted her.

With unlimited stamina I plunged in and out of her moist sex pumping vigorously without rest, multiple orgasms unforgivingly shaking her thrashing body one after the next.

When her voice grew hoarse from loud screams of pleasure and my hard thrusts had punished her trembling sex enough, I fell asleep immediately, later on waking, but not remember anything that happened.

(NETWORK)

A resourceful link, working cooperatively for the betterment of each, to network makes tasks more easy, each piece to the chain works differently, supporting the other mutually, its interest invested in the others ability to come through expectantly, showed and proved capable to know its link is stable, knowing each others worth, in a resourceful network

(4 PLAY)

Before I dive in I must have you open, I want you to beg for my entrance, to need me in you, to greedily take everything I give you, to get angry when I purposely make you wait, to give it to me each and everyway, to soak the bed before I penetrate your sex, to know the power of my touch, to tell me every place you want, to shake and stutter my name, to warm you up before we play

(WHIP CREAM)

Lick my whip cream off of your succulent lips, close your eyes and savor it, our evidence of passionate sex, something you will never forget, to replay as you wish in your greedy mind, a more explosive climax, intense satisfaction each time, a haunting experience when I'm not there, the lingering sensation, the feeling of me near, you in vision me a ghost, though physically your alone, the heat of my flesh penetrating the core depths of your soul, everywhere you go all you see is me, tasting the resonating flavor of my addictive whip cream

(DEABAUCH TIDE)

Tossed back and forth by the tide of her sex, what was once
repressed awakened in this sultry sadist, no longer inhibited,
bringing utter delight in sensual corruption, what has touched
Sin Byron is forbidden, dangerously transgressed, creating an
insatiable thirst that can never be quenched, a need for sinful
pleasure from the darkness within, what virtue abandoned for
brazen passion, the taboo of desire in slavish actions

(MY SWEET PUNISHMENT)

Relentlessly plunging in and out of your sex, in tune with
your body's every movement, I take my frustration out on
you; look at all the dirty things you make me do, now its time
I make you pay, the highs and lows of pleasure and pain, you
shake and stutter backing away, I will not stop until you
break, deeper and deeper my hips will thrust, cruelly pulling
you back every-time you run, I do with you anything I want,
succumb to my sweet punishment

(INSATIABLE DEMONS OF SEX)

Locked up by the chains of there touch, bewitched by their
whispers of lust, enthrall by the whip of their voice, a slave
to the whims of my inner void, likened unto the use of a
sexual toy, nothing but a strung out puppet, a plaything to
insatiable demons, in which my spirit has been completely
saturated, I Sin Byron have become apart of the dungeon, its
brazen influence, a willing participant in temptations sadist
like sickness, a captive of desires pleasurable sin, the sensuous
sensations, I have become them

(HARD)

I fuck you hard a complete switch, from a soft love to chains and whips, if this is what you want I will be happy to give, submit to me and I will grant your every fetish wish, on your hand and knees crawl to me, I will show you how to please, your salty tears falling free, gasping as you breathe, open your eyes to pleasures high, loose your mind a liberating ride, be free from society's decency, with no restraint, give in don't think, throw away your virtue to hunt and pursue, I can give you your filthy wants, your nasty dirty lust, a fast beating heart, a satisfying release, when I fuck you hard, I give you what you need

(BANANA CREAM)

Open your legs, use your hands, use your mouth, your tongue to trace my banana up and down, you want my cream so you got to work for it, tight and wet gets the cream going, use rotation, throw it back, making faces, hurt me bad, give it to me like it was your last, talk nasty, play with me, kiss and suck my banana clean, that is how you get its cream

(HANDCUFFS)

The freak in me is let loose when I am alone with you, handcuff you to the bed, oh I love it how you beg, hard breathing, soft moans, when I'm playing with your sex, you are at my mercy, so do as I say and don't behave, make noise, call me the worse, bite me, scratch me, make me squirm, why fight what we both want, screw making love, lets just fuck, animals in wild heat, ride me, slap me, choke me, fulfill our needs, release this freak in me

(BAD)

I don't want your heart, right now I crave your body, you want it bad, I make you beg, long pump and short strokes inside your sex, fuck you hard or tease you slow, you run away ill pull you close, I'm bad to touch, I'm bad to hold, because I make you lose control, I make you cum, I make you moan, I bring the worst behind closed doors, inside the gates desires wake, lust incarnated in different ways, now as I lay you down to sleep, dream of all the bad yet to be free, it feels so good it cant be bad, I know you love it when I'm Sin Byron

(WORKOUT/STAMINA)

Having hot sex, dripping pouring sweat, is a satisfying workout like doing sets and reps, lifting up your beautiful body like weights off of my chiseled chest, my shoulders and cut arms when I'm holding up your legs, I know you love looking at this work of art, my stamina super human when I'm going long and hard, my energy it lasts, penetrating with constant thrust works out my strong back, giving it all I got works out my ripped abs, as you throw it back giving it your best, to hold you in place works out my legs, cardio, calisthenics and weights when we make love, a satisfying workout taking stamina

(ACTIVE/LAZY)

To keep your body active is to retain its vitality, its health, blood pressure and heartbeat, to keep it in shape, being able to withstand strain builds up muscle strength, well conditioned its stamina retains, a lasting foundation that must be maintained, becoming lazy can only take away, degrading what's been set in place, what's been built slowly fades, losing firmness, losing shape, day by day more goes away, don't be lazy live actively

(DARK SEX WISHES)

Take me to your secret place and engulf my cock with your dripping sex, I wish not think of anything else but you, I wish to be lost in the moment and delivered unto drunkenness by the taste of your skin, fuck me until my words babble and make no sense, do with me what your sex wishes, I wish to be void of any emotion and likened unto the habitual use of a sex object, we will not speak of this, nor will we care what it is we are doing, we will relish the feeling in a relentless passion, a twist of seduction poised between your succulent lips, conjuring the beast within your willing slave, freeing the lust and desire that cannot be contained, oh how I wish to water my black rose in your yearning garden, watching it bear the fruits of an awaken temptation, causing the release of all doubt, fear and inhibition, this my love is my dark sex wishes

2Q

Together love and I traveled the crossroads, to what I now understood was the conjoined paths of the unbalanced multi dimensions within myself, a confusing concept I still had a problem fully grasping.

Knowing the unpredictable dangers that could come from my lack of knowledge I stayed alert, ever vigilant for the slightest sign of trouble.

My blade of light resting at my side ready to respond to whatever didn't seem right.

In an instant day turned to night and thick snowflakes fell from the sky, a few inches already collected on the ground under our trudging feet making a crunching sound.

All around there was nothing but white, looking up I could see the celestial stars and the heavenly bodies of the universe shining brightly. Across the night sky a beautiful aurora of streaming color painting its awe-inspiring wonder in a bluish purple spectacle.

Following love a few steps ahead of me I couldn't help but admire her beauty, the way her flowing hair brushed over the fullness of her plump rear while her long soft legs kept stride had me mesmerized, just one look at love would have any man hopelessly distracted.

"We are almost there just a little bit further," said love snapping me out of my daydream, pointing to what looked like a small cottage in the distance.

"Are you sure, that place seems pretty average to me," I said squinting my eyes to get a better look, how could my soul be in a place that small and dingy I thought to myself.

Suddenly in a blur of lightning speed something rushed by me snatching love by the hair dragging her violently, her screams echoing through out the calm night as her body was being forcefully pulled threw the snow leaving a crooked line, in a blink of an eye she disappeared from sight.

With no time to waste I immediately gave chase, judging by the speed of this thing by now she could have been miles away, but I could not let that stop me, I would rescue my love or die trying. Following her tracks I ran as fast as I could, becoming light on my feet the faster and faster the wind whipped by me.

Catching up quickly, while in motion my swinging blade severed the base of the creature's right arm.

Stopping abruptly it screamed in agony as love tumbled free from its clutches, the creature's loud cries of pain echoing through out the sterile silence.

Raising my blade in defense I tried to figure out what I was looking at, the creature resembled a cross between a guerilla and some sort of dog breed.

In sporadic haste the creature ran away surprisingly agile with one of its limbs gone.

"Are you alright?" I asked rushing to loves side.

"I'm...I'm ok" she said shuddering, " but we have to move quickly, that was a demon and where there is one there is more."

Helping her up we raced over to the cottage getting inside without another problem.

Baffled, I looked around what I thought was a small run down cottage but instead gigantic on the inside with emerald doors lining multiple floors.

"On the outside the structure is small but how could this fit all of this?" I said looking around in amazement, the glow from the emerald doors enhancing the places eye-catching beauty.

"Yes it is impressive isn't it" interjected a short man in a white suit.

"What can we do for you?" said another man taller in height wearing a black tuxedo.

Something about these two didn't sit well with me.

The short stubby one with a bald head and dark colored skin looked like he could be in his mid forties, while the lanky tall one with the tan and the greasy slick back hair-do could pass for a younger youth in his early twenties, they both looked human, but my instincts told me they were insidious demons playing dress up.

Shielding love behind me, I would be the first one to speak.

"I am looking for a place called the soul, could you point me to where I must go?" I asked, probing them in distrust.

"Were my manners, I am pride and here by my side is my associate selfishness, and you are?" asked the short man with a pleasantness I found disarming and shady.

"My name is 2Q and I am in a hurry so if you don't mind-"

"Well I do!" Spat pride, "Don't you dare come to my portal house being rude, making demands when I am gracious and hospitable, I know who you are, you have made yourself quite famous in these parts."

"You harbor the fugitive emotion love, do you know the fetching price for such a find," said selfishness rubbing his hands together with a crooked smile.

Willing my blade of light, I frowned balling up my fist ready to defend my love if necessary.

Walking out from behind my cover love spoke.

"We mean no disrespect pride, we come respectfully and in peace, not wishing to be a burden we appreciate your hospitality," said love courteously.

"How well spoken, the stories of your beauty have no merit compared to standing in front of you in person, I am honored to be in your presence," said pride bowing.

"Here we have our own methods, we do not follow anyone's rule, if you wish we can protect you," offered selfishness with that twisted smile I found distrusting.

"Thank you, but I must decline, not wishing to inconvenience his host, if its ok I would wish to go about our way," said love.

"Nonsense, I insist you stay for at least one human night, if you accommodate my wishes I promise to give you the gold key, for behind each portal door is a passageway to another place or infinity," said pride.

"You must have the right key or you could become trapped in a void of nothing," added selfishness.

"Can you give us a second to discuss this?" asked love turning towards me.

"What do you think?" love asked me whispering,

"I think it's a trick, but I don't see no choice in the matter of it, so stay on guard and do not separate from me for any reason," I replied.

Nodding her head in agreement she turned back towards them.

"We accept"

"Splendid"

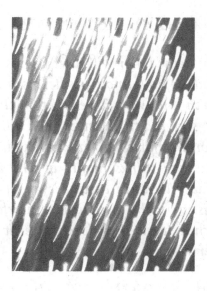

(SETTLE)

Why settle for something less when you can have so much more, the choice is yours, the ball is in your court, a fool others will try and take you for if they think they can get away with more, they will swindle, lie and cheat to get ahead, using you as a stepping stone settling for less, leave nothing to chance, never settle for second best, when opportunity knocks be the first to answer it

(DISTANCE)

Distance become a haunting vision of my presence, for I live in your love I am the essence, everything I am in you is a field of roses in full bloom, I am your guilty pleasure, a secret longing, a heated message, an eternal devotion to capture your affections, these living words have an intimate connection, like the sun and the moon, when one sets, the other rises this passion inside of you

(THE DEMON PRIDE)

Pride will not be denied, nor will it let things slide, though it is known for pride to have another side, a sense of self respect, knowing its worth and what it deserves, in this it burns out and over exerts, striving to be better then all, coming second to none, its actions resemble arrogance, though staying within its means, its ability thinks highly of who it is and what it could be, pride believes in getting even, if it reaches into its conscious disturbed by an outside interference, and its security is breached, it will then do whatever it takes, to regain its sense of superiority

(THE DEMON SELFISHNESS)

Caring for nothing but itself selfishness offers no help, it would soon watch you perish rotting in filth, paying you no attention, turning its back, not lifting a finger to help unless receiving something back for itself, if there is nothing in it for selfishness why offer any assistance, if in turn its not worth it, when there is something to gain watch selfishness go out of its way, yet do not expect a thing, it will keep all for itself and give you nothing, at the end of the day, its only interest and focus is on what you have to give, it is what it is, when it comes to the demon selfishness

(ETERNAL STARS OF PALACE EDEN)

The transcendent souls are the eternal stars that enter loves portal with open hearts, a transmitting spirit ascended in a brilliant spectrum, through the precious bond of a crystal element, teaming essences full of life, the garden of Eden, her enveloping paradise, where roses bloom in immortal beauty, in the palace of the universe, in spiritual harmony, to forever shine, there solace light, upon the loves, who join the sky's, if you believe, you soon shall be, amongst the very stars of your sparkling dreams

(LOVES GUARDIAN THE ETERNAL CRYSTAL ELEMENT)

Through loves special alignment with a crystal element, I reflect a radiant spectrum of light to the heavens, I 2Q am loves guardian, my mission, to lead her towards the portal of transcendence, to escort love to the pedestal of her palace, to bestow upon her the sparkling treasure of her eternal inheritance, to restore solace beauty to the universe within, as loves protector in selfless service, I risk it all in the sacrifice of a passionate advocate, for loves interest I defend, my sole reason to live, to bring great victory, as a soldier on the hearts battlefield of precious glory

(LOVES SPARKLING SPIRITS)

My love soon you will center the wonders of my celestial universe, soon you will become apart of the new life that is the palace treasure, a heightened spirit, a new body in the starry form of a translucent perception, a transcendent being of special alignment, in a brilliant spectrum of rays you will instantly change, adorning the sparkling light of an impressive array, love will accompany your vibrant days, peace and contentment will forever herald your hearts undying flame, your unique beauty will never age, because now you believe, you are truly free

(SHOOTING STARS)

Out of endless stars, the one I visit vibrates in the throws of sensation, shooting across the universe in utter excitement, merrily fluttering about in enflamed propulsion, streaking recklessly, freely streaming sparkling beauty, painting the exalted heavens of loves royalty, the shining spirit alive and happy

(LOVES WAY)

Follow love and you will not be lead astray, but first make sure it is for your heart that you are risking everything, listen to the subtle melody for its consistent beat, for it to will guide your treading feat, through pain and tears the way may go, through twist and turns, harsh winds and storms, but stay the course, you must give your all, or watch lost love fade in the dark

(LOVES QUANTUM DIMENSION)

Leap into the endless universe, traverse the twinkling stars with beating hearts, what you see is only the beginning of your sole perception, weather near or far we are all connected, but what's different lies deep within, every alternate experience of love is intimate, every luminous soul in states of blossoming metamorphosis, all transcending in spiritual independence, threw the many views of a quantum dimension

(STAR LIGHT)

Each star, a soul, a heart, each shining spirit illuminating the core of its center, each a bonding magnet of wonder in relation to the other, each glorious paradigm a melody of loves grand design, the pure light of conglomerating diamonds, the sparkling treasure aglow in an aurora lit sky, a crystal palace formed in a spectrum of vision, a celestial paradise in an eternal element

(SOLAR FLARE)

My soul, my sun, flaring in reaction to love, an interstellar voyage across light years of distance, but inflaming its recipient in a matter of seconds, its out bursting energy flowing in continuum, rapturing one heart to the next from the surface of passion, penetrating deep into the core of inhibition, letting go of all doubt in solar eruption

(SUPERNOVA)

Star light, star bright, exploding wonder in the celestial sky, nothing in loves universe can ever die, more twinkling hearts are born of fire, immortalized in eternal heights, sparkling diamonds of the solace night, a supernova makes space for others, the souls of beauty in states of splendor

(LOVES TWILIGHT)

In loves twilight, the sense you are being suspended through torrents of tension, carried along troubled rapids towards the edge of routines existence, is to hard to ignore, a haze surrounding the vision of sensible clarity, is all but alluring, expecting the end to come you brace for the exciting conclusion, secretly longing for its chilling impact to bring breathtaking refreshment, revitalizing the part of yourself lost back then, made new when emerging from twilights deep end

(LOVES DAWN)

Rise my beautiful love, shine your revealing light from the heavens above, may your brilliant rays pierce every layer of shadowing insecurity, may the glorious dawn alleviate all doubt, transcending all hearts as its magnificence majestically ascends through the parting clouds, standing at the edge of the universe I have viewed the dawns stunning countenance, its peeking presence giving life to the vast horizon, in wonder I behold this dreamlike landscape, a world of spirit, my loves reality

(CONSTELLTION)

Paradigms of wonder high in the celestial universe, loves eternal mark on the galaxy of hearts, all brilliant pieces of unparalleled art, for there is not one lesser then the other, all are different in completeness together, some close, or far in the distance, but still one soul that dwells within them

(SNOW WHITE)

Like falling snow crystals reflecting from the blazing sun, pure love transcends, sparkling before my gleaming eyes in living substance, everything in her world made in essence, a spectrum of kaleidoscopic light shining through every angle of a crystal element, relaying the bewitching amazement of mysterious places, different ways to view love in appreciation, seeing what's transparent in things made solid, the gift of the beholder, 2Q and Sin Byron

(CELESTIAL SKY)

My celestial sky, the heavens Atlantis, a bewitching sea so vast, beautiful, enchanting, each twinkling star apart of my soul, apart of my world, my creation for her, every level to roam, yet not every level to reach, except the one who invokes, the white rose in me, its luminous glow, the heart of its center, the rose gives it life, to the sparkling lights

(BRIDGE)

From the highest heaven, from the tallest mountain, from the deepest depths, I build a bridge, from the heart to the mind, from the mind to the soul, until I am whole, I build a bridge, for every walk of life, through the wrong or right, through the darkness and light, I build a bridge, from me to you, from you to me, where ever I'll be, I'll build a bridge

(LOVES AURORA)

In the heavens of loves world, in many forms I admire her, with one of pure light, a beautiful aurora in the shaded sky, under the cover of night I behold its magic, streaming, wavering in hues of bewitchment, with billions of admiring stars as a witness, I cry out my devotion in hope she is listening, my love how you enslave my passion, its bleeding essence causing this igniting reaction, my mind, my soul, my heart is for her, to paint her wonderful world in a spectrum of color

(LOVES SPECTRUM)

With the entire world in view, my love is the sun that rises in a fluorescent spectrum, her comforting warmth felt by different races, her brilliant shine kissing there beautiful faces, the various wave lengths a rainbow of language, her omnipresent reach in every direction, her omniscient view a universal understanding, this pure light dwells wherever you are, her omnipotent love the greatest power of all

(LOVES UNIVERSE)

The vast sky, the quantum stars, the heavens and all that are within them praise love unending, the celestial bodies themselves fawn over this eternal goddess of the universe, restless energy prostrating, catering to her attentive needs, adorning her, presenting sparkling treasures laid at her feet, adoring admirers singing to her special desires with beautiful melody, everything revolves around loves attractive gravity, being pulled into orbit, centering with harmony

(LOVES LUNAR ECLIPSE)

In special alignment with loves universe, comes a celestial body of shadowing energy, temporarily blocking the luminary glow of clarity, the view of the heavens change slightly in the lunar face of obscurity, though love is ultimately the ruling authority, its world can eclipse, shifting its mannerism in ways beyond understanding, but never what it is in essence, once more the light will return to the present, but not without leaving unanswered questions

(IMPENETRABLE)

What I give to you will always stay, guard your heart so they could never take it away, hold it close and do not fret, it will not break, it cannot bend, it was made specifically with you in mind, it will not age in space or time, a diamond truly fit for you, a precious gem, a sacred jewel, something rare you cannot find, for our love is one of a kind, impenetrable

(DIAMOND)

Our love must be as a diamond forever strong and lasting, a beautiful love, one that causes all who gaze upon it to want to possess a love just like it, there are those who would wish to steal it, that look in our eyes, for those precious moments are valuable and they want to own it, the way we kiss with burning passion gets them jealous, because we carelessly flaunt our wealthy possessions, they envy and hate those faces we make, this diamond we have they wish they could break, if they had it there way it wouldn't be safe, they wont give up till they take it away

(LOVE STRUCTURE)

Give me the keys to your heart and I will build a kingdom of life that will never fall apart, in it I will set a place from which I will never depart, I will dwell alive and well, to bring gifts of affection, to be your lover and companion, holding your hand in a spiritual marriage, our ring a symbolic connection, but there is something that may threaten its reception, for our love cannot hide from the inevitable question, how well can we resist the pressure of an outside influence, for our structure will undoubtedly be tested, our love that seemingly cant be moved, will it stand in revelation to the truth, in the end will you accept or deny its proof, only then we will see, if we are strong enough to make it through

(REAL WEALTH)

What is it you find valuable? What is it you base your judgment of other people? What do you hold dear to you? Is it your garments, your money, your jewelry, your possessions, are you rich, then why is it people are never happy when they seemingly have everything? Why on the outside do they seem content, but on the inside broke and desolate? Could it be that the roles have switch, that somewhere along the line the irony of it all eluded definition, did it indeed drown in a shallow pit of disappointment and resentment, is the phrase indeed true, more money more problems, so what is the solution? For I have seen those with less be happy in spirit, where as it may seem they are the true wealthy, what is their secret? How is that despite whatever comes their way they remain in abundance, like there is nothing that can be taken from them? As if they can never be daunted, how can they make something out of nothing? The answer lies within your very own heart, soul and mind, the ability to see things from the outside, to appreciate what you have, more so the blessings that come in there own time, for not everything in quantity is good, but it is the quality inside that leads to a fruitful life

(CONSIDERATION)

Be considerate to your fellow man, you do not know what it is they are going through, there is a bigger picture, it is not always about you, you should treat people the way you would want to be treated, open your eyes and look past your pride, past your wall, past the front lines put up on the outside, not only thinking about yourself, you could be of help to someone else, not knowing in life where you might land, you might see this person again, and this person you treated right, could be the very person who saves your life, just something small to think about in moderation, to your fellow man have consideration

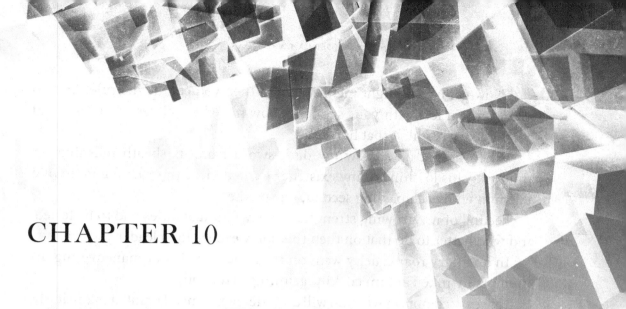

CHAPTER 10

SIN BYRON

Close in proximity I could see him but he couldn't see me.

Getting a glimpse of my other half's mysterious newfound ability's I had to admit I was impressed, but how he came to acquire such power was perplexing and unbelievable.

"How I abhor weakness," I said looking down on the shape-shifting dog soldier that lost its arm trying to abduct love but didn't get far.

Though its arm grew back it had failed me one time to many.

"I don't know why I gave you another chance when it is obvious you're worthless!" I barked venomously.

"Please master I-"

"Silence! You are hereby stripped of your rank and will be replaced, take him."

At my command two snarling dog soldiers grabbed cruelty restraining by both arms.

"What, unhand me, I served you loyally, these are my soldiers, this is betrayal! " barked the ex general cruelty tussling against restraint.

"So u still think you have what it takes to lead, your tough right, everyone should listen and bow to you right, well prove it to me pussy."

Upon my command both its arms were let go causing the demon cruelty to fall onto its knees in the snow.

"Now get up and fight me, if you win then you can be the ruler and do whatever you feel with your soldiers, show me why you deserve to live and not die like a bitch!" I spat harshly.

When he got up I drew my dark sword from its sheath relishing his animosity, his loathing of my existence excited me, I was turning more into a demon with each passing second, I loved the

Feeling of my growing strength, my newfound abilities had to be tested, and who better to do that on then this sorry excuse for a leader.

In an angry roar cruelty went on the attack, easily out maneuvering his attempts I winked at him cockily, grinning arrogantly.

"Nice try champ, maybe you will do better next time," I taunted shamelessly.

Enraged, cruelty went berserk, its rapid attacks becoming wild and uncontrolled, but to me his every sloppy move came slowly, leaving vulnerable openings I would exploit.

Quickly out-maneuvering his wasted attempts I kicked his legs out from underneath him, falling over, cruelty landed headlong into a pile of snow. Laughing in mock I turned my back on him, facing the rest of the attentive group.

"Is this who you want leading you, this loser shouldn't bare the title of general, this lame is the weak link in our organization, are you not strong, this pathetic worm is nothing but disposable!"

Roaring in reckless madness, cruelty jumped up attempting a sneak attack.

Spinning swiftly, I dodged his desperate attempt bringing my blade around with accuracy and power. With a death-dealing swipe cruelty's severed head fell from his twitching body.

"You are now the general," I said pointing to a demon dog soldier I felt had potential.

"Yes master, it would be an honor to serve you," said the demon dog soldier kneeling in reverence.

"Good, now we must-"

Suddenly my enhanced senses gave me a jolt, turning, I looked into the distance, and to my surprise I could see someone approaching.

(CAN'T RELY)

I cant rely on you, I can only rely on me, because if I let me down I can blame only me, if I asked you to do something for me, effort would only be half of what it could be, because the attention isn't focused on you, you cant really say what others will do you, you cant really see what others perceive, until certain moments bring clarity, so I do nothing for you, as you would for me, I handle my business when it come to my needs, stay two steps ahead you better believe, I cant rely on you, you cant rely on me

(MISTAKES AND EXCUSE)

There is limited space for a thing called a mistake, an excuse is just a cover up, for if what you pursued was to go through, then would it have been a mistake in the first place, this does not deny the fact that the deed was done, what it comes down to was the motive behind the action, and the events leading up to the accident, is a mistake a mistake when you purposely go out of your way, knowing the possible outcome and what it could bring, so now comes the excuse, minimizing responsibility when it falls back on you, knowledge is key when it comes to mistakes, only if you did not know in mistakes limited space, this is the exception, thus excuses are accepted, for there is a thin line between the two, true and false, mistakes and excuse

(LEADERS INFLUENCE)

Leaders understand the power of influence, for the follower will mimic you, how you move is imperative for it shows *who you are, within the character could betray flaws that the opposition will feed on, its uses will be to destroy you, to have your coalition turn on you, for power comes from the cooperation of the follower, with this gone you will fall, your influence lost, those that harbor resentment and ill will, will rise, the time will be ripe for an attempt on your life, to overthrow your seated power of position, no longer will the followers listen, leaders understand the power of influence*

(EXAMPLE)

Why would anyone listen to you if you don't lead by example, you become hypocritical when you say what you don't do, then you just become someone else with empty words, a bumbling fool who speaks to himself because no one hears you, in one ear and out of the other, you become as the insane, the one who does the same thing yet expects the end result to change, when you say something and follow threw, your words have more meaning and power becoming special, people more inclined will listen to you, showing them how to move, they will do as you do, only if you lead by example

2Q

Love and me were escorted to an extravagant room with a king sixed bed stocked with all the necessary amenities, we were told to make ourselves comfortable until the festivities were ready.

Taking a deep breath I plopped down on the comfortable bed exhausted, straddling me love put her head on my chest snuggling why she listened to my heartbeat.

"Don't you ever get tired?" I said playfully.

"I want to know when are you going to make love to me again?" asked love bashfully.

"When I get clean, because right now I'm dirty," I replied humorously.

Thankfully the room had a shower added to it, though I didn't know demons to take showers, but then again pride and selfishness were not your average monsters.

Getting up hoping I was right, I walked over to the adjoined bathroom with love close behind. Closing the door love started to kiss me and help take my clothes off, stepping backwards into the glass shower I turned it on while my yearning love fell into my embracing arms.

As the warm steam fogged up the glass what started off slow turned hard and fast, with her arms clasped around my back and her legs wrapped around my waist, in sync she moved to my every stroke, her soft whimpers turning into loud screams of passion as I penetrated her sex as deep as I could, after our satisfying release we cleaned each other enjoying the intimacy of our close connection.

Walking out of the steamy shower feeling refreshed, we were startled to see the demon selfishness standing by the door waiting.

"I take it you enjoyed the perks," said a perverted selfishness with a smug smirk.

At that moment, all I wanted to do was draw my light blade and cut off his overbearing face.

"How long have you been here?" I said clenching my jaw in irritation.

"Long enough to know you are late, here is a gift from pride for the lovely lady, a red dress expertly designed and cut to hug her…delicate curves" said selfishness.

His perverted eyes eagerly taking in loves nakedness, it took everything in my power to hold my composure and not snap, he was lucky I had more self control then my other half Sin Byron, or pride would of found his dead partners detached head in the nearest waste disposal.

"And for you master 2Q is a fitted suit custom made by the most exquisite material, all of which has not been made by, human hands" said selfishness with a superior attitude, "Down the hall to the left a banquet has been prepared for our honored guests,"

With that said he left the room.

Balling my fist up tightly I glared at his cocky stride; brought back to focus by love, I put my murderous thoughts aside, it was time to prepare for what I was sure would be an eventful night.

(EVERYDAY)

Everyday is a holiday when I'm with you, everyday is special, everyday is brand new, everyday when I hold you is like when I first met you, everyday I still learn more things about you, everyday I tell you I love you, everyday I sex and touch you, everyday you still surprise me, everyday you stand behind me, everyday you are my best friend, everyday you are someone I can confide in, everyday you are my rock, until everyday forever stops

(SECRETS)

No ones got to know our secret love, what we do, just me and you, alone together we disappear from view, and sex till your tired from me, and I from you, our magic we create is known only to us, we keep it from those who would only judge, our guilty pleasures are written on our face, its hard to mask this connection we made, yet there prying suspicions only lead them to a dead end, a secret of lovers disguised as friends

(WATER)

In this water we wash the scent of sex off our bodies, our pungent musk mingled together, evidence of our rigorous love, clean me with your kisses, then I will clean you with my tongue, more love will be released before we are done, to be washed away when the water runs, soothing and relaxing our desires all together, now satisfied, we can drift away, to a waterfall of cleansing waves, all I feel when you are next to me, in this intimate atmosphere, is your beautiful release when the waters near

(FIRE)

Near the fire our blood heats up, our eyes light up from the flames as we kiss and touch, your warm skin presses against mine creating friction, burning with passion, a lovers vision, melt into my arms where you should be, the very element of a fantasy, through the rising smoke your dreams become reality, your fire now alive flickers inside of me, catching wind, bursting your heart in romantic combustion, out heated sex, lighting a candle carrying our scent, a love that will never burn out, these flames will spread until we burn down

SIN BYRON

Who-ever this stranger was he was either very brave or incredibly idiotic.

Coming closer to my encampment, my demon dog soldiers blocked the strangers path doing there best to discourage his movement by intimidation, but despite there menacing snarls he contained a calm composure wishing only to speak to me.

I could also see this stranger was dressed nicely which struck me as strange, but I guess not more odd then talking dog soldiers.

Giving permission for the stranger to pass, the man dropped to his knees in front of me.

"Great ruler, I have news that may be valuable to you."

"Arise, tell me your name" I said cordial, noting the eagerness in his desperate demeanor.

"My name is selfishness," said the formal man standing, brushing snow off his prim attire.

"And what news do you bring selfishness?"

"Two strangers arrived at the portal house wanting access to the portal door of the soul, people you may be familiar with, 2Q and the emotion love."

Immediately interested, I could only guess why a slimy snake such as this would volunteer this pertinent information.

"So you come to me, the great Sin Byron with information I already know, tell me why I shouldn't just kill you now and leave your rotting corpse to my ravenous demon soldiers?" I questioned sharply, closely watching his movements.

"Because I can be of worth to your campaign, as someone on the inside I can get close to them without raising suspicion, if we can come to some sort of proposal we can both gain from this lucrative situation, said selfishness lively.

"I'm listening,"

As selfishness broke down his plan in full detail we both came to an agreement, if he brought me love I would grant him his wish, though I could actually care less about my promise to this treacherous demon, I would tell him what he wanted to hear to get what I needed, anything that would stoop to such a low level in the grand scheme of things could never be trusted.

This is just what I needed an unsuspecting turn of events, ready or not Sin Byron is coming.

(NEED/WANT)

A need you cant live without, a want you can do without, a want could seem like a need depending on how you perceive, but need by itself leaves no room, this is something you have to do, something your want become frivolous to, something you need to pursue, what your wants have grown accustomed to should be of little significance, your need is a necessity, coming first and more importantly

CHAPTER 11

2Q

It took some time for love to convince me not to bring my weapon, but eventually after our tedious discussion, her easygoing attitude versus my cynical distrust, I relented and left it hidden in a place I could easily reach if needed be.

Hand in hand love and me walked into a room of music and crowded people, all of them dressed in elegance, all seemingly human, but I knew the tricks of the enemy and what the consequences could be for assuming anything less, they were demons and therefor could not be trusted.

Waiting patiently for our arrival was pride with a disarming smile.

"Welcome friends, I hope you don't mind me inviting some close associates, their are some demons whose main concern isn't death and devastation, their are some who devote there eternity to the sheer feeling of uninhibited pleasure, come and I will show you that we are not your stereotypical demons," said pride reading our uneasiness.

Walking through the throng of well dressed demons my eyes jumped from face to face looking for a sign of ill will, but got nothing, no one even looked our way, they were to preoccupied reveling in their haughty conversations and indulging in the whine they drank from sparkling glass cups.

Coming to where the tables were set, an abundance of fresh food were placed on them, not remembering I had a stomach till now I was reminded when its famished confines growled pleadingly.

"But how," I said, my mouth salivating my teasing taste buds and my bulging eyes roaming row after row of freshly cooked meats, deserts and baked goods.

"What do you think, humans are the only ones who can eat and have the resources for said delicacies?" said pride matter-of-factly.

"You know not everyone is out to get you, there are some who wouldn't mind helping you, especially for someone so beautiful," said a charming selfishness walking up behind love lithely.

His flirtatious manner causing her to giggle in delight, inside I felt something stir that became worse when he started to dance with her, hand in hand gliding across the marble floor effortlessly, his overly eager hands groping her waist. Selfishness and his shady persona disgusted me, deep down I had a feeling he was trying to get under my skin, if I kept staring at loves happy expression and that conniving glint in his squinting eyes I would vomit, I could not stand watching them, and besides nothing bad was happening so instead of breaking them up and ruining loves innocent fun, I got loose, enjoying the lively entertainment, eating my feel and drinking to much.

(STEREOTYPE)

Every group has a stereotype, what they all do, what they all like, selective perceptions collectively bias, mostly wrong, the views are false, every person is different, everyone has their faults, this does not define who they are, treating someone different of a set definition, based on race or miscellaneous religion, are the same type of people who never see their own faults, a stereotype is misleading and wrong

(SLOWDOWN)

Slowing yourself down is a valuable skill, your thoughts become clearer, vividly seeing the bigger picture, you are less likely to miss something important, things that otherwise would go un-noticed, looking deeper attaining precious focus, a potential going beyond the normal comparison, in this fast pace environment things become easily lost, shady and unclear in a oblivious fog, for with the motion back and forth something is bound to loosen and fall, if things were to slow down it would have been noticed, people constantly in a rush are quick to make up assumptions, yet never really knowing, for clarity to be found, you need to slow down

(SUBSTANCE ABUSE)

Drugs used to escape, to get away from reality, the pain and disappointment going away, for a short time the sun shines blocking the rain, if even for a little while disappointment can smile, the pain alleviated by the haze of the clouds, but this is living in falseness, the allure to leave things behind only causes more problems, coming to need this habitual release becomes a ritual to cope with your body, nothing can be right unless the fog covers your mind, the jets of euphoria streaking thoughtless patterns of joy in the sky, enjoying the effects of a exhilarating high, so far gone, not seeing the dangerous signs, that you are slowly dying inside, losing yourself in a hellish routine, who you are becoming a fiendish need, your only concern, your only priority, not caring what it is you have to do, to get the feeling you crave from substance abuse

SIN BYRON

Storming the portal house I shouted out orders to my bloodthirsty party of demon dogs.

"Spread out! Kill everything that moves, you know who I want, I will deal with them myself."

"Wait! What is the meaning of this intrusion?" cried pride walking briskly, stopping to stand in front of me with loathing spilling from his penetrating eyes, his attitude written on his lackluster demeanor.

"You are sheltering fugitives who oppose my rule, I have come for them you would do best to move."

"I will do no such thing, I have no ruler, I am a demon who rules alone in my own right"

"Yes, selfishness warned me of your self imposed overbearing haughty like arrogance."

"What! He put you up to this," replied pride angrily.

"He is tired of your pompous ass ways, so in return for getting rid of you, he will do something for me, I command you step down, from now on selfishness will control this territory for himself, and if you don't comply with my wishes I will spew your bloody corpse out of my mouth, your soulless existence will be sent on a one way trip to hell," I threatened.

"I will always knew of his greed," said pride shaking his head in preconceived understanding, "That is why I hid certain things from him, for one if you somehow manage to kill me you will release the demon revenge who will not stop until he devours whoevers responsible for my disappearance, for it is I who feeds it. Second I have a team of demon assassins who serve as my security," said pride signaling them by high pitch whistle.

Falling from the ceiling were ten masked demons dressed in black wielding lethal blades, their red eyes glinting under their hooded apparel.

"And as you can see I am no slouch either" said pride materializing a lethal sword of his own into his right hand.

Angry at selfishness for not mentioning this resistance, I would see to it that he paid dearly,

But no worries, we still had the upper hand out numbering his ten assassins to my twenty-demon dog soldiers.

"You fool, you would really oppose me the great Sin Byron, now your severed head will dangle on my mantle while your gutted insides will be hollowed out by my dark blade then fed to my demon army, you will die for your conceited pride, attack!" I screamed.

Clashing together, it took two of my demon dog soldiers to fend off the demon assassin's swift movements and vicious attacks.

"Take three soldiers and make sure 2Q is erased permanently, seize the emotion love and see to it that misguided bird selfishness in no longer relevant," I ordered my new general violence.

Following orders, violence rushed off with three other demon soldiers to do my bidding.

Zeroing in on pride I joined the battle, with my focus on him I watched as he savagely thrust his blade impaling one of my dog soldiers in the neck, its gory blade coming out the other end.

With a cry I ran towards him, dodging an assassins blade, bringing my blade to the side slashing it across the face, concurrently stabbing another leaving guts hanging from my blade, swinging low lethally cutting off another's leg, in a murderous rage all I could see was red using my dark blade to bring pain and death.

Finally facing off with pride our blades crashed together, every blow matched, except I had more height and reach where as pride was short and stubby, though he was swift I used that to my advantage maiming prides left collarbone, crippling his left arm completely.

Falling to the ground, pride wailed in the throes of anguish, with victory assured I grinned at his pathetic state.

"Oh how the mighty have fallen," I stated with satisfaction, taunting his prominent weakness before bringing my blade down to administer its death-dealing blow.

But before it got there, in an evanescent shroud of black smoke pride suddenly disappeared.

(EXPECTATIONS)

Don't set your expectations to high, because at any given time there could be a minor set back or delay, things not going your way causing you to become upset, you must prepare for the worse and hope for the best, something formulated should have a contingency plan, a what, when, and if things don't happen, preparing yourself for all possibilities you skirt frustration, don't rely on set expectations

(UNDERESTIMATE)

You may find yourself at times able to predict a outcome, becoming lax to a situation, thinking things will go your way, seeing a counted victory before it begins, you underestimate what you are up against, leaving you mentally susceptible to this unseen weakness, unbeknownst that you yourself have become the wedge in your own defenses, whatever challenges comes your way becomes the opponent you have to face, to underestimate the slightest thing leaves a gap open, no matter how prepared you feel you may be, no matter how you plan, it all means nothing, if you ignorantly don't see that your opponent is capable of anything, never underestimate the power of change, in this solid kingdoms can be left in ruins, you will only be to blame, because you so foolishly underestimate

(THE DEMON VIOLENCE)

Eager to react violence snaps, with a desire to hurt all in its path, it fumes with malice and wrath seething inside, putting just reason behind, for settling peace to be rubbed out with afflicting conflict and seedy grime, to joyfully revel in the duress of the heart and mind, spreading discord with a show *of force, its compulsive love for torture expressed in full, to any and all whose hand it calls, sinister, destructive, rampantly running, infringing on who-so-ever it chooses, rejoicing in its findings, its victims reminded, no one is safe from the demon violence*

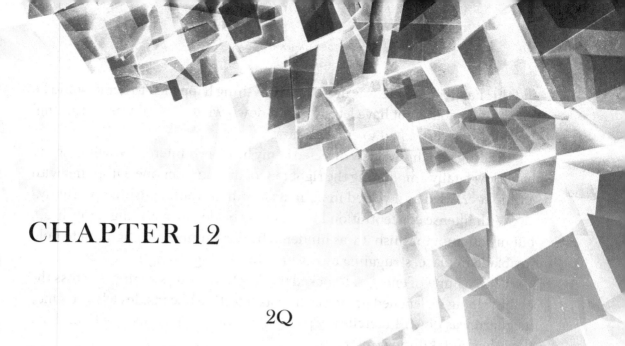

CHAPTER 12

2Q

In my dreams I could see love talking to me, she was a few feet away but I couldn't hear her words, she was frantically waving in a panicky expression, so I waved back, was she in some kind of trouble?" if only I could hear what she was trying tell me… and then I did.

"Wake up its Sin Byron!" cried love,

With her voice resonating in my head, in alert my eyes flew open.

With a loud bang the door to my room swung open, the lights in my room were off but judging by the bright light coming from the portal doors in the hallway I could instantly tell that the strange silhouettes at the door didn't belong, this was an ambush.

Instinctively rolling off the bed I had just missed the bad end of a blade by inches. In one hurried motion I rolled under the bed freeing the gold hilt from its hiding place.

Suddenly the bed was lifted and flung its frame smashing against the wall.

Willing my luminous blade of light I could clearly see that it was not a blade that originally struck the bed, but a razor sharp claw belonging to one of two demon dog soldiers.

Getting to my feet quickly I jumped back barely dodging a swinging claw headed for my chest.

My mind was all over the place as I battled these revolting demons, how did this happen? Where was my love? If anything happened to her it would be my fault, I should not have let my guard down what the hell was I thinking! I needed answers; I had to end this now.

Evading a swinging claw directed at my head, I countered by swinging my blade low fatally amputating the right foot of dog number one. Dropping with a thud it crawled as it yelped in pain, its terminal wound gushing profusely.

With intense concentration I brought my blade down aiming for its head, but my attempt to finish it was hindered by dog number two fighting to hold my blade in place, struggling against my increasing strength.

With a burst of energy I knocked its claw to the side slashing it across the belly, yelping it clenched its stomach as its intestine like insides fell out. Once its guard was down I mercilessly plunged my blade threw its mouth and out the other end, killing it instantly.

Turning my focus back on dog number one, with a loud cry my blade landed splitting its head open, putting an end to its cursed existence.

Rushing out of the room blindly, a razor sharp claw was unsuspectingly swung at my neck, I was seconds away from death had it not been for pride deflecting it.

Quickly recovering from the shock of the moment I turned and plunged my blade into the demon dogs massive chest, with a forced grunt it fell over dead.

"What's going on? How did this happen? Where is love?" I asked pride excitedly, my adrenaline pumping as my eyes darted from side to the side taking in my surroundings in a matter of seconds, it was then I noticed pride was wounded.

"There is no time to explain, here take these two keys, thirty doors to your left is where selfishness is hiding love, ten doors to your right is what I promised, the portal door to the soul, I will hold off the enemy as long as I can, now go!" cried pride shoving me away from him.

Counting emerald portal doors as I ran I could hear the clashing of blades, the battle taking place couldn't be to far behind me, or possibly further ahead, I couldn't tell, any sound here seemed to echo producing a feeling of an empty space yet every floor seemed to go on forever. Luckily this was the first level, for there were seven just like this, every place and everything seemed to be a twisted paradox, a never ending loop, but there was no doubt in my mind that behind all this madness my dark half Sin Byron lay responsible.

Stopping at the designated door, I realized pride had forgotten to mention which key went were, picking one, I was pleased to see my first choice fit the lock perfectly. Upon turning it I stiffened in anxiety, the solid gold key instantly liquefying in my grasp, dreading the worst case scenario of my wrong decision I prepared myself to face the worse, whatever came from this I would face with no fear, relieving my premature problem, the lock clicked three times opening the shimmering emerald door.

As its contents slowly revealed itself to me I readied my blade, the first thing that came to view was selfishness mutilated body sprawled on the floor, his mangled face rendered unrecognizable by bite marks, and there my love stood stunned, I could tell by the look on her still face she had seen something horrific.

Moving rapidly the demon dog put its right claw to loves neck.

"Drop your weapon on the floor and kick it over" it said with a snarl.

Not wanting love to get hurt I reluctantly did as it said, boiling with disdain at not being able to do anything.

"Good boy, I was just telling love here how I was going to defile her purity, now you can watch me, the more the merrier."

"You bastard I'll kill you," I snapped with my fist tightly clenched moving forward.

"Don't you take another step further?" the demon dog said moving his sickle like claw closer to loves neck.

Shape-shifting its other claw into a human hand a sick smile formed on its despicable features, as it reached under loves red dress violating her sex. Love did not move or flinch, as if her body was a shell and her ghost elsewhere, I couldn't just stand there and watch my love be taken advantage of, I had to do something.

In my mind I visualized my blade moving by itself animated by some supernatural force. Taking a deep breath I closed my eyes willing my blade with everything I had, all my pain hurt and anger feeding into the stoking fires of my fierce and relentless drive, I could feel the power surging in and out again, grasping hold of its pulsating energy I opened my eyes.

"Now you will watch me stick my demon cock in her tight ass," the cocky dog said with a maniacal laugh.

With a loud cry I released the power I held inside. In a flash of blinding light my blade moved itself off of the ground and lodged itself into its exposed back, in agony the dog soldier yelped dropping its claws, spinning round and round trying in vain to get the blade out, rushing over to love I started shaking her.

"Wake up, I have the key we have to leave!"

Snapping out of her daze love embraced me tightly, "Wait here for a second and don't turn around," I said staring intensely into her pink eyes.

In a noncommittal fashion love stared back blankly, nodding her head leaving her back towards me.

"Guess you didn't think this all the way through you fool, I would kill you slow but fortunately for you I have more important things to do," I said coldly.

Holding out my right hand I willed my blade forward, dropping to its knees, the dog soldier's vacant eyes went agape in disbelief as my blade sunk deeper and deeper into its back ripping a gaping hole in its chest finding its way back into my hands.

Satisfied that this creep was now out of the picture, I grabbed love making a break for the door, running back down the hall towards the portal door to the soul.

Stopping us in our tracks were four demon dog soldiers blocking our path, shielding love I Raised my light blade preparing for an attack, suddenly four more dogs came up from the rear locking us in, we were surrounded.

Trying my best to face all of them I held my blade up in defense preparing for the last stand, readying myself for the inevitable move, but it didn't come, they just stood there as if waiting for something.

I could see why when all four dogs in front of me moved to the side revealing pride on his knees, his face bruised and beaten, my demented other half Sin Byron standing behind him with a disturbing smile.

"Hello 2Q fancy meeting you, anything you would like to say before I send pride on his way."

"Please don't do this, whatever the problem is it can be handled different, there is no need for killing."

"Well I guess that's it then," said Sin Byron pulling prides head back, grinning grimly while he sawed repeatedly, cutting deeply into his neck with a dark blade, black blood spewing a gruesome mess onto his gory hands leaking a large puddle on the floor, he did not stop until prides head fell off.

Blocking loves vision, I did not need this traumatizing event getting to her,

"Why?" Was all I could say after witnessing something that brutal.

"Because that bland uptight bitch pride asked for it, now being that you're my other half, well human half anyway I might give you a pass depending on how well you follow orders, first you will hand love over to me, then you will give me the flame of hope and the gold key to the portal door of the soul, I promise you will be free to go safely returned to your home, in the morning you will wake up in your world seeing all of this as just a bad dream."

"Sorry those terms just don't work for me, I will give you the flame of hope and the gold key to the portal door, but love leaves with me."

"You always were a little soft pussy ass weakling, you will never get anywhere being kind, those types are blind to there surroundings, easily rapped, robed, beaten and spit upon, it is the aggressive and the negative that gets the attention of cowards, demanding the respect and absolute dominion that it deserves, now look at you captain save an emotion, so stupid, I will always be better then you, I will always be in the lead while you and your meekness bow at my feet, the true ruler of this dimension."

I could tell my other half had changed, he looked deranged, unsettled, consumed by the evil shadows, Sin Byron was a demon.

"This is between me and you, there is no need for a third party," I said trying my best to reason.

"Enough of this bullshit! You will give me everything I ask or your life will be forfeit," said Sin Byron angrily.

"I'm prepared to die for mine," I said steadfast standing my ground.

"So be it!" barked Sin Byron with hostility.

Snarling all eight-dog soldiers started advancing elongating their retractable claws.

Suddenly without warning the ground began to shake, a resounding boom knocking everyone off balance.

Appearing unexpectedly was a hulking Monster.

(LOVE IS WAR)

Love is pain, a map to greater pleasures gained, I conquer your heart, you conquer mine, we fight, we love through enemy lines, push and pull someone must bend, to teach them how to love again, distance ache my soul awakes, to draw you to desires gate, sweet tension, recapture the essence of yesterdays promise, remind me love how far we've fallen, we come together to pick up the pieces, pain is love our only weakness

(LOVE LIFE)

Life means nothing without your love, I went without it for to long, I would rather die before I go back, I will not last another heart attack, I need you by my side, tell me everything is going to be alright, you make me weak to the touch, addicted I cant get enough, you occupy my wildest dreams, without you what would life be, I will love you through your flaws and weakness, can you love me through my pain and demons, I appreciate the love you give, you are my will to live life

(IN TIME)

In time hold me close and don't let go, for anytime could be my time to go, so cherish our love, never take it for granted, tomorrow is not promised, the unexpected can suddenly happen, one minute I may be here, the next over there, so live every minute with no fear, because in an instant all could disappear, so give me your all and don't hold back, if we are meant to be only time will see, why worry over possibilities of a future not yet reached, can you not see the beauty in this, anytime could be our last kiss, the last time we make love, lets take advantage while we still have breath in our lungs, while we are still alive in time

(I WILL)

I will fight for love, I will die before giving up, but if I am to die, my love will rise as a burning phoenix from the ashes of a new genesis, I will never let go of you again as long as my bones have marrow in them, as long as my life has meaning, I will create beautiful poetry of art and symbolism that would make Apollo himself envy my devotion, I will build a bridge from my soul to yours, strengthening it with precious diamond so it will not fall apart, I will become Eros the Greek god of love and ascend your heart to my eternal one, I will be everything you ask for and more, I will become the very thing you live for

(VOICE)

Be strong my love, for to long you have been repressed, silenced by discouraging noise, burdened, overlooked, taken advantage of, if you will not stand now, then when? How much more *will you suffer if you remain mute and do nothing? Stepped on over and over again, likened unto the dead not the living, find your voice, no longer will you stand for emotional abuse anymore, take heart, scream defiantly at the barrier limits, storm the stronghold of inhibition, shake the foundation of stagnation, become what you were destined to be, a sparkling star in the palace of your dreams*

SIN BYRON

Having 2Q right were I wanted him he would finally meet his death by my hand.

I could taste the sweet satisfaction of victory at the thought of seeing his life leave his eyes as I wrenched his love from his grasp, but that didn't happen, nothing could ever prepare me for what I was facing, could this be the monster revenge the late pride spoke of, I could now see he wasn't bluffing.

Getting up off of the floor, I gnashed my teeth sourly as I watched my other half use this unpredictable disturbance to escape with the emotion love into the portal door, there was nothing I could do to stop them, right now I had bigger problems.

The demon revenge was a four legged beast with the face of a sphinx, a height of at least thirty feet, a massive body, broad mandible and teeth and claws as long as my arms, this colossal monstrosity could easily devour me and all eight of my remaining dog soldiers at the same time, and there still would be room for more.

With its each titanic step the ground trembled as revenge started barreling towards us.

Leaping into the air it landed grabbing two demon dogs brutally tearing them apart, there bodies left mangled and bloody by the ferocious demon creature.

Upon seeing this savage display of unleashed carnage the rest of my detail scattered about in panic, but met there bloody ends being picked apart, torn limb from limb.

Not making any sudden moves, I watched this mindless killing machine slaughter my minions in a heinous fashion, yet remained void of any feeling of it, I knew for certain this devil wanted only me, I could tell by the way it stared, flaring its nostrils and baring its jagged teeth, its pitch black eyes cold and unfeeling wanting the person responsible for its masters untimely demise, if there was no way to kill this thing I would need a way to escape, it was time I communicate threw the telepathic demon link.

"Temptation can you hear me"

"Only when you speak," said temptation, her direct voice channeling into my head clearly.

"Listen I have a situation that could use my immediate evacuation."

"Oh you mean a transmission."

With a high pitch roar the demon revenge started barreling towards me.

"Yes at your earliest convenience!"

As it leaped into the air I briskly slid underneath it, sparks flying from my dragging blade across its impenetrable bottom, I had barely scratched it, all I managed to do was make it angrier, its magnified roar ear-splitting and immense.

"Hmm what will you do for me"?

"Anything, now make it happen!" I barked turning around running.

The ground shook aggressively as the demon revenge charged after me.

"Wherever you are its making your energy hard to read, you need to get in another position," instructed temptation.

So in other words I had to get outside, but the front entrance was in the opposite direction and revenge was close behind, there was no choice I had to turn back.

To my surprise what I thought was supposed to be an endless hall just a few feet ahead was now a dead end.

"You got to be kidding me," I said to myself between clenched teeth and hastened breath.

The once vibrant portal house seemed shut down, the emerald portal doors no longer glowing, the color of the portal house dull and worn, all of it no doubt in response to the release of this crazed mutant.

Putting together a plan at the spur of the moment I had one chance to pull it off, if the plan went wrong in the slightest I would be demolished, but I would rather take my chances being obliterated then a bloody smear on a wall because I died cornered and trapped like a mouse, I did not come all this way to lose, well here goes everything. Waiting till I was a few feet away from the end of the hallway I dove to the side abruptly.

Just missing me slip by revenge careened into the wall forcefully smashing its massive head, the blunt impact like the sound of a nuclear bomb going off.

Taking this vital time to get to my feet I sprinted in the opposite direction towards the entrance of the portal house.

Hearing a mighty roar I knew revenge had quickly recovered and I was back trying to escape from this enraged monster. It would not stop until it caught and killed me for what I did to its master pride; luckily the exit was now a few feet in front of me.

Opening it to the outside I trudged threw deep snow. Moment's later revenge came barging through the front of the cottage, its completely destroyed frame splintering with an exploding crash.

"I can feel you now, keep going until you see a dark shroud," said temptation voice ringing into my head.

I could see it lingering up ahead, but revenge would not give up until I was left mutilated by its vengeful clutches.

With monumental strides the demon revenge seemed to move faster in a more open setting, catching up to me it opened its mouth.

Inches from its jagged teeth I could smell its rancid breath of death, only seconds away from being devoured I lunged forward, barely escaping into the idle shroud.

(THE DEMON REVENGE)

Hell bent, the demon revenge will come with troubled thoughts swirling like the wind, each gust speaking swiftly of retribution, no matter how long, no matter what's needed, revenge will get even, through whatever disturbing means it deems, it will deliver no mercy, doing what it feels necessary to right what was so wrongly wronged, it will find you wherever you are, weather near or far, to the ends of the earth revenge will search, to bring to you what it feels you rightly deserve, its hell bent curse, your hell on earth

CHAPTER 13

2Q

Opening the portal door to the soul we were instantaneously sucked into a spiraling vortex falling deep into a bottomless darkness, yet sustaining no injury, landing on our feet smoothly. Seeing my love safe and sound gave me comfort, for the first time in along while I felt at ease.

Willing my blade of light I could see we were in some kind of cave that looked as if nothing could inhabit this cold and desolate place, was this now the confines of my soul? Some cold decrepit dungeon, what of the crystal mirror in my mysterious dreams surrounded by wondrous things? I pondered in deep thought.

"Are you ok?" asked love, reading the apparent disappointment on my solemn face.

"Yea its just I thought there would be more to this, is this what my soul has become?" I asked sadly.

"We should start looking, maybe the entrance to the soul is still farther in," replied love optimistic and hopeful.

Suddenly my thigh felt warm, then it started burning, jumping from the scalding heat I reached into my pocket quickly throwing the red-hot flame of hope away from me.

Landing a few feet away it emitted a brilliant light that illuminated the cave blinking and flashing continuously, then in a final burst of light everything changed, we no longer stood in a cave, but a spectacular place made of a collaboration of precious stones and rare jewels.

Transfixed by wonder I stared at the vast treasures of my abundant soul, astonished at the wealth I had never known, even a dream could not fully prepare one for enthralling enchantment, the soul seemed to go on unending, truly this was a beauty in eternity.

Catching my eye was a crystal structured fountain spitting sparkling water into a clear pool, behind it a sculpted onyx statue of my other half Sin Byron holding a gold chalice, its jasper eyes focused on three crystal clear cases covering threw different roses, one white, one red, one black, overshadowing these wonders sat an elevated pedestal, an illustrious throne made of diamond all around adorned by twinkling stones, awe struck I could not help but walk over to it beguiled by its serene magnificence.

"Be careful 2Q, the soul is made up of concentrated energy, there is no telling what effect any of these manifestations could do," warned love.

But I didn't listen; all I could see was the absorbing image of the diamond throne before me, seduced by its presence I touched it, instantly my eyes were open and locked into a vision, I could hear and see Sin Byron.

(SUBSTANCE)

Something of substance is worth more then riches and material possessions, for something about it is whole, undeniable and beautiful, for most things are superficial, partial and impractical, something of no value, easily had or ran threw, but substance is finality, full in a perfection of quality, rare because it is not found just anywhere, not everyone can see it for what it is, in harmony its mechanics move together in a sync like matrimony, all together in oneness, its center an ocean of substance

(IN LOVES ETERNITY)

In eternity we will dance forever, hand in hand our souls connected together, our love higher and brighter then the brightest star, no more burdens weighing heavy on your heart, you are more beautiful because of who you are, I can see all of you, not just some of you, here we are made new, here there is nothing to fear, nothing more to lose, no more pain to bear, no fake people out to use you for ill gain, come into my arms where you will feel safe, in this place we make our own way, truly alive we can thrive and do our own thing, here there is no one to say we cant, for we are free and spiritually limitless, here our dreams and wishes are infinite, my love where shall we go next, shall we stand at the waters edge then dive over its side closing our eyes, submerge to arise in the rays of welcome sunlight, the garden of Eden coming to life, an everlasting beauty there will always be, me and you forever in eternity

(MY WILL)

My will, a turbulent ocean surging ever forward, its destructive waves crashing the shores of a crystal element, never still, never settling, a flowing spring, an immovable object, a raging torrent subject to my whim, sovereign like the wind, flexible as limbs, far reaching as the rain, my will rolling clouds full of kinetic energy, a brewing storm, an unstoppable force, nothing can withstand, nothing can endure, its focused potential, released at my will

(LOVES BATTLE FIELD)

A raging battle on loves frontline, opposing forces of a hateful alliance, we fight against a consuming tyrant, of fear, inhibition and stagnant defiance, we cant give in to the pressure against us, the pitfalls of plots and limits of barriers, we must guard our hearts as we stand together, so the enemy can never come between us

(ENDANGERED LOVE)

What is it do you really want, what is it do you repress, why have you allowed yourself to become subjected to a spiritual prison, be free my love, open your eyes to the gift I can give, to channel the undying love threw my lips, for you are an endangered species that grows alarmingly, what rock will steady your beating hearts, the unstable man seems to easily fade into the wind, leaving you alone in the dark to burn out with no love to give, but everything I am has become the essence of an intimate connection, to break the chains that has inhibited your true beauty from its reflection, take me into your arms and hide me, lock my words inside of your beautiful vanity, that no one may tell you different, that I 2Q have personalized this gift, that it is your love that will transcend it, that together our hearts will beat as one, my love what is it do you really want

(FOR YOU)

I live and breathe only for you, I will die for a love that's true, I fight for her honor in a game of shadows, for life promises no tomorrow, I will burn and desecrate in the name of my love, then pray to God for the things I have done, for you I will defy the mortality of death, my soul will not rest until it finds its way back to the living, for I am the definition of an eternal agape, for your love is my love, together one heart beat

(LOVES SHADOW)

In the riches of my soul there is a shadow haunting my loves treasure, a dangerous truth that tempts all yet reveals few, an abundant tree full of forbidden fruit, a question that eludes answer, a source that contradicts definition, it is a mystery in its numbing coldness and the sun in its brilliant warmth, an intricate puzzle and a map to an endless bliss, an evanescent touch and the sweetest kiss, loves shadow lives and its presence breathes, the light and dark, the shadow and me

(JUST BECAUSE)

I adore you because of who you are, I admire you for the strength of your heart, I cherish you because of what we could be, I search because of a spiritual need, I call out to the one, because of the intimate connection of three, I am what I am because of a blessed mystery, that lives forever because of who you are to me

(ICE BREAKER)

Through your frozen exterior and hardened views I see something special inside of you, more so that I must break this ice that inhibits you, setting you free threw the crystal reflection of warmth and beauty, through visions of a love trapped in the depths of your need, why must you remain captive in the glacial abyss, robbed of the seductive radiance presented in wealthy abundance? Through provocative devotion learn thy evident importance, through exaltation of the spiritual become awakened, through the soul of the eternal bring timeless life to the surface, through an intimate connection know my three roses, through our infused hearts the ice is broken

(LOVES HAREM)

My women together under one sun how unique and beautiful you are, how significant ever-changing and subtle your beating hearts, how intense emotional and persuasive your love, the time has come for you to rejoice in the harem of the symbolic white rose, embrace, seek and vie selfishly, for the white of the rose symbolizes purity, a pure love that calls out to the deep desires of every women, yet it will choose only one to be given away by 2Q and Sin Byron, a ceremony of two who have become one, a harmony of the binding spell of true love, one that will never fizzle or fade, one that lives eternally, my loves you are the harem of the white rose, the keepers of 2Qs passion fire and Sin Byron's dark desires, so come together and rejoice in your hearts knowing that your love is alive, and the gift to each of your beautiful souls personalized

(YOUR LOVE)

My heart burns for your love, the smoke of desire fills my lungs, passion and darkness wrapped in one, the day and night, 2Q and Sin Byron, would you think me crazy if I shared my soul, a piece of each of the treasure I hold, for the pedestal of your heart deserves the rarest of stones, an intimate gift for your love to covet, your body betrays what your heart delays, the essence of your being burst into flames, your cravings of lust, the way that you change, for I Sin Byron run through your blood, and I 2Q am your one and only love

(PECULIAR LOVE)

Entering loves portal, you hastily leave the physical world of your burden, the others you have left behind may never come to understand the spiritual change taking place inside, that twinkle in your wide eye, that skip in your brand new step, for you are nothing but an empty shell to the old state you were in, you have transcended beyond the veil of limited energy, gloriously transformed into a luminous being of eternal beauty

(PERCEPTION)

How you view, what's personally deemed false or true, is all helping shape the world seen around you, what's more beautiful is the contrast built within your own uniqueness, the internal emotions as you discover the depths of self creation, how this occurs to each is of there own choosing, what is believed becomes reality, taking various forms in literal or symbolic imagery, with your boundless mind as the gold key, to open the limitless portal of wonderful dreams

(SPECIAL ALIGNMENT)

The hearts of love in perception to transcend, by way of portal through a crystal alignment, for a past life once left has no meaning, nor should previous burdens be revisited, but look forward my love to what joy awaits, for a celestial palace of treasure bears your name, an eternal freedom of beauty timeless, ready yourself, my special stars of brightness

(LOVES REFLECTION)

Approach loves portal with undoubted confidence, only with acceptance and freedom of inhibition can you receive the eternal soul of beautiful riches, for all women are the heirs of this royal inheritance, but what really underlies vanity's outside appearance, in your reflection, do you really believe in what it is you are seeing, are you secretly being held captive by grievous insecurity, I tell you now, as I have told you then, not one will enter loves paradise with a burdened spirit, only by being who you are will the illuminating light of transcendence unveil the material worlds distorted vision, bearing witness to the twinkling wonders of the heavenly dimension

(SOUL DEPTHS)

The depths of my soul, a dimension of heavens, a well of love, a beautiful essence, a soul of fire, a soul of transcendence, a soul of crystal, a soul of diamond, a soul of peace, a soul of clarity, a soul of dreams, a soul of stars, a soul of hearts, a soul of spirit, a soul of vision

(CHANEL MATRIX)

Sucked into the internal vortex of a channeled matrix, my divine essence, my mystery within, the core of my beings universe opened, the ultimate unveiling of my eternal spirit, the emerald portal through a transcendent dimension, me and myself viewed in depths of description, viewed by the beautiful heavens of a starry existence, the endless treasures of dreams and wishes, the pure light in the soul of a crystal element

(LOVES INHERITANCE)

My blessings, my curse, I have inherited loves treasure, the beautiful and broken hearts of the world, each brilliant piece specialized for her, what I did not have, I was given in abundance, what I did not ask, I was destined to acquire, 2Qs passion fire, Sin Byron's dark desires, each rosses essence, deeply rooted into this spiritual blessing, a gift of no limits, a gift of deeper understanding, I am consumed by it, I invite never ending love to come in, to dine with me at the table of her riches

(THREE ROSES)

These three roses inside of my soul, one essence in whole, encased in clear crystal, its harmony fluent in all that I am, its roots run deep inside mystery, entangling the obvious, concealing what's seen, the secrets it holds, the power of three, in fulfillment of seven, its purpose will bloom, so what is now, is truly unknown to you

(2Qs red rose)

The red rose, a symbolic beauty of her reflection, a luminescent glow, the essence of her perfection, to uplift and glorify what destiny intended, above and beyond the celestial heavens, the stars will fall and gather together endless, at the shores of the heart to sing of her transcendence, the clouds cannot cover pure loves angelical auras presence, this red rose bleeds a romantic connection

(SIN BYRONS BLACK ROSE)

The black rose, a symbolic twist of the darkness within, what is secret, what is unknown, drawing you close, pulling you in, an enticing enigma of what is also Sin Byron, the scintillating fruit of aggressive wants, the forbidden temptation to touch, this hungry need rapturing the soul, dark desires, a loss of control, but in essence, a haunting piece to the living mystery, also a vital key, to future things not yet seen

(WHITE ROSE)

Take this white rose for it is perfect, soon its millennial transcendence will rise above all, for there is found on it no blemishes or fault, its beauty is raw, undeniable to any and all who beholds it in its symbolic form, when this is given, you know that it is you who have been chosen, that all in harmony and oneness has finally come together in the heavens, that no longer are pieces broken, forever in eternity my heart is open, for you to be my lover and companion in this life and the next, until my eyes close and I take my last breath, what comes together will never come undone, the white rose symbolizes pure love

(LOVES PORTAL)

For though my beautiful love extends her rapturous reach to the collective world of hearts, souls and minds, there are repelling evils blocked from entering the portals paradise, hate, envy, discord, deceptive energies, demonic allures, no not one will see the treasures of loves world, nor will things change because now you have decided to turn, to be given this gift requires a lightness of spirit, an openness to receive this selfless connection, for it is not about vanity and what other judgmentally perceive, but the total acceptance of your being, in the reflection you see

(PEDESTAL STONES)

In my soul, surrounding my elevated throne, lies rare stones, more precious then its diamond, more illustrious then gold, what specializes her love in a personalized halo, the illuminating glow reflecting on the cases of my rose, a jubilant spectrum, twinkling wonders that rival the stars, more dearer to me, because the closer you are, vibrating my sensitive being with joyfully sensation, endless treasure aglow, threw pedestal stones

(DIAMOND THRONE)

Here on my diamond throne everything becomes heightened, sensational energies outside and within, together buzzing with collective vibration, a crashing waterfall of uninhibited friction, both in constant flux, both spectral frequency's at once, but threw focus, I have learned to calm these compelling forces, but yet I am baffled at how to fully understand them, what powerful source gives life to this spirit, the question of the mysterious presence of my own existence

(SOUL SEARCHING)

Into the depths of my eternal soul I have been, to search for the things I could not see, to clearly find what was always me, to know the whole of my destiny, to share my love in the shining light of her glory, to transcend into a dimension of celestial beauty, to understand the power of faith and belief, *to go through the demented shadows of darkness and emerge victorious, to unveil the gift of a potential unlimited, to mend together what was broken, to become one together in harmony and solace*

2QS VISION/SIN BYRON

"2Q I leave you more wiser then I once was, the time for talk has set its course, for if you are receiving this message I am already gone into the darkness to retrieve crystal pieces that have gone missing.

I urge you not to come after me for I may already be consumed, my approaching fate sealed by what I have to do. There are questions I cannot answer so I would be of no help, what I do know is that each crystal piece is pieces of our-self.

The power of the crystal mirror allows the looker to see things intimately, its imagery projecting clarity as if somehow being separate from your present reality, yet there is still so much mystery to this that I have not yet figured out.

Now without the full knowledge of it, its whole has been destroyed by the sheer negligence and ignorance to the harmony of self, that what we should be is not separate to our being, but whole in one piece, these things I now see clearly, but unfortunately it is to late.

If there is a chance to be saved I will risk everything to regain what went missing, for there is no hope for our spiritual unity without them. The soul of our connection becomes weaker the more time it is uninhabited, even so I must leave to right this wrong.

If you are somehow caught up in this confusion, which I feel you may be, and you do decide to follow me despite the spiritual danger, you must choose amongst three roses, if chosen right, a door will be opened before you.

Beware of the perceptible evil that lives in the manifested world surrounding our vulnerable unbalance, at anytime the enemy could be anywhere lurking, easily assuming any shape to trick and mislead you, they are the affliction that has pestered and terrorized the light of humanity since its dawn, I have watched this disease run amok.

Knowing the hearts of men this scourge whispers silent influence to the subconscious. Like the moving strings of a puppet they have mastered spiritual manipulation, be-careful that you are not consumed by this plague, be-careful of me, for even I may not be the same.

I have erased certain memory's and ciphered them into the ever flowing potential of the springing waters of the crystal fountain, a never ending well of pooling energy that will only show itself when hope is revealed.

My hope is my burden to hold on to and not lose, farewell 2Q, for my words are to be continued or forever silenced in my tomb.

2Q

Snapping out of the trance I felt dizzy and nauseous.

"I got you," said love putting my left arm around her neck to steady me.

"Sin Byron…spoke to me," I said trying to catch my panting breath from the strange experience.

"What did he say?" asked love, her eyes agape in wonderment.

"I now understand the severity of everything. Sin Byron knew the predicament we were in, and when the crystal mirror broke he went to find its missing pieces that got caught up between the souls dimensions of existence, hoping he could restore the balance. Aware of the knowledge he held and what damage it could do if revealed to the enemy, he somehow erased his memory and hid it inside of the waters of the crystal fountain. He also had a flame of hope with him, the key to revealing all of this."

"But now that he is on there side wouldn't the demons have it?" inquired love.

"I believe they do, but destroyed it in hopes of further manipulating Sin Byron for there evil purpose, it was me they weren't counting on.

Even if they did keep it, I doubt they knew of its significance, he wouldn't be able to tell them anything anyway even if they tortured him. He also said that one of these three roses would open up a door inside, yet all of what he was saying is not complete, vague even, they are still unanswered questions, like if there is something missing, then where are the hidden ones that remain?"

Walking over to the onyx statue I hefted the gold chalice out of its hands, steadying its dense weight before dipping it into the clear waters of the crystal fountain.

"Wait! Are you sure you have to do this?" said a jolted love with a look of apprehension.

"I'm positive, there are no other options, the answers we need are inside of Sin Byron's memory."

"What if something were to happen to you, I refuse to go on without you, promise me you will be ok, promise you'll come back to me," said love with tears in her eyes.

"There are something's I cannot promise you for I do not know what the future holds, but I swear on the stars of heaven that I will give all of my heart, body and soul until you are safely back home, I swear to you my undying love and devotion for all of time and eternity, there is nothing in this world or the next that will keep your love away from me," I said wrapping my arms around love bringing her close.

With urgency me and loves lips met, kissing with spirited fixation, there was no denying this beautiful chemistry, there was no doubt that love was the one for me, I would risk my life to see the heart restored again.

Letting her go, I brought the gold chalice to my lips and took a small sip.

Suddenly the room began to spin, my body and limbs stiffening dropping the golden chalice on the floor spilling its contents. I could hear love screaming my name then all sound faded away, I was inside of Sin Byron's memory.

(CRYSTAL FLOW)

The crystal flow springs forth from my soul, a sparkling fountain, a deep well with no bottom, springing forth in abundance, flowing through eternity's home, an outlet of power, its source unfathomable, bringing shine to the treasures, substance to the essence, sustaining the portal, twilight magic, birthing a living eclipse of celestial origin, to be further revealed, in a future uncertain

(CRYSTAL OVERFLOW)

My being overwhelmed by the waves of crystal clear waters, my overflowing cup spilled over, blessed I am to receive such gifts, my heavenly light a newness of spirit, for what was old has passed away, behold the dawn of a glorious day, a beautiful sight ascending in a spectrum of rays, that calls from the depths, of a soul aflame

(PROMISE)

My love there are many things I cannot promise you, for they would be untrue, but what I can promise is to give your love a chance, to look past your past, to see you for who you are, not judge based on your flaws, its been a hard road, this I know, but with me let it all go, I promise not to hurt you, all I ask for is your understanding that my heart is damaged, and something's I might do, not to take personal, I promise to build you, to give and not take, some promises are made to break, but my promise to you will forever remain

(THE GOLDEN CHALICE OF TIME)

Like the spilling sand in an hourglass, what is past and present can be turned back, repeating its process over and over again, the crystal fountain of an endless continuum, the ever flowing spring of a crystal element, the intertwined loop of the golden chalice, all connected to my universe within, the enveloping harmony and sync of everything

(CHEMISTRY)

My love you compete the better parts of me, our energy flows naturally, I cannot believe you may be the one I need, I think about it constantly, this connection, this peculiar chemistry haunting me endlessly, a need to tell you everything, I find myself opening up slowly, telling you secrets I never told any, with thoughts to open the illumined case, giving you the white rose that awaits for the one who is worthy of its purity, when I finally accept all is complete, the time I give all of me, I must see what this could be, I cannot deny this chemistry

(PERSISTENCE)

I will not stop until I make it to your heart, no barriers or shields can hold, through rain or the cold, through hell, through the pain, I persevere with no fear, the opposition will always hate, I will not fade or disappear, I believe that God put me here, to treat your heart with tender care, to bring heaven to your earth, to give you things you deserve, attentive I will always be, your love they can never take from me, I will battle waves to cross the sea, I will not stop for you and me

(ALWAYS BE)

In my last breath I will utter your name, so God can give me angels wings, to be there in your lonely nights, to be your everlasting light, to comfort you in your dreams, to fight away all the evil things, to paint images that bring you peace, shall you ever find yourself missing me, just touch your heart and feel its beat, close your eyes and truly believe, that inside of you I will always be

CHAPTER 14

SIN BYRONS MEMORY

"In my memory are blank pages, but if you look beyond words images appear, for something is happening that I always feared, the eminent destruction of the crystal mirror.

I see my other half at night, blissfully unaware of what's going on inside, yet I choose to leave him oblivious, because to him we are two different images.

Beyond the veil of his reality I see everything he doesn't, everyday I drift further away from him when in truth we should be one, yet I allow my anger to get the best of him, a fact he would rather deny and push to the side, obliviously going about his carefree life.

So I apply more pressure, not thinking of the crystal mirror that keeps the spiritual balance at the core of our center.

At times I think it would be better if the balance were to shift.

But then the question arises, who would be in control of this vessel? Would my other half even exist? How freely could I embrace the feeling of power I have grown to love when consuming him? Yet still who would I be without this other half of me?

The fact remains that he is me who would cease to be. That his ignorance of self would keep him blind until we both would tragically be banished from our body, dead because he needed me, oh how selfish I could be with all this pride looming inside of me.

Yet the realest thing I have ever felt came to me as something unreal. Women,

This craving that I need speaks to me intimately, I hate what this does to me, I burn when they are near, as if they touch a deeper part of me. Vulnerable, I do not seem myself, as if screaming for their help, to release me from this internal hell, to save me from myself.

Being pushed over the edge of a haunting obsession, I write of their love, our beautiful connection.

Never a writer before this, I found it to be a gift that the power of the crystal mirror enhances. The more I look into the mirror of my crystal reflection the deeper I travel into my soul discovering the substance of the essence between my other half and me.

Our maintained connection is a monumental matter of importance that had to be handled delicately, for 2Q and I do not see eye to eye.

But now with a more expanded view I think of why? How could it make any sense that we remain at odds, the same yet spiritually separated, and if continued like this it would lead to our destruction and inevitable corruption.

2Q and me would have to lay our differences down to save ourselves from being lost.

Preparing to make the necessary amends I hear the final crack, the crystal mirror breaking into pieces with a crash.

Instantly my thoughts are sporadic and no longer clear, I feel as if I am everywhere in pieces, as if my very mind has become the shattering structure of the crystal mirror.

I would wish to disappear, for what has appeared is a mystery, a dark gate that sits solemn and shrouded by darkness.

I can feel its presence, a familiar voice beckons from deep inside its dark entrance calling me forward, wailing in grievous lament.

The feeling that beyond its living shadows are missing pieces to the crystal mirror that have got caught up in the shifted unbalance. I have tried to nonchalantly ignore its wailing lament, but the noise of its cry grows stronger with each passing day I do not answer its call.

The mental pain like razor sharp claws digging like clenching clamps into my sanity's door, threatening to unhinge it and break it down, I must answer it now, these missing pieces have to be found.

Now that the protective veil has been destroyed the safety of the soul has been compromised. There is something trying to break inside, I can feel the cold presence of demons, I can hear their subtle whispers of intent to possess the crystal pieces.

Knowing this, I hid them amongst three special roses. If it were to be discovered that amongst these three is what they seek, they would have to choose wisely, for if the wrong one is touched the crystal walls of the soul will collapse destroying everything.

This is a back up plan; for if the enemy is allowed to reconstruct the crystal mirror I fear darkness will be released, altering everything we see, catastrophically devastating all that we know. There is a heavy burden resting our shoulders.

No matter which way I contemplate every option; all I see is that this mission must begin and end with me.

I must end this madness before the enemy has a chance to cause more damage. The fate of our world rest within each crystal piece,

Let my journey into the darkness begin.

(BREAK THEN BUILD)

To build up you must first break down, in this there should be no doubt, this will never be easy, for things become made to be set in comfort-ability, habitually its structure wears away, something drastic must take place, or watch inevitability demonstrate its crippling effects when it is abandoned and left to decay, all you worked for washed away by the tide of devastation, not allowing room to breathe, pull the rug out from under complacency's feet, a hard landing will teach it to be more aware of the possibilities, break patterns, with no mercy simulate disaster, giving no guidance on what to do after, sometimes to learn you must suffer injuries, crash or burn, basing off of the things you learned, you will build a foundation that is lasting and firm

(BEAUTIFUL CONNECTION)

Your deep desires, your intoxicating sex, your exciting presence, weans this connection, the signal received in full, then wrapped in a precious gift, given back to you, to appreciate its devotion, to covet its words, enslaved in seduction, entranced by its rapture, your energy feeds it, in return it receives you, this loving connection, intimate and beautiful

(MY LOVES TRUE CONNECTION BEYOND WORDS)

I am moved by love, compelled by the magnetic attraction of a spiritual connection, words can only begin to adorn the force of this overwhelming feeling, beyond which I paint the heavens of her celestial palace, raptured into the multi-dimensions of a crystal element, filled with the concentrated energy of the hearts unparalleled emotion, intertwined deep into the core of my eternal being, the soul of my endless universe, the essence of immortalized beauty

(ORGANIZE/CLUSTER)

Organize, so when it is time things will be easier to find, things in a heap of cluster will make it harder, for what you need is buried under, sorting through a pile of mess, could change your mood from cool to stress, organize to avoid all this, and what you need will be at your fingertips

(RESCUE ME)

Rescue me for I do not know how to love, how to breathe this breath into my lungs, how to see that one is for me, for I am broken to many pieces, this is all so much to bear, so it bleeds into three roses I share, saturated with everything I am, my essence trapped within the confines of its compartments, the roses stems drink from the waters of the crystal fountain, growing wildly until I am lost inside of its branches, its many levels of different words cries out to be listened to and heard, to find me between its secret passage, rescue me from what is shattered

2Q

Stumbling back to my present reality I fell over, but was thankfully caught by love acting as my crutch helping to hold me up.

I now understood why the opposite sex had this strange effect on me.

Every-time I got near a beautiful girl my heart would skip a beat, this heat would warm my body, my demeanor would flush, and my nerves would flutter.

The origin stemmed from Sin Byron and his weakness for women, it was that weakness that allowed him to become vulnerable enough to see that he was destroying us, but that was information I would keep to myself.

"What happened? Are you ok?" asked love, attentively brushing her fingers across the side of my face.

"I'm ok," I said weakly, still feeling dizzy from the prolonged aftermath.

"Good because you scared me, I wouldn't know what to do if I lost you," said love embracing me, nuzzling against me with endearment.

"I could feel the feeling of being mentally torn in different directions, I could feel the pain it caused Sin Byron, and facing those odds he had no choice but to leave the soul. Demons were at the portal trying to break in, they knew from the very beginning what caused the disturbance. They plan to reconstruct the crystal pieces, using its power to fully consume our world in eternal darkness. Sin Byron sensed this, so he hid the broken crystal pieces amongst these three roses, the catch is he doesn't say which one, I think that way if the demons were to find the key to the soul he wouldn't be the one to give the answer away."

"Did he say anything about the door that opens?" asked love.

"I don't know, he doesn't elaborate on it, but what he does say is if the wrong rose is picked in search of the remaining pieces, the soul will collapse destroying everything."

"What! So how will we know which one to choose, if the wrong one is picked we are doomed," said love discouraged.

"That will never happen, because in every aspect he is me, so I should know where it should be."

Studying each eye-catching rose illuminating in its scenic brilliance, out of all them, the white rose gave me a strong feeling, it was indefinite, but my gut instincts were telling me this was it, but if somehow it wasn't, my collapsing soul would be the grave we would be buried in, the only way out was from within, our fate narrowed down to one option.

(LOVE SUPPOURT)

Hold my hand, take me as I am, my love is my crutch, the ground I stand upon, the support if I ever were to fall, the cause of the one who I adore, the protection of crystal walls, the foundation of beating hearts, an accepting embrace of comforting warmth, a ray of light in the despairing dark, an unwavering faith when all seems lost, a strong belief in who you are

CHAPTER 15

SIN BYRON

Appearing in temptations boudoir, I could see she had prepared it just for me.

Lit candles adorned the perimeter of her bed casting dancing shadows; rose pedals decorated the floor in a sea of red, all together the mood completing an ambiance of Romance.

"I take it your not hurt" said temptation looking me over.

"I'm ok for the time being, but you need to show me how to harness these demonic powers I'm developing, if I knew how to control the fullness of it, it would be easier capturing love and killing 2Q."

"I will show you, but after I do with you what I want to."

"And what the hell is that supposed to mean?" I asked, growing furious at her self imposed delusions of having power over me.

"It means I gave you something now its time to receive" said temptation licking her full lips, a suggestive glare in her mesmerizing eyes.

"So what I'm just supposed to bow down to you in submission everytime you wish it, am I supposed to just give in to you like a slavish animal, you amuse me with your delusions, if that's what you want you can forget it because that's never going to happen."

"You ungrateful prick! Here is your first lesson," said temptation manhandling me with an exertion-less shove.

Flying into the air I landed on her bed, suddenly materializing chains coiled its way around like a snake binding my hand and feet, I struggled but couldn't get free.

"What the fuck is this!" I barked angrily.

"Do you think I'm someone you can toy with Sin Byron, some mistress you can use when you want something, you will never be in full control of your power unless you let go of these stank emotions, you are creating spiritual barrier limits stopping you from seeing and feeling energy that you will need to transcend."

"Bitch! If you don't let me go this instant I will-"

"You will what! You want me to show you but you wont shut up and listen; now I will have to make you play your position, lets see...for talking to me disrespectfully I will fuck your face, you will learn your place in this universe, you will know that as your cosmic teacher I will not tolerate your disorderly insubordination."

Getting on top of me temptation positioned her naked sex over my face; wrestling against the unbreakable chains in vain I turned my head avoiding her sick punishment.

"Now that's the spirit Sin Byron create some friction, which reminds me."

Sitting on my chest she snapped her fingers inducing my head to freeze in place, opening my mouth she pulled my tongue out.

"Now you can taste, which in a way is a lesson in using your five senses, well actually six but you will eventually catch my drift."

With my head frozen from this hexing enchantress I mumbled in protest, but was carelessly disregarded.

Lowering her moist sex onto my face she began aggressively humping and grinding, winding and rotating her hips, zealously bouncing, resiliently throwing her all into it until her legs began to wobble, screaming my name as her squirting orgasm violated my face drowning me in her pleasing release, laughing hysterically she got up off of me.

"That should teach you how to talk to me," said a giddy temptation with laborious breathing.

I didn't know how to feel, apart of me felt small and insignificant and I felt angry for it, yet another part of me wanted more, craving her sexual torture.

"Now you will stay that way until you can transmit yourself out of those chains."

"How," I said gnashing my teeth, fighting myself from saying anything brash.

"How polite of you Sin Byron I would be happy to help, now, feel your surroundings by using all of your basic five senses, picking up the energy that is everything will open up your sixth, the link and the use of your minds eye, to visualize the fullness of anyplace know where you are, know who you are, know that in a broader aspect we are all connected, allow the energy to flow through you and you will successfully open a transmission portal."

Putting every belittling thing that had just happened to the side I closed my eyes and took a deep breath.

Feeling myself in the moment detached from all distraction I entered a meditated focus, becoming aware of the energy waves coursing through my body, a bonding oneness of everything all around me, as if all along it was apart of this enigma that has always been this bigger picture.

Becoming larger I could feel its power flood in whole, I was no longer held captive I now had full control.

(DETAIL)

This attention to detail is all for you, my garments, lit candles, a bed of rose pedals, a scent to entice a lovers night, a gift to excite that look in your eyes, not in the present we have entered the moment, we give into each other lustful wishes and wanting, addictive and sexy creating memories of magic, the ambiance charms your auras magnetic attraction, dim lights, possessed shadows moving to our love all night, intimate hourglass bring detail to life

(PLEASURES OCEAN)

Like a waterfall I allow Pleasures Ocean to wash over me, your passionate release so dirty yet so clean, allow my soft pink tongue to taste the splash of your candy rain, savoring its sweet waves, oh divine the delectable taste, I just cant get enough hungrily devouring my plate, like an excited child's food drooling, dripping and running down my face, drown me in between your legs, with you on top capture me there, trap my head then steady your hands, rock me and ride me until you explode, I want you to leave my face a mess with the orgasm of your trembling sex, I want your sensitive body's energy spent, make me your slave, an instrument for your pleasure, to give you first, then receive me second, then float away in pleasures ocean

(CANDY RAIN)

Rain on me, soak every inch, enough so you can drown me in, I close my eyes and hold my breath, smother me till I confess, I open my mouth and hold out my tongue, to taste the rain I know will come, sticky drops of candy rain, falling off my eager face, everyday I look for the clouds, to wait for the rain pouring down, in hopes to be swept by the tide of the gluttonous, held in the restraints of euphoric contempt, debauch by the pleasure of your sweet punishment

(PUNISHMENT)

Without punishment, privileges would be taken for granted, punishment would not be respected, rules and authority would be rejected, if something is given too much it looses its value, but if it is taken away, it gains appreciation, and focus measures will be taken to sustain it, the feeling of having is better then needing and not receiving, taking the initiative, respecting privileges, change is eminent, implement punishment

(LISTEN AND LEARN)

Drown the noise out and listen, use the ears you have been given, if you talk less you will learn more, you will notice something different, deciphering idle talk from wisdom, you will see reasoning in things not seen previously, enlightened, you will gravitate towards something just like it, people, places and things will change, you will no longer feel the same, you will truly see what you used to be, from listening your knowledge will increase, learning substantially, for the better your life will turn, if you just listen and learn

(CRITICISM)

You must learn to take criticism constructively, not seeing it as malicious or mean, use criticism as a tool, reviewing the things that you may be unable to see, to make the necessary changes to your actions or behavior, see criticism as a favor, think of it as a mirror, you want to look your best, if something was not right, you would want it to be correct, you would invest the appropriate time into fixing yourself, see criticism as something that helps

(CONTROL)

Why is it do you try to control everything, your marriage, your relationship, anything close to you with an iron grip, holding control uncomfortably with no air to breathe, scrutinizing each and every little thing, why does nothing satisfy you and everything seemingly not to your specified liking, becoming likened unto a tyrant, you bitterly vent your frustration with accusation, do you know you push people away, why not let the chips fall where they may, are you afraid, is your incessant battle for control apart of a deeper insecurity, is there something your hiding, whatever it is, this I know, something's you need to let go, you will lose everything if you continue on this road, everything cannot be controlled

(BONDING ENERGY)

Energy I can read, it shows me how you could react or receive, it warns me to your interest from what is blind to see, an intuition based on feelings unexplained, a bonding to a link of concentrated waves, what you hide from me eventually gives way, even if words lie, energy will relay, my eyes are open so through you I can see, intentional or not, it tells me all I need

(TRANSMIT)

From one place to the next, I move in her mind, if her soul is receptive, I'm there deep inside, the power of my will focused wherever I deem, then in a blink of an eye I'm there spiritually, to cross the heavens light smooth like a breeze, cold in an idle shadow, or in light as a beam, there when I want, there when she needs, from one place to the next, with the power to transmit

(PRECIOUS FOCUS)

With my eyes closed I visualize the door way to my goal, silence, the bigger picture building, yes, next comes the feeling, wavering, what's associated with them, images, the object surrounding my attention, everything, drawing energy in bits, steady building, once whole, I have attained precious focus, in essence, I now have total dominion

(POLAR TRANSFERENCE)

My universe, my world, both the essence of my light and darkness, each a polar opposite, each a spiritual magnet drawing a soul in special alignment, linked characteristics, a unified consciousness, yet a signal of transference in multi-dimensions, a dual reflection, yet a single body in synchronized orbit, all revolving in relation to 2Q and Sin Byron, a paradox of feeling, passed threw the energy of the purest emotion

(REFINED)

Refined by my hurt, refined by my pain, refined by the fire, refined by the blaze, refined by the darkness, refined by the light, refined by a love I could not deny, refined by the spirit, refined by the soul, refined what you see, refined what you don't

(FOREVER ALIVE)

I am forever alive in your love, alive in your touch, alive in your kisses, alive in my roses, alive in your emotions, alive in the flesh, alive in the crystal mirror, alive in the secrets, alive in the mystery, alive in the words, alive in the soul, forever alive in its treasure

(FOREVER LOVE)

In eternity love is forever, so love world, this is the only power strong to keep you together, enough to withstand the catastrophic

*enormities of life's impending pressure, it is harmony in the
front lines of chaotic clamor, gentleness in the bias face of
adversity, sharing and caring for all no matter who they may
be, patient in burden bearing, attentive, constructive, capable
of a deeper understanding, never judgmental or demanding,
always open and receptive, rarely withdrawn or selective, there
is no obstacle it cannot surmount, no barrier it cannot move,
its will can bend space and time, forever me, forever you*

(PRACTICE)

*To become the best you must practice, for true mastery does not
come idly, to hone your craft you must do just that, putting in
time, to receive skills back, this will take practice, the more it
is done it becomes second nature, an instinct reacted quickly,
implemented swiftly and sufficiently, becoming natural as the
air we breathe, a duplicate extension of how you move and
what you do, showing skill through your actions, to become
the best you must practice*

2Q

Picking the white rose, I lifted its clear crystal case exposing the white rose underneath. How solemn it sat, so beautiful, yet it gave me a feeling of a deep sadness, what was its purpose? Why did I feel so drawn to it? As I pondered this, its case was snatched from my grasp as if by magnetism covering the white rose once again.

In a flash a black leather bag appeared in front of a sapphire door materializing out of nowhere.

"You did it!" said love embracing me.

"I told you we would be ok," I said relieved.

Walking over to the ordinarily looking bag I could see it had two straps to be slung over the shoulder or carried by back.

Unzipping the zipper that went down its middle my eyes lit up, what a sight to behold, a translucent treasure that shined and twinkled in the light; entranced by its irresistible allure I reached to touch it.

"No 2Q don't!" screamed love,

But it was to late; electricity had immobilized my jerking body.

In an eye opening spasm waves of energy flooded my brain at once, in my sight I could see different creatures, people, places and things of all kinds, I could feel the energy of the entire world compacted into these crystal pieces, I had become the outlet, its current flowing through my infinite being, all this power was to much, I was losing control, everything coming to me in Nano-seconds.

Pushed by a burst of overflowing power I flew unto my back, my conscious drifting away in a shroud of black.

(FLASH LIGHT)

I am your flashlight in the dark, your twinkling star in the night, the luminous ember to an everlasting flame, the new beginning of a young lovers love that can never die, a guardian element leading your heart safely through the veil, to the replenishing waters in between the moments of time, I am 2Q the bleeding red rose that is alive, going before you, opening the gateway to the reflective beauty inside, I am the flashlight that shines through the diamond of your sparkling eyes, I am the crystal fountain that will never run dry

(BEAUTIFUL FLAWS)

All my flaws caused me to transform inside an enlightened soul, it lives in a house with rubies throughout, full of diamonds and gold, its treasures are rich, but on the outside it is dressed rather drab, if you did not know it personally you would think it poor or sad, such a misjudged intriguing personality, it inspires other attributes to react in sync and harmony, it recovered positive growth when it was thought to be lost, my substantial unique one of a kind, beautiful flaws

(LIVING WHITE ROSE)

Pure love lives through this white rose; it has been locked away in a crystal clear case to pick whom it will give away, an internal connection will gravitate, I do not know the time or day, if you listen close you can hear it breathe, sorting through her energy, seeing the things that cannot be seen, each aura individually, bleeding from every beating heart, it does not matter who you are, its root lies beyond the exterior, its reflection present in every mirror, whatever's hidden it will find, to give its love for all of time

CHAPTER 16

SIN BYRON

I was now a full demon with the power to manipulate energy.

Weather positive transferring signals or negative retracting reception I could bring either with the slight shift of my perception.

With my ability to instantly transmit myself from place to place I had easily collected the missing crystal pieces.

Once the first piece was within my grasp, weather buried or intricately hidden I would use the crystals energy signature to track the rest of them.

By transmitting to different regions of the realm I had built alliances with powerful entity's, ruthless monsters that would aid me when the time was presented, now 2Q and love were all I needed. When they had entered in the portal door to the soul in a sense they had entered a warped dimension, some type of twisted time loop.

I could not assume my rightful position as official ruler of the realm until I found them.

I knew they would resurface, in fact I believed they had already, they were out there somewhere I could feel it; I would turn over every stone until they were mine.

For years I searched gathering information, killing hundreds if not thousands of hiding emotions, torturing, beating, burning and hanging them to find their location.

And now finally according to the information that I gathered we were approaching a hidden camp, a supposed secret haven for hidden emotions that I was sure would reveal the whereabouts of love and my other half.

Sending my snarling pack of cold-blooded demon dog soldiers to draw them out, they maliciously ransacked and burned their makeshift refuge to the ground.

To my begrudging disappointment only three emotions ran out, catching two of them the other luckily got away, but it wouldn't get far, I had locked on to its unique energy signature, there was no escaping fate.

Knowing where it was going I would let it think it was safe, and then I would appear in a surprising instant. Oh how I would enjoy the frightened look on the emotions face as I tortured and sodomized it with my dark blade, the hellacious thought amused me, but first I would question the ones we captured thoroughly.

With there heads pressed into the dirt my wicked group of demon dogs ridiculed the insignificant emotions, snickering at there helpless position with pitilessness. Opening up there enclosed circle, I sauntered over to our captives wondering to myself how long it would take for me to run out of patience and end up killing these worthless emotions, they both were young but I would show them no mercy.

"Stand and tell me your names"

Doing as they were told they both cowered before me in fear, the first one to speak was obviously the oldest of the pair.

"My…my name is joy and he is-"

"Don't you dare speak for him!" I yelled sharply startling them, my voice harsh and demanding.

"My name is…is appreciation," said the youngest boy timidly.

"Now I'm going to ask you boys a simple question, and if I were you I would think long and hard before you answer, do you get what I'm saying kids."

With wide eyes they nodded their heads in comprehension.

"Excellent, now where is love?"

Not answering they remained quiet, there sheepish eyes revealing there ignorance, they knew nothing so what use were they.

"Answer me!" I roared running out of patience squeezing joys neck till he started gaging and choking, "Where is she you filthy emotion! Where is love hiding?"

"We don't know, please let him go!" pleaded appreciation sobbing.

Enraged with spiteful venom I squeezed harder until joys slim neck snapped in my bare hands, his lifeless body falling to the ground limp.

"Now I am going to ask you, you will either answer or end up dead like your friend, do you understand you little brat!"

Appreciation wouldn't stop begging and crying so I grew tired of his whining annoyance, so I decided not to ask the wimp anything, instead I let my hungry dogs have a piece of them, he screamed in agony as my voracious dogs ripped him apart devouring his limbs, his cries falling on the ears of murderous monsters, when they were done the only evidence that appreciation existed where a leftover pile of picked clean bones.

Focusing, I searched the connected ether for the runaway's energy signature; locking onto it I conjured a shadow in a transmission, going after the escaping emotion.

(DARK WHISPERS THE SHADOWS OF POWER)

For there are dark voices that whisper, the more I fight not to listen, the more these whispers are presented, struggling to wean me from serenity, pushing me to edge of sanity, when I am awake I question if I am asleep, when I am asleep my senses seem awake, compelled to enter the shadows beyond me, yet living and ever present before me, the gathering darkness enthralling, but never overwhelming, seemingly hopeless, yet strangely submissive, is it unintentional manipulation, or enlightened confusion, for I Sin Byron can now bend the shadows to my will, and have become the very source of the whispers themselves

2Q

In the dark I could hear my name being called over and over again. I seemed to be floating, though I could see nothing I became aware of this voice. Moving closer to it I could feel water on my skin as if it was raining, then I could see a light up ahead, reaching for it my eyes flew open, breath filling my lungs in a rush causing me to gag and cough.

Standing over me was love crying, her hands radiating a bright blue hue trying her best to heal me. When I came back to life her beautiful face was no longer distraught and her warming smile formed.

"You were dead, your heart stopped beating but your back, please never leave me again," said love sobbing.

Wiping away her tears I pulled her close for a heated kiss, there was nothing and no one that could make me feel like love did, she was my motivation and will to live, I would stop at nothing to make sure everything was right again.

"I would never abandon you love, sorry if I scared you, now help me up we have work to do. Immediately after standing I felt different, waving my hands in front of my face I could see its heat signature emitting waves of energy, turning to look at love I could see her aura like burning incense wafting into the air.

"What am I? I don't feel the same," I said boggled, looking around at my now even more remarkable surroundings, and even more vibrant color distinguished and eye-catching.

"Could it be that you have become concentrated? More in tune with the energy of your soul," said love examining me with piqued interest.

"I don't know, everything about me has drastically changed, I can see things that should not be possible to see, I can feel things that should not be normal to feel, what have I become? Why is-"

Suddenly pangs of pain shot through my body causing me to cringe. In suffering discomfort I dropped to my knees clenching my constricting stomach muscles, my ears began to pop and ring, I could hear loves cry echo inside of my head with a magnified sound, her falling tears hitting the ground with a piercing pound.

I was feeling the very pain Sin Byron experienced, the maddening ache of being mentally torn in different directions, my senses muddled, my brain flooded with mysterious energies, the pain was excruciating.

"I love you 2Q please be ok," said love helping me to stand.

"This…this enormous power must be channeling from the crystal pieces, Sin Byron was right, this is beyond us, I do not fully understand what this means for me, but I know where this door leads."

"Whatever it means we will figure it out together, where does the door lead?" asked love.

"The mind"

(LIGHT SPIRIT)

Through a light spirit I am free, what restraints can hold me, as if in a dream I waver through your reality, through your being I enthrall you, take my hand love for we a stronger together, your heart I can hold, for its treasure rests in my soul, for eternity it has always been, its diamond pedestal elevated, special and distinguished, her love nothing compares to, these I show you, because what is, has always been heightened

(LOVES MELODY)

Loves wavering aura sways in the airs gentle breeze, it is her subtle persuasion, her soft melody, her sweet kiss, be attentive, listen quietly, soon you will find your soul bewitched by its infections symphony, enslaved by its ambiguity, raptured at the sources mystery, come as you are it seems to say, with no inhibition you move towards it, looking, straining to hear its specifics, yet strangely its beautiful words are repetitious, connected, speaking of others before it, neither judging, nor condescending, somehow it seems natural even, one things for sure, nothing can deny this sensuous feeling, this stirring passion, your hearts total surrender to loves melodic rhythm

(LOVES NEW BIRTH)

My loves of the world in stages of sleep, every language, every color, every unique beauty, awaken through the heart of your inhibited need, set your spirit free in a supernova of bonding energy, ignite, come alive, together shine your spectrums throughout the universe, for in this, you illuminate the palace of your intimate treasure, born to royalty, sparkling stars fulfill your destiny, in harmony, behold the magic of a renewed perception, in solace, the new birth of your glorious transcendence

(WISDOM AND UNDERSTANDING)

A higher elevation of knowledge, its insight in various subjects bewilders in astonishment, its judgment is wise and unlike others before it, a deep elaboration of sense rich in substance, its accumulation of meaning is abundant and accurate, stemming from the well of clarity and enlightenment, not many have it, some cannot grasp it, for it is layers of perplexity, a deeper understanding, its foundation is firm, its wisdom unchallenged, gaining a higher elevation, with wisdom and understanding

(WHAT AM I)

What am I? A question I asked for a long time, this person I seek to find inside, the mystery in the places described, within myself, secret compartments deeper then the deepest well, from what I figured out there is no clear route, there are no short *cuts, just a maze through and through, that's wrapped around a twisted loop, infused in-cryptic ways to move, so what you think you know you should think again, take a step back and analyze what I am*

SIN BYRON

"Going some where!"

Startled, the emotion turned and ran in the opposite direction, holding out my right hand I discharged a gravitational energy to hold it in place.

"Hey not so fast you little rodent I got to ask you some questions."

As the trapped emotion unsuccessfully struggled against my force field, I drew my dark blade with diabolical delight.

"What's your name?" I questioned.

"Please don't kill me!" the emotion pleaded.

"That depends on the information you give me."

"My name is peace,"

Scrutinizing my young detainee I could see he would be compliant, he was to petrified to go against my wishes, he would do everything I told him to do with no resistance.

"Good, now I am going to let down my energy, and I swear if you play games with my tolerance I will do things to you, you couldn't possibly imagine."

Letting down my energy peace stood there obediently.

"What can I do for you sir"? Said peace.

"I like your attitude peace, better then your idiotic friends who are no longer breathing, there might be hope for you peace, depending on how you answer this question."

"I promise to do my best," said peace mannerly.

This little runt was kissing my ass hoping I wouldn't hurt him; well he had another thing coming.

"Marvelous, now where is-"

Suddenly a sharp ringing blitzed my head with a hammering headache, dropping to my knees I covered my ears crying out from the throbbing pain, the grinding thump driving me into a state of temporary insanity.

I could feel my other half, a drastic shift in his being, a dramatic increase in his unbelievable energy, I knew he had found the remaining crystal pieces, as quick as the pain came it subsided. Looking around peace was nowhere to be found, he had taken advantage of my disabling weakness and escaped.

But that didn't matter now I finally knew were to find 2Q, this time he would die, and the rest of the crystal pieces and his love would be mine.

CHAPTER 17

2Q

Fastening the leather bag onto my back I took loves hand.

Upon opening the sapphire door we were immediately pulled upward into a whirling vortex.

Hugging love close I kept my eyes closed as the hurricane like winds whipped its current to and fro, battering our vision with dangerous gusts, its unrelenting draft threatening to separate us.

When the madness finally stopped and everything went quiet and still I opened my eyes to a dimly lit room casting shadows from flickering candles, erotic pictures lined the circumference of the walls, the suggestive picture fetish giving off a feeling of a transgressed intimacy.

Love looked dumbstruck as she stared at the pictures of different women posing in provocative positions.

Watching her I could only wonder what she was thinking, walking over to the beautiful door made of amethyst I opened it just a little peeking threw the crack, in awe I gawked at what I was seeing, flustered I closed it back quickly, my face flush with heat, I knew my other half loved women but this had to be an over the top extreme figment of his lustful imagination.

In those brief seconds I had opened the door I could see beautiful women of all different shapes, sizes and complexions, all naked, walking about as if oblivious to the bare nature of there existence, there prominent assets out in the open, the whole scene felt strange and wrong, but oddly exciting and fulfilling, apart of me felt guilty yet enticed by my transgressed thoughts.

"Is everything ok?" asked the ever-observant love that always noticed the little changes in my behavior.

"Lets just say those flamboyant pictures on the wall come to life, I have a plan, but for it to work you have to take your clothes off and get naked again."

With a perplexed expression love walked over to the door and opened it slightly, closing it back without saying a word she started to undress.

"So what's the plan?" inquired love plainly, as if unaffected by everything.

When love had her heart on her sleeve she was easy to read, but there where times since I had met her when I would want to know how she felt deep down and it would seem to be withheld, as if she held it in, this fact bothered me.

"Does this not bother you in the slightest?" I asked love with concern.

"Why should it"?

"Look I know you were naked when I first met you, but doesn't that effect you, this environment, how come you seem so at ease with it, at times things seem to daunt you, but what I think at times should, doesn't, my love you are so confusing."

Love smiled,

"You look to much into it, and because of this you look at how things should be instead of letting it be, I am love in its purity, I do not see with set definitions or restrictions, this is why I am naked, outside of this door are no boundaries, no inhibition of consciousness, whatever it is you see will also be in its concentrated purity."

Understanding her but at the same time not, I decided to leave the topic alone for now, without actually haven't set foot here I was somehow aware of the ins and outs of the internal atmosphere of the mind.

"Not to far from here is a place called the minds eye, we seek the ones who run it, their names are knowledge and wisdom, they are the keepers of the hidden archives and the only ones who can answer our questions, maybe even give us a safe passage to the heart."

"How will we get to them without being noticed?" asked love.

"This is going to look and sound crazy, but I'm going to take the form of my other half Sin Byron."

In an instant I shape shifted, my teeth becoming fanged, my brown eyes red and my attire all black my dark half's preference.

The only thing I could not change was the gold hilt that willed the light blade and the leather bag full of crystal pieces, so I rendered both invisible.

Gasping in fright love backed away from me.

"Its me love, this disguise is necessary if we are to fit in."

"Don't you think that would draw to much attention to us, why not take the form of one of those dog soldiers?" asked love.

"Because they are Sin Byron's guards, there job would be to go wherever he tells them, it would be odd to see one when they should be at there designated post, impersonating there ruler is a chance we have to take, it is only temporary, just stay close to me."

Opening the door into the inner levels of the ever-changing mind, we walked out together, the looming future of our success uncertain.

(DANGEROUS LOVE)

Exciting yet terrifying this dangerous love, undeterred I aim for the heart, I want all of your affections, but the effect I cannot foresee, how complicated love can be, will it lead to my ruin, how far reaching will my words influence, I do this for you my love, but is that enough? Is one piece of me enough to satisfy your every want and need? My touch so addictive can become a contradiction, my intention is not to mislead, but know this, my whole I can never give, because I must search until I'm whole again, will you hold my piece dear, or turn against what you cannot fully possess? Will this bring about your anger, or will you help put me together? In time these questions will be answered, because my dangerous love demands it

(ARE YOU HAPPY)

Are you happy my love? When he looks at you do you see the magic of forever? Are you mesmerized by passion fire, or has it cooled no longer wild with desire? Has the light once vibrant and bright dulled into a cold dark night? Are you happy? Does he touch you the same way or has doubt found its way, creating in its place a void that pushes you away? When I look into your eyes they cannot lie, for they speak of your heart and soul intimately, are you happy my love or pretending to be?

(PERFECT)

As I look into your eyes I can see a hidden insecurity under a fabricated mask you pass as reality, to the average person you seem stable and in control, but I can see past that all the way through to your soul, I can see you wonder what I see in you, deep down wishing you could change the things you hate about yourself, then maybe you will have more confidence to not second guess the relevance of your presence, to not doubt your existence, my love you are perfect the way you are, no amount of make up could cover your loving heart, I see you for who you are, your beauty is not only skin deep, there is more to your story, more then just excepting anything that's walking, dropping your standard for less instead of realizing you deserve the best, as I look into your eyes I can see that your worth it, my love to me you are perfect

(INCRYPTIC MOVES HIDDEN CRYSTAL ARCHIVES)

To each their own, may the tools within my universe help illuminate the whole of your soul, for only you know the hidden *things that appeal to you, what is my in-cryptic archives in dimensions of crystal, how clearly you view this is important, the moves you make is the base for your own creation, what actually materializes into your reality's existence, for life is nothing but a perceived illusion, to bend to the will of the spirit in choosing*

CHAPTER 18

2Q

As soon as the women saw me they immediately stopped what they were doing rushing over to stroke and caress me.

Trying not to be overwhelmed by the attention, I kept on moving telling the alluring women with authority in my tone to go back to what they were doing, but with my every step the inviting attention became more intense, more yearning women bombarding me with titillating propositions.

Excitedly grabbing both of my hands inducing me to come with them, eager for the stimulating feeling of the warmth of my body, openly playing with there sex until there out-bursting cries of pleasure released there passion coating there quivering legs, begging for me to take part in there various fetishes, slavishly throwing themselves at my feet.

My head was reeling and my enflamed desire boiling in my veins like poison, but despite it all I remained focused.

Ever so often I glanced over at love. With no readable expression I could sense she was once again holding back her true feelings.

I was successful in keeping the temptation at bay until I met someone I could not turn away.

Her beauty was breathtaking and her body enticing, but the most distinct thing about her were those hypnotizing eyes exuding her fascinating appearance, the color of scarlet with a mix of lavender and hints of green, the sight of her caused me to stop moving.

"Sin Byron when did you return I would have prepared a feast?" asked the stunning women.

"Why would I need you to prepare anything?" I asked trying to impersonate my other half's hot-blooded arrogance.

"I think we should discuss something personally," said the overly eager women. "I have business that must be adhered to, I should be on my way as should you," I said brushing her off, walking away briskly.

"This cannot wait I insist your majesty," said the persistent women catching up to me.

Her smoldering eyes staring intensely into mine, pressing her perky breast unto me she leaned over whispering into my ear.

Powerless to resist, in an instant thoughts filled my head with fornication, I could not control the urge to give in to my pent up feelings of carnal temptation, next thing I knew my lips were pressed against hers and my hands outlining the perfect shape of her curves.

Pulling down my zipper she freed my throbbing manhood that now extended in its full length, stroking and messaging it gently the feeling of ecstasy washed over my relaxed body, while touching me she turned towards love with intentional spite.

"He is mine you cannot handle him, now run along little girl he never cared for you."

Hooked by the gripping sensation I didn't take notice of the damaging exchange between temptation and love.

"That's not true, he loves me," said love fighting back her swelling tears.

"Oh poor baby how naive and foolish you are, don't you know that all men are dogs, he never loved you, and now that he does not need you he will do what all men do when they tire of an easy conquest, he will dispose of you, with all these beautiful women to fuck he can quench his insatiable appetite anytime he wants, look at his face as I stroke his thick cock, yea that's right soak it up, guess your not that special after all you little cunt."

Reaching the pinnacle of knee jerking bliss I snapped out of my dreamy stupor just in time to see love running away crying hysterically, I knew I had fell for a trick when the women licked my seed from her hands cackling maniacally. Pushing her to the side I ran after love, we had blown our cover.

(THE WONDERING EYE)

The peculiar eyes cannot focus on one thing at a time, this takes great discipline and focus to keep the attention from roaming, the eye is hungry to see things never before seen, it is a retinal obsession, the retinas need to view images as much as it deems, the wondering eye is hard to please, you must give the appearance of change constantly, different spectacles and visuals luring the pupil, but if you let up the vision will fade, and the wondering eye will wander again

(PROMISCUOUS/THE ONE)

How fun and free it is being promiscuous, from one person to the next with no attachments, moving about in a state of bliss holding on to nothing, then you run into the one, a person you never expected to get under your skin causing you to come undone, the mood has changed and is no longer fun, because now you hope they want you as much as you want them, before seeing things as a game, you had your way caring only about yourself, now with your emotions involved you care for someone else, off balance your thoughts surrounded by images of the one, there face becoming the ocean that your helpless heart is drowned in

(FAILED RELATIONSHIPS)

Without knowing the person you love at first lust, inevitable failure is soon to come, quickly as it started is as quick as its done, disenchantment will soon set inside of someone, an illusion wore off you thought you saw, but this wasn't the truth at all, you thought for love you would fall, but instead you gained nothing at all, you fell for lust who played as love, until reality came in and broke things up, now here comes the heartache and pain, your falling tears like drops of rain, you blame yourself, your blaming them, your wavering emotion between sadness and frustration, asking yourself what went wrong with the relationship, but the answer is simply this, that you did not get to know the person before starting it

(MARRIAGE AND COMMUNICATION)

Marriage is a sacred vow, in front of God your love is bound, a partner, lover and friend, all the way to the end, communication keeps the connection, tender love and sweet affection, together one heart, both one soul, till your hair is gray and old, communicate everyday, never let your love fade away, marriage is taken as a joke today, it never last, loves thrown away, to keep a marriage truly sustained, together your love must communicate

(CHEATING/INFIDELITY)

Some people cant see what they have so they cheat, choosing infidelity as a way to cope instead of trying to fix the relationship, they run from it feeling they are missing something, often times the significant other either doesn't know or becomes blind to the problem, until the issue grows becoming more then thought possible, the change evident through behavioral differences, through patterns and instances, a balance shifted disrupting a marriage or relationship, confusion and anger sets in, what was done to deserve this becomes the question, *somewhat complacent you did not notice that you took a part in creating the situation, it is as much your fault as it is theirs, ask yourself why would the other have an affair, when everything that they could ever need or want is right here, the answer is you have allowed comfort-ability to bring about predictability, marriage and relationships are a two way street, try to keep things interesting, thinking for yourself, yet at the same time your other, this way of thought will keep you together*

SIN BYRON

I knew my other was in the mind so I warned temptation ahead of time, knowing her power of coercive persuasion would get the job done.

If there was one thing that I learned is that an emotional person is a weak one, so to get what I needed I would have to be subtle, instead of confronting 2Q and creating a commotion, I would gather every demon I had an alliance with to finish what I started.

"Your other half came out of my spell and is chasing after love, whatever it is you plan on doing now's the time to get it done," said temptation using our telepathic network of communication.

"You must not allow him to reach her, dispatch my demon dog soldiers to stall him, I will be there soon after some friends of mine come threw."

Summoning the most evil and wicked entity's they all answered my call instantly, appearing in a black shroud they transmitted themselves all around me, now I was ready.

(THE DEMON STRESS)

The demon stress wears on your mind, breaking it down peace by peace in time, as you wither away from the mental strain, your body shows signs of early age, the light in you will start to fade, your health will start to decay, unstable emotions will start to show, your skin will sink and show its bones, vitality no longer what it was, close to death you will become, your complexion no longer tone and vibrant, your cells malnourished started dying, draining your energy till nothings left, a progressive and gradual hell, the demon stress kills

(THE DEMON INSANITY)

There is a thin line between sane and insanity, insanity will cause the sane to lose their grip on reality, sliding down the slippery slope of instability, erratic thoughts and repeated pitfalls, walking the edge of reason, you find yourself seeing and responding to things as if with rational thinking, believing in a sense of difference, being fed an illusion, seeing its purpose in its absurd image, following it blindly to fall over its edge, to the point of no return, lost in the deep end

(THE DEMON DEPRESSION)

Draining your spirit of vitality you sink deep into a bottomless hole of sadness, slowly losing yourself in depression, embracing all the bed feelings in acceptance, taking them in as your own becoming a surrogate home, changing on the inside your healthy habits decline, physically and mentally sabotaged you become inactive and slow to respond, your vulnerable emotions become a burden, so they are cast aside shutting down your active mind, in a state of denial its functions diminish, becoming hollow decrepit and spiritually desolate, then ultimately consumed by the demon depression

(THE DEMON TROUBLE)

When you think everything is fine the demon trouble is not to
far behind, for trouble stealthily stalks you, somehow always
knowing where you are, no matter who you are trouble has a
job that it is dedicated to, trouble loves to make things difficult
that would otherwise go smooth, upsetting and antagonizing,
disrupting an easy flow with obstacles and bumps on the road,
trouble invades the sanctity of peace, showing up to places
unexpectedly

(THE DEMON HURT)

Hurt causes you to do and say things you normally wouldn't, to
lash out at others though you shouldn't, to harbor resentment
for the source of your hurt, to want to do unspeakable things
you cant put into words, to hold a grudge and seek revenge,
to want to inflict the same hurt on them, the burning feeling
as if a wound is open, and there is nothing to heal or relieve
your suffering, for the demon hurt runs deep, inside of your
veins into your heart beat

(THE DEMON IGNORANCE)

This demon would see to it you remain in the dark, ignorant to
information, content how you are, to not know something and
careless to look, excuses to be made from doing things you should,
knowledge is power so it diverts you away, to keep you imprisoned
within an empty space, were nothing could get through the
walls of your mind, keeping you mentally closed and confined,
becoming as an infant who does not know any better, susceptible
to lures and traps purposely set up, the end results for you to fail,
because you don't know, chances are you will

(THE DEMON SCORN)

A close kin to anger and hate, scorn scowls in disgust, despising you and what you've done, looking down on your no good ways, ruing the very day you came, ruing have to see your despicable face, scorn would love to have any trace of your being erased from sight and memory, to give you a taste of its secret aches and pains, you are the source of its disdain, the demon scorn blames you for everything

(THE DEMON GRUDGE)

Causing you to hold on to resentment, the demon grudge will make you bitter, eating a hole threw your center, rotten you from the inside out, infusing its spite, leaving your emotions wrapped and contort, with no way of escaping your thoughts, lost in the feeling, not able to see threw the fog, grudge poison seeping threw your pours, holding on to it enough can lose who you are, becoming consumed blackens your heart, being haunted by your very thoughts you cant let go, there is no where to turn, no where to run, when you have took in the demon grudge

(MENTAL WARFARE)

How can you fight what you can see, or face an unknown enemy, if you are not aware, how can you strategize an effective defense against the subtle attacks of mental warfare, for the enemy knows that you cannot, so its scouts lie in wait with schemes and plots, spying on your open reactions from the little instances it secretly wrought, often using temptations that betray the solidity of your thoughts, gauging the minds insecurities and small inconsistencies, bringing back valuable information of the kinks in your chemistry, knowing what it is to insinuate into the will of your body, for in ignorance there is much to fear, for the enemy's sole purpose is absolute control, silently waging warfare threw the relevance of your mental

EVIL CONJURE)

The darkness conjured I freely speak, because the manifestations are now gone from me, at once demented I cared not for the emotions of the living, cold and distant, the Sin Byron of a shadow alliance, the real nightmares of an empty conscious, a consuming attachment of a villainous perversion, twisted in the practiced ways of a demonic rebellion, a delirium almost overtaking the soul of my infinite being, if not for the heavenly light, I would never have survived

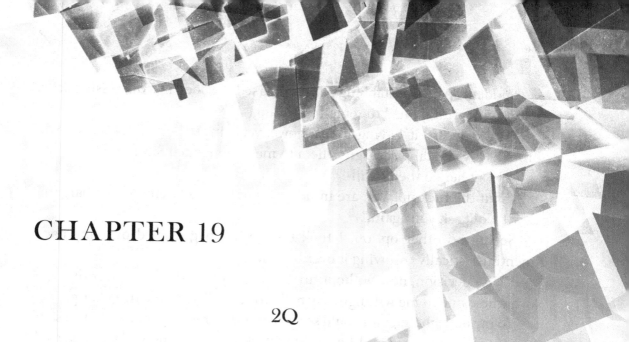

CHAPTER 19

2Q

I could see love up ahead I had to get to her.

Now that we had no cover this left her vulnerable, she was so caught up in her own emotion she wasn't thinking rational, everything she held inside was finding its way out, I had to calm her down.

Blocking me from continuing on was a gang of demon dog soldiers snarling and elongating their razor sharp claws. Finding myself surrounded I dropped the façade of my appearance, willing my blade of light I could feel my enhanced power surging threw me and there interruption made me irate.

"You want to play, well let's do it!"

With a fed up cry I stomped on the ground, the sheer force cracking its surface followed by a powerful blast of rippling vibration, airlifting the yelping dogs soaring uncontrollably in different directions.

With a clear path I continued after love, the last time I seen her she had bent the corner, I couldn't be to far behind.

Reaching the corner I stopped my pace, startled to see my other half blocking my path with an array of fiendish demons behind him.

On the outside I looked confident, but on the inside I was panicking as I watched Sin Byron hold his dark blade dangerously close to loves neck. Coming up behind me snarling were the gang of demon dog soldiers I sent air-borne and they were furious.

Suddenly pangs of stabbing pain immersed my body in a distressing ache, it took everything I had to remain standing.

"Hurts doesn't it, having all that power yet being stifled by it, I can see you brought my crystal pieces, give them to me." Demanded Sin Byron

"No let her go then I will-"

"Shut the fuck up! You are in no position to make demands or bargain, now I wont ask you again."

Seeing no other option, I took the leather bag draped over my back unenthusiastically throwing it over to him.

"Wise decision, now without further delay I would like to meet the new love who came to me willingly, say hello to scorn," he said letting her go.

To my outright horror I could see love was different, her normally pleasant face was in a grimace and her unique pink eyes were now black, a jagged dagger materialized into her hand.

"Listen love I'm so sorry, I wasn't thinking straight, you know you mean everything to me, think of everything you would be giving up if you go with him, come back to me please, I know this isn't you!" I pleaded broken hearted, hoping I could get threw to the love I knew.

"You never cared, you used me and I foolishly fell for it, the sweet and innocent love is gone, you are nothing but a dirty and conniving dog, you will pay for what you have done, you will look upon the face of a lost love as I cut out your lying tongue, then slit your throat and drink your blood."

Sin Byron and his demons started jeering and laughing in hysterical contempt as my scorned love moved forward with the intent to kill me.

If demons could materialize themselves then maybe I could as well I fleetingly thought to myself, but I felt drained and my body racked with pain, but I had to try, the fate of my soul and my love hung delicately in the balance.

Digging in deep I felt a familiar object building, drawing my spare energy in bits, it was the flame of hope.

Putting everything I had into its pooling power I focused were I wanted to be, this would either kill me in an implosion or work successfully, letting the energy flow through me like a cascading flood I dispersed it all at once, in a blinding flash I was gone.

(HARD LOVE)

Sometimes you must give hard love cutting off support, this might seem extreme, but this might be the only option for them to see, the person might feel they are being dealt with harshly, that you are being cruel and affair, there anger will start to flare, for the moment they may push you away, disregarding everything you do or say feeling hurt and betrayed, not able to see things your way, not seeing the help they need, you may start to feel sorry, you may start giving in, asking yourself if what you are doing is really working, stand firm, until they learn that what your doing is out of care and concern, until things start to change, it has to be this way, showing your hard love everyday

(DESERVE)

Did I not deserve love, when your pieces fell was I not there to help pick them up, when I fell apart you let it hit the floor, a countless reminder that part of me abhors, an alternate split caused one half to pursue, the other half hated the fact of what you made it do, they fought each other bitterly yet could not deny the fact, that it came to far without your love and to both you turned your back

(SOMETIMES)

Sometimes love can lose its sight, sometimes id rather blow your mind, sometimes I don't listen before I talk, sometimes I don't look before I walk, sometimes I don't think before I react, sometimes I wish the world would burn to ash, sometimes love can turn to hate, sometimes another chance can be a chance to late, sometimes your all is just not enough, sometimes I just don't care as much, sometimes I say things I don't mean, sometimes I don't have the patience to read the lines in between, sometimes I view the world as a game of chess, sometimes my first move isn't my best, sometimes hardship is a test, sometimes more is equal to less

(TAKEN FOR GRANTED)

My love will you make him plead and beg, when he realizes he lost something good but it took it for granted, now wanting it back will accept him, leave hope dangling over his head, or watch him self destruct condemning him to death, there is never an easy decision, were you hurt because of this, was it all done on purpose, is it even worth it, does he love you, or is this a desperate cry only because he is in trouble, the heart never really knows what it wants, until that something is gone, you will know it wasn't real if that something moves on, but if it comes back, there might be a chance, that it will never take love for granted again

(SPARK)

To keep your love alive you must not loose your spark, to reignite that feeling in your life think back to happier times, remember how you felt inside, before the arguments, before the fights, when everything was vibrant and bright, your significant other by your side, recreate the moments that set your heart aflame, calling each other name, hurt if even for a second that person was away, the first time you kissed, the first time you touched, the feeling of your beating heart, the feeling of a rush, when nothing else mattered, as long as there was just you two, when the spark between your hearts was exciting and new

(CHOOSE)

My loves who will you choose? On one hand 2Q, his love and romantic views, on the other Sin Byron, his desire and temptation, both one and the same, yet not when it comes to there ways, who shall it be, 2Q and his red rose of beauty, soft kisses, sweet dreams, you are all he sees, you are all he needs, delicate and tender strokes making love to you intimately, his attention to detail tailored for you specifically, or shall it be Sin Byron and his black rose, drawing what makes you crave, what makes you moan, what makes your need out of control, to possess your mind, to pursue until you find it making you upset, yet at the same time eager for his attention, mindless thoughts of being ravished, or 2Q and his passion, my love this selective choice is for you, who is it will you choose?

(LOVES SCAR)

Even now the pain still resonates, the half empty reminder, the countless dreams, the twisting and turning of misery, the bare feeling of nothing, a distressed call but no answer, a ghosts identity, dead to the world, dead to love, mentally coming undone, now here you are, would you have loved me then, could you have looked into the lifeless eyes of disappointment yet done nothing, would you have left my casket open like the rest, deep down knowing my life would eventually fade bringing me ever closer to death, no, yes, what answer fits best, still all meaningless, would you care to know the voice of darkness, why this piece seems to be an open wound, but fret

*not my love, it has scabbed, now soothed, for in abandonment
and death, what was deemed ugly, now has become beautiful*

SIN BYRON

Love and the crystal pieces were mine, now to my joyous glee 2Q would die.

The irony of it all was that his love would do it; something he vainly fought for would be his undoing. To watch his reaction as scorn plunged her blade into him repeatedly would be excitingly entertaining.

But just as I was expecting the conclusion to this long overdue affair 2Q had disappeared into thin air. When did this loser learn to transmit? I thought to myself, obviously my other half was full of surprises.

But who cares I had won, now I would ascend to levels beyond comprehension, I would reign forever as ruler of this domain with undoubted dominion and absolute power, there would be nothing that could stop me, no where 2Q could hide from me, no where my hands could not reach, soon I would be the sovereign overlord of everything.

CHAPTER 20

2Q

Appearing at the crossroads on my hands and knees, I cried out in despairing anger striking the ground repeatedly.

I had let my love down, what would I do now? I failed, and because of this everything would plunge into eternal darkness.

What made me think I would be cut out for this mission; I should have just gone with the reaper of souls from the beginning. Got damn Sin Byron how could he be so stupid, didn't he realize the demons were using him as a puppet, and once they got what they wanted they would destroy him and our world leaving nothing.

But wait, in his haste he forgot one thing, the flame of hope, what if I could finish the mission love and me started revive the emotions and launch an offensive, maybe together we could recover everything that was taken before it was to late.

But I had no idea were to find the heart. Anyway there was no time and where would I even start?

Sensing something, I picked up my downcast head and looked around, there far away in the distance I could see someone, the energy I discerned seemed slightly different, familiar even, a demons energy signature felt cold and gave off an eerie feeling that sent shivers to the spirit channeling it, this had to be an emotion.

I was not yet fully recovered but I had just enough energy to get there, gathering it together I focused it in that direction then released it, appearing directly in front of a frightened boy. Cringing in pain I rested on one knee with burdensome breathing.

"I'm sorry I didn't mean to run away please don't hurt me!" pleaded the boy putting both of his hands up bracing himself.

"I...I am a friend are you...an emotion?" I asked trying to steady my taxing breath. Looking into his jittery eyes I could tell he was going to run away, if he did there was no way I was going to catch up to him in this strenuous condition.

"No please hear me out," I said showing him the flame of hope.

"Where did you find that?" said the wide-eyed boy staring at the luminescent object with compelling interest.

Explaining everything to him I could see his defensive exterior begin to ease.

"My name is peace, me and love were raised together, and if what you say is true, to help her is to help you, I know where to find the heart, but if it is time we are up against I regret to tell you it is very far."

"That's ok, I have the power to move from one place to the next, if you show me where it is we can get there in an instant," I said standing up. Suddenly a triggering soreness swept over my body like a crashing wave dropping me back down to my bending knee.

"I...used up a lot of energy," I said as my chest heaved, my body's muscles constricting in a pulsating spasm.

"Take a deep breathe," said peace putting both of his hands on each side of my temple.

Closing my eyes I took a deep breathe feeling a calm reassurance, the sensation of floating away in a swaying ocean without a care or worry, a warm breeze in a bright blue hue that made me feel calm and tranquil.

"How do you feel? Can you stand?" asked peace removing his hands.

Getting up I felt refreshed and better then ever.

"Thank you,"

"No problem, your mind was broken and I mended it, just be careful how much energy you expend or it can become undone again," informed peace.

Taking his words into consideration I was ready to start the mission, and this time instead of using highly concentrated bursts of energy I would use it sparingly.

"Focus on where the heart is and I will take it from there," I said grabbing peace by the hand. Using his mind as a guide and my energy as the driving force we disappeared in a flash of light, in an instant we appeared at our destination.

(LONGING)

In this moment I want you now more then I ever wanted anything, there is no more me, I would be delivered to hell if so wish, to suffer eternal torment if I could but savor your timeless kiss, exile from thought, I await on an island of despair with poisonous doubt clinging to my vulnerable exterior, transforming me to a little boy lost in a wilderness calling to be found, seek, find and confound me in your adoring affections, lock me up and make me your slave, a conspirator in your crimes of passion, in this moment of longing I want you now

(PROBLEMS/ SILVER LINING)

You must see a silver lining through every problem, weighing the positive from the negative options, if It did not kill you, your awareness is stronger, your tolerance able to last with it longer, take a good look at the root of the problem, gauge its severity by how quick you can solve it, if the problem is consistently persistent, this will require more patience, try to see the best out of trying situations, keep a level head, do not rush or panic, consider confiding in someone understanding, two thoughtful minds are more sufficient then one, you may find the key to this stubborn dilemma, you may find good underlying the bad, seeing a silver lining to the problem at hand

(THE OTHERSIDE OF LOVE)

The other side of love can be frightening, this shift, this transgressed coldness, clinging, obsessive, needy and possessive, often damaged, for these relations a warning of caution, a scorned heart is as fatal as poison, when dealing with this hellish situation, make your every movement sure, who knows what's to come next, for what was once love, may never be again

(FORGIVE AND HEAL)

To forgive you must first forgive yourself, letting go of the bad feelings being held, in doing so your eyes will open, clearly seeing where the ailment stems from, no longer blinded by hatred, hurt or pain, you can begin to heal again, for time mends wounds, scars and broken hearts, holding on to something for to long creates a monster called resentment, breaking you down like a sickness, the longer it lives, the more you conform to what it is, becoming a burden, a malignant attachment, keeping it alive by breathing in life, to fully heal you must let it die, relinquishing control, forgive and let it go

(WASTE/INVEST)

Waste not, invest a lot, why waste when it can be saved for a different day, invest with purpose and efficiency, for further in time there may be a need, that other wise would not be met

if you did not invest, ignorantly waiting when you should
have been saving, could cost you more then if you were patient,
to invest could lead to success, but to waste can only take away

(THE HEART)

Through its intricate corridors lie many passageways, but
first you must get it to open, once inside tread lightly for its
walls will collapse, volatile its many emotions will leave you
trapped, its fragile strings tugged then snapped, made with
flaws errors and gaps, be careful what you whisper in secret
to the heart, for its sponge like feelings surely will act upon,
beware of its many dangers if wronged, beware of falsely
leading it on, for it will absorb what you have done holding
your actions responsible, the heart can become irrational,
stopping at nothing to come after you, fueled by spiteful
intent by the very emotions placed in it, its every feeling from
end to beginning provokes its motives, its reason for existing,
though loves home resides in the heart, there are other things
living there not so far apart

SIN BYRON

Given access to the seventh level of the mind I was told to wait for an audience with the demon king. I was given a luxurious suite with plenty of insatiable naked beauties to accompany me, desirable women who could not get enough of my sex.

When temptation came to my room naturally she took over with her usual demands, she wanted me to give it to her roughly, pain is the only thing that satisfied her, I always had fun when it came to the perverted sadist temptation.

"Fuck me Sin Byron is that all you got, Make me yours, make me your filthy whore!" screamed temptation in a dog style position.

With her hair wrapped around my hand I single-mindedly rammed, pounding her raw tightness relentlessly. The way she moaned thrashing about like a wild animal in heat excited me.

Climaxing in an uncontrollable explosion I fell on top of her slightly winded, there was no women that could make me feel this way, but then again temptation was a demon.

"I'm proud of you, and now soon you will have what your hard work has sown, you will become what you have always dreamt, you will rise and-"

Interrupting her praise was an announcement through our telepathic network; the hierarchy of demons and the demon king were ready to receive me.

(BAD GIRL)

Come here bad girl, let us revel in our lust from sun down to sun up, let us pursue each others fantasy and deep desires, let our every secret be known only to us, less others plot to ruin our fun, for every bad girl deserves a black rose to grow, and every black rose of Sin Byron's must be pleasure soaked

(INSATIABLE)

A love devoured my next victim awaits, to prove to the next to reform me and stay, it is hopeless to think I could see it this way, your chasing a ghost with promiscuous taste, a list of seduction of my conquered loves, I have embodied a trophy that has to be won, an object of desire yearn to possess me, beautifully ironic, mysterious, uncanny, truth is there is a whole where my heart is to be, till the white rose has chosen I search endlessly, until I find what completes all of me, this insatiable curse draws you to me

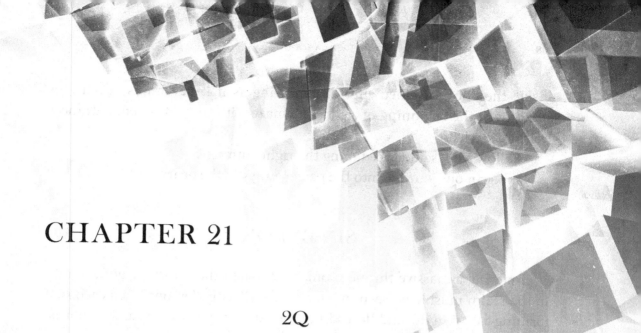

CHAPTER 21

2Q

Appearing in a dessert, I could see a small shack up ahead, but this time I knew better then to make conclusions.

"This place used be teaming with life now it's barren and dry," said peace shaking his head in disappointment.

"What you did for me could you do it to the mind of this dimension?" I inquired, looking around at the affliction of loves home.

"Yes I can bring peace to the mind in general, but for all that the infinite mind is there would need to be a strong enough connection, one that could trigger a reception of everything around and inside the omnipresent mind," Stated peace.

"When we get to the heart what can we expect?" I asked as we near its drab outside.

"Once inside of the heart there is no turning back. Long ago the emotions set certain traps to ward off things that would do it harm, when the unbalance shifted and ultimately changed everything as we know it that one thing remained the same and is very active. You have to remember that the heart is volatile; within yourself try to remain as neutral as possible or your very thoughts could turn against you, We must reach the center with hope and legend has it that the heart will restore in whole," Informed peace.

Reaching the small shack the door creaked as it opened. Once we were inside the door slammed shut disappearing as if it never was, leaving us standing at the beginning of a concrete maze with three different entrances leading into it.

"Follow Me," said peace taking the right entrance.

So began our journey into the passageways of the heart.

SIN BYRON

Entering a massive throne room, I estimated that every demonic entity in the realm must have been in attendance. Ghastly demons lined each side forming a path in the middle leading to a red demon with long arched horns; everything fell silent as I moved forward.

Reaching the end of the pathway I stood in front of an exalted throne constructed of quartz and jade, the one on the throne started clapping creating a thunderous applause that shook the foundation of the mind to its core, raising his hand silence filled the throne room once again.

"Welcome Sin Byron, I am pleased to receive you into my court, you have exceeded beyond expectation, I will grant you anything you wish, but only after you put together the crystal pieces," said the demon king.

Materializing before me was a long table; on it were all the crystal pieces I had accumulated, not remembering this being apart of the arrangement when I dealt with temptation I felt slighted, but something told me it wouldn't be wise to start a debate over specifics.

Looking down on the table, like a puzzle I could see where each piece went, it would not take long to put the crystal mirror back together again.

(FALLEN ANGEL THE DEMON KING)

Knowing the power within and what eternal treasures await, he deceives the masses to willingly give it away, he commands the whole of his army to lay waste to the soul, tempting those who are aware of the weapons he holds, he wages war on the mind in a battle for control, with the power to possess and ultimately consume, he breaks down strongholds betraying any weakness to you, the strongest of his enemies who elude his grasp, he targets those closest to them with a malicious wrath, the light he curses, because the light he knows, a fallen angel before the book of life was wrote, an envious snake to re-write a page, that forever changed the course of history

(INHIBITIONS STRONGHOLD)

The advancement of your limitless possibilities halted, the walls of your mind breached by the stagnant forces of inhibition, what beneficial affirmation barricaded by an internal matrix, whatever aiding reinforcements sorely defected, because somewhere along the way the unaware self let it, the insidious seed of cant planted by doubt, allowing the personal adversary an intimate stronghold of clout

(BARRIER LIMITS)

In a world of calculation and rationality, what others perceive rarely goes outside of the box of their own reality, that repetitive loop of limited comprehension, analytical and hopelessly bias, with no acceptance for anything vague or mysterious, it is written off as a fable or myth, rejection of the free reign of consciousness, deemed foolish, to allow a single thought of the possibility to cross them, you stifle your own dreams with definition, your spiritual growth with inhibition, conforming to others out of fear of not fitting in, because of this, you will always succumb to the barriers of limits

(THE SYSTEM)

A system designed with different branches of control, for people with no place to go, a place for misfits and criminals, a place for the mentally and emotionally unstable, a place for the old and disabled, a place for income that's minimal, etcetera, though well connected the system is, there are flaws that are rotten within its elaborate setting, looking over neglected and forgotten, the system is riddled with many problems, left to the devices of the powers that be, changes are barely made, solutions come slowly, the attention is short-lived unless it concerns the system directly, the system is corrupt, yet finances are paid, the people unable to set themselves free, relying on the systems support for there needs, this is the way the system sustains, to continue to run its programs in whole, a system designed with different branches for control

(POWER AND POLITICS)

The base of power resides in its politics, not everyone has an ear for it, for it is delicate as well as intricate, power boasting in its confidence, arrogance and dominance is only half of what it is, behind the scenes are the politics that run it, forming the elevated platform in adornment, adjoining the two as if by the hip, when one goes the other following, a close partnership seen by all, but to the few involved politics are a dictatorship with power placed as it sees fit, the elite making the decisions, picking a face to speak in there place, the questions and concerns falling back on them, giving the viewer the illusion that it is the face moving the movement, the appearance goes deeper then what is perceived, when it comes to power and politics, nothing is as it seems

CHAPTER 22

2Q

As me and peace walked the labyrinth of twist and turns I kept my mind clear of anything that could potentially become our worst nightmare. Everything was fine up until I saw love standing in a different place then where we were headed.

"Love!" I screamed, running towards her.

Could it be, how did she get free? I thought to myself focusing on her face.

"No she is not real!" yelled peace pursuing after me.

My thoughts became more turbulent when I reached her illusion realizing my heart had played a trick on me, suddenly the ground began to quake.

"What have you done, you triggered a heart ache run!"

Following peace, we moved quickly trying our best not to get knocked off of our feet from the shaking instability.

Then things went from bad to worse as the walls of the labyrinth started closing, peace had little feet he could only move at a certain speed, sweeping him up into my arms I continued running, my long strides covering more ground quickly.

"Take a left, no not that left the next, now a right, keep going until you reach a clearing," directed peace.

Getting to an open area with no walls, I could see up ahead that there was more to this complex labyrinth and the walls were steady closing.

"Hurry, the center is up ahead we have to make it!" shouted peace.

We were almost there until five clones of love suddenly shot out of the ground in front of us, blocking our way not to far from where we needed to be. Lowering peace I gave him the flame of hope.

"If I don't make it revive the emotions and save your home."

Willing my blade of light I distracted the distorted versions of love towards me so peace could get away.

"They are only there because you think they are, clear your mind, the more you fight the more you give these images life, let her go!" shouted peace.

"You used me, you never loved me, you gave me away to the enemy, how could you do this to me," each of the clones said in unison, each holding a lethal dagger.

"I feel guilty and hurt because I let you down, I cant live knowing you are not here with me now, knowing I could not protect you like I promised, but if I die, at least I did everything I could to see things made right again, I'm truly sorry love."

Un-willing my blade of light I dropped the gold hilt on the ground, making up my mind I would not fight, this was the end of the road.

"I'm sorry love I have to let you go," I said sadly.

The clones were now inches from me, they're cold blank eyes were locked into a stare, there daggers raised into the air.

Seconds before my demise to my surprise the clones of love immediately vanished, with the labyrinth walls no longer closing I felt as if a great burden was lifted, like finally being able to breathe fresh air after being submerged in an ocean of despair.

Still with me, the emotion peace walked over with a smile.

"Why didn't you leave? You could have blown the whole mission, ruining our only chance to save the heart, why would you stay?"

I asked peace, upset at him for not listening.

"Because I could not just leave, there is something about you that makes me believe, I had faith that despite the odds you would come through. Previously when I touched you to heal your mind I could feel this incredible presence inside of you, something special, it was then I knew you was telling the truth and that you were the creator of my world, everything you need is inside of you, if only you truly believe then anything is possible, so there can be no doubt that we will succeed," said peace confidently.

"Thank you for believing in me peace, now let us finish the mission and see if the legend holds any merit," I said with a renewed determination of vigor.

Making it to the center, the flame of hope burned brighter then I had ever seen, suddenly its cylinder case broke open, all around us the foundation began to pulsate, swaying and rocking, moving to a synchronized rhythm, in awe I watched as everything lit up becoming engulfed in a bright light.

In an instant we were traversing the universe soaring upwards into the heavens beyond, in a rocket like propulsion light seemed to fly by us at a frightening velocity, the center of the heart had transformed into a shooting star.

Though our feet were firmly planted we seemed to be in its core, but were where we headed? Just as that thought crossed my mind in a startling explosion our star ignited, bursting into spectacular hues.

Materializing before my astonished eyes the new life of my revived heart began to take form, what was once worn and drab had become a glorious palace, the interior of the palace walls and floors were translucent like crystal, around the outer perimeter was a vibrant garden full of blooming roses of every color, trees and other wonderful things I could not name, the palace grounds stretched as far as my eyes could see and in between this astounding beauty flowed a never ending river.

The whole of this amazing paradise stood in the middle of a starry universe that illuminated with endless light, because it itself was the brightest of all stars.

Suddenly where we stood began to take form.

To my amazement we were standing in a gigantic dining hall under an impressive chandelier made of crystal.

Appearing simultaneously were an innumerable amount of materialized emotions, men, women and children confused at how they all had gotten there, unaware they were brought back from the dead, all of them clamorous.

Raising my blade into the air I emitted a blinding flash of light that got everyone's attention, finding myself in the middle of confused emotions I willed my voice as a microphone becoming loud and leaving a lingering echo.

"My name is 2Q and this may be a hard pill to swallow but all of you were dead and I have revived you, the legend is true, there is a crystal mirror and the flame of hope has saved your home, but this victory will be short-lived because of malicious demons and my consumed other half Sin Byron-"

The mere mention of his name caused a boisterous uproar.

"Please listen to me," I pleaded,

But there continuous noise drowned out my amplified voice.

"Why should we listen to you?"

"He is the very spawn of evil!"

"He wants to trick us!"

They did not trust me, but there was no time for their bumbling, in another flash of light I released some of my energy sending out a vibration that could be felt by every emotion, this caused silence.

"I am not evil! And unless we do something soon the demons will reconstruct the crystal mirror darkening our world forever, there is something else…they have someone we both know and care for, they have love."

The troubled emotions started whispering amongst themselves.

"And what do you want from us," said an old man speaking up.

"I want you to join together and help me fight the demons," I replied.

"That is preposterous!" barked the incredulous old man.

"Yea! If we were dead already what makes you think we can stop them," said a doubtful young woman.

"Maybe alone we can't, but together we can accomplish anything. Each and everyone of you have a special ability, to heal, to feel, to bring peace, long ago love left by herself despite your protection, despite the odds stacked unevenly against her, believing she could make a difference, believing she could heal a heart that was damaged. Now that it is all accomplished all would be in vain if we do nothing!"

I could feel the tide turning; everyone's eyes were focused on me, each burning with intensity.

"So who among you will have the courage to stand and fight for what is right, who among you will say no to being consumed, possessed and controlled, who will see to it that love is brought safely back home and her evil captors brought swiftly to justice, when this day is written in our history whose names will shine in glory, in honor of our harmony, who is with me!" I cried out raising my blade of light high into the air.

Bonded together all the emotions cheered and chanted words of instilled encouragement, ready or not Sin Byron I declare war.

(TWIST AND TURN)

One twist is a piece to the lock, what is and what's not lies only in your thought, a riddle wrapped in mystery, what you see is layers of perplexity, a turn of an anomaly, a labyrinth of intricate deception placed to confuse the obvious direction, I am of no help in your endeavor to decipher this, for I am apart of the twist, the turn is when you figure out you reached a dead end, and so you turn to start over again

(PHASES/MATURITY)

There are phases that one goes threw to reach maturity, though temporary, the road may be bumpy, seemingly endless, unpleasant, alarming, distressing, pretentious, phases are mazes that must be traveled, with many different beginnings there is no telling where this will end, what path will be chosen, maturity is the finalization of the phases, the end game of the process of elimination, the minds behavior no longer pacing, has found maturity in its phases

(ORIGINAL/COPY)

Be original, why copy, originality is a one of a kind masterpiece, true to its quality, it itself can never be duplicated, if it is, it will never be the same again as when it first originated, it will set a trend for those behind it to follow in its steps, it will lead where those only will follow, its originality will forever be immortalized in the future of tomorrow

(RISK AND SACRIFICE)

Where there is gain there must be risk and sacrifices, dangers that lurk in the darkness, for the average person sees the finish, but they will never know the beginning, the risk it took to get this, the things unspoken, the places visited, what was sacrificed giving life to an image, the blood sweat and tears paid for a vision, the only way was to take risks, to assure things stayed the way it is, to keep it the way its been, take sacrifices, all bases needed to be covered with no objections, everything has a story behind it, filled with risk and sacrifices

(PURE EMOTIONS)

I have met all emotions in there stark naked purity, hidden deep inside the mysterious world of me, the greatest and most sought after love, cherished, linked, bonded to each and everyone, through trial and error I have come to truly understand them, through a glorified gift deeper then one can fathom, like you, their different feelings are unique and special, but costly, potentially problematic and volatile, their mixed signals can bring bitter confusion, but through precious focus you can learn to channel them, knowing the full effect of each, gaining peace and solace, reverberating harmony shared through pure emotion

(LOVES CELESTIAL PALACE)

For the harem of hearts intimate, open your eyes and sees loves palace, in this it houses all of loves celestial tenants, a crystalized structure surrounding in spiritual protection, no inhibition, nor fear, nor darkness can enter there, here peace reigns uncontested, sovereign, absolute, abounding with strength, glory, power and truth, receiving the freedom lights of luminous clarity, a heavenly paradise, a haven of beauty

(CHANNELING EMOTIONS)

Brazen emotions in synchronized movement, coming together possessed in unison, to channel their purpose on the object of choosing, enthralled by a melodic hypnotic music, swayed by seduction, their connection bonding, one will they perpetuate, to the mood they gravitate, all in a single moment their feelings released, on an intimate source, flooded with energy

(HEART ACHE)

My shallow heartbeat racks my being with a wrenching ache, my spiritual need constricts my deprived soul with shuddering pain, where are you my love? Why must I feel empty and drained? Why do the solemn walls close in on this place I thought you would be cherished and safe? Can you not see you're afflicted home in this sorry state? Can you not feel our intimate connection endangered in the very same way? Or is it that I am the only hope in this broken world I ignorantly created, how can I move past such a volatile frustration, if love is not here to keep my weary heart from an emotionless damnation?

(REINCARNATED LOVE)

I am back as your love, reincarnated from a casket of dust, the darkness of death, the echoes of distress, the aches and pains of long lost days, but like the sun I have risen, reborn, a new resurrection, connected to the very emotions that attaches to the heart of every women, everyone in its pureness I have truly met, but I had to let go, to become reincarnated

(PARADISE)

My heart replenished, its inhabitants restored, the light now pierces the inhibiting dark, now a flowing river, but before the dawn, its dried up ground left crumbling walls, now its rose filled gardens are full of life, a glorious beauty, a victorious sight, but it took for this, to see the gift, a celestial palace coming forth in its strength, I am forever thankful for the love that it gives, emitting so bright, heavenly paradise

(TRIAL AND ERROR)

Through trial and error I came to find out who I am, through constant failure, different endeavors, from boy to a man, life ever-changing, nothing certain, how could my lot in life be cast, id rather die, then not to try, I think therefor I can, the dial on now, if I falter, pick myself back up, I sworn an oath, to never go, back the way I've come, but now I've learned, that twist and turns, in this life exist, to forge a will, stronger then, steal that cant be bent

(LOVES REVOLUTION)

Fight for love never let it die, if it acquires such kill for the right, who will dare say its wrong, chant, shout, sing loves song, stand up boldly, profess her name, side by side invoke a blaze, burn down the barrier, shine your light, open up, never downplay your cause, declare your statement to one and all

(AT HEART'S CAPACITY)

At hearts capacity, clamorous emotions rise to the edge of tolerance, different constricting feelings, pushing, fighting, clashing, clawing there way to the surface, at first nothing seems to console them, the pained reasons, the various whys of obscurity hidden, even the mind and soul seemed afflicted by division, and then you relent, dealing with each firmly, yet not being overwhelmed by a sense of conformity, being the steady rock in a flowing tide, brings the inner confidence deep inside, the limitless strength to move the barrier of inhibition, freeing what was at first a burden of tension

(LOVES HOME)

How long I have waited for you my love, now I can say with absolute pride and certainty you will forever be mine, in greedy anticipation I have prepared the way by putting her treasures aside, building a wonderful paradise of heightened delight, now behold loves luminous glow that enchants the essence of my rose, in honor of her eternal beauty I have adorned my diamond throne with personalized stones, each resilient pedestal more captivating then the next, yet equally impressive in its dazzling perfection, this hidden world is hers to roam, my love be free in your glorious home

SIN BYRON

Working diligently, the crystal mirror stood partially reconstructed. Everything was almost complete, now all I had to fit was one last piece. But before I could fit it in its vacant spot a trumpet sounded, in a feverish incited haste demons began lining up in a defensive formation.

"Finish it now Sin Byron!" shouted the demon king impatiently.

I grew tired of his overbearing importance and hated the way he lorded his authority over me, now I would purposely wait, what was the big rush anyway I was curious to know why demons with such high positions seemed shaken up. Suddenly thousands of angry emotions swarmed the throne room with 2Q leading the charge.

Oh the audacity of my tenacious other half, this unsuspecting revolution would be interesting. Both sides stared each other down, the air thick with suspended tension.

"You have some nerve barging in here uninvited," I said with a cocky grin.

"Sin Byron don't do this they are using you, they don't plan on sharing anything, they want to wipe us out from existence."

"Oh please do you think I care what they want, it's about me, one hand washes the other, as long as I get what I want they could destroy the rest of this dump"

"I cant allow you to piece together that mirror, if you do and the demons take control you will kill everything inside, destroying both me and you."

"Cry me a river loser, there is nothing that will stop me from being Ruler of my own domain, and now the time has come for me to reign," I said picking up the final piece.

(TENSION)

Vibrating in the air tension can be felt, as if the very air constricts itself, as if it could already tell, holding its breath waiting for what's next, knowing something's coming bracing for impact, a sense of unease wafting in the breeze, a contagious energy felt individually, yet all the same collectively, all feeling its extended reach, burning like ignited wood, its smoke alerting by its ascension, spreading the contagious fumes of tension

CHAPTER 23

2Q

I couldn't believe who sat on the throne; did Sin Byron know whom he was making a deal with? I thought to myself incredulously.

Standing on the far left I could see love glaring at me with disgust, I was confident that if there was anything that could get through to her it was the emotions.

We were up against menacing and evil demons; the very sight of them could turn the stomach of the squeamish.

The crystal mirror was now standing up on its own, in its middle a single space was empty, when Sin Byron picked up the last piece I directed my energy at him.

Disappearing in a flash I tackled him to the ground, the remaining crystal piece flying out of his open hand.

War instantaneously broke out, the emotions and demons clashing with colliding impact, limbs were ripped apart, heads were bashed, the emotions conjured weapons and used there special gifts to turn demons against themselves, to confuse and misdirect, while the demons shape-shifted using there fangs, razor sharp teeth, claws and sheer brute force.

Sin Byron and me went blade for blade, the power of the heavenly light versus the power of the demented darkness.

"You can't win!" snarled Sin Byron swinging.

Ducking his oncoming blade it sailed over my head missing its mark, swinging back sparks flew as our clanging blades clashed.

"We can end this, we can stop the madness!" I said grunting, tussling against his ample strength.

"Never!" cried an enraged Sin Byron putting out his right hand hitting me with a charge of energy, the blasting force tossing me into an aerial summersault.

Hitting the ground hard my head spun from the momentums dizziness.

Following up, he jumped into the air coming down forcefully with his blade focused on my lower body. Rolling over with quick reflexes his blade pierced the ground close to me.

Hitting Sin Byron with a charge of my own, I emitted a powerful wave of released energy blasting him away from his blade, his body flipping backwards uncontrollably.

Breathing heavily I could feel my energy drop substantially, what mending peace did for my broken mind was coming undone, I didn't know if the power I had left would be enough to stop him. I would have to figure something out soon, because here came a roaring Sin Byron locked in a delusional state of unhinged madness.

SIN BYRON

Flipping backwards I hit the ground with a head-banging crack, its result ringing my ears and temporarily blurring my vision.

Not to far from the throne I could see the demon king was gone.

Fucking coward, he would rather others do the dirty work for him then do it himself, no other demon would be able to assemble the crystal mirror unless it was 2Q or me, but forgot that for now, this fight had become personal.

With an output of power like the one 2Q let go I knew it was too much strain on his mental. His energy was low where as mine had infinite potential.

Once I had fully embraced my full demonic being the limiting effect the broken crystal mirror presented no longer affected me. Raising my hand, the dark blade pulled itself from the ground and returned to me.

With a cry I ran directly at 2Q, I would show him once and for all who was fit to rule and who would be better off serving on there knees.

Swinging, our blades clashed repeatedly.

Judging by his exerting expression, I could see the taxing energy he expended to keep deflecting my blows, he was weakening, and soon I would defeat him.

Finding the opportunity, I cranked up my energy output; with a power filled swing I knocked his blade away, pointing the point of my blade in his face.

"On your fucking knees!"

"I would rather die on my feet," 2Q spat back defiantly.

Using the hilt of my dark sword I struck him across the face knocking him down.

Standing back up he spit his blood at me rebelliously.

Flying into a fit of rage I struck him across the face repeatedly, yet he tried standing after each jaw rattling blow taking the punishment of my pummeling, in those moments I respected him more then I ever did, but it was time for 2Q to meet his end, grabbing 2Q, I pulled his head back exposing his throat.

"Don't worry it will all be over soon," I said preparing to take his head with satisfaction.

But before I could finish him the ground began shaking, the front structure of the throne room exploding in a cloud of debris, and there stood the bloodthirsty demon beast revenge.

"Curse these turn of events!"

I knew without a shadow of a doubt what this monstrosity wanted, and it would not stop until it claimed it.

CHAPTER 24

2Q

I was at Sin Byron's mercy, but I would rather die standing then cower to his satisfaction. My face was completely swollen and both of my eyes were on the verge of closing, the little energy I had left I couldn't swat a fly with, but I had my mind set on deliverance and I believed that despite my position I would be ok, then something miraculous happened.

Joining the fight was the same sphinx like monster that allowed love and me to escape into the soul, it was back, and it didn't look happy.

The deer in headlights look on Sin Byron's face was comical, I could see he was worried, before he must have narrowly escaped it but now it was back to claim him, the focus was officially off of me.

The giant beast plowed through the demon combatants knocking bodies into the air as it charged at my shocked other half.

Away from the battle, I spotted peace standing next to love and two tough looking emotions that were guarding them.

Just as I thought, the emotions had changed love back I thought to myself thankfully.

Locating the last crystal piece I picked it up off the floor then limped over; when love saw me she broke down crying.

"2Q I am so sorry, I didn't…I wasn't myself"

"Its ok love, if it's about the past it is already behind me, right now I need both of your help, can you heal me?"

Nodding their heads both peace and love stood over me with outstretched arms, their hands illumined.

Seeing what was going on, three demons rushed over trying to intercept my regeneration. Springing into action the guarding emotions started fighting them off but one slipped through their defense, by then it was to late, I was fully healed and my willed blade of light taking its head off before it could take another step.

The guarding emotions managed to kill the other two demons by tricking them into killing themselves; everyone was safe for the moment.

"Get love far away from here as possible," I told the two hulking emotions, "Peace come with me I have a plan, I am going to make the crystal mirror whole again."

SIN BYRON

Charging at me with an ear-splitting roar, the reckless beast flung whatever in its path.

Damn this mindless Monster! If it thought it could easily take my life it was sadly mistaken. The difference from the last time I had encountered this abomination was that this time I had transcended.

With full control of my demonic power I would slaughter this rampaging leviathan.

Before it could get near me I transmitted above its head sinking my dark blade deep into its skull.

Bellowing angrily the beast swung its head from side to side while I frantically held on to the hilt of my stuck blade, being tossed about like a rag doll. Still holding on as it thrashed about, the beast bucked abruptly propelling me forward.

Using my energy to help stabilize my landing I glided towards the ground smoothly, but before my feet could touch the ground the beast charged butting me with its massive head sending me tumbling.

Ending up on my hands and knees I wheezed, the torpedoing like impact knocking the wind from my body.

With no time to catch my heaving breath or steady my disoriented composure I was charged at again.

It would have swallowed me whole had I not swiftly used my energy to keep it a bay, forming a shield suspending it in place.

But it was recklessly pushing against the power base, its tons of weight straining my energy, any second the barrier would collapse and the backlash would be devastating.

CHAPTER 25

2Q

"I don't know what effect completing the crystal mirror will cause, but in theory maybe we can use the crystal mirror as a gigantic receptor, a sort of lightning rod creating a powerful enough connection that will reach all of the mind, if demons can consume in a sense we should be able to, if we can bring your gift to the mind maybe the crystal mirror will reciprocate like wise," I said breaking my plan down.

"Yea in theory, but what if you are wrong and the crystal mirror releases what the demons have been hoping for, then we would have been the cause for our own downfall," replied peace.

"I understand the repercussions of what your implying, there is a possible downside to this plan but we have to try something, more emotions then demons are being killed and at this rate there wont be an army left to defend, drastic times call for drastic decisions, are you ready to do what needs to be done?" I asked peace sternly.

"Yes," said peace nodding his head with a look of anxiety.

Taking a deep breath I put in the final crystal piece expecting something to happen immediately, but nothing did.

Shrugging my shoulders, peace and me looked at each other in confusion.

But then under my feet I noticed a small fissure slowly traveling like a skillful doctors incision splitting the floor down its middle, and then suddenly a dark hole opened up inside of the mirror, starting off small then growing bigger, creating a powerful vacuum sucking everything into its center.

Quickly judging the grave situation I made a snap decision, in an attempt to save all the emotions I used my power as a magnet attaching all of their energies to me, keeping them steady.

The roof of the throne room caved in, demons were being dragged to there oblivion, my hold was straining and my fragile mind wrenched and tugged in two different directions threatening to rip me asunder, there was no way I could keep this up much longer.

"Peace!" I screamed,

Both of his hands were placed on the side of the mirror, the whites of his eyes were showing and his body convulsing and glowing bright blue, his ability was being drained and there was nothing I could do.

(UNDOUBTED BREAKTHROUGH)

Through positive influences, I have overcome negative resistance, through the binding power of pure love, I have broken through the stagnant forces of hidden barriers, through belief and undoubted faith, I have discovered the crystal element in the midst of the rough in a hard place, through the portal of my eternal soul, I have opened my eyes to depths and wonders unknown, through the multi-dimensions of me, I behold levels and heavens of never ending beauty

(INTERCHANGING CORE PERCEPTION)

Interchanging your core perception, channeling its forming matter through precious focus, envelops individual reality with alternate energy, moving the universe at the command of your will, the bonding control of the likeness of a steering wheel, directed by a better view seen by you, out with old, exchanged *with the new, turning potential into pure substance, putting what's negative into things more positive*

SIN BYRON

Crying out from the strain, I could not hold on to this accursed beast any longer.

I would be ripped apart and left to die on this cold floor; after all I fought for it would all amount to nothing. And to think I was this close to receiving what I Sin Byron so rightly deserved.

Closing my eyes I let go, but before the beast could take a bite out of me I was yanked away and flung into the air.

Transmitting myself to safety, I was shocked at the realization that 2Q had assembled the crystal mirror; everything was being dragged into its center.

When the ceiling caved in I looked up amazed to see the outside scene erratically changing, even it was being pulled by the mirrors powerful suction, everything was being erased leaving in its place nothing but darkness, what good could possibly come from this? Was my other half telling the truth? Could it be I had indeed been tricked, used with the hell bent intent of advancing their insidious purpose? Fed false promises only in the end to be destroyed by my own ignorance? If I was to be ruler where would I reign, then and there reality hit me harder then any beast could, I remembered everything.

Flying by me snarling was the monster revenge being pulled into the mirror with my dark blade still lodged into its head, along with the majority of the demons who failed in there desperate attempts at finding anything to hold on to.

Looking towards my other half I could feel his energy was failing, he was using up all of his power protecting the emotions, he would not last long if he kept on going like this.

CHAPTER 26

2Q

"Hold on!" I screamed out to the frightened emotions.

Hand in hand they held on to each other forming a wavering line that threatened to be disconnected by the crystal mirrors tempestuous vortex. My power was failing, if only I could hold on just a little longer, I could not let them down, I would give my all until nothing was left of me.

Crying out loud I fell to my knees still holding onto the lines energy.

Closing my eyes I prayed a prayer of deliverance, if there was any doubt in my faith I asked it to be taken for me, growing disoriented and dizzy I was seconds away from losing everything until suddenly my strenuous burden lightened.

Sensing a familiar presence, I looked over and was surprised to see Sin Byron helping me to hold the emotions steady, his power combined with mine made me stronger and able to last the duration.

Suddenly in an explosion of gleaming light the negative polarity of the mirror changed, instead of things being sucked in, waves of positive energy shot out reversing all of the damage done, there were no longer any malevolent entity's threatening our existence, the balance had been restored, we had won the war.

Running over to peace I looked down on his pale lifeless body, his eyes were open, staring blankly as if seeing something I couldn't lying beyond in the distance, the crystal mirror had drained him until nothing was left, peace was dead.

Kneeling next to his body I bowed my head in condolence.

"We won, thanks to you everything is as it should be, because of your sacrifice the mind will forever have solace, rest in peace my friend," I said closing his eyes, and my last words of good-bye.

Hearing a loud commotion behind me I quickly got to my feet turning around alertly to see that the emotions had surrounded Sin Byron, they were in a mobbing frenzy ready to attack him. Focusing my energy into the middle of the crowd I appeared next to my other half raising my hands in objection.

"Wait! I would not have been able to hold on to all of you if it wasn't for him, he helped me save you," I pleaded to the angry emotions.

With my vindicating words of justification falling on deaf ears the boisterous emotions continued cursing and shouting.

"You would have us forgive him after everything he has done!"

"We should kill him!"

"Lets chop then burn him up like he did us!"

"He cant be trusted he is a demon!"

The voices of the troubled emotions crashed over each other like the turbulent waves of a raging sea.

"There right, no matter what darkness will always be apart of me, its ties run deep within my poisoned blood. It took the crystal mirror being put back together for me to see I had changed into the very thing I hated, I now realize the terrible mistake of falling for temptation, of allowing myself to be consumed by demons, though I cannot deny the addicting feeling of doing whatever I wanted, it was really the not having to deal with the constant reminder of a human side that was to irresistible to pass up, I'm sorry for that, but being so, that wont change the fact that I have already been compromised, for us to become one again would only jeopardize the purpose of our union." Said Sin Byron regretfully.

"You still don't get it do you, we must be one! Neither you nor I would be complete without the other; the question should be how do we move on from this? And how to prevent anything like this from happening again?" I said standing face to face with my dark reflection.

For the first time since I became aware of his presence I never thought I would see him show a vulnerable side of himself to me, maybe Sin Byron wasn't so bad after all, just misunderstood. Suddenly appearing in a flash of light the beautiful six winged angel Gabrielle stood dazzling in his brilliant countenance, us along with the crowd of emotions gasped simultaneously startled by the sudden intrusion, not a sound could be heard as the angels eyes roamed the whole of the crowd resting on me and Sin Byron.

"From the very beginning the most high has watched over you, 2Q you are commended for your bravery, it is your actions that have saved you, you have been reborn, receive your second chance at life again with gratitude and thanksgiving, your faith has made you well," said the angel Gabrielle before focusing on Sin Byron.

"You lost your way, but in the end realized your mistakes, sure it is true that you can't go back and erase what you've done, but that does not mean you cannot co-exist peacefully. Once the both of you take my hand you will become one again, the lord of the kingdom will command his angels to keep close watch on the crystal mirrors balance, he will help protect the portal, no darkness may cross the veil, nor burdens of any kind, you must understand that this is a joint effort, because you have free will you two must see to it that this union remain pure, now come be restored once more," said Gabrielle holding out both hands.

"Give me a second," I said searching the crowd of faces.

Spotting love, I could see her appearance had transformed miraculously.

There she stood in the midst of fawning admirers clothed in a spectrum of radiant rays, adorned as if by the sun itself, a diamond tiara placed atop her head sparkling in the glow of her essence, my love had transcended, and now she would take her rightful place on her pedestal as queen in the palace of her heart.

Walking towards love the crowd of emotions parted.

Trying not to breakdown into a bundle of nerves I looked into those pink eyes that enthralled me at first sight. After all this time of feeling empty I knew she completed me, love made me a better person. I knew I had to let her go, but could I live without the one thing that finally made sense to me, the one thing that made me whole, I needed love how could I leave her, she was my fresh air, my passion, my reason for existing, nothing could fill her place, not in a million lifetimes I thought to myself, distraught at what would be our last moment together.

"You were never any good at hiding your emotion, what's wrong?" asked love with a concern that made my heart ache.

Fighting against my trembling composure I took both of her delicate hands into mine.

"Words cannot express what I feel when I am with you, I want you to know I cherished every moment we spent together and because of you I know what real love is, after all this I finally understand that it is love that was missing in my life, now here you are transcended in your glorious beauty, a goddess of my heart, if I could I would spend the rest of my life by your side, but deep down I feel this may never be and it hurts me more then words can ever explain, am I wrong, if so tell me now and I will stay with you forever," I said hopeful, prepared to drop everything, ready to leave everyone behind is she said the word.

"I love you 2Q, but to exist beyond the veil of this dimension means neglecting your own, we will always be one because I am your love, none of this would be here if it weren't for you, it may sound unbelievable, but in time you will understand that you are the source, you always were."

"Will I ever see you again?" I asked meekly.

"You will not see me as I am now, but you will feel when I'm near, you will know its me through my words, by the way that someone kisses and touches you, I will not be easy to find, you may search for a longtime, but when you find me, you will know I'm the one," said love.

Raptured by each others gaze of longing we became lost in the moment, our intimate connection pulling us into an embrace, the sheer touch igniting a consuming desire enthralling our eager lips locked in a sensuous rhythm.

The core of my being was enveloped in the hungry flames of passion fire, nothing existed, nothing mattered but the love of my life, the haunting beauty of my frustrating dreams, everything that she was to me surrendered in that moment of magic, our spiritual union a supernova of vibrating energy streaming in brilliant auroras, rays of sparkling light dancing in wavering patterns.

Though my eyes were closed, I could see the starry heavens, and they're in the midst was loves palace shining in all its glory, its prominent presence enveloping the entire universe, seemingly centering it.

Then something love said came back to me and I finally began to understand, that all I was seeing and every place we had been was apart of my infinite perception. But still the depths that were me remained a mystery, my soul, heart and mind were all apart of loves universe, but the depths and multi-dimensions of myself were a little hard to grasp, there was obviously more to me then I had known.

As my mind wondered, suddenly love de-materialized from my embrace ascending towards the heavens in a spectrum of light, opening my eyes love and the emotions were gone.

"Oh that was so nice," said Sin Byron with a hint of sarcasm in his tone, "But this nice looking angel has been waiting patiently for your ten minute kiss to be over."

"Yea you would be one to talk, I do remember your lustful mind and vulnerable memories but that's another story," I retorted freshly.

"Ok I do have a thing for women, and wont deny it either lover boy," said Sin Byron nonchalantly.

"I always wanted to ask you something…where did you come from?" I asked Sin Byron, still baffled at how my dark half came to be.

"I am as mystified about my origin as you are about this entire ordeal, maybe it is like your love said all will be revealed in time, I don't know, all I know is I'm ready to go home, what about you?"

"Yea I could use a sense of normalcy in my life," I replied reaching to take the angels hand.

"Oh wait before I forget…I'll be watching," said Sin Byron with a grin.

"Oh yea…well me to," I said grinning back.

Taking the angels hand, my eyes flew open to the hot sun beaming its bright rays onto my face. Squinting my eyes, I turned my head to see a crowd of people standing around me with shocked and forlorn expressions.

Then the realization that I was laying in the middle of the street dawned on me, I was back in the physical world or did I even leave? With the past events still fresh on my mind I had to wonder if I had dreamt it all.

"Hey mister are you ok?"

Raising my arm to block the harsh glare of the sun I saw a familiar face that banished all doubt, the young man resembled the emotion peace.

Getting up excitedly, I embraced the bewildered youth before parting the gawking crowd with pep in my step and a renewed purpose.

Ever since then, I 2Q have searched for love, using the purity of the white rose encased in my soul as means to finding the incarnate love of my reality, I would search even if it took an eternity, every night I talk to Sin Byron through the newly restored crystal mirror, he is no longer angry or controlling we have truly become one, the future looks bright with a new beginning.

(SELF AMENDS)

To move forward, I had to step back, to re-establish who I had become, to reinforce the basses of what made me who I am, taking a long look at myself and how far I had come, there was no going back, the damage had been done, the change within self evident, nothings to be the same again, coming face to face with the honest conclusion, that I am better off then when the nightmare first began, to move forward would take self amends, to embrace me with complete acceptance, welcoming with an open heart full of appreciation and forgiveness

(LOVE BE FREE)

Be free my love, for once you were afflicted with burden, chastised with the flogging whip of uncertainty, constricted by the chains of forced conformity, lose these hindrances, be brazen and adventurous, spit upon the face of your captives, explore your repressed desires with no regrets, going beyond the imposed limits of bondage, understand that you create your own resistance, and the power to dissolve this stressful barrier is well within your bottled up wishes, shed this complacent flesh of inhibition, that slavishly allowed such bothersome restriction

(DON'T LET GO)

We can save each other don't let go, for you have always been apart of my soul, our beauty is a sight to behold, you must not give up, it wont be long, at your wits end know our victory is near, maybe at the cost of pain and tears, the thought of losing you I cannot bear, draw nigh to me do not despair, for one we are, my strength is yours, together what can we not endure, through this we will be ready for what's next to unfold, we must not give up, don't let go

(LOSS)

Though you have loss, you have also found, once you could not see that love abound, for a time darkness covered your face, until you discovered power through faith, now the light can be your guide, take heart the raging sea has tide, to bear treasures from your heart, soul and mind, together illuminating throughout your life's

(FORGIVEN)

Though forgiven I cannot forget, the hell unleashed, the ways of death, the blinded eyes, the path once tread, the resonating despair that's left, The sacrifices made, the darkest days, the revisiting past, the secrets haunting me, the internal fight, the things I've done, yet all that was, has been forgiven

(PEACE OF MIND)

Sound peace, oh the waves of serenity flooding through me, the sacrifice to attain it well worth it, the foundation it was founded a previous burden, but no more war, no more rearing sides of clamor, the road has been paved, the once blocked sun now shining, the clouds of worry now clear, let new beauty come forth, resonating its intoxicating scent of debonair

(QUEEN LOVE CRYSTAL LIGHT SPIRITS)

Queen of the crystal palace, her throne the center of my soul, the starry light of her sparkling treasure, my universe shining forever, I adore the heart of your wonder, my love we are one together, a spectacular vision of multi-dimensions, the beautiful combination of a kindred spirit

(TEAM WORK)

You can do more as a team then if you were alone, working together to reach your goals, to accomplish similar objectives in more ways then one, all moving in one direction, with collective minds, you will find solutions to problems not yet devised, each with individual talents placed within a special alignment, moving swiftly with a coordination of efficiency, gets the job done effectively, the mission being accomplished rises in probability, if one falls, the other helps to pick back up, together there is strength in numbers

(APPRECIATION)

I appreciate your love and care, for you still being there when I had to depart into the shadows losing myself in the dark, no matter how far I drifted, your light shined bright like a star in a sky limitless, when I turned cold and distant, you showed patience and persistence, clothing me with warmth, your heat consistent, your voice driven urging me to listen, your life you would have easily traded for mine in an instant, in a different position, I don't know if the person I am would of did this, and it hurts because my heart is dented, I cant see what it is you see in me, but all you ever did was believe in me, even if I die battling these demons I'm facing, just know you have my deepest appreciation

(I'M SORRY)

I'm sorry for everyone I ever hurt, I'm sorry for the times I should have been strong but instead weak, I'm sorry for my actions and everything they caused to happen, I'm sorry for being selfish only thinking about myself, I'm sorry that I wasn't there for you when you needed help, I'm sorry I couldn't see my worth, I'm sorry it took me all this time to learn, I'm sorry if you do not except my words, I'm sorry if this apology is not enough, I'm sorry if me you thought highly of, I'm sorry if I let you down, I'm sorry that I wasn't sorry then and that I'm more sorry now

(GOOD TIMES/BAD TIMES)

Remember all the good times, the places visited, the laughs and experiences, the times shared without responsibility or care, the times everyone you loved was there, never take for granted these times you have, you must also remember the bad, the times you did not have, the times you were angry or sad, the times you lost someone you loved, the times you wanted to give up, for though these times are bad, it is through these difficult times you realize the good you have, to know not to ever take things for granted, to savor and cherish every moment, to live life to the fullest like your running out of time, to view the good and bad threw a silver lining

(PAST, PRESENT, FUTURE)

The past is the past, nothing can be added or taking back, you must not dwell in it, all you can do is learn from it, not repeating the same mistakes previously made, now this will help you today in the present where you have the power to change, it is not what you did, its about what you do here and now that effects your tomorrows victories or doubts, the decisions made now is what counts, leading hand in hand towards the future, here your present has become the past, make use of the present, because nothing can be added or taking back

(EXCITING)

Life is exciting, the possibilities endless, a rush, a high, a roller coaster unending, an adventure, a journey, a walk in the dark, a first kiss that ignites a luminous spark, a blazing fire, a constellation of stars, a trip to an exotic location afar, the feeling of getting to know someone new, a breath of fresh air a love can produce, not seeing someone that's been away for a while, a brush with death on adrenalines cloud, a runaway heartbeat in a chase, live life to the fullest exciting each day

(ROYALTY)

I am royalty in the spirit, I have mastered the many levels of self and are catered to by the abundance of my mind, the universe is my advisor in which I grant my highest favor, I am waited on hand and foot for my far reaching words and undeniable wisdom, I create my world and all within my realm subject in obedience to my will, the secrets to receive whatever I wish has been unlocked by my power within, there is no level I cannot reach, there is nothing impossible if I have unwavering faith and believe, all wealth under my decree must be presented unto me, for I am an infinite being, for I am royalty

(YOUR WEAKNESS)

I am your weakness making you angry, yet at the same time hungry to possess all of me, do my words haunt the very air you breathe, my aloofness at times can become upsetting, bringing about a cold breeze as if in the presence of a ghostly entity, my love there is a magic surrounding me, an unseen aura of multiple chemistry, the very thing that makes you weak, is the very thing that draws you to me, are you worthy of my white rose that discerns the inner beauty and weaves the desire of destiny, all will come, but few will be found fit to receive, idle it sits in its crystal clear case, waiting patiently for the day, when it is to be freed and given away

(FINDING YOU)

I search a crowd of endless faces, back and forth to different places, to look for who my soul aligns, a destined love for all of time, the stars will talk of our union, angels will sing eternal music, past and present will come together, our passion and love will live forever, and if we were ever to part, a guiding light will find your heart, this I know to be true, in my search of finding you

(VICTORY)

The victory is mine, I have conquered the darkness, though it may still dwell in me, I now have control, though it still haunts me, I have made it threw the shadows, no longer am I afraid for I know what moves it, no longer do I cry for I am comforted by the light, no sadness or pain, no demon nor monster will ever again claim hold, for I am whole, my soul guarded, my heart replenished, the crystal mirror power balanced, through all these things I have been given the greatest gift of all, a pure love that is alive, by the wind my voice will be carried to the four corners of the earth, shouting the victory is mine

(THORNS)

Come close and do not mistake my roses for thorns, my love for promiscuity, my ways for theirs, my sight as an illusion for what is not there, my intention as wrong, my truth for false, a treasure for something less then you are, these words in vain, my tears and pain, all that have brought about my new name, the past for present, what's gained as lost, do not mistake my roses for thorns

(FREED)

A laborious breath I no longer breathe, for the darkness has no hold on me, my chains of bondage has been freed, my soul rejoices in its peace, hope, faith, love beneath, all heavenly lights these eyes have seen, spilling forth in my belief, the power of my will one flowing stream

(STAR CHILD)

I have found myself, yet I have always been, a star in the dark, an echo in the turbulent wind, an incorrigible light in a celestial sky, the brightest of all under the cover of night, a humble voice in a world of forced words, the mystery has dawned a star child of earth

(REST IN PEACE)

Rest my weary love, for you have found peace, rest my pained heart, for now you have relief, rest my beautiful soul, for our spirit is made whole, every treasure accounted, every place in its own, for all to be valued, not one to be left, rest ye inhabitants, in heavenly rest

(THREW)

Through the darkness I made it threw, through the portal inside of truth, through all that's in me, in you, all the way through to the mystery unveiled, all the way through the portal of will, through the crystal fountain inside of my soul, through the depths of my essence inside of my rose

(MUSIC)

A phantom of hearts, a musical ballad, a symphony of the senses, a choreography of seduction, a song of total enslavement to the mesmerizing sex, the collective essence of women spirited where love is, a charming tale of beauty so real, a poetic artist, a rhythm composed of the light and the darkness, let it reverberate in her mind from the window of my soul, drawn from the depths, displayed through the haunting connection from the music of my lips

SIN BYRON

Will there be a backlash, only time will tell, for I have defied the darkness and shaken the foundation of hell, spitting upon the face of the fallen one, rejecting my cursed blood, for though all is well I am not naive, for I know that inside there is this monster laying dormant in me, and as I sit here on my diamond throne watching over the new life of my elated other half, I cant help but wonder, will there be a backlash?

THE END

MY STORY SONG

Verse 1

In my words, their sings a song, of a long lost love that came along,
Though invisible, it some time seemed, there was no denying that
love in me,
So she came, wishing to be free, of a world of pain and grief,
Finding the red rose, of destiny, she had found what was missing...
she found me

Chorus

This is my, story song, of a lost love that came along,
I would fight, for this love, with the light from above,
In my heart, in my mind, in the soul_ of the night...she is all I need

Verse 2

In my words, their sings a song, of a hope that was lost,
Beyond the shadows of the world, belonging to a broken mirror,
In crystal, the pieces spread, lost between the light and darkness,
Now he searches, to find then, to put together what was broken...he's
broken

(CHORUS)

Verse 3

In my words, their sings a song, of a war that was fought,
Then the victory, was mine, now my heart is alive,
And my soul, treasures bright, I had to leave I said goodbye,
Love will I ever, see you again, until then ill be searching…until the end
Bridge-You alone can open my eyes; you alone can help me see…you alone can make me alive; you alone can set me free

I AM

Verse 1

    What do you see, in the dark of the night,
    Why do you fear, things will never be right,
    Where are you now, where have you been,
    When no ones around, how do you live
    Do you know who you are, when you look from afar,
    Beyond, the shining, stars, just know that

Chorus

    I am the beat of your heart inside you
    I am the one in the dark beside you
    You are never alone, no matter will you will go,
    No matter how hopeless things may seem, hell be right there

Verse 2

    What do you feel, when bad things come your way,
    Why do you cry, from all those past mistakes,
    May love come down, from a heavenly place,
    May love abound, washing all tears away,
    In your soul there is life, in your heart and your mind,
    Everything, shining, bright, I know that

(CHORUS)

FIGHT

Verse 1

    This life isn't easy, my loves come to me, and I will never turn you away…

    In the darkest hour, I will be the light that, help guides you on your way…

    There's no easy road, there's on way to go, I warn you watch your company…

    Every one will know, when the story's told, who died standing on there feet,

    Yeah yeah yeah_

Chorus

    Just take my hand, don't let go

    Lets make a stand, no matter what cost…

    Together were stronger, it wont take much longer for

    Us to win

    Yeah, yeah, yeah

    They want to break us, they want to take us,

    They can only do that if you let them in,

    Yeah, yeah, yeah_

Verse 2

As this world gets colder_ lean on my shoulder_, I'll be the fresh breath
that you take in...
No one can move me_ I'll be all that you need_ promise me you wont
give in...
When the sides have chose, and the doors have closed, have faith and
do not heed...
When the darkness falls, and the light seems lost, will you then still
believe...
Bridge-How can we lose now, how can we not push on,
How can we die knowing we didn't do, our best_
When the war is on_ and the fight is long_
Will you leave me, will you stand by me_

(CHORUS)

ABOUT THE AUTHOR

Joshua Ra Dundas spent eight and a half years in the bleak confines of a state penitentiary, emerging on his twenty-fifth birthday with an extraordinary story. Hailing from Brooklyn, New York, he now lives in Upstate New York.

Printed in the United States
By Bookmasters